A. G. Paddock

The Fate of Madame La Tour

A Tale of Great Salt Lake

A. G. Paddock

The Fate of Madame La Tour
A Tale of Great Salt Lake

ISBN/EAN: 9783337192310

Printed in Europe, USA, Canada, Australia, Japan

Cover: Foto ©Andreas Hilbeck / pixelio.de

More available books at **www.hansebooks.com**

THE FATE

OF

MADAME LA TOUR

A Tale of Great Salt Lake

BY

MRS. A. G. PADDOCK

NEW YORK:

FORDS, HOWARD, & HULBERT

1881

LETTERS

CONCERNING THE TRUSTWORTHINESS OF THE AUTHOR OF THIS BOOK.

From GOVERNOR MURRAY.

TERRITORY OF UTAH, EXECUTIVE OFFICE, SALT LAKE CITY, April 16, 1881.

I look with interest for the publication of Mrs. Paddock's promised book. Her writings attest her capacity, which, joined with her long residence in Utah, and access to reliable sources of information, suggest a true story well told.

ELI H. MURRAY,
Governor.

From J. S. BOREMAN, ESQ., *late Associate Justice of the Supreme Court of Utah.*

SALT LAKE CITY, UTAH, April 27, 1881.

I learn with great pleasure that it is the purpose of Mrs. A. G. Paddock to publish another volume giving some pictures of life among the Mormons. I know of no one better qualified for that work than Mrs. Paddock. She has been here for some years, and I know from numerous articles which have appeared from her pen and from the active life among these people that she has gathered a vast storehouse of information. . . . I have resided in Utah eight years, and been on the bench of the United States Court for seven and a half years of that time, and believe that I am tolerably familiar with the Mormon system.

JACOB S. BOREMAN.

From HON. G. S. BLACK, *Ex-Secretary of Utah Territory.*

UNITED STATES MARSHAL'S OFFICE, ⎰
UTAH TERRITORY, ⎱
SALT LAKE CITY, April 28, 1881.

MESSRS. FORDS, HOWARD & HULBERT, Publishers, New York City :

GENTLEMEN : I take pleasure in saying that I have known Mrs. A. G. Paddock for the last ten years, six of which I was Secretary of the Territory. I know of no person in the Territory who has given the situation here, and Utah affairs in general, more study than Mrs. Paddock, and her advantages for gaining and ability in imparting information have been the envy of us all.

GEO. S. BLACK.

From MRS. S. A. COOKE, *President Woman's National Anti-Polygamy Society.*

SALT LAKE CITY, April 16, 1881.

I have been a resident of this city since 1852, and have been personally acquainted with Mrs. Paddock since 1871, and believe she has access to *reliable* sources of information on matters connected with Mormonism. She mentioned my name in her former book, " In the Toils," as a lady who had care of two boys saved from the Mountain Meadow massacre. The eldest of the two boys had a perfect recollection of the scenes in that most horrible tragedy. I do not think Mrs. Paddock would overstate the facts respecting that or many other deeds that have darkened the history of this Territory.

MRS. SARAH A. COOKE.

From JOHN GREENLEAF WHITTIER *to Mrs. Paddock on receipt of a copy of her former book on Mormonism.*

DANVERS, MASS., 8 Mo. 18, 1879.

DEAR FRIEND : I thank thee for a copy of thy story " In the Toils." I had read it in the *Alliance* with a deep and painful interest. It seems scarcely possible that such a state of society as is there depicted so graphically and forcibly can exist in our country. Yet all history tells us that there are no limits to atrocities and cruelties which even those who are naturally good and gentle may commit under the influence of religious fanaticism.

How to deal with this great evil I confess is to me a difficult problem. While it exists I trust that Congress, however demoralized by party politics, will not admit Utah as a State into the Union.

Thy friend,

JOHN G. WHITTIER.

PREFACE.

THE present tale, while following chiefly the fortunes and misfortunes of a single family (the main incidents of which are only too truthfully related), traces the development of the Mormon system in those distant " valleys of the mountains," and shows some of the ways and means of its workings. I do not pretend to tell the worst of the doings of the Saints, for no decent pen could describe and no decent reader would peruse the shocking facts. On the other hand, I have carefully avoided all such elements as would tend to have any corrupting influence or to offend the sensitive and pure-minded.

Louise La Tour is not a creation of fancy. Her story is true ; her sufferings were real ; but I have only

> " Hinted, with delicate half-words
> And scrupulous reserves,
> What no one scrupled she should feel in full."

For my sources of information, I have my own personal observation during a residence of ten years in the city of Salt Lake. I have boarded in Mormon families, have had Mormons living in my own family (though neither my husband nor myself have ever been Mormons), and have had Mormon neighbors on every side. I have also enjoyed the acquaintance and the confidence of many of those who have represented the Federal authorities here. My husband has been in the Territory since 1858, and has personal knowledge of many matters herein described. I am especially indebted to him for the material of the chapters relating to life in Oregon and California and on the plains ;

as he himself passed through most of the experiences and adventures there set down, the pictures may be relied upon as true to life.

The two hundred thousand Mormons of Utah and its neighboring States and Territories are by their religion the sworn enemies of the United States Government ; the married women are voters, who follow the orders of their husbands, who in their turn elect the " chosen of the Lord," as directed by the hierarchy ; and by way of strengthening this political, spiritual, social, independent despotism, there were more polygamous marriages during the year 1880 than in any previous year since the settlement of Utah by the Mormons. These three facts make the *topic* of this book one of importance to every thinking man and woman in our common country.

To myself, the construction of this story out of realities existing on every side of me, which far surpass in strangeness and romance any fiction that could be invented, has been a matter of intense interest. I cannot hope to have done justice to the materials, but if my story shall succeed in arousing people to think, and to examine into the facts of the unnatural problem of Mormonism, I shall be content. I call it a " problem," because it is not easy among the elements of this theocratic despotism to find a " Republican form of Government," nor out of the debasing results of polygamy to develop a community of Christian American households. In reality there is no " problem" about it, for no such solution is possible ; but the public indifference seems to take it for granted that these things " will all come right some day and some how," and therefore it is that I ask a consideration of the system, its ways, means, and results.

CORNELIA PADDOCK.

Great Salt Lake, Utah Ter., June 1, 1881.

CONTENTS.

CHAPTER I.

THE ADVANCE GUARD.

IN the early spring of 1847 a body of armed men were gathered on the west bank of the Missouri River. It was not the Missouri of to-day, spanned by railroad bridges, plowed by steamers, its shores bordered with fertile farms, and dotted with cities and villages, but the Missouri of thirty-four years ago, wending its tortuous and solitary way between high bluffs that echoed to the howl of the wolf and the war-whoop of the savage.

Most of these men wore the homespun dress of the pioneers ; but a few were clad in the buckskin suits adopted by hunters and trappers. Besides the rifles in their hands, more than half of the company carried small arms in their belts, and to a man their faces expressed a grim and fierce determination.

Viewing them thus, as they stood there in the early morning, the solitary bluffs of the Missouri on their right, the boundless, silent prairie on their left, the spectator, had there been one to note this extraordinary group, would have carried the picture away in his memory as that of a band of outlaws about to start on some desperate errand, with but faint chances that so many as half their number would ever return.

Still, there were accessories to the picture which forbade the supposition that they were ordinary brigands, bound on an expedition of robbery and murder.

A few rods distant about fifty wagons were ranged, some of them filled with supplies for a long journey, others loaded with farming implements and sacks of grain, and near these wagons more than three hundred horses and mules were picketed.

The men, about a hundred and fifty in number, were leaning on their rifles and listening to one of the band, who was evidently their leader.

He stood on a little hillock, a few feet above his auditors, whom his fiery words held spell-bound. He was in the prime of life, of medium stature, but powerfully built, and his face bore the stamp of an iron will to which all must bend, and of that inflexibility of purpose which annihilates all obstacles. His deep-set eyes told of greed, both of money and power, as plainly as the square mouth and heavy jaws revealed the savage in his nature, at once sensual and cruel.

He talked rapidly, and his diction was that of a man of the people—unpolished, uncultured, and ignorant of even the alphabet of such learning as is garnered in books, save such as he might glean from the Scriptures ; but his rude and forcible eloquence swayed his listeners as a northern gale bends the pines, and when from time to time he exclaimed, " You who are with me, raise your right hands," all hands were uplifted simultaneously, as though some secret spring moved the whole company like one man.

Pointing eastward, he denounced in scathing language the nation whose frontier settlements lay beyond the river, and invoked upon the people the curse of famine and pestilence, of fire and sword.

A deep " Amen" from all his listeners answered him.

Then stretching out his hand toward the West, he exclaimed,

" Yonder, a thousand miles beyond the borders of this accursed people, lies the land that is given to us for an inheritance, and there we will build cities, and plant vineyards, and dwell in peace, while the vials of wrath are being poured out upon the nations of the earth.''

He continued to talk in this strain for a few minutes longer, and then, lifting his hands, pronounced a benediction on the armed band that had echoed his curses. The discourse was apparently a preliminary of the real business of the morning, which now began in earnest.

Teams were harnessed and attached to the wagons, single horses saddled, arms and ammunition looked to, and the train put in marching order, the men being divided into companies of fifties, and those again into squads of tens, each with a captain, through whom the orders of the chief were carried out in detail. · By the time the sun was well above the eastern bluffs, teams, horsemen, and footmen were moving westward. Civilization was behind them, the desert before them, and a savage foe on their route; but not a man hesitated or faltered. Faith in their leader, and a form of fanaticism which made them regard themselves as under the special protection of Heaven, sustained some; but others, and these by far the majority of the company, were already outlaws, whose presence civilization refused to tolerate, and to them the wilderness offered the only safe refuge.

Counterfeiting and theft were the least of the offences laid to their charge. Many, if not all of those thus outlawed were accused of the darker crimes of bigamy, treason, and murder, and the rude pioneers of the border, meeting violence with violence, and punishing glaring outrages by mob-law, had driven them from their midst.

No fair-minded historian will attempt to cover or palliate a resort to mob-violence. In a country where the courts are open to all, and where, as a rule, any criminal may be tried and punished according to the established forms of law, those who take the law into their own hands are inexcusable—and yet the peculiar circumstances attending the expulsion of this band of outlaws from the community on which they had preyed make one hesitate to condemn without reserve those who drove them out.

The company leaving the banks of the Missouri this morning had no fixed destination. They were scouts whose business it was to discover and take possession of some tract of land that would furnish a refuge for themselves and those whom they represented, and a home for their families. A few of them may have believed that their chief would be divinely guided to the spot that Heaven had set apart for them—some Promised Land, flowing with milk and honey—but the greater number relied on the sagacity of their leader, and on a certain trapper and plainsman in their ranks who knew the country.

The first month brought them no hardships. The well-watered plains of Nebraska afforded abundant pasture for their animals, and favorable camping-grounds for the train. There were no hostile demonstrations on the part of the Indians. Game abounded, and good rifles, in the hands of men who knew how to use them, kept the company supplied with meat.

They reached the crossing of the Platte in advance of the June freshets, and were therefore able to ford the stream without serious difficulty. The river, not more than three fourths of a mile wide at the crossing, and but little more than two feet in depth at this season of the year, is yet a formidable stream to ford, for two reasons. It runs with extraordinary swiftness, and the fine white sand in the bottom, packed hard by the action of the water, forms a thin crust over the treacherous depths beneath—shifting, dangerous quicksands, 'in which the wheels of the loaded wagons sink and cannot be withdrawn. Footmen and horsemen may cross without danger, but if the loaded teams are allowed for any reason to halt, the wheels break through the thin crust of the river-bottom, and the wagon begins to sink—continues to sink until, in a little while, no force can extricate it.

In the present company there were plainsmen familiar with the crossing, and the method dictated by their experience was adopted. The teams were unhitched from all but ten of the wagons. To each one of these wagons four teams were attached, and a spot previously tested by the horsemen was selected for crossing. The teams entered the water in single file, the drivers walking on the upper side, with a horseman for each team riding the stream below. All the speed that the swiftness of the current would allow was now made, to avoid the quicksands, and when the last of the ten wagons was safe on the opposite bank the teams were unhitched and driven back to aid in bringing the other wagons across.

Conducted in this manner, the fording of the stream occupied nearly the whole of two days.

The teams attached to one of the last wagons at the crossing becoming unmanageable in the middle of the current, the driver, who walked beside them, was thrown down, and as he rose to his feet the blood that trickled from a wound above the temple mingled with the stream. Was it a foreshadowing of the day, not many years later, when, tracked and followed by his " brethren" to this same river, his life-blood should stain its waters, and the treacherous sands beneath become his grave ?

When the train resumed its march, after camping for the night on the bank of the river, the one man in the company whose trapping expeditions had led him into the regions beyond, was made their guide across the vast expanse of rolling prairie stretching westward to the Rocky Mountains.

No pillar of cloud by day or pillar of fire by night was vouchsafed to lead them ; but, as before stated, the majority of this band of scouts were men uninfluenced by fanaticism, or any other motive beyond that of placing a safe distance between themselves and civilization, and the buckskin-clad trapper who guided them served their purpose quite as well as an angel going before them to point out the way.

Six years before the time of which we write, emigrant trains had begun to cross these prairies, and the mountain regions beyond, on their way to the coast, and four years previous to the date of the present exploring expedition the regular annual overland emigration to Oregon and California began, so that a trail which could be easily followed was already marked out,* and the trapper, who had accompanied such trains more than once, was able to assist the leader of the band by suggesting the principal features of the "vision" which was to decide the company in their choice of a location. It was the first of June when they reached the South Pass, a park or mountain valley many thousand feet above the level of the sea. Here, within three hundred yards of each other, are two springs, the one the source of a little creek that, flowing eastward, joins itself to streams that become tributary to the Missouri, finding thence an outlet by way of the Mississippi to the Gulf of Mexico ; the other, the head-waters of a rivulet that widens and deepens as the snows continue to melt and other rivulets join it, until it becomes a river, and its waters, by many and devious channels at length reach and mingle with the Pacific.

In these springs the leader of the band found an omen of the destiny of himself and his people.

* See Appendix, Note A, page 328.

" Here," he said, " we leave the East forever—leave it under a curse. We follow the waters of this stream, whose course is toward the West. There is our inheritance. There we will set up a kingdom that shall yet destroy and break in pieces all the nations and kingdoms of the earth. The land is ours, and woe to the man or the nation that tries to take it from us. We will never be driven out again. *From this time forth it belongs to us to drive others out.*"

To the few fanatics in the company these words were a prophecy—a message from above. To the others they were a revelation of the ambitious plans of their leader, who nourished the hope of setting up an independent government somewhere in the fastnesses of the Sierras.

Let those who exclaim against the idea that a plan so preposterous could ever have been seriously entertained by a man possessing the known shrewdness of that leader, look over the history of the community he ruled, and ask themselves the question whether, in point of fact, it has not been an independent state for more than a quarter of a century.

Beyond the South Pass the train made excellent time. The weather was everything that could be desired ; game abounded, their animals were in good condition, and as it was yet early in the season there was no scarcity of water or grass. At a few points along the route the Indians showed faint signs of hostility, but by the sagacious management of their leader trouble was avoided.

It was about the middle of July when they entered the mountain passes west of Green River. Here the main body halted for a time, and half a dozen picked men, guided by the trapper before mentioned, were sent out to prospect for a location possessing the advantages of water and a fertile soil.

After a few days' absence the scouts returned with good news. They had found the very spot which their leader assured them he had seen in a vision—the site of the future kingdom.

No time was now to be lost. On the very day that the scouts returned the train was again put in marching order, and on the twenty-fourth of the same month the whole company entered the Promised Land through a wide pass leading by a gentle descent into the valley.

They came in through this pass in the morning, and before nightfall they had pitched their camp, taken formal possession of the country, and commenced breaking the soil for the autumn crops that they proposed to put in.

The valley was watered by a score of mountain streams, which were fed by the melting snows. The soil was deep and rich, needing only irrigation to make it immensely productive, and with a promptness and energy which promised well for their future success, a dam was built at once, and ditches dug as soon as the seed was put in.

- Then, as the thousand miles or more which they had traveled must be retraced before winter set in, the main body hastily prepared for their homeward journey, leaving about thirty of their number to hold possession of the country, and do what they could toward building houses for the families that were to come on the next year.

There was no timber for building purposes nearer than the cañons, and to these the roads had yet to be made ; but the settlers, profiting by the experience of their Mexican neighbors, made use of an excellent building material that they found ready to their hands. In many places near the site of the " city" their leader had laid out, there were large tracts of the clay used for making *adobes* or sun-dried bricks. These bricks were easily molded, and, in that climate, soon dry enough for use ; and in the absence of lime a serviceable mortar was made by mixing sand with the mud of the adobe pits, and in a little while, to the surprise of the red man who came down from his tepee in the hills to interview the new arrivals, the walls of a dozen cabins were taking form and consistence under the busy hands of the colonists.

Meantime the returning pioneers were experiencing all the hardships of travel on scanty rations over the plains parched by the heat of midsummer. The grass that made such excellent pasturage in June was withered, many of the streams were dried up, and before half their journey was accomplished the rations they carried with them were so reduced that they had to depend almost wholly on their rifles for food. To add to their trials, the Indians stole many of their horses and harassed them in various ways ; but they finally reached the frontier without the loss of a man, and on the last day of October stood again on the banks of the Missouri.

CHAPTER II.

MADAME LA TOUR.

SPRING has come again in the valley of the Missouri. The vast, treeless prairies on the western shore are a tender green. As far as the eye can reach, north, south, and west, the grassy sea extends until it meets and blends with the blue of the clear May skies.

About a mile west of the bluff, and on the north bank of a small stream that empties into the river, there is a settlement which, from the nature of the buildings and the character of the surroundings, is evidently temporary, being little more, in fact, than the camp of a people who for years have had no certain dwelling-place. There are a large number of rude log-cabins, bearing every mark of the haste with which they were constructed, and of the indifference with which their owners regard them. The logs, obtained from the cottonwood grove on the river-bottom, a little to the north, are still incased in their native bark, and the buildings are roofed with poles and brush, held down and made water-tight by a coating of earth. The circle of cabins is interspersed with tents, and in the rear of each one stands a covered wagon, its white top visible above the low roof, so that at a little distance the whole settlement presents the appearance of one of those canvas towns which, a few years later, sprang up everywhere throughout the West in the wake of miners and railroads. The cattle belonging to the encampment are feeding on the prairie beyond in the care of the herders, but, with the exception of the men thus engaged, the whole population of the settlement are assembled in an open space within the circle of buildings, to listen to their chief and receive his orders.

The speaker is the same individual who, a little more than a year ago, stood on the bluffs of the river a couple of miles farther south, and prophesied to the band of scouts he led that they should find in the heart of the desert a land flowing with milk and honey. This prophecy he repeats to-day to a company of two thousand souls, men, women, and children, who to-morrow are to break camp and turn their faces westward.

Among these are many sincere souls, who regard their leader as inspired, and who are ready to follow him to the ends of the earth if need be.

There are men of wealth camping in those mud-roofed log-cabins, who have offered all their possessions on the altar of their faith, and there are chaste wives and tender mothers, whose presence in the outlawed band can only be explained by their sincere though sadly mistaken belief in the divine mission of the man who stands before them.

Still, as already stated, the fanatics and those sincere believers in the New Gospel who do not merit that title, are not in the majority. There are scores of women in the encampment who are there only because their husbands have chosen to follow the leader who is about to conduct them into the wilderness ; and there are other women— many of them—whose relations to the leader and his satellites are such as could not be maintained openly in a civilized community.

More than half of the mixed company are children, to whom the journey across the plains presents itself in the light of a long summer holiday, and babes in arms, happy everywhere so long as they can look up into the unclouded heaven of a mother's face.

When the speaker concluded his address, the " Amens" were less hearty and general than when he spoke to the band of picked men who were to go before the people and prepare the way. Many of the present company were already restive under a despotism which they foresaw would become absolute, when the proposed colony should be established a thousand miles from civilization ; but what could they do ? Some of them were already outlawed by their own acts ; others had surrendered all their possessions into the hands of those who controlled the organization, and even among the disaffected the feeling prevailed that they had now gone too far to retreat.

After the assembly broke up, the speaker, disengaging himself from those who pressed around him with eager questions, walked toward the open door of one of the cabins, which, while it differed in no wise from the others outwardly, within was comfortably and in some respects even luxuriously furnished.

A handsome carpet hid the rough floor, a silken coverlet was spread over the bed that occupied one corner, and the three or four chairs in the room were of costly make and material, though bearing unmistakable marks of having been brought to their present destination under difficulties.

The only occupant of the place was a lady, still in the prime of life, and with a face whose beauty must once have been of no common order, though stamped now with the ineffaceable marks of years of suffering. Her dress, like the furniture of her room, was strangely out of keeping with her rude surroundings.

She was in deep mourning. A robe of soft cashmere trimmed with heavy folds of crape trailed on the carpet as she paced the floor with slow steps.

A widow's cap covered the heavy coils of hair, once jet black, but now thickly sprinkled with silver.

The face was perfect in outline, but colorless as though carved out of marble, and thin and worn, as though with long illness or hopeless sorrow—perhaps both. The eyes, large, dark, and lustrous, were cast down and half hidden by the long lashes.

A certain air of proud patience, the offspring of a spirit that disdained complaint, marked both her face and her manner, yet when the eyes were raised for a moment the smouldering fire in them told of passions that, once roused, would brook no control.

As the leader of the people paused at her door, she inclined her head slightly, but gave no other sign of being aware of his presence. His face darkened. It was not such a reception as he was accustomed to ; but mastering an evident inclination to resent the disrespect shown him, he said, in bland tones,

"We missed you much this morning, Sister La Tour. I am sorry you were not able to be out."

Madame La Tour (for by this name she was known in the world she had left) turned her dark eyes full upon him, with a look under which he quailed for an instant ; but recovering himself, presently he added,

"I want to speak a few words to you in private, and by your leave I will come in ;" stepping across the threshold as he spoke, and closing the door after him.

Madame La Tour neither answered nor turned her head, but continued to pace the floor with slow steps, her eyes once more cast down.

Her unbidden guest seated himself in the nearest chair, and making an effort to appear unconscious of her manner, spoke again :

"Sister La Tour, we start at an early hour in the morning. All our arrangements are made, and every one except yourself is ready. You are not going to rebel against the Spirit of the Lord, and at the last hour refuse to go with us ?''

In spite of his assumed ease, there was an undercurrent of anxiety in the tone in which he put the last question. The woman stopped suddenly in her walk and faced him.

'' Tell me first,'' she said sharply and sternly, '' what you have done with my daughter.''

'' Your daughter is in good hands,'' was the reply. '' I will myself be responsible for her safety.''

'' *You !*''

It would be impossible to describe the concentrated hate and scorn in her voice as she spoke this single word. She crossed the room again once or twice, then, pausing before him, changed her tone.

'' Only give me back my child,'' she said, clasping her hands imploringly, '' and you may keep all else that you have taken. Will not my money satisfy you--all of it ? Why should you rob me of my daughter ? What have I ever done to deserve it ?''

The man's deep-set eyes flashed, and his cruel mouth closed firmly. For some moments he regarded the ago- nized face, the suppliant attitude of the proud woman be- fore him, with savage satisfaction. When he spoke again, it was to say, in his coldest tones,

'' Whether you ever see your daughter again or not de- pends entirely upon yourself. She is going with us, though not in this company, and if you give over your sinful oppo- sition to what the Lord has revealed, and join the train to- morrow, you will meet her in the place that He has given to us for an inheritance. As for your money''—here he dropped the hypocritical cant which he knew was thrown away upon his listener—'' your offer is liberal, very, consid- ering that I have got it already, and that you have nothing to show for it.''

Madame La Tour made no reply. Her face settled into the expression it had worn before the entrance of her un-welcome visitor, and she recommenced her walk across the floor, taking no farther notice of him. He sat a few minutes in silence, then, rising, opened the door and passed out, saying,

" You can let us know your decision this evening."

A little group of women stood at the door of the next cabin, and as he came near them he stopped, and, glancing backward, said,

" Some of the sisters ought to keep an eye on Sister La Tour. She grows worse, and I am afraid will never be right here again," touching his forehead significantly as he spoke.

" Poor thing !" said one of the women compassionately, as he passed on ; " I didn't know she was so bad as that, though, to be sure, she has never been like herself since her husband died."

" His death was very sudden, wasn't it ?" inquired another of the group, a tall, sharp-featured woman.

" Well, yes, rather " the first woman answered, hesitat-ing a little, and looking around as though to ascertain who might be listening, "and there was considerable talk at the time."

This vague statement appeared to convey a meaning which the tall woman understood, for she raised both hands with the exclamation,

" You don't say, Sister Merrit," and then relapsed into silence.

" I'll tell you what it is, Sister Merrit," interposed the third sister, who had not yet spoken, " I think she sees more trouble about her boys going off with that Gentile emigrant train, than about anything else."

" Nonsense, Sister Purdy," answered Sister Merrit sharply, " she's glad to have her boys get away. If they hadn't joined the train she would have sent them back home to Canada, and she'd be on her way there herself now if it wasn't for this trouble about Louise."

"Who is Louise?" asked the tall woman.

:"Don't you know? I thought you did, or I wouldn't have said anything. Louise was her oldest daughter, and a proud, headstrong piece she was too ; but a great beauty, as they say her mother used to be in her young days. After Brother La Tour died his widow was obliged to go to St. Louis on business, and while she was away Louise boarded in Brother Joseph's family. When the mother came back she got it into her head somehow that there was something wrong ; but the Prophet was killed that same month, and we all had too many troubles of our own to think much about Sister La Tour's affairs. For the next two years, and until we left Nauvoo, the girl stayed with her mother, and seemed somehow greatly changed. She was only fifteen when her father died, and not much more than seventeen when I saw her last ; but it seemed as if she had grown old in two years. Her mother was more wrapped up in her than ever, and would hardly allow her out of her sight a moment ; but when we left Nauvoo (Sister Purdy can tell you what a time we had crossing the river on the ice, and what hardships we went through afterward), a good many families were separated for a while on account of the confusion and trouble. Among the rest, Sister La Tour and her daughter were parted accidentally, and," lowering her voice to a whisper, "*she has never seen the girl from that day to this ;* but she has got it into her head that Brother Brigham has her hid away somewhere, and that's why she never speaks to him if she can help it."

"But, Sister Merrit," interrupted Sister Purdy anxiously, "you know the poor woman is out of her mind."

" She was all right before this last trouble," Sister Merrit answered, " and if that ain't enough to drive a mother out of her mind, I don't know what is."

" H'm ! seems to me there's a good many queer things happening among us. If I'd a known before I left Vermont all that I know now I wouldn't be here."

It was the tall woman who spoke ; and she finished her remark in spite of a warning gesture from one of the others, who perceived that a stout, bullet-headed man, one of the original pioneers, was approaching within hearing distance. He passed them, however, with only a civil " Good-morning," and when he was out of sight the woman who had given the history of the missing Louise said, in a low tone,

" Sister Wade, we all have a right to our opinions, but sometimes it's just as well to keep them to ourselves. We are out of the States now, and after to-morrow morning it's hardly likely that many of us will ever see them again. I found out, even when we was where we could turn back, that it didn't pay to make enemies of the heads of the Church, and I'm sure that after we start on this journey we'll *have to* keep on good terms with them."

" If *I* thought that," Sister Wade answered, " I should not start at all."

" Yes, but," rejoined the other, " could you persuade your husband to give up going with the rest ?"

Sister Wade's countenance fell. She looked like a resolute woman ; but it was plain that she was now confronted by a difficulty that could not be easily disposed of.

" I've never talked to him about it," she said evasively ; and after a few more words the conversation dropped, and the women separated.

Meanwhile Madame La Tour's guest was walking rapidly toward his own domicile, a building constructed, like the others, of logs, but larger than any of them, and divided into several rooms. His face expressed the consciousness of a hard-won victory, and as he passed out of the hearing of the women to whom he had spoken, he said aloud to himself,

" She will go."

The front door of his own house was open, and within a plain-looking woman was busily engaged in packing.

He passed her without speaking, and knocked at an inner door. It was opened by a tall, handsome, well-dressed woman, whose face indicated in a marked degree the same traits which his own looks revealed—pride, ambition, and unconquerable self-will.

This woman, who had forsaken husband and children, and thrown position and reputation to the winds for his sake, had meant to rule the man who ruled all others ; but while she was conscious that she had failed in this, she was wise enough to make the most of his confidence, and of the degree of influence she possessed.

As he closed the door behind him, she asked, with evident anxiety,

" Have you succeeded ?"

" I have," was the answer. " She will go with us to-morrow, and, what is of more consequence, her money and her family go. I have no wish to see her return to Canada to spread an evil report ; but still she will always make trouble, and we could have spared her better than we can spare the children or the property."

" What do you want with the children ?" she asked, eying him keenly.

" What does any one want with children ?" was the rejoinder. " How could the kingdom be built up without them ? Philip is a likely boy, who will be a man in three or four years ; and, boy as he is, he would cut off his right hand for me to-day. The little girls will be women by the time we get fairly settled, and they will have their mother's beauty, though, it is to be hoped, not her temper."

"I see." The woman's face was a study as she pronounced these words. "But how did you manage to get the mother's consent?"

"I told her she should see her daughter in Zion, but never anywhere else. She made me no answer, but her face showed that she was conquered. We used to think Brother Heber a fool, but he was wiser than any of us when he carried off the girl."

"Brother Heber thought only of himself," the woman answered, her lip curling slightly as she spoke; "but how about the money? Those boys who have gone through to the coast may make you trouble about that yet."

"They are welcome to try, *after they get there.*"

The tone in which the last sentence was spoken, and the look that accompanied it, conveyed a meaning not to be mistaken. The woman turned a little pale.

"There are risks," she said.

"Not for me," he interrupted; "I never take any risks."

Has not history—the history of a long succession of crimes whose responsibility was always shifted upon others—borne out this assertion?

The remainder of the day we are describing was a busy one in the settlement. Goods were packed, tents taken down, wagons loaded, and before the sun set all the preparations for their long journey were completed. Their flocks and herds, which were to be taken with them, were corraled near at hand, and the horses picketed outside, so that there need not be an hour's delay in the morning.

The family of Madame La Tour, consisting of a boy of sixteen, two little girls of ten and twelve, and a couple of servants, had been busy as the others, and by the time darkness settled down on the encampment nothing remained in their house except the bed, which the mother occupied on this last night with her little girls. Philip, the son, slept in the ambulance in which they were to travel, and the servants, Pierre Roche and Joan his wife, who had come with the La Tours from their old home in Quebec, kept guard over the goods in the wagons.

Before following the fortunes of the emigrants any farther, it becomes necessary that we should give a brief history of this family, whose members will occupy a prominent place in the present narrative.

Francis La Tour was a descendant of one of the oldest French families who were among the founders of Quebec, and for nearly two hundred years there never lacked one of his name and blood to fill the honorable place which his ancestors had made for themselves. The family were Catholics, and in his youth Francis, at that time their only male representative, was strongly inclined to a monastic life ; but the beauty of a neighbor's daughter won him from his resolves, and after his marriage, as sometimes happens, he passed from one extreme to the other ; and whereas he had begun by yearning for a monk's cell he ended by casting off the faith of his fathers altogether. The consequence was that a coldness grew up between himself and his old friends, and he decided at length to seek a home elsewhere. The point he selected was St. Louis ; and when he settled there he had already a family of six children, three sons and three daughters, growing up around him. His children were bright, handsome, and affectionate ; his wife was devoted to him ; he had every good that wealth can bestow, and yet Francis La Tour was an unhappy man.

In casting off the faith in which he was reared, he had by no means cast off his religious aspirations, and his state now was that of a man seeking rest and finding none in any form of belief.

It was at a time when his mind was in this state which I have tried to describe, that the emissaries, sent out by the community calling themselves " Latter Day Saints," found in him a willing hearer. He was disquieted by doubts: they offered him a certainty. He was tired of comparing the rival claims of the systems of religion that were taught in books : they would lead him at once to a living prophet, through whom Divinity would speak directly to him. His case was met.

Whatever faults these missionaries may have had, diffidence and hesitation were not among them, and the certainty that they assumed, the boldness with which they spoke, and the promptness with which they acted, had their effect. Francis La Tour was among their earliest converts, and within six months after his baptism he removed to Nauvoo, and like one of old, sold all his possessions, and laid the price at the feet of those who did not display the least unwillingness to receive it.

Strangely enough, however, as soon as his property was in the hands of the Church, his health began to fail, and he died after a short illness, leaving his widow, whose faith was by no means as strong as his own, to make the best terms she could for the support of her children with those who held her property in their hands.

The two older sons were, like their mother, only partially convinced of the truth of the New Gospel ; but Louise, the oldest daughter, and Philip, the third son, shared their father's faith, and looked up to the Prophet Joseph as almost divine. It is true that Philip was little more than a child, but he was one of those who are religiously disposed almost from the cradle. Louise was differently constituted, but her father was her idol, and anything that *he* believed was sacred in her eyes.   It was her own wish to board in the family of the Prophet after her father's death, and her mother gave a reluctant consent only when Louise urged, as a final argument,

"If father could speak, he would say that was the place for me."

The business which called Madame La Tour to St. Louis detained her nearly six months, and when she returned to Nauvoo the air was rife with whispers of strange doctrines, chief and most repulsive of which was that of Celestial Marriage ; for it was in the State of Illinois, and as early as the year 1843, that this doctrine became one of the cardinal features of the religion of the Saints of the Mormon Church, and there is abundant evidence to prove that the practice antedated the promulgation of the doctrine by half a dozen years at least.

CHAPTER III.

MADAME LA TOUR, like most persons reared in the Catholic faith, had exalted ideas of the sacredness of the marriage tie, and when the report (only too well authenticated) came to her ears that the Prophet Joseph had taken a score of young girls as his spiritual wives, and that a number of women already married had been "sealed" to him for eternity, horror and loathing took the place of the kindly feeling she had entertained toward him for her husband's sake. Her daughter was no longer an inmate of his house. She had taken her home on the day she returned, and she now felt that her child had been rescued from the brink of destruction. This comfort, however, was short-lived.

Within a month after her return, the Prophet, exasperated by a report that Madame La Tour was about to go to St. Louis with her family for the purpose of denouncing him, sent her a message, the import of which was that she might go when and where she pleased, but she could not take Louise, who had been sealed to him; and Louise, when confronted with the messenger, did not deny it.

The unhappy mother never recovered from this crushing blow, and the kind-hearted women who thought her "a little out of her mind" were not altogether wrong. Her daughter's disgrace bowed her proud spirit to the earth, and when Louise, now thoroughly cured of her infatuation, begged that she might not be forced to go back among those whom she could never look in the face again, her mother yielded so far as to consent to remain in Nauvoo until they could find some retreat far from all who had known them in the past.

. The one thought of both was to hide forever from the world ; and the mother, thrown back in her grief and despair upon the faith of her childhood, vowed herself to a life of prayer and penance in the refuge that she hoped to find.

At this time, however, all their property was in the hands of the authorities of the Church. Indeed, if it had not been for a small annuity which Madame La Tour possessed in her own right, they would not have had the means to live from day to day.

Matters were in this state when the Prophet Joseph, with several of his counselors, was arrested by the civil authorities and conveyed to the prison, where he met his death at the hands of an infuriated mob. His murder had the effect that might have been anticipated. In the eyes of his devoted followers it crowned him with the glories of martyrdom, and the whole people, accepting it as the gage of open war between themselves and the world, saw the necessity of a closer union among themselves, and began to look forward to the establishment of a commonwealth of their own, at a safe distance from their enemies.

Madame La Tour found her embarrassments greatly increased by the Prophet's death and the consequences that ensued. Her only home was among his followers, and in the eyes of the world she was identified with them. Her daughter refused to return to their former friends, and her property was still held by the Church. Besides all this, the man who from the first had determined to succeed to the dead Prophet, and who already, within six months after his death, exercised a greater power over the people than Joseph had attained to in a lifetime, was her bitter and unrelenting enemy.

By means best known to himself, he had become the trustee of her property, and conceiving the idea of securing it as his own, proposed to make her his spiritual wife. The unmeasured scorn and indignation with which she repelled the first intimation of his purpose, he could neither forget nor forgive, and while outwardly patient and considerate in his manner toward her, he only bided his time to wreak on her such a vengeance as she never dreamed of.

Long before they left Nauvoo, he began to prepare for the accomplishment of his purpose by throwing out artfully-worded hints regarding her insanity.

He intrusted the abduction of her daughter to other hands, upon his established principle of taking no personal risks ; but it was his act nevertheless, and only the beginning of his vengeance.

At first, Louise's separation from her family was so arranged as to appear accidental, and her mother hoped to find her somewhere in the company of fugitives who were making their forced and perilous march to the next halting-place chosen by their leaders. It was not until they reached the western bank of the Missouri that she learned the truth. There, in an Indian country, where redress was impossible, and where her enemy had already strengthened himself by an alliance with the chiefs of the savage tribes around them, he sought an interview with her, and obtained it by the promise of giving her news of Louise.

The substance of his communication, when made, was that the spirit she had lately shown rendered her an unfit guardian for her daughter, who besides being the child of the Church, left in its care by her father, was the wife of their martyred Prophet, and as such the especial charge of his successor.

The bereaved mother did not break out into ravings, as

her tormentor hoped she would ; the blow was too direct
and stunning. For a time all her faculties seemed benumbed, and during most of the years that followed she
appeared as we have seen her on the day preceding the
departure of the emigrants for their new home in the heart
of the wilderness.

*   *   *   *   *   *   *

It will be perceived that Brigham Young, in the character of successor to the murdered Prophet, assumed powers
that the former never pretended to. Already, within less
than a year from the time that his claim to the office on
which he had seized was confirmed by the people, he had
entered upon the exercise of that absolute temporal power
which afterward grew to such proportions that he felt himself able to defy the Government of the United States.

And yet, not one of all those who have attempted to
analyze his character has given a satisfactory solution of
the secret of his extraordinary ascendency over his followers.* A man of the people, born and nurtured in poverty,
barely able to read and write, living in obscurity until
nearly forty years of age, and moreover quite destitute of
personal courage,† for nearly a quarter of a century he
held the lives, liberty, and property of the Saints in his
hands, and exercised in all things the power of an absolute
and irresponsible despot. At the time of which we write,
his complete domination over his followers (numbering
many thousands in both hemispheres) was shown by the
fact that, while he led in person the small company of two

---

* See Appendix, Note B, page 331.

† The present writer has seen Brigham Young in the hands of the
Federal authorities, pale, trembling, and suffering all the agonies of
extreme physical cowardice ; and it is notorious that in the zenith of his
power he never ventured outside his own gate without an armed
guard.

thousand souls which composed the van of the moving army of pilgrims, the marching orders which he left behind him were obeyed to the letter by the Saints who were settled in comfortable homes, as well as by those who tarried in camps, and thenceforward the plains were white with the wagons of the emigrants, who came at the call of their leader from almost every country and clime, to gather round the standard which he had set up in the wilderness.

The first company, with which the Prophet traveled, was provided with everything necessary for a speedy and prosperous journey, and as many of the men in this company were already under the ban of the law for various offenses, the Zion toward which they journeyed was to them a city of refuge, which it was desirable to reach as soon as possible.

There was another reason which operated still more powerfully with their Prophet to urge forward the company he led. Among the spiritual wives who had been sealed to the Prophet Joseph were a number of married women, whose husbands knew nothing of their relations to him. In some cases the deceived husband was absent on a foreign mission, which would keep him from his family four or five years. In other instances, though the husband continued to live with his wife, concealment had been so successfully practiced that he did not even suspect her of infidelity ; but in either case a discovery which could not fail to be attended with unpleasant consequences was to be guarded against just now.*

Injured husbands had made much of the trouble which resulted in the downfall of Nauvoo, and the Prophet Brigham, who in the character of Joseph's successor claimed and appropriated a number of his wives, meant to estab-

* See Appendix, Note C, page 331.

lish himself securely in the mountain fastness which was to be the seat of his kingdom, before the husbands of these women learned the truth.   Then, being clothed with absolute power, he would acknowledge them openly as his wives, and make them members of his household.

*   *   *   *   *   *   *

Madame La Tour felt keenly the degradation of being forced to make her journey with this company of outlaws, and of women who had sacrificed truth, honor, and virtue on the altar of their false faith ; but there were others among the emigrants whose sufferings in this respect were far greater than her own.

Polygamy had been secretly practiced, not only by the leaders of the people, but by many of their followers, for six years past, and now, having left the farthest borders of civilization for a home in the wilderness, all disguises were thrown off, and women who had been wholly ignorant of the acceptance of polygamy by their husbands were confronted with the "spiritual wives" (and in some cases with their children also), and requested to receive them as members of the family !

In Nauvoo, women who refused to accept what was known there as the spiritual wife doctrine could only be subjected to ecclesiastical penalties, and threatened with eternal punishment ; but here, in the heart of the Indian country, with no human tribunal to which appeal could be made, with no help at hand, the penalty which the Mormon code prescribed * could be visited on offenders by abandoning them to the tender mercies of savages and wild beasts.

---

* If a woman refuse to give other wives to her husband it shall be lawful for him to take them without her consent, *and she shall be destroyed for her disobedience.*—REVELATION ON CELESTIAL MARRIAGE, Section 25.

There were many wives in that company who could not otherwise have been brought to submit to the indignities heaped upon them ; and among these there were some who would have chosen to perish in the wilderness rather than to continue their journey with the women who had robbed them of their husbands ; but these wives were also mothers, many of them with babes at the breast, and for their children's sake they endured all things.

It was for her child's sake that Madame La Tour had undertaken her dreary pilgrimage across the plains, in the company of those she despised and loathed. The word of the Prophet alone could not have convinced her that Louise was to be taken to the place to which the emigrants were bound ; but what he had said to her was only a confirmation of what she had learned from other sources, and she had now no reason to doubt that her daughter, if not already in the mountains, would be carried there some time during the present summer.

A mother's love triumphs over all difficulties, and perceives no impossibilities. She did not ask herself how she should rescue her child when found. Surely, after all her sacrifices and sufferings, God would provide a way.

There was no one near her in whom she could confide, or of whom she could ask counsel. Her son Philip, though affectionate and obedient to her, looked up to the Prophet as a divine being, and the latter spoke truly when he said that the boy would cut off his right hand for him. Catherine, her second daughter, inherited her mother's spirit, and if she knew the truth about her sister, would say or do some rash thing which would bring trouble upon all of them ; and Blanche, the youngest, was only a child.

Her servants, it is true, were faithful and attached to her ; but they were stolid specimens of the Canadian peasantry, whose slow wits were of little use in any matter not connected with their daily tasks.

She had one friend in the company outside of her own family, but just now this friend had sore burdens of her own to bear.

Helen Woodford was the wife of a high priest whose place was near the Prophet, and whose counsel and aid had been of the greatest value to the Saints in their past difficulties and perils.

He was a man of more than ordinary ability, and by far the superior of their leader in birth and culture; but he was one of the few who merited the title of fanatic. He had already sacrificed fortune, friends, and social position for the sake of his faith, and the event proved that he was ready to do much more than this at the command of the Prophet.

He had always been proud of his wife, who was a woman of fine mind and noble presence, and apparently their marriage was in every sense a happy one.

They had three boys, bright, handsome children, idolized by both parents, and so far as their friends knew, their domestic sky was without a cloud ; but in reality, the storm which finally wrecked their home began to gather as far back as the days when the Prophet Joseph first whispered to those nearest him that he had a " revelation" commanding the Saints to take unto themselves many wives.

Woodford, from the fact that he occupied a position of trust and confidence, was one of the first to hear of this " revelation," and although the immediate effect of the disclosure was to shake his faith in the new religion and its Prophet, he was finally brought to accept the doctrine of celestial marriage as true. Still his affection for his wife, and perhaps also a little wholesome fear of consequences (for it must be remembered that at this time and for some years afterward the Saints were, to a certain extent, amenable to the civil law), kept him from putting his belief in practice.

It was not the will of the Prophet's successor, however, that the " revelation" should remain a dead letter, and a strong pressure was brought to bear upon the leading men of the Church who had still some love for their wives, and some regard for decency and good morals, to bring them to practice its teachings.

Woodford was among the number of those who, as a test of their loyalty to the Church, were required to take more wives, and in the end he consented to do so, and two young girls were sealed to him on the same day, " for time and eternity."

The need of secrecy, however, was still recognized, and for many months Helen Woodford knew nothing of the irreparable wrong done her.

When her suspicions were at length awakened, her husband was absent on a missionary tour, from which he did not return until the day when the first company of emigrants were preparing for their march across the plains. Long before this the quick eye of the wife had discerned a change in him for which she was at a loss to account ; and now, while he was, if possible, more tender in his manner toward her than ever before, she could not help perceiving that he was ill at ease, and oppressed by some unusual anxiety.

Still, strangely enough, the fears which she had begun to entertain during her husband's absence did not now trouble her, and after they started on their journey she did not once suspect the true cause of his gloom and restlessness, until the day came which he had determined upon for ending all concealment.

The emigrant train had now been about a week on the

road, and was a little more than a hundred miles west of the Missouri. It was near sundown, and they had camped for the night, when Woodford entered the tent in which his wife sat, accompanied by two young women, one of them carrying a baby in her arms, and the other leading by the hand a child a little more than a year old. Helen rose with a feeling of surprise, but still with no premonition of what was coming, and at the same moment her husband led forward the woman on his right, saying,

" This is my wife Mary, and this is our child."

Then turning immediately to the one on his left he added,

" This is my wife Emily, and the little one in her arms is our child."

Helen did hot break out into reproaches, nor did she scream or faint. She walked quickly and silently out of the tent, and continued to walk until a little rise of ground hid the camp from her sight. She was following the course of the stream that ran near the tent. Somewhere, perhaps, it might be deep enough to afford her a resting-place under its waters. Still farther. She was now a mile from camp, and yet the peaceful stream, creeping between its grassy banks, was so shallow that she could touch the bottom with her hand. She sat down beside it, and gazed into the water.

" There are other ways," she said aloud, remembering the pistol that was lying in a corner of her trunk, with a sense of disappointment that she had not brought it.

How long she sat there she did not know. She was not thinking ; she was not even conscious for a part of the time ; but at last her trance was broken by a voice that she knew —the voice of her first-born.

" Mother ! mother !" the boy called, in accents of agony and terror.

He did not see her. Darkness was settling down, and the fringe of willows on the bank hid her from view.

" Mother ! mother ! where are you ? Oh, she is lost !" and then sobs drowned his voice.

That sound called the mother back to life. She rose slowly to her feet. " Here, my son," she called, and in a minute more the lad was clinging about her neck.

" Oh, mother, why did you go so far ?" he said through his tears. " Edward and I have hunted everywhere for you, and the Indians are all around. Poor little Arthur is alone in the tent crying for you. Come, mother ;" and leaning on her son, henceforth her only stay in life, Helen retraced her steps. Half way to the camp they met the second boy sobbing and wringing his hands, while he continued to call for her, and little Arthur, her baby, had cried himself to sleep in the tent.

She lifted the little fellow, sobbing even in his slumber, from the cold ground on which he lay. Of what had she been thinking ? Was her life her own to end when it became unbearable ? No. It belonged to her children, and for their sakes she would live it out.

She sat down on the side of her bed, with her boy in her arms, and rested the little sleeping head on her bosom. There was healing in the touch of the baby hands. There was balm in the soft breathing close to her bruised and bleeding heart.

The older boys moved about quietly, building the campfire and cooking the supper, and when all was ready, Robert, the eldest, said,

" Shall I go and call father ?"

" No," the mother replied, wondering at herself that she could speak so calmly ; " he has something to attend to, and will come by and by."

She did not ask the boys whether their father had sent

them to search for her ; and it was well perhaps that she
knew nothing of what passed in the tent after she left.
Emily, the younger of the two women, looking at her as
she passed out, was terrified by the expression of the
white, set face.

" Go after her quickly, Brother Woodford," she said ;
" she means to put herself out of the way."

" You do not know Helen," he answered.   " This is a
heavy cross for her, and she wants to be alone for a little
while.   She needs to pray for help to receive you in the
right spirit."

" You don't mean to say," exclaimed Mary, " that she
knew nothing about us until you brought us right in before
her ?"

" Brother Brigham counseled us to reveal nothing before
the appointed time," was the answer, " and I have obeyed
him."

" Then I must say, Brother Woodford, I don't wonder
that she went out in the way she did, and for my part I
wouldn't have stirred a step to come here to-night if I'd
known that she had never been told a word before. It
wasn't treating her right, nor us either."

" Mary," said Brother Woodford severely, " such language in reference to the counsel that is given us is most
unbecoming, and I cannot allow it in any member of my
family."

Mary looked subdued.   It was plain that she stood
greatly in awe of her lord, who according to the teaching
she had received held her salvation in his hands.

Both she and Emily were simple-minded, unsophisticated
girls, whose credulity had been their undoing, and they
were not so lost to all womanly feeling as to wish to force
their presence upon the wronged and outraged wife. It
had been Woodford's purpose to follow the example of the

Prophet, and make them members of his household at once ; but they both refused to remain that night. They had made the journey thus far with a relative, and they announced their intention of returning to his camp for the present. " We will give Sister Woodford a little time to get reconciled ; I know I should need it in her place," Emily said, with a touch of genuine feeling.

CHAPTER IV.

MYSTERY BEGINS.

THE days lengthened into weeks, and the weeks into months, but the emigrant train had not yet come in sight of the mountains that girt the Promised Land.

Incumbered as they were with women and children, with flocks and herds, and with heavily-loaded wagons carrying all manner of supplies for the new settlement, their progress was necessarily slow, but there was little sickness and no death in the company, and the savages who had annoyed the scouts did not show any disposition to molest the train—a fact which the devout believers in the new gospel regarded as a sign that Heaven had interposed specially in their behalf.

At length, late in August, and near the close of a long day's march, dim, bluish masses began to appear upon the western horizon. They might have been taken for clouds, so faint and far-away they looked ; but as the sun sank out of sight among them, their jagged outlines were clearly defined, and the light of the next morning showed plainly what they were—the rocky peaks of the mountains about whose base wound the trail followed by the scouts the year before—the mountains which were to be as a wall between the inheritance of the Saints and the world with which they were at war.

About a dozen men, mounted on the best horses in the train, were now dispatched in advance of the main body to give notice to the colonists in the valley of the approach of the emigrants. The difficulties of traveling with so many incumbrances increased greatly as they entered the mountains, but the certainty that they would reach the end of their journey in a few days at the farthest lightened all burdens, and the whole company seemed cheered and inspired by the near prospect of rest from the fatigues of their toilsome march.

It was the first of September when the train reached Emigration Cañon, for so the pass leading into the valley had been named by the scouts. The day was one of the loveliest of the year, and the scene that burst upon their view as they emerged from the cañon was such as to leave no doubt in the minds of the faithful that their Prophet had been divinely guided to the spot, while the large number of his followers, to whom a remembrance of the world they had left was unpleasantly associated with the idea of sheriffs, prisons, and the penalties of violated law, regarded with the greatest satisfaction the defences which nature had built up around this new stronghold.

The improvements made by the colonists in the valley were not very extensive. About a dozen adobe houses, and as many more log-cabins had been built ; the fall grain put in the year before had been reaped and threshed, and a few acres of ground planted with potatoes and other vegetables.

The square set apart for the Prophet (a plot of ten acres in the heart of the city) had been partly surrounded by a rude fence, and an adobe house had been built in the center. In one corner of this square was an inclosure known then (and ever since) as the Tithing Yard. Into this inclosure those wagons whose freight was most valuable were driven, and a guard was placed over them " that the Indians might not be tempted to commit depredations :" so the owners were told.

The wagons loaded with Madame La Tour's goods were taken to this place, and also the ambulance in which she had made the journey.   A smaller wagon, containing their camp outfit and a few necessaries for daily use, was unloaded at the door of the cabin which was designated by the Prophet as the one they were to occupy.

Madame La Tour had been ill during the last week of the journey, and when her bed was made up in the cabin, and her children had done what they could for her comfort, she sank into a stupor from which it was difficult to arouse her.   She continued in this state much of the time for ten days, and Philip was obliged to go to the Tithing Yard in search of medicines and other necessaries which were in the wagons left there.

The Prophet, who supervised the smallest details as well as the largest undertakings of the community, was the person to go to—so the man on guard informed Philip when he made known his errand.   Accordingly the boy waited on his Prophet-master, who received him very kindly, but told him the wagons must not be unpacked until his mother was able to look after her own business.

" And meantime," he added graciously, " I will lend you anything and everything you may need."

With Philip the word of the Prophet was law, and he accepted this arrangement without question.   When his mother was able to sit up, she learned for the first time where her property was, and immediately sent Philip and Pierre with a written order for the wagons and their contents.   This order was received as civilly as Philip's verbal request of the week before ; but the Prophet assured his young disciple that they could not deviate from the rule they had adopted, which was not to deliver up anything until identified and claimed by the owner in person.

" In a few days at the farthest your mother will be able to come herself," he said ; " and, as I told you before, I will see that you have everything you need."

Madame La Tour made no comments on this message when she received it. It was, to her, sufficient evidence that her enemy meant to hold everything and reduce her to a state of complete dependence on him ; but no good could come of talking to her son about anything that she felt or feared. Now, when it was too late, she saw that she had placed herself wholly in the power of the man whom she knew to be an unrelenting tyrant—cruel as death, remorseless as the grave.

Only a single faint gleam of hope lighted the dark prospect before her. Her elder sons, who had rebelled against the Prophet's rule, and who hated everything that pertained to this false faith, might yet be able to help her. As before stated, they had gone through to the coast with an emigrant train in the spring. To their mother, who was ignorant of the geography of the country, it seemed that the place to which they were bound could not be very much farther west ; perhaps it was just on the other side of the mountains. If it were only possible to communicate with them, they would find means to bring her out of this valley, the air of which seemed already poisoned.

And yet, even if a way of escape opened, she could not avail herself of it until her daughter was found—her daughter whose fate she dared not conjecture.

Louise was not in the valley. It is true, her mother at first entertained a suspicion that the pioneers had taken her with them the year before, but she had given up this idea months ago. A much larger company of emigrants, composed chiefly of those fugitives from Nauvoo who had remained east of the Missouri, was now on the way.

It was expected that the train would arrive some time in October, and from information furnished by Mrs. Woodford, Madame La Tour was confident that her daughter would enter the valley with this company.

Yet, supposing this to be true, her mother might never see her face. The valley of Great Salt Lake, the site of the city the Prophet had laid out, was by no means the only spot selected for settlement. Even now, before either men or animals had recovered from the effects of the long march across the plains, scouts had been sent north and south to prospect the country. The colonists who came in the year before had wonderful stories to tell of the beauty and fertility of other valleys farther south, while the trapper who had acted as their guide, and who still remained with them, assured the new-comers that there were thousands of acres of rich grass lands a little to the north.

It was the policy of the Prophet to take possession of these lands and settle them as rapidly as possible ; and about twenty families in the present company had already been detailed to colonize the valleys lying south of Great Salt Lake, while a still larger number of the company expected in October would be sent north as soon as they arrived.

Fortunately for the prosperity of the new settlement, many of the colonists were practical farmers, and this year as well as the year before a number of the wagons in the train were loaded with agricultural implements, and with seed for the ground that was already broken to receive it.

Necessity is a stern taskmistress, and under her compelling hand the settlers worked as probably few of them had ever worked before. Buildings went up as if by magic, irrigating ditches were dug, and a large area of ground was ready for the fall planting by the time the second company of immigrants arrived.

Meanwhile the La Tours continued dependent on the Prophet, who under various pretexts delayed the surrender of their goods ; and while their neighbors were breaking ground to plant the grain for the next year's bread, or building themselves comfortable houses, they remained in the cabin which had been assigned them on the day of their arrival, without the means of improving their present condition or making any provision for the future.

Pierre Roche and his wife had been ordered to accompany the colonists sent south, and they had gone, taking with them, by the Prophet's direction, the wagon and ox-team which were the only vestiges of Madame La Tour's property outside the Tithing Yard. Soon after they left, the Prophet sent for Philip, " to talk matters over," as he said. Assuming a most fatherly look and tone, and putting his arm around the shoulders of his young disciple, the leader of the people began.

" My dear boy, what I have to say to you to-day is of a very painful nature, and because it is painful I have foolishly put it off from time to time ; but now I feel that something must be done, and for this reason I have sent for you. You know that your mother's health has been failing for two years past ?"

" Yes."

" You have also noticed that she is greatly changed in other respects ; but you are so young, and the change has been so gradual, you do not see as others do that her mind is quite gone."

, " Are you sure it is so bad as that ?" The boy's face was white with distress and fear. " I know she is not as she used to be ; but she is not—my mother cannot be—mad ?"

" I could not bear to say the word, but that is just the truth. She is mad, and unless she is watched very carefully she will do something dreadful to herself or other people. You cannot be with her all the time, and your sisters are not old enough to take care of her, so I have engaged Sister Purdy, who, you know, is a very good woman, to stay with her and watch her, and help your sisters about the house. For yourself, though you are so young, you must be a man, and take a man's place. The support of your mother and sisters and a great many cares besides will now fall upon you, and because I love you for your father's sake as well as your own, I want to help you. You have proved before this that my counsel is worth something.''

Beginning in this strain, the Prophet detained his listener for two hours, while he poured into his ears '' counsel'' upon every possible subject connected with his present or future life.

When Philip at length started for his home the sun had set, and he felt a little troubled at the lateness of the hour.

He never left his mother and sisters alone after dark ; but he comforted himself now with the thought that Sister Purdy was already at the cabin, as the Prophet had assured him that she would go there before night.

Still, in spite of this assurance, he was uneasy, and as the shadows settled down upon the valley he quickened his steps. When he came in sight of the cabin no light was visible, but this did not seem strange to him, as he knew his mother usually hung a blanket inside of the one window, in which a square of muslin did duty in the place of glass. He hurried on, and was soon opposite the door.

Here he stopped, as though a strong hand had arrested him. The door, which opened outwardly, was swinging on its hinges, and there was neither light nor sound from within. At another time this might not have alarmed him ; but now, with the Prophet's words, '' Your mother is mad,'' still ringing in his ears, he stood rooted to the spot by a vague terror. Then, before he could collect his scattered thoughts, two figures, which in the increasing darkness he did not at first recognize, ran toward him, and in a minute his sisters stood beside him.

"Oh, Philip!" Blanche exclaimed breathlessly, "we have run so fast, and we were afraid mother would be angry with us for staying so late; but indeed we.could not help it."

"Why, where have you been?" he asked.

"Oh, only for a ride with Brother White and George and Dolly. We had gone around the corner just for a little walk, when Brother White came along with his wagon and told us to jump in. We said we must ask mother first, but he told us he stopped at the house and asked for us, and she said we might go. Then we rode—oh, ever so far; and when we got back to his house he took us out and told us to run home as fast as we could."

"You did very wrong to go without asking mother yourself," Philip said severely, and yet hardly knowing why he blamed his sisters. "Come, let us go in. Poor mother is alone, and has no light. The candles must be all gone. I forgot to ask this morning;" and with a feeling of self-reproach, much too poignant for the apparently slight cause, he led his sisters to the open door.

Within all was silent and dark.

"Mother," he called gently.

There was no answer.

"Mother! Oh, mother! Where are you?" all three cried, this time, aloud, and in terrified tones.

Still there was no response.

"Where can she be? Oh, something dreadful must have happened!" Catherine exclaimed, and Blanche began to cry.

"Hush, girls," Philip said authoritatively, though his own voice trembled a little. "I have a match in my pocket, and will make a light. Catherine, you feel for some paper on the box by the door, while I gather a few splinters.''

In a couple of minutes, and with the exercise of much care lest the one match should go out, the splinters were lighted, and Philip, taking a couple of them in his hand, entered the cabin, followed by his trembling sisters.

Everything was just as when they left in the afternoon. Their mother's bed was undisturbed, and her hood and shawl hung on a nail above it. Philip drew aside the blanket which served as a partition between the front room and the shed in the rear. That, too, was silent and empty.

'' Mother is lost,'' Blanche said, still crying.

'' You talk like a silly child,'' Philip answered sharply. '' We all stayed away so late she did not like being alone, and she has gone to Sister Woodford's.''

'' Then,'' said practical Catherine, '' why did she leave her hood and shawl ?''

Philip was about to answer when he made the discovery that the splinters he carried would not burn a minute longer, and Catherine, who thought she remembered seeing a candle in the box that served them for a cupboard, began to search for it.

'' Here it is,'' she exclaimed presently. '' Now, at any rate, we shall not be in the dark.''

When the candle was lighted Philip said,

'' Girls, you must stay here quietly while I run over to Sister Woodford's. I will not be gone long, and you can fasten the door till I come back.''

The words were scarcely spoken when they heard a step outside, and Sister Purdy appeared at the open door and began to make hurried excuses for being so late ; but noticing Philip's pale face and his sisters' frightened looks she stopped short, and exclaimed,

"Why, children, what on earth is the matter, and where is your mother?" glancing past them into the empty room.

"Mother has gone to Sister Woodford's, I think," Philip said.

"She has not, for I stopped in there myself as I was coming down ; I don't see what you were all thinking of to leave her."

Philip checked the incautious woman by a whispered word, and then said aloud,

"Sister Purdy, if you will stay here with the girls, I will go and find my mother."

He spoke quietly, but his heart throbbed so it almost seemed to him that the others could hear its beating ; and not daring to trust himself to utter another word, he hurried out into the darkness.

He was only a boy, and he loved his mother dearly. If harm had come to her, was he not to blame for taking so little care of her? Why did he not beg the Prophet to allow Pierre Roche and the faithful Joan to stay with them ? The Prophet loved him like a father, so he kept saying to himself, and would not refuse anything he might ask.

Bitter self-reproach mingled with the grief and dread that oppressed him ; but he never for a moment dreamed of reproaching his leader, to whom he was now hurrying as fast as his trembling limbs would carry him. To-night, as in every other trouble of his life, he turned to this hard, remorseless man, who, to him, was always so tender, and whom he regarded as almost divine.

The Prophet listened with an air of profound solicitude to Philip's hurried and agitated recital, and as he finished sighed heavily.

"That which I have feared so long has happened at last," he said. "Your mother has wandered away, at the very time when I was planning to guard against such a thing. Sister Purdy is much to blame for not going to her at an early hour as I directed ; but, my dear boy, don't be too much cast down. I will have the settlement searched thoroughly, and will send parties of men beyond the limits to look for her in every direction."

"Will some one start out with me now ?" Philip asked eagerly.

"You could not do a great deal to help," was the answer. "You lay your trouble too much to heart. Go home and take care of your sisters, and leave the search to me. You know I will do everything that can be done."

With this assurance Philip was forced to content himself. He had never disobeyed the Prophet or questioned his decisions, and he could not begin now ; so with a heavy heart he returned to the cabin to wait and watch alone through the long hours of the night, after his sisters had sobbed themselves to sleep ; for Sister Purdy left as soon as he came in.

There was nothing for her to do there, she said, and she might learn something by inquiring around.

The night seemed endless to the lonely watcher. He was so young, barely sixteen ; and though he had known sorrow before, he had never been called to bear anything so hard as this. Long before dawn the single candle burned low in the socket that held it, and went out.. Then he watched the stars and waited for day, his ear strained meantime to catch every sound.

With the first hour of daylight a messenger came from the Prophet's own household. The settlement had been thoroughly searched long before midnight, he said, and at daylight parties of men had gone out in every direction, through the valley in the foot-hills, and toward the Jordan. As soon as either party found any trace to follow, they would send a man back to the settlement with word ;

meantime the Prophet especially required Philip not to be anxious or alarmed. They were all doing their best, and without doubt his mother would be home before many hours.

The messenger brought a basket of provisions and other necessaries, and added many kind and sympathizing words on his own account. Philip needed all the comfort that was offered him. He looked haggard and ill after his long night-watch, and when his sisters waked and found their mother still away, he had all he could do to soothe and quiet them.

Blanche cried incessantly, and Catherine made remarks quite in keeping with her temperament, which shocked and distressed her brother.

"Mother hasn't been ten steps from the door since we came here," she declared, "and she wouldn't go away from the house unless somebody took her. Besides, if she went out of the settlement she had to go past some of the houses ; and don't you suppose they would notice her, walking bareheaded, and with her silk wrapper on ? That was the dress she wore yesterday, and all her other dresses are here, and her shawl, and everything. There's nothing gone except what she had on when she sat in that chair," pointing as she spoke to her mother's empty seat, at the sight of which Blanche's sobs grew louder.

Catherine was three years younger than her brother, but tall and well developed ; almost a woman already in appearance. Her mind, too, seemed of late to have matured rapidly, and she often surprised those around her by the expression of ideas quite in advance of her years. She had, moreover, as we have previously noticed in these pages, her mother's spirit, and she had imbibed from her a distrust of the Prophet and his teachings. Now, in spite of her brother's efforts to check her, she continued to express her opinion that her mother never left the house alone, and that nobody had taken much pains to find her.

"Catherine," Philip said at length, when at the end of all patience, "if anybody is to blame it is yourself. I left you here to take care of mother. You knew she was sick and needed you, and you ought not to have gone outside the door until I came back."

This reproach silenced the girl, who loved her mother above everything, and who had all the time been secretly blaming herself for leaving her alone, though when she went out with Blanche the day before, it was at her mother's request.

Meanwhile the day was passing, and there was no news from any of the parties who were supposed to be searching the valley ; but late in the afternoon Philip was again summoned to the Prophet's residence. This time he was received with expressions of the deepest sympathy, and with an exhortation to lift up his heart in prayer for strength to bear whatever might come.

"It was not until past noon," the Prophet said, " that we got the least clew to follow. Then Miles Hayward, the trapper, who was leading the search in the direction of the river, came upon foot-prints here and there. The marks were those of a woman's foot, small and delicate, but the track was not easy to follow, on account of the bunch-grass and the loose sand. Still, as all the marks seemed to point toward the river, they thought they could not do better than to follow it up and down, and in the willows near the bank Miles found this."

He took something from the table, unfolded it, and held it up before Philip's eyes. It was a fine cambric handkerchief with a monogram in the corner. Philip knew it only too well, and reached out his hand for it with a cry of anguish.

" Stop," the Prophet added, retaining the frail token ;
" I have more to tell you.

" Near the place where the handkerchief was found,
there were more foot-prints, and just at the water's edge
the bank was broken, as though by some person slipping
down.

" Now, my dear boy, I have done my duty. I shall pray
for you, and all the people are praying now that you may
have strength to bear your affliction : but more than this
we cannot do. A dozen men are already dragging the
river, in the hope of recovering your mother's body, but if
they fail (and I own I fear they *will* fail), try to be resigned to the will of God. It is in times of trouble that the
true Latter Day Saint shows the strength of his faith. Go
home now to your sisters, and comfort them, and let everybody see that your religion is worth something."

CHAPTER V.

CELESTIAL MARRIAGE.

MEANTIME, where was Louise La Tour, the daughter for whose sake the mother had risked all, and, as it seemed, lost all ?

She was not in the valley, nor had she been there. She had remained with those followers of the Prophet who had temporary homes east of the Missouri ; but in order to understand her condition and surroundings it will be necessary to go back to the time of her father's death.*

To-day, men and women who were among the disciples of the Prophet Joseph in his lifetime, but who have since then renounced Mormonism, account for the influence of this man, coarse, ignorant, and wicked as he was, over a multitude of followers of a far different character, by saying that he possessed wonderful mesmeric powers.

While he lived, his strange gifts were supposed by them to be supernatural ; and men whose sense of right compelled them to denounce the wickedness which they afterward discovered in him were at a loss to account for what had seemed miraculous powers, conferred on him from above.

Whatever may have been the secret of this power, the fact, which cannot be disproved, remains on record, that for many years he exercised an almost unlimited influence over persons who were greatly his superiors in mind and

* See Appendix, Note D, page 333.

education, and whose previous lives had been irreproach-able.

When the doctrine of Celestial Marriage was first taught by him, many of those who listened to his teachings sup-posed that they referred to a union purely spiritual ; and when the truth at length came out, numbers forsook and denounced him, but among those who remained his adher-ents there were hundreds whose motives and character had hitherto been above suspicion. And, stranger than all, many of the women who became his plural wives were of good families and, up to that time, of unblemished fame.

Wives whose fidelity to their husbands had never been questioned, and young girls who had been watched over from infancy by Christian mothers, were among his earli-est victims.

When Louise La Tour became a member of his house-hold she was only fifteen. She had been carefully brought up and tenderly watched over by both parents, and in heart and mind was still a child, as ignorant of evil as her five-year-old sister Blanche. In stature, however, she was a woman, and already the perfect outlines of her supple form, the contour of her lovely face, the soft rose-tints of her cheek, and the liquid luster of her dark eyes made a pic-ture so fair to look upon that, had not the mother been blind to the fact that the child who was but yesterday in the nursery was no longer a child to any except herself, she would never have risked such priceless treasure unguarded for an hour.

Louise, who saw the Prophet only through the medium of her father's faith, was all docility and obedience when placed in his care, and at first received whatever he taught without question.

When he told her that, to secure her future salvation, she must be " sealed " to him for eternity, and that it was her father's dying request, she consented to the ceremony, without understanding in the least what it meant.

When she received the first intimation of the Prophet's real designs, she was in a room in the Endowment House, to which she had been carried in a fainting state. The barbarous rites in which she was forced to participate, and the fearful oaths she was compelled to take,* had the effect of paralyzing her faculties, and long before the conclusion of the ceremonies (which lasted eight hours without intermission) she was nearly insensible through fatigue and terror.

*   *   *   *   *   *   *

Even to her mother Louise could not repeat the history of the weeks that followed that dreadful day. She was in the power of her destroyer. It seemed to her that he held her, body and soul, and when her mother came to take her away, she had sunk into the lethargy of despair, and prayed for nothing but death.

Madame La Tour saw that her child was ill and wretched, but she had not the faintest suspicion of the true cause until the day when the Prophet claimed Louise as his wife. Then, as we have seen, her plans for escaping from Nauvoo with her family were frustrated, and they were compelled to remain with the Mormons until they fled westward.

On the day that the fugitives crossed the Mississippi, the greatest confusion prevailed in their ranks, and no better time could have been chosen for the abduction of Louise, which had been resolved upon months before.

It is a historical fact, perfectly well authenticated, that the large number of women who were sealed to the Prophet Joseph during the last two years of his life were

* See Appendix, Note E, page 334.

divided after his death among those nearest him in office, and that such as were thought most desirable were appropriated by Brigham Young, the Prophet's successor, and by Heber C. Kimball, his First Councilor.

The unhappy Louise was apportioned to Kimball, a coarse, brutal wretch, whose name deserves to be handed down to everlasting infamy. The promise from Brigham Young, that he should be allowed to add her to the number of his wives, was quite sufficient to induce him to take all the risks attendant on carrying her off, and months before the exodus from Nauvoo he had a place prepared for her in Iowa, where many of the fugitive Mormons found temporary homes.

Louise's prison (for such it proved to be) was a three-roomed log-cabin in a small clearing. The building, though rudely constructed, was tolerably comfortable and well furnished, and she was told that her mother and the children would make it their home for a time.

For a couple of months she saw nothing of Kimball, and knew nothing of the motives of those who brought her to the place. Like her mother, she at first supposed that her separation from her family was accidental, and as she was kindly treated by the couple who had charge of the cabin she felt no uneasiness except that caused by not seeing her mother as soon as she expected.

When Kimball at length found time to visit his captive, and the knowledge of the fate to which she had been consigned burst upon her, the shock was too much for her reason, and for many weeks she raved in delirium.

The brute to whom, according to the decree of the new Prophet, she was now bound for life, took a savage pleasure in making her feel that he was her master, and that she was wholly in his hands, without the faintest hope of escape or redress.

During the whole time that her mother and brothers remained in the Mormon settlement on the west bank of the Missouri, she lived in this cabin, not fifty miles from them, as ignorant of their fate as they were of hers. Kimball visited her frequently during the first year, but long before the end of the second year he grew tired of her, and when in the summer of 1848 she was taken across the Missouri to join the second company of emigrants to Salt Lake valley, she had not seen him for months.

The unspeakable fear and loathing with which she looked forward to his coming never failed to make her ill when the time at which she expected him drew near, and at the close of her first year's imprisonment no one would have recognized in the pallid, hollow-eyed, wasted woman who still answered to the name Louise, the beautiful girl whom her mother remembered so fondly.

Now, however, six months' respite from his hated visits, together with the dawning hope that he had grown tired of her and would come no more, seemed to have given her a new lease of life, and with returning health a little of her old beauty and spirit came back also.

Kimball was not in the company with which Louise was to cross the plains. He had gone on with the first train, taking several of his wives with him.

As those who knew him best will testify, he had one good trait—that of providing abundantly for the physical comfort of all dependent on him. His numerous families were always well housed, well fed, and well clothed, and Louise's custodians, John Burch and the woman who held the relation to him of fourth wife, were supplied with everything necessary for themselves and their charge upon the journey. When they reached Salt Lake they found comfortable quarters ready for them ; but Louise was kept a closer prisoner than when in Iowa. Kimball did not come near her that autumn, nor the following winter, and for many months she saw no one except her jailers. She was still ignorant of the fate of her family, and knew nothing of what took place in the settlement.

The slow months followed each other, with nothing to mark their lapse except the change from autumn to winter, and from winter to spring—changes which she watched wearily from the one window of her room. Once a day, when the weather permitted, she took a short walk with her keepers along a solitary path leading to the bench north of the settlement. She met no one during these walks, and had she done so she would not have thought of making any appeal for help. She knew that she was in the heart of the wilderness, a thousand miles from the borders of civilization, and that the only human beings near her were the slaves of the Prophet, whom she believed to be the author of her past sufferings and her present imprisonment.

All hope of escape had long since died within her, and she had nothing left to look forward to except the possibility of meeting her mother, whom she felt sure the Prophet would yet find means to bring to the valley, if he had not already done so.

The winter which, mild and short as it was, seemed interminable to the captive girl, came to an end at last. With the opening of spring the whole settlement was alive with the work of preparation for planting a large area of ground. An additional immigration of several thousand souls was expected early in the summer, and as the colony was forced to depend mainly on the season's crop for food, the entire laboring force of the settlement was taxed to its utmost during the process of breaking ground and putting in the seed.

At this time Louise's keepers were also fully occupied with outdoor work, and as she showed no disposition to wander off, she was allowed the liberty of the house and lot. The ground belonging to the cabin was not inclosed, and there was nothing to mark the existence of a street near it except the path mentioned before, which led up to the foot-hills. Late one afternoon in March, when Burch and the woman who kept the house were away, Louise was sauntering listlessly about the borders of the spot of ground that had been plowed for a garden, when she saw a slender, girlish figure hurrying down the path toward the cabin.

There was something strangely familiar in the outlines of this figure, in the poise of the head, and the free, alert movements—something that made Louise's heart beat quickly, and drew her toward the path.

The person she was watching came a few steps farther in the direction of the cabin, then turned and seemed about to take another way, when Louise, hardly knowing what she did, called,

" Catherine !"

The girl stopped abruptly, turned round and looked to see from whom the call came, then moved toward the speaker in a hesitating manner.

" Did you call me ?" she asked.

Louise, without a thought of consequences, sprang across the ditch that divided the garden from the common, and hurried to the spot where she stood.

" Catherine ! Sister ! Don't you know me ?" she said, holding out her hands.

" *Louise ! Ma belle sœur !*"

The language of their childhood sprang unbidden to the lips of the younger girl, as with a glad cry she threw herself into her sister's arms.

It was some moments before either spoke again. Then Louise, with a caution born of experience, cast her eyes in

every direction in search of a possible witness of their
meeting. No one was in sight, and winding her arm
about her sister, she said,

"Come, *chérie*, let us go into the house. I am all alone,
and I can see from the window if any one comes, and let
you out of the back door."

"Poor sister ! Then you have to watch and listen too.
I am learning to do so ; but I don't like it one bit. When
I begin to talk about anything, Philip says, ' Hush ! some
one might hear you,' or ' Look out ! there is somebody
coming ! '"

By this time the girls had reached the cabin. Louise
drew her sister into her own room, carefully closing both
doors after her. When they were seated she clasped
Catherine's hands, and with her whole heart in her face and
voice asked,

"Our mother ? Is she here ? Is she well ?"

It was a hard question, but Catherine answered it more
wisely than many an older person might have done.

"I believe mother is here and well ; yet I don't know in
what house she is. But see ! I did not know in what
house you were until now."

"Tell me all that you do know," Louise urged, with
feverish eagerness, holding her sister's hands so tightly
that she hurt them.

"I will, but first—you do not believe in the Prophet, as
Philip does ?"

"Believe in *him ?* No !"

Something of her old spirit flushed Louise's cheeks and
gleamed in her dark eyes as she gave this answer.

"I am glad of that ; and now, I'll tell you what I know
and what I think. We came here with the train from winter quarters early last summer. Mother was sick at first,
but she got better, so that she could walk about the house

and lot. We were not very comfortable, for our things were all in the tithing-yard, and they would not let us have them. Philip had to go up every day, nearly, and ask for a little something that we were obliged to use.

" One day, when he was gone, mother told me to take Blanche out for a walk. We meant to be back in half an hour, but when we were out of sight of the house Brother White came along with his children in a wagon, and told us mother said we might ride with him.

" I thought then that he told the truth ; but now I believe it was something made up, and you will see why. He took us a long way from the settlement, and did not bring us back till after dark. When we got home we met Philip at the door (the Prophet had kept *him* till after dark too), and mother was gone. They pretended to believe that she was out of her mind, and had wandered away to the river and been drowned—said they found her handkerchief on the bank, and I don't know .what else. I did not believe it at the time, and the next week little Benny Spiers said to me,

" ' I was playing below the hill when your mother went away, and I saw her. Brother Atwood was with her.' ·

" I hushed the child up, for I knew it would be a bad thing for him and for me if it was found out that he had told me such a thing.

" I have never breathed a word of it to Philip nor Blanche ; but in my heart I am sure that mother is alive and somewhere in this country, though maybe not in this settlement ; and I mean to keep looking for her till I find her, if it takes years and years."

Louise heard her sister through without attempting to interrupt her. When the story was finished, she sat silent, her face white and rigid, her large dark eyes unnaturally bright.

" Why do you look so strangely ?" exclaimed Catherine.

" You need not feel as though what the people say might be true. Mother is alive, and we shall find her."

" Yes, you are right, *petite sœur*. Mother is alive, or if—"

Louise stopped. The dark suspicion that had crossed her mind must not be breathed to any one, least of all to her young sister, who was comforted and upheld by the hope of finding the mother alive and well.

" Tell me something more," she said, after a moment's hesitation, " I cannot understand why mother came here. Surely it was not her own wish."

" No, it was not. I know something about that which I cannot tell to Philip. On that last day at winter quarters, when everybody was getting ready to start, the Prophet came to our house. Mother was alone in the front room, but I was in the little shed at the back, and I heard him tell her that she might see you here, but never anywhere else. That is why she came."

" And our brothers, Charles and Francis, are they here too ?"

" No. They left winter quarters before we did. They are somewhere west of this place, with the Gentiles. They think of the Prophet just as you and I do."

The sisters talked for a few minutes longer, Louise evading a direct reply to any of Catherine's questions relating to herself. Then, as the sun sank lower, and the time of her keeper's return drew near, she repeated her caution not to let any one know of their meeting, and sent her sister away by another path in the rear of the cabin.

Catherine was to come up the hill again the next day if possible, and Louise was to let her know, by a sign agreed upon, whether it would be safe for her to venture near the house.

That night, as it happened, John Burch was to spend

with one of his other wives, and the woman Hannah came home alone, and in a rather despondent mood. She was a simple-minded creature, who had been sealed to Burch because she thought her salvation depended on him, and who manifested a dog-like attachment and fidelity to the master, who treated her much as he might have done if he had bought her in the market-place. She had been hard at work all day with him in the field, and would have counted it a privilege to cook his supper and wait on him at night; but of course it was quite right that he should go over to the other house, where Abigail and Sarah were living with his first wife. Abigail had one boy, and Sarah two, and poor Hannah bewailed her own childless condition as she and Louise sat alone at supper.

"Brother Brigham says it's want of faith," she observed. "He was a-preachin' only last Sunday in the Bowery, that if a woman hed all the faith in plurality that she orter hev, her reproach would be took away, an' she'd be the mother o' thousens. I've prayed an' prayed fur more faith, an' I've tried an' tried to be reconciled to Brother Burch's stayin' over to t'other house so much as he does lately, but some way my heart ain't right."

Louise felt called upon to offer some comfort to the poor creature, who had always been kind to her.

"You are doing the best you can, Hannah," she said, "and I would not worry. There is Eliza Snow, whom you all look up to. She has no children, and nobody blames her for want of faith."

"Oh, but, Sister Louise," the woman answered, lowering her voice as though there might be listeners even there, "You don't know all that I do about Sister 'Liza. You see she went into plurality when everybody was agin it, an' when the Gentiles an' the law an' all was after us. That was a time when it took a power o' faith to kerry a woman through, an' Sister 'Liza hed faith ; but in them days the sisters that was in plurality didn't dare to own their children, an' the trouble that Sister 'Liza went through, no tongue could tell. It ain't a mite of wonder that she hain't hed no children sense."

Hannah was growing unusually communicative, and Louise thought that by drawing her out she might learn something to her own advantage.

"On these lonesome evenings," she suggested, "I would like to sit with you, if you are willing, and to pass the time you might tell me something of the sermons at the Bowery, for you know I have never heard one."

"I'm sorry I didn't think of that afore. 'Twouldn't a' bin near so lonesome for neither of us. But after this you're goin' to the Bowery on Sundays. Them was the orders Brother Burch got yesterday."

Louise did not know whether this change boded good or ill. If she was to have her liberty, the time might come when she could meet her brother and sisters unhindered ; but such meetings, if allowed, might be used to entrap them or herself in additional difficulties.

For her own part it seemed that she had little more to fear. Her enemy had done his worst, and she could think of no deeper pit that might be dug for her. But the others ! She thought with a throb of fear of Catherine's beauty. She was growing tall and womanly too. Oh, why had she ever been brought here ?

Hour after hour, during the long night, Louise turned upon her sleepless pillow, calling up and dismissing one plan after another for escaping from the valley with her sisters.

She did not share Catherine's belief that their mother still lived. Indeed she was not sure that she wished to believe it. Better, far better, that she should be dead and safe in heaven, than alive and in the power of the remorse-less, unpitying tyrant who had already brought such miseries upon them.

But the girls, her innocent sisters ! It seemed almost as though she could hear her mother's voice bidding her watch over them,

Then another Voice, one that had saved her from despair, whispered,

" Fear not, for *I* am with thee."

In the darkness and silence of the night, in that lonely cabin, the helpless girl, cut off from all human succor for herself or those she loved, turned toward the unseen, mighty Helper.

She had drifted far, very far, but not beyond the reach of the Hand that built these mountain walls, which had seemed to shut her in, away from hope or help.

" *I* am with thee."

It was as though all the resources of heaven and earth had been placed within her reach. A great peace fell upon her, and, laying her head once more upon her pillow, Louise slept as she had not slept since the day she left her mother's roof.

CHAPTER VI.

FORTY-NINERS.

THE sunny August day was wearing to a close. The scattered clumps of fir and mountain-laurel cast long shadows across the rocky trail, up which a heavily-loaded wagon-train was slowly winding.

A couple of women and half a dozen very young children sat on rolls of blankets in front of the canvas covers, but with this exception, all belonging to the train—men, women, and children—toiled up the steep ascent on foot.

It was a rough way to climb, and a long one, but all were cheerful and hopeful, for the fertile valleys of Oregon lay just beyond, and the stout-hearted pioneers, who had traversed the prairies and forded the rivers west of the Missouri when the snows began to melt, crossed the Rocky Mountains before summer had softened the winds that swept down from their peaks, encountered the perils of the Desert, threaded with alkali streams—of the Snake Plains—and the bands of alert and dangerous savages on their borders, were not to be discouraged by any difficulties so near the journey's end.

Moreover, the summit was close at hand, and the sun yet two hours high. If they pressed forward steadily they might view the land of promise from that Pisgah before the darkness hid it, although it was not promised by a "Prophet."

The women of the company fell a little in the rear of the wagons. The children made frequent excursions into the chapparal, returning with their arms filled with flowers and branches of blossoming shrubs. About half of the men were occupied with attending to the teams and loose cattle belonging to the train. The remainder walked, some of them in advance of the wagons, and some a few yards in the rear, with their rifles in their hands.

At the head of the advance guard two young men paced side by side. They were of the same height and build, and performed the difficult feat of keeping step along the rugged trail with military precision.

Of the two who walked behind these, one was a tall, loose-jointed Missourian, clad in jeans, and carrying a gun as long as himself. The other was a small, wiry man, whose grizzled locks were covered by a cap of panther-skin. The tail of the panther depended from the rear of the cap, serving the double purpose of an ornament and a trophy.

His buckskin shirt and breeches were trimmed with a profusion of beads and fringes, and in addition to such arms as the others carried, a tomahawk with a handle two feet in length was fastened to his belt. Just now his keen black eyes were fixed on the summit before him, as he observed to his companion,

" It mought be a bad job for us to git over thar jist dark, with all these wimmen folks on our hands. Ef I was alone on the trail, I wouldn't see a mite of trouble about the time of day, but with wimmin an' babies to take care on, I'd like a few hours more o' daylight to look for Injun signs."

The Missourian, who answered to the name of Long John, gave a backward glance toward the men nearest the wagons.

" 'Twouldn't do no good to broach that idee to any of *them*," he said. " You an' I an' the boys ahead, bein' single men, hain't so much to lose if the Shastas should cut up rough, but them that owns the wimmen an' babies are a borrerin' trouble enough without our sayin' a word to help the thing along.

"That's so," assented the other ; "but it mought be as well to speak to the boys about bein' on the look-out ; I'll jist mention it to 'em anyhow ;" and raising his voice a little he called,

"La Tour !"

Both heads turned simultaneously.

"Thar, I knowed it," he chuckled. "It's jist the same as pullin' the string that ties 'em together."

In response to his signal the young men now halted for him and the Missourian to come up with them.

As we have said, they were exactly of a size, and one face was so like the other that it seemed as if their own mother would not have been able to distinguish between them. There was the same clear olive complexion, the same liquid black eyes, soft as a woman's, and the same features. Their comrades had long since given up the effort to tell them apart in any other way than by their dress. Both wore gayly-braided hunting-shirts, but the one was blue and the other gray. As they stood side by side, tall, erect, with their rifles poised lightly over their shoulders, the trapper's eyes dwelt on them admiringly.

"If them two was gals now, what a fortin' they'd have in their faces," he observed *sotto voce* to the Missourian.

"Yes," answered Long John ; "but neither on 'em carries a gal's heart under all that braidin'. There ain't a man in this train that I'd rayther have with me in a life-an'- death tussle with Injuns or any other varmints."

"That's so," replied the trapper heartily, ignoring the fact that his own merits as an Indian fighter had been passed over. "They're clear grit, both on 'em, an' long-headed too, for youngsters."

By this time they were within a rod of the young men,

who advanced a little to meet them, still keeping side by side.

"What is it, comrades?" asked the wearer of the blue hunting-shirt.

"The matter is, Francis, my boy," answered Long John, "that we want to take a observation from the peak without makin' any stir in the train. Carter, here, thinks that ef the Shastas air goin' to cut up at all, we kin look out for 'em in these mountaings, an' we four kin push on a little ahead an' watch fur signs."

"All right"—it was still Francis who was spokesman—"but see the sun. We have no time to lose. Shall we lead on?"

"Go ahead, boys," answered the trapper. "We'll be right with you."

The little party quickened their steps until a bend in the trail hid the wagons from them.

"I don't deny," said the trapper, "that I'm some oneasy about this late crossin' of the divide, but jist at this time the Shastas is more likely to be on their huntin'-grounds than on the war-path, an' they hain't troubled last year's emigration, neither on the way nor sence they've took up their land."

"Mebbe that's because there was nigh onto three hundred rifles, an' three hundred good shots to use 'em, in last year's emigration," observed Long John. "An Injun hez as much sense as a white man about takin' too many chances."

"There's somethin' in that, I know," answered the trapper; "but then, Injuns hez other kinds of sense too— more'n they git credit for. They don't, ginerally speakin', go on the war-path for nothin', an' they know what good treatment is. Now, most folks thinks that all the good Injuns is six foot under ground, but I've lived alongside of 'em too many years to believe that. Jist to show you what I mean, I'll give you a little experience I had last winter.

"I was trappin' on the Rattone Mountains, an' I'd built me as tight a cabin as you'd wish to see, an' had everything comf'table. One night, jist as I was cookin' my supper, two Injuns come to the door, an old one an' a young one. They looked more beat out than I ever see Injuns look afore. They'd been out a follerin' elk, an' had the worst kind of luck, an' the old Injun had had a fall an' hurt his leg.

"I took 'em in, cooked 'em a good supper, give 'em my two best bar-skins for a bed, an' sent 'em off in the mornin' with a tip-top breakfast an' provender enough to last 'em that day.

"Well, about a month afterward the same thing happened to me. I was out after elk ; follered 'em all day with no luck, made the best shift I could for the night, an' next mornin' started for my cabin, but lost the trail somehow.

"I tramped all day, till late in the afternoon, an' I kin tell you it wa'n't much of a pleasure trip. At last, when I was about to give out (for to make bad wuss, the weather had turned colder 'n the North Pole, an' it was a snowin'), I struck a wickiup that was by itself in a little gulch.

"I didn't know what kind of a welcome I'd git, but the smoke a-curlin' from the top was sech a temptation that I jist walked right up to it—an' what do you think ? it was the lodge of the old Injun that I'd took in a month afore.

"Well, you may say what you like, but that thar Injun 'peared as glad to see me as ef I was his brother. He brought me right in, give me the best he had to eat, kep' me over night, an' sent his boy with me for a guide next day."

"I don't dispute that there's good Injuns—a few of 'em

—above ground, though, bein' so scattered like, they must have a powerful lonesome time," remarked Long John.

" I can't say as any of 'em ever put theirselves out to cook my vittles for me ; but I've seen the day when they mought a' took my skelp as easy as fallin' off a log, an' they didn't do it. It's nigh onto two years ago that it happened. I was with the ox-train that was haulin' freight to Santa Fé. Me an' Tom Bradshaw was the extry hands that trip, an' we was full three miles behind the train, a-drivin' the animals, that had got to be tender-footed.

" We was joggin' along careless like, thinkin' mostly of camp an' our supper, when all of a suddent we heard a noise like thunder or the tramp of the biggest kind of a herd of buffaloes, an' lookin' away off to our right, we see a terrible cloud o' dust a-risin.' A minute afterward a band of twenty-five or thirty Injuns galloped out of the dust an' made for us. Behind 'em, as fast as the dust cleared away, we could see more Injuns, all of 'em ridin' like mad, straight onto us. If ever any fellers' hair stood up, it was mine an' Tom Bradshaw's jist then, an' when the head Injuns got to us, they jerked their ponies up till they a'most stood straight on their hind feet, an' give a yell—seems as ef I could hear it now ! The screech of a thousand painters would be the softest kind of a hush-a-by alongside of that Apache whoop ; for they was Apaches, as we found out afterward ; somewhere near a hundred young warriors. Our poor, tender-footed cattle, that could hardly creep along, was that scared that they broke into a gallop, an' Tom Bradshaw an' me jist stood stock still, a-waitin' to have our hair lifted, it seemed like ; but after a bit we found out that the Apaches was only havin' a little fun of their own.

" They jabbered a few minutes in their own lingo, then treated us to all the English they knowed, which was the cuss words they'd picked up from the freighters, an' wheeled round an' galloped off as they'd come."

By the time that Long John's narrative was finished the party stood on the summit, about a quarter of a mile in advance of the train. The trapper's keen glance swept the horizon, and rested finally on a peak to their right. A less practical eye would have perceived nothing there, but Carter had spent twenty-five years in the mountains and on the plains, and his sight and hearing were those of an Indian. He descried a thin blue column of smoke rising skyward, and announced to the others :

"A signal-fire ! The Shastas air a-givin' notice to the bands to the north an' west that we're a-comin'."

"That means war," Long John remarked, though more in the tone of one putting a question than asserting a fact.

The trapper shook his head.

"No, not for sure, by no means. You see, Injuns don't go much on ·station-*ary*, an' post-offices is skurse betwixt here an' the line ; consequently they does their letter-writin' by lightin' a little brush on the peaks, an' considerin' that any one on 'em kin see that thar smoke fifty miles as the crow flies, it ain't a bad way."

"Then you do not think the Shastas are hostile ?" inquired one of the young men.

"No ; an' I'll tell you why. Ef you look sharp, you'll see the tops of their wickiups a-showin' in the chapparal down there on the foot-hills. Now when Injuns is hostile there ain't nary lodge in sight, an' you won't come across no warriors neither, except it's a little party of three or four that meets you an' makes a show of bein' friendly, to find out how many men there is in the train ; but when you see their tepees right along the trail, you don't need to borrer no trouble, for there won't be no fightin'."

Long John confirmed this statement, but added, as a

conclusion deduced from his own experience, that the savages were " onsartin critters," who might be friendly to-day and on the war-path to-morrow.

By this time the men who were acting as the advance guard of the train had reached the summit. These men were husbands and fathers, who had lives far dearer than their own to protect, and one after another approached the trapper with anxious inquiries as to the look-out ahead. His cheerful assurance that there was no danger, and that good treatment would keep the Indians friendly, was received with expressions of relief and thankfulness, and the whole party, freed from the apprehensions that had kept them on the look-out for signs of trouble, directed their attention to the view before them.

The valley, which lay almost at their feet, stretched away to the north as far as the eye could reach. On the south it was bounded by a spur of the range on which they stood, and twenty miles to the west a succession of grass-covered benches led up to another chain of mountains, whose sides were hidden by a heavy growth of fir and cedar. The sun was already dipping behind these western peaks as the rear guard of the train came up, and it was agreed on all hands to defer further observations until morning, as, according to Carter's reckoning, they had barely time before dark to reach a spot of which he knew, that would afford a favorable camping-ground.

The whole company began the descent in good spirits, and the animals, as though they realized that plenty of grass and water would be their reward, behaved admirably, so that by the time the first stars began to twinkle faintly in the sky, the train entered the park or mountain valley in which they were to camp for the night. On three sides of this park the rocky peaks of the range rose like a wall, and through the pass by which they entered, a clear stream, fed by unfailing mountain springs, leaped and rushed downward on its way to the valley below.

These emigrants were not outlaws fleeing from just punishment, or fanatics seeking some spot in the wilderness upon which to erect the altars of a faith at war with the spirit of the age and the genius of civilization. They were the sturdy yeomanry of the Mississippi valley, themselves the children of pioneers, bred on the frontier, and trained to combat the difficulties and face the dangers of border life. The wonderful reports that had reached them of the beauty and fertility of the valleys of Oregon, together with the inducements offered by the Government to settlers, were to them a sufficient reason for undertaking the perilous overland journey of more than two thousand miles, with their wives and little ones.

Brave, hardy, and adventurous, the very children partook of the spirit of the enterprise, and talked wisely of the land that father was going to take up, and of the way they would work to help him put in the crops ; and if the young mother with her baby at her breast quaked inwardly at the thought of the savage bands, the original lords of the soil, who still roamed over the fertile valleys in which their cabins were to be built, she gave no sign of her fears.

Thus far all had gone well with the train. Sickness had not thinned their ranks, and they had escaped the bullets and arrows of the red man. Now the goal of their hopes lay before them : the beautiful valley stretching away to the north, the richness of its soil proved by the tall grass which waved over it, the foothills clothed with luxuriant pasture, the cañons and mountain-sides covered with timber and abounding in game, and the streams stocked with fish. The land was theirs. They had nothing to do but enter in and possess it, and they well deserved this goodly heritage. As we have noticed previously, all of them except Long John, the trapper, and the brothers La Tour, were men of families, and they brought with them the wish and the determination to rear their children as worthy citizens of a great and free country. To-night, as they sat round their camp-fires, they talked not only of the farms they were to acquire and the homes they would build, but of the churches and school-houses they hoped to see in the valley before ten years rolled round ; and those who know the history of the State they helped to found, know too how nobly the men of Oregon have redeemed the pledges of those early days.

The La Tours had joined the company, not so much for the land they might acquire as for the sake of escaping from the bloodhounds that the Mormon priesthood set on the track of their recalcitrant followers ; and the emigrants, with ready sympathy for refugees from tyranny of any sort, had received them with open arms. Their bearing since they joined the train had been such as to make them general favorites, and honest Dick Bradley, the happy owner of a pretty little wife and a sturdy year-old youngster, expressed the sentiments of the whole company when he said,

" Better boys than them thar never saddled a horse nor drawed a bead, an' ef the redskins sh'd pop me over, I'd trust 'em to bring Jinny an' the baby through safe."

Yet the brothers, though outwardly cheerful, and always ready with an encouraging word for the despondent, and a smile so sunny that the youngest toddler in camp would run to meet them, carried a heavy load of concealed anxiety under the brave exterior they maintained. They were "mother-boys," both of them, to the very core of their affectionate hearts, and " *La belle mère*," whom they worshiped with what has been truly and beautifully called the fairest type of first love, was a prisoner in the hands of her enemies. They had meant to carry her with them, but all their entreaties had been powerless to move her to take a single step without Louise. They thought of her still as on the banks of the Missouri, not dreaming that she could be induced to accompany the Mormons to their new home ; and their hope, a faint one it is true, but still something to cling to, was to make a home here to which they might yet bring all of their scattered family.

The number of acres which a single man could take up was only half the liberal grant made by the Government to the head of a family ;' but the two brothers had been as one ever since the days when they lay in the same cradle in the old home in Quebec, and the land of both would make a noble farm—a little kingdom for the mother when they should bring her here. So, comforting themselves with a dream that was never to be fulfilled, happy in their love for each other, and pleased with the life of freedom and adventure that opened out before them in the new North-West, they joined heartily to-night in the rejoicing that filled the camp.

"Tell ye what," observed the trapper, as he poised a slice of venison on the end of the sharp stick that answered for a spit, " this here valley is jest as nigh bein' the Gar_ding of Eden that the Good Book tells about, as any land that lays out door. I was raised in Vermount, an' I hate to speak disrespectful of the country on account of the old folks, that lived an' died thar, so I alwuz make a pint of sayin' that Vermount is a mighty nice State to emigrate from ; but when I look at this here country, an' then think of the rocks an' stumps an' stone-heaps that had to be plowed around for every bushel of corn that was raised back thar, seems as ef the old folks, ef they know it, won't blame me for advisin' everybody raised thar to emigrate *young*. You see, the old man was a deacon, an' never said nothin' worse in his life than ' I declare,' besides bein' one of the patientest souls that ever drawed breath ; but I've seen him look as ef it would a' bin a powerful relief to his mind to make some onscripteral remarks when he was a plowin' the side-hill above the barn.

" You've heerd the story, most likely, of the traveler in Vermount that seen a man a-scoopin' somethin' out of a crevice between the rocks with a long-handled hoe, an' asked him what on arth he was a doin'.

" ' Doin' ? ' says the man, ' why, I'm a tryin' to gether up dirt enough to kiver them pertaters. You don't s'pose they'd grow ef I left 'em bare to the sun ? '

" Now I ain't a-goin' to say I know that to be so, because its somethin' I didn't see myself, but there's enough that I *hev* seen to make me thank the Lord that the way opened for me to move on toward sundown as soon as I got to be a man. I'd ruther have a hand-to-hand tussle with the varmints in this country than with the rocks an' stumps back thar ; an' seems as ef I relish the game I shoot out here more'n I used ter the sheep an' cattle we killed on the farm. I alwus pitied the poor things, they had sech a hard time a-pickin' their livin' where there was two stones to one blade of grass, an' it seemed cruel to kill 'em after they'd made out to grow up on such pastur."

CHAPTER VII.

THE BROTHERS.

THE emigrants, safely sheltered by the walls which nature had built around their camp, slept the sound sleep they had earned so well, undisturbed by dreams of their savage neighbors in the cañons below, and rose when the earliest signs of dawn appeared in the sky, to prepare for the last stage of their journey.

Daybreak in these primeval solitudes seemed like the birth of light in a new world. All the shy wild creatures whose haunts are in the forest and the mountains came out from their coverts. The deer bent their beautiful necks to drink of the little lake that lay in a basin half way up the gorge. The rabbits nibbled the short, sweet herbage, or sat soberly on the bare hillocks, gazing about as if admiring the landscape. Every leafy shelter was alive with birds, whose chirpings and twitterings, beginning before the stars faded, swelled gradually into a triumphant chorus of song as the sun cast his earliest rays upon the fleecy patches of cloud that hung over the mountains.

No human sound came up from the valley below. No sign that man had invaded this corner of nature's domain was visible from the spot where the new-comers had rested for the night ; but as they left the park and began to descend the pass they perceived tiny spirals of smoke, curling upward from unseen fires, and in another half-hour the deer-skin lodges of the nomads of this western wilderness were in plain sight.

The Shastas, the emigrants' nearest neighbors for the

present, seemed to have confidence in the peaceable intentions of their visitors, for the village beside the trail was tenanted only by the women and children of the band, who showed a mild curiosity with regard to the appearance and belongings of the pale-faces, but manifested no signs of fear or displeasure. Through the trapper they communicated the information that their braves had gone to the hunting-grounds, which were five suns distant, and that if deer and elk were plenty they would be home before two moons. A little trading was also done, a few well-dressed skins being exchanged for the trinkets dear to the savage heart, and a bright brass kettle, which was regarded by numbers with covetous eyes, was left in the chief's lodge as a gift. Then the train moved on, followed for a mile or more by a procession of scantily-clad, dusky juveniles, who were loath to lose sight of the wonderful pageant.

By the middle of the afternoon they reached the end of their journey, and camped in what seemed the richest portion of the valley. There were about one hundred and fifty families in the company, and it was necessary that they should keep together as closely as possible for mutual help and protection. Their claims were staked out in the best way for the accomplishment of this object, and in the center of the land thus taken up, a fort, surrounded by a stockade, was erected while the cabins of the settlers were going up.

Long John was a millwright, and the wagons in the train belonging to him were loaded with the necessary machinery for a saw-mill, one of the first wants of the new settlement. The useful trades were well represented among the colonists, and not only every man and woman, but every child in the company above the age of seven, knew enough of farm work to lend a hand in some department of what was to be the principal industry of the settlement.

Thirty years ago, and on the frontiers, life was simple, and artificial wants were few. It is really surprising how much comfort and happiness our colonists managed to extract from a mode of living whose details would appall the stoutest-hearted of those philosophers who are wont to advise their friends to "go west."

If in the press of work attendant on breaking ground for putting in the crops, no time could be found to have lumber sawed for flooring, the good housewife got along very well with a floor of earth, hard packed and well swept. If glass was wanting, a doeskin, dressed thin and oiled, took its place in the window. If the supply of dishes fell short, the youngsters of the family ate with excellent appetites from blocks of wood nicely hollowed and scraped smooth. When the small store of groceries they had brought with them began to fail, and the nearest trading-post was more than two hundred miles away, the honey which the bees, with commendable forethought, had laid up in hollow trees for just such an emergency, supplied the place of sugar, and if the women missed their cup of tea they did not say so.

Spinning-wheels and hand-looms, which had already grown obsolete in the East, were among the most valued possessions of the colonists ; and as the years passed and their flocks of sheep increased on the range, and acres of flax blossomed on their farms, fathers, mothers, and children were clothed from head to foot in suits, by no means to be despised, that had been " raised on the land."

Game and fish abounded almost at their doors ; wheat that was sown the first autumn yielded a bountiful harvest that was ready for the reaper by the following June ; and the crops of all sorts that were gathered from the ground planted in the spring filled their bins and granaries to overflowing.

And while outward prosperity attended the colonists, the roofs of their lowly cabins sheltered scenes of domestic peace. No baleful shadow, the outcome of a faith that crushes the purest instincts of humanity, sat at their hearthstones. No tyrannical priesthood made the people its slaves. No " blood-atoner" dogged the steps of those who saw fit to go elsewhere.

The next year and the year following witnessed a still larger immigration, the beginning of that steady influx of population which, in the course of a decade, covered the whole country with farms, and built up scores of busy towns where only a little while before the red man had been the sole tenant of the soil.

Early in the fall of 1852 a small train from the States arrived, which had come by a different route from that taken by the first settlers. They had encountered many difficulties on the way, and by the time they reached Echo Cañon their animals were so jaded and footsore that they feared they would not be able to get through. They turned aside, therefore, into the Mormon settlements, to exchange their nearly worn-out teams for fresh ones, and to get such supplies as the settlers might be able to furnish.

They represented the Mormons as numerous and apparently thriving, but by no means disposed to entertain strangers. However, by the exercise of a little strategy, which Ward, the captain of the company, said he thought entirely justifiable under the circumstances, they obtained what they needed by paying two prices for everything, and went on their way unhindered.

" I don't think nature intended me for a hypocrite," Ward said, " for the bit of acting I went through with in Salt Lake was the hardest work I have done in twenty years. You see, as soon as we struck the settlements, we could tell by the atmosphere of the place that we were not welcome. The men gave us black looks, and the women disappeared in-doors as soon as the train came in sight. No one would talk with us, until after a time I got a small boy to direct me to the Bishop's house.

I knocked at the door boldly, and the man who opened it proved to be the Bishop himself. I stated our case to him, enlarged on the reputation of the saints for hospitality and generosity, said we knew if we could reach their settlements we should be cared for, and finally begged of him a letter to President Young.

"The old fellow was completely won over. He ordered his people to let us have the supplies we wanted (for which, by the way, we paid a big price), and invited me to breakfast in his own house. After breakfast he made up his mind to go with us to Salt Lake, and through him I obtained the privilege of paying my respects to the Prophet.

"To him I praised everything that I saw in Utah, and, as I flatter myself, made so good an impression that I had no further difficulties. I think if the folks at home could know what diplomatic abilities I developed out there I should get a foreign mission at any rate."

"But with all yer diplomatic abilities, ye didn't git ahead of that old coon on a bargain," drawled Jim Badger, one of the party. "Our hosses an' cattle wor blooded stock, wuth a mint of money, ef they *wuz* tender-footed, an' we hed to trade 'em fur mustangs an' the orneriest horned critters that ever lifted a hoof; an' fur the garding truck an' other provender they sold us, we paid 'em in hard cash more'n would hev bought a good-sized farm out here."

"That's all so," answered Ward, "but I saw we were in a place where it was Hobson's choice. One of these days I'll get even with them on the animals."

The La Tours, as soon as they heard that the strangers had stopped in Utah, paid a visit to their camp, in the hope of learning something of their relatives, of whom they had never been able to hear anything since the day that they parted with them at winter quarters. Though they did not think that their mother and the younger children would go with the Mormons except upon compulsion, they were by no means so sure about Philip, and they believed also that Louise was in the Prophet's power, and that she was in Utah, if alive.

Captain Ward could give them no information, but while they were talking with him another of the company came up—an Illinoisan named Spencer, who had relatives among the Mormons.

"Here is a man," said Ward, "who had a better chance than I to look around, and he may be able to tell you what you wish to know."

As the brothers stepped forward to meet Spencer, he exclaimed,

"I have surely seen one of you before; but no—stop. It was a younger man; only a boy, in fact."

"Where did you see him?" In their eagerness the brothers both spoke at once.

"In Salt Lake. He was a youngster of about eighteen, I should say, but as tall as either of you, and so like you that the resemblance quite startled me at first."

"Did you talk with him?"

"No. I did not even hear his name mentioned. You see, the Mormons don't encourage sociability between their people and outsiders. I know them of old; and when they are fixed so that they can have things their own way, it won't do to ask too many questions about their affairs. I would have liked to question my own relatives, especially the women, who looked downcast enough to make me sure their lot was a hard one; but I was certain that I should make trouble for myself and for them too by doing so."

"The fact is," interposed Ward, " we found ourselves in the hands of the Philistines, and were forced to remember that discretion is the better part of valor. A little imprudence would have cost us a great deal more than the garden truck that Badger tells about. We none of us dared to appear as though we were inquiring into their concerns, but if you have relatives there and wish to find out about them, I think I know of parties to whom inquiries could be addressed.

"You know we came in by the southern route, and in Shasta valley we met some old friends of mine on their way to the diggings in Yreka Flat. There were half a dozen apostate Mormons with them—fellows who had got tired of Prophets and polygamy and all that sort of thing, and left Salt Lake without bidding anybody good-by. From the stories they told I should say they had a lively time getting away. They started out to hunt stray stock, and it appears they managed to have the animals stray a good ways, and timed their search so as to fall in with a train bound for California. They were young fellows, all of them, and from what I saw of Utah I can't blame them for leaving."

That night, when the brothers were alone, they talked long and earnestly about the advisability of disposing of their land and going over into California, where they might possibly hear something of their family. There were many recruits from Oregon in the army of California miners, and the La Tours had more than once been on the point of going ; but now, as on many other nights when they had talked the matter over, they went to bed without reaching any conclusion.

The brothers still slept side by side, as they had done all their lives. Their claims adjoined each other, and a cabin built upon the line answered the legal requirements of a dwelling upon each farm.

The unexplained physical and mental sympathy that often exists between twins was so strong in their case that in many respects they could hardly be said to have a separate existence. They dropped asleep together, waked at the same moment, and even their dreams were alike. To-night, going to bed at a late hour, they slept until long past midnight, then both waked with a shudder of alarm.

" Dear brother," said Francis, " I have had such a dreadful dream."

" And I," answered Charles. " I dreamed that I saw our mother in a little room, cold and bare like a prison-cell. She sat on the edge of a narrow bed, and when she tried to rise I saw that there was a chain about her waist that fastened her to the spot. Her hair was white as snow, and her face pale as the dead."

" I saw all that too," interrupted Francis, " and yet in spite of everything there was a peaceful, almost a happy look in her eyes, as they met mine. What can it mean ?"

" I do not know any more than you, and we shall not find out by staying here. Let us not wait any longer, but start for California at once. If we cannot sell our land, we can rent it."

" I was thinking just the same. If we meet those young men from Salt Lake we can at least find out whether our mother and the little girls are in Utah. Philip is there, without doubt. It could have been no one else that this man Spencer saw."

" And the little girls are almost women now. Think what a place that must be for them, with no one able to protect them !"

The brothers slept no more that night, and the next morning set about making the necessary arrangements for leaving. It was not a difficult matter to find a purchaser for their land among the late arrivals, and with the price of it safely stowed away in the leather belts which enabled the men of the Coast in those days to become their own bankers, they started on their journey, carrying with them the good wishes of the whole settlement.

In 1852 the road over the Siskiyous was not what it is to-day, but it was a very good road of its kind nevertheless. Up and up the steep sides of the mountain, now winding to the right, now making a sharp turn to the left, here creeping along the edge of a precipice, and yonder sinking almost out of sight in a narrow defile, the trail led at length to the open plateau overhung by the frowning summit of Pilot Knob. Here our travelers caught their first glimpse of the Land of Gold —that wonderful country whose hidden treasures are covered, not by desert sands and bare, bristling rocks, but by an emerald carpet, embroidered with all the hues of earth and sky.

The brothers lingered on the plateau until the declining sun warned them that it was time to be on their way, if they expected to reach the valley by nightfall ; but the picture spread out before them was one which might well excuse delay. Who that has even looked upon it can forget it ! What traveler who has explored the valleys and climbed the mountains of the Pacific Slope can lose the memory of the charmed landscapes that make all other scenery appear tame and cold !

A little way from the foot of the mountain they began to perceive signs of human occupancy. Herds of cattle were grazing on the slopes, trails branched off from the main road in different directions, and finally the rock chimneys and clap-boarded roof of a long low building came in view. Our travelers' horses quickened their speed of their own accord, and even the pack-mules began to move more nimbly as they came in sight of the watering-trough, hewn out of an immense log, and filled by a pipe leading from one of those mountain springs whose clear waters show the form of the tiniest pebble or insect at the bottom.

The building needed no lettered sign to announce " Entertainment for Man and Beast." More than a dozen wayfarers were resting in various picturesque attitudes on the porch, while in front of the stables a small band of horses and mules were being divested of packs and saddles.

A number of the travelers were Oregonians, who, after a prosperous summer in the mines, were returning to their families, and among these the La Tours found one or two acquaintances who had spent the last six months on Yreka Flat. They confirmed Captain Ward's account of the Mormon boys who had lately come to the mines, and were able besides to give the names of some of them—names which the brothers remembered in connection with the flight from Nauvoo, and the year they had spent at winter quarters.

The company that filled the inn was a genial one, the supper was good, and the stories of the " diggin's" which followed it were well flavored with the marvelous ; yet the brothers, who were eager to be on the way, found the evening a long one, and by sunrise next morning they were ready for their journey.

A ride of ten hours through a rolling country covered with grass, with here and there a patch of timber, brought them in sight of their destination.

Yreka Flat, in those days, came under the head of " new diggings." About half a dozen cabins of the rudest construction were scattered around, but the majority of the miners had been too busy during the summer to think of building cabins ; and besides, what need was there of a house in those months when rain never fell, and the air was as soft as a baby's cheek ?

The day's work was over, and all along the gulches camp-fires began to gleam, casting a bright glow on the faces of the masculine cooks, who were making coffee, frying bacon, or engaged in the more arduous task of mixing bread in their prospect-pans.

They were a merry crew, these miners. They sang and whistled as the cooking progressed, and when supper was ready seated themselves comfortably on the ground, with no complaints about the absence of tablecloths and napkins, and ate and drank with an appetite that it was worth crossing the Sierras to find. There was no trouble about clearing the table after the meal, and dish-washing was a brief and infrequent ceremony, observed chiefly out of respect to the traditions of the past.

Our travelers were received with that open-handed hospitality which was a distinguishing characteristic of the " Forty-Niners," and before the evening wore away they were rechristened according to the custom of the Coast. Every man in the camp bore an appellation which had a distinctive meaning, the arbitrary title by which he was known in " the States" having been dropped, along with other relics of an effete civilization. Henceforth the new-comers were to be designated as the " Turtle-Doves," and if a necessity arose for speaking of them separately—a thing which rarely happened—they were distinguished as Number One and Number Two.

Early the next morning Christopher Columbus—so named because, according to his own version of the history of the Coast, he was the original discoverer of all the rich diggings known to fame—proffered his services to the late arrivals in the capacity of instructor and general adviser.

" This here camp is gittin' considerable played out," he remarked. " Diggin's was struck last spring, an' sence then there's been nigh onto a thousand of the boys at work

on the Flat.   Mebbe a hundred out of the lot has made a
clean-up of from three to ten thousand dollars, an' ef you
count alongside of them all the claims that's bein' worked
now, you can see with half an eye that the ground's bin
pooty well prospected.   The pay streaks is worked out, an'
by the time snow flies these diggin's 'll be as lonesome as
a last year's bird's-nest ; but I'll tell you what I'll do,''
lowering his voice to a confidential half-whisper ; '' I've
got a big thing on the crick, jest the other side of the
mounting.

'' I reely don't like to tell it as big as it is, because you
mought think I was a-lyin'.   I hain't done much work on
it : jest staked out the claim, an' sunk a shaft eight foot, to
the bed-rock.   Well, now, you heerd the boys talk last
night about half a dollar to the pan, as though that was big
pay.   I didn't want to say anything to discourage 'em, but
ef I thought I hadn't got nothin' to look forrerd to but a
pay streak that u'd average half a dollar to the pan, I'd
throw up the sponge an' quit the country.

'' As I was tellin' you, that there claim of mine ain't had
much work done on it ; but the dirt I took out of the bottom of the shaft went fifteen dollars to the pan.''

'' Mining is new business to us,'' Francis ventured to
suggest, '' and we want to look about a little, and get
what information we can before deciding upon anything.''

'' Well, ginerally speakin', that's the best plan ; but
when a feller that's new to the diggin's has a chance to go
in with some one that's bin on the Coast since airly in the
spring of '49, an' took out more dust than a mule-train
could pack down-hill on the ice, it's different.   Now, I
don't mind sayin' that I've kinder took to you boys, an'
I'll make *you* an offer that I wouldn't make to everybody.
Ef you've a notion to go in with me on that there claim,
you kin have a one half intrist for five hundred dollars, or

a two thirds intrist for a thousand. You see, two thirds gives you the control, an' that's a big thing for you."

At this point the conference was interrupted by loud calls for "Christopher" from a neighboring group of miners ; and with a hasty apology to his new friends and a promise to see them again, the proprietor of the rich placer claim on the "crick" moved away in answer to the summons.

The young men looked after him with a mingled expression of amusement and relief. The fortunate owner of the wonderful gold deposit was a trifle seedy in his personal appearance. The rim of his hat had disappeared, with the exception of a single piece which hung down behind, while a bristling crop of sandy hair showed through an aperture in the crown. His flannel shirt, his sole upper garment, had evidently been fashioned from the half of a pair of blankets which had seen long service before relinquishing their first form and design. His breeches, skilfully patched with remnants of flour-sacks, stopped half way below the knees, and were met by the tops of boots that had never been a pair.

The brothers were still following the receding figure of the great discoverer with their eyes, when a friendly hand was laid on the shoulder of each, and turning they confronted Lucky Jim—a blue-eyed, jovial ne'er-do-weel, who had followed up all the strikes on the Coast without making a dollar, but who seemed nevertheless as happy and care-free as though he had found the world an oyster already opened for him.

" The boys noticed Columbus going up your way," he said, " and they sent me around, not to notify you that he's the biggest liar on the Coast, for they reckon you can find that out for yourselves, but to tell you how to get rid of him.

" When he comes back with an offer to sell you two

thirds of his claim—he'll ask a thousand dollars for it at first, and finally drop to a hundred or less—just tell him you'll take an interest if he can get the Professor to go in with you. You see, he swindled the Professor out of five hundred dollars when he first struck the diggings, and came mighty near getting the top of his head shot off when the ' Golden Treasure ' turned out to be salted.''

'' That is a good idea,'' said Francis, who usually spoke for both. '' We were wondering how we should answer him ; for no doubt if we declined buying an interest in his claim on the ' crick,' he would bring forward a dozen others, each one better than the last.'' Then after a brief pause he added,

'' May we trouble you to assist us in another matter ? We came here hoping to find three young men from Utah, who, so we were told, were in this camp.''

Jim nodded. '' I know the boys you mean,'' he said, '' but they're with a party that's gone over the mountain for supplies. They will be back in about a month. You have just missed seeing them, for they left only four days ago.''

CHAPTER VIII.

THE PROPHET'S PROFITS.

THE spring of 1853 opened with every indication of a prosperous year for the Mormon settlements in Utah. The heavy overland emigration to California during the two previous years had been of great benefit to the Saints. Many large companies were compelled, on reaching Salt Lake, to make such exchanges and purchases as Captain Ward's train had made, and it is scarcely necessary to add that the Mormons always had the best of the bargain. Many other companies had unwisely loaded their wagons with supplies of all kinds that their jaded teams could not possibly drag across the desert, and these supplies were unloaded in Utah and sold for a trifle, or, in many cases, given away.

There were still other small companies that entered the borders of Utah and were never seen again. This was especially true of returning Californians, who attempted to cross the Territory with the treasure they had taken from the mines of the Coast.

At this time Brigham Young was at once the ecclesiastical, civil, and military head of the colony. He was Governor of the Territory, by Federal appointment, *ex-officio* commander of the military, and he assumed also to be the vicegerent of the Almighty. His power was that of an absolute and irresponsible despot,* and this power he exercised for more than twenty years, without let or hindrance from any quarter.

* See Appendix, Note F, page 337.

To say that he held the lives, liberty, and property of the people in his hands is to make an assertion that falls short of the truth. He had it in his power to condemn those who fell under his displeasure to a fate more terrible than death, and to cause the slow years of a wretched life to drag out in the midst of tortures such as Loyola never dreamed of.

And like the savage tribes of the American wilderness, he punished those who offended him, not merely by causing them to suffer in their own persons everything that his cruel spirit could devise, but by putting those who were dearer to them than their own lives to torture and shame.

Because Madame La Tour had incurred his bitter hate, it pleased him to sacrifice her daughter, who had never offended him. That he might torture her mother through her, Louise La Tour, beautiful, gifted, and refined, was made the slave of a brute whose very presence was an insult to a pure woman. Then, when this wretch tired of her, and wished to throw her aside, he was prepared to give her to another of those beasts in human form who were among his familiars ; but here, it seemed, his hand was stayed. He who sent His angel, and shut the lions' mouths ; He who walked beside His chosen ones in the furnace seven times heated had heard the cry that went up in the silence of the night from a soul bereft of earthly hope : Louise was no longer alone. She realized the encompassing, all-pervading presence of the Helper of the helpless ; she felt that an invisible Hand was turning aside the shafts aimed at her. Her first encouragements were that about that time human friends were raised up for her in unexpected quarters. The first wife of Kimball, known among the people as Sister Vilate, whose sufferings had not yet culminated in the madness that preceded her death, was moved with a strange pity for the hapless girl, whose history she knew only too well. She visited her in Burch's cabin, watched over her like a mother while she remained there, and finally induced her husband to give Louise her freedom.

In Utah, as in Asia, a man who is displeased with one of his many wives, or who has grown tired of her, gives her a bill of divorce and sends her away,* and Sister Vilate was able to persuade Kimball to give Louise such a bill ; but could not procure for her the privilege of living with her brother and sisters. As soon as she was divorced the Prophet had her removed to his own household, ostensibly to act as governess for some of his children, but really that there might be no hindrance in the way when he should see fit to marry her to one of his followers.

She had now been two years in his family, and, as yet, no further harm had befallen her. She attended faithfully and quietly to her daily duties, and won the hearts, not only of the children under her care, but of the women in the Prophet's household. She was always gentle and patient, and, so far as those around her could see, content with her lot.

In the mean time both her sisters had grown to womanhood. Blanche, at fifteen, was as tall as Louise herself, and Catherine, though only seventeen, had the face and manners of a mature woman. They still lived with their brother, and the little household, as Louise found out at an early day, was often in straitened circumstances.

Madame La Tour's effects, which were brought to the Territory, had never been restored to her family, but the Prophet had continued his plan of " assisting" Philip by furnishing him with small supplies from time to time. He had also loaned him a team, and with this and his own labor the young man had done his best to support his sisters.

* See Appendix, Note G, page 342.

His loyalty to the Prophet never wavered, though his inherited pride made him restive under what seemed his constant dependence on others. At length, one day, when emboldened by some unusual kindness on the part of his leader to speak freely to him, he ventured to ask some questions about the money which his father at his death left in the hands of the authorities of the Church, to be held in trust for his children.

" My dear boy," the Prophet said, in his most paternal tone, " have you ever asked yourself how much it has cost the Church to provide for all of you, and take care of you as you have been taken care of ever since your father's death ?"

Philip was silent and abashed for a moment.

" I thought," he faltered at length, " that my mother had a small income which lasted as long as she lived. I know she had still a little money when we came here."

" Yes, money which I loaned her," was the cool response. " The fact is, Philip, it is now ten years since your father's death, and he left a large, and in some respects a very helpless family to be cared for. All of you had been used to luxuries, and we did our best to provide for you in such a way that you should not feel the loss of anything. We would have been glad to take care of you without using any part of the little sum which your father left ; but that was not possible."

" Do you know what that sum was ?" Philip wondered at his own boldness as he made this inquiry. It seemed to him like calling his Prophet to account.

" I cannot give you the exact figures without consulting my books," was the answer.

" I have heard my mother say something about thirty-five thousand dollars," Philip began, more timidly than before.

"Thirty-five thousand ! Why, your father did not have one third of that sum when he came to Nauvoo. As I have said, I cannot tell you the exact amount he left, but this much I do know, there is only five hundred dollars coming to you. That was just the balance in your favor the last time I looked over the account, and I calculate to give you a deed for the house and lot you occupy for the five hundred. To be sure, the place is worth more than that, but you are like a son to me, and I am glad to do you a favor, no matter what the cost may be to myself."

What could Philip say ? In his heart he knew that the Prophet was doing him an injustice, but he would not admit the fact even to himself. The man who stood between him and God, who was the mouthpiece of the Almighty, could do no wrong. He felt as a Christian might feel, when tempted to question the ways of Divine Providence, to ask, "Why hast thou dealt thus with me ?"

But more severe tests of his loyalty awaited him. During the summer of '53, in spite of his utmost efforts, he could not keep want from his door. His own and his sisters' clothing grew shabby and worn, and their meals were coarse and scanty. Catherine fell sick, and their prospects became more gloomy than ever, when a company of returning Californians stopped in Utah on their way to the States, and brought Philip the first news he had had of his absent brothers since the day that he parted with them. They brought also what, in the present distressed condition of the family, was a most welcome gift—namely, a hundred dollars in gold, which Charles and Francis had sent to their sisters. The next morning, while Philip was consulting with Catherine as to the best manner in which to lay out the money that had arrived so opportunely, a messenger came to summon him to the Prophet's presence.

"Philip," said his leader very gravely, as soon as the

youth stood before him, " I have sent for you and for a good many of the younger brethren to-day, to remind you that the work of the Lord is standing still, because you do not bring your tithing into His storehouse. Thousands of poor Saints are waiting to gather to these valleys of the mountains, but we have no means to help them on their way. We are commanded to hasten the building of the Temple, but the Church has no money—no, not so much as to finish the foundation. I grieve to say it, but I feel that the wrath of God will be poured out on this people if their tithes are not paid in full. I have looked to you to set an example to the others ; but you must know yourself that your tithing has not been paid for many months."

" We have been so very poor," Philip began humbly.

The Prophet's eyes flashed. " Take care," he said. " You can't deceive the Almighty. This very minute you have one hundred dollars in gold in your possession."

" It is not mine," Philip found courage to say.

" Yes, I know," was the triumphant answer. " It is not yours, but the Lord's. Are you going to keep it back ?"

" That is not what I meant to say. The money belongs to my sisters. It was sent to them."

" And you are going to make that an excuse for with-holding your tithing ? Ah, Philip," shaking his head mournfully, " I did not expect this of you. I am afraid your heart is not right."

" I want to pay my tithing," Philip answered, " but you do not know how destitute we are, and Catherine is sick."

" More excuses ! I thought I had taught you to give up everything to the Lord, and trust Him to provide for your wants."

Philip was silenced. The pale face of his sister, the vision of his home, so bare of comforts, and his own sense of right availed nothing against the subtle arguments of his chief, backed by the assumption of divine authority, and in the end he not only paid over all the money his brothers had sent, but drove his only cow to the Tithing Yard to settle the arrears which the Prophet declared to be still due.*

Louise knew all this, but she could not interfere in any way, nor had she any means with which to help her sisters. She taught the Prophet's children, and was boarded and clothed for her services ; but she had no money. Catherine seemed nearer to her than any other member of their scattered family, and the thought of her sickness and destitution wrung her heart ; but she was not even allowed to visit her.

How Philip accounted to his sisters for the disposition he had made of their money she could not learn ; but she heard enough from others to know that he redoubled his own exertions to provide for them, so that before winter set in they were at least saved from actual suffering.

Early in December, Philip, whom she sometimes saw at the Prophet's house, brought her word that Catherine was to be married at Christmas ; and to her great relief, when the name of her intended husband was mentioned, it was that of a young man who, as she had good reason to believe, was thoroughly cured of his faith in Mormonism. As a matter of course, this was not a thing to be talked of publicly. No man in Utah who valued his life ever uttered a whisper of dissent in those days, except to friends whose faith in the Prophet was as weak as his own ; but Robert Kenyon had never been suspected of heresy, and for a year past he had been employed much of the time about some buildings that were being erected upon the ten acres which were set apart for Brigham Young's private grounds. In

* See Appendix, Note II, page 343.

this way it happened that he often met Louise, and the free-masonry which existed among the disaffected soon made them aware of each other's views.   His acquaintance with Catherine had been short, but it seemed to be a case of love at first sight on both sides.   The Prophet, for a wonder, had no objections to make to the marriage when Robert, with due humility, asked his consent, and he was likewise gracious enough to grant their request to be married by him in his office, without going through the Endowment House, Kenyon alleging Catherine's delicate health as a reason for wishing to put off receiving their endowments until spring.

Soon after the marriage the Prophet, in a fit of good nature, gave Louise permission to visit Catherine in her new home.   This was almost the first opportunity that the sisters had enjoyed of talking freely together since the memorable day when they met on the path above Burch's cabin.   On the few occasions when Louise had been allowed to visit her family, Philip had been at home, and when she and Catherine met elsewhere it was always in the presence of others.

To-day Louise found the young wife alone.   They talked long and earnestly of their own affairs, and of their mother, whom Catherine, with strange persistence, still spoke of as living, though she admitted that she had never been able to find the faintest trace of her existence since the day that she disappeared.

" And I have tried too," she said ; " secretly, of course. One must be secret about everything in this miserable country.   I feel as though I was breathing an atmosphere of lies all of the time, and it suffocates me ; but I have worked in the dark, and in underhand ways, like all the rest here, because I wanted to find mother."

" And you have discovered nothing ?"

"No, nothing ; but, my dear, I must not make you unhappy on this first visit, by dwelling on a sorrow that cannot be healed. Come, let us talk no more about it. I will get dinner, and you shall help me. We will take our dinner alone, because Robert will not be home until long after dark to-night."

While they were sitting at table, Catherine asked suddenly,

"Have you heard the news about Margaret Denys ?"

"No. What of her ?"

"She was sealed to Apostle Woodford yesterday."

"I can't say that I am surprised," Louise answered, "for nothing that is done here surprises me ; but her husband will be home in a few days, and unless he has changed greatly there will be an outbreak that will end just as that affair of the Penfields' ended last year. George Denys is not the man to stand quietly by and see his wife given away to another, even though that other may be an apostle."

"But in this case there has been no giving away," Catherine answered. "It is all Margaret's own doings. She asked for a divorce herself, and asked several times before she got it. For my part, I wonder how a man like George Denys ever came to love such a woman ; but I suppose he was taken with her pink cheeks and blue eyes, just as Apostle Woodford is taken with her now."

"Margaret is weak, not wicked," Louise said earnestly. "I believe she really loved her husband once—loved him even when he went away on this mission ; but he has been gone three years, and during all this time she has been listening constantly to such talk as we are all compelled to listen to every Sunday ; and being, as I said, weak and easily influenced, she believes that the apostle will give her a place in the next world that she could never reach as the wife of plain George Denys."

"I have no patience with such folly," Catherine began ; but she stopped short when she saw the pained look on her sister's face. She did not know all of Louise's history, but she had heard enough and guessed enough to be aware that she too had once listened willingly to teachings that afterward bore bitter fruit.

"I hope some person who has a little influence with Denys will be the one to break the news to him when he comes," she said after a few minutes' silence.

"So do I," Louise answered. "I don't want to see him throw his life away, as he will be sure to do if he acts as a husband would act anywhere else under the same circumstances."

"Louise, you know what became of Penfield. Is not that true ?"

"Don't ask me." Louise shuddered, and her pale face grew still paler. "What I know I cannot help knowing. I would be ignorant if I could. I would gladly be blind and deaf while my home is inside those walls, but what I am forced to know I do not want to recall."

"I should be afraid in your place," Catherine said, "that since I was not blind and deaf, the Prophet would take a sure method of making me dumb."

Louise shook her head. "Brigham Young fears nothing from one like me. He thinks that I am completely crushed —that I am his slave, body and soul, but even if this were not so, I should not feel myself in any danger."

"And why not, pray ?"

"I believe in God."

Catherine made an impatient gesture.

"Don't misunderstand me," Louise continued. "I was not thinking of the God these wretches worship—a God of blood and cruelty—but of our mother's God—of the God she taught us to pray to in the dear old home. You have not forgotten, have you, the nursery with the high windows and the crimson hangings, and the bed by which we used to kneel ? I could not forget it if I should live a thousand years."

Catherine's face softened. "I remember," she said gently, "though it is almost like a dream now ; but you know that ever since I was eight years old I have heard the name of God used as a shield for all manner of wickedness."

"Yes, I know," Louise answered, "and I have seen hands that were red with murder raised in prayer ; but is that a reason why I should not pray to the God who abhors the evil that is done in His name ?"

It is not to be supposed that at the time referred to a conversation like the foregoing could be safely carried on under ordinary circumstances. The system of espionage adopted by the Mormon leaders at the very outset had now been brought to such perfection that every person's comings and goings were strictly watched, and the private affairs of every family were as well known to the priesthood as their place of residence. No one dared marry or be given in marriage ; move from one place to another, buy or sell, or make any business or domestic changes whatever, in opposition to " counsel."

Husbands and wives, parents and children, friends and neighbors, were required to be spies upon each other, and the secret police shadowed every man's steps.

Louise's visit to her sister, however, was made by the Prophet's express permission, and neither she nor Catherine were suspected of the slightest leaning toward apostasy. Louise said rightly that her own spirit was supposed to be completely crushed, and in general her master took no more notice of her and attached no more importance to her presence than if she had been a five-year-old child.

Robert Kenyon's house was not watched as that of a suspected person would have been, and the sisters, seated in an inner room, with closed doors and windows, knew there was no danger that their low-toned conversation would be overheard.

They would have been bold indeed if they had uttered such opinions or mentioned such facts where there might possibly have been unseen listeners ; for no one's life was worth an hour's purchase who was known to question the authority of the Prophet, or to denounce the crimes of the priesthood. And then, too, the Mormon hierarchy knew how to take life with unheard-of refinements of cruelty.

Oh, if the dark recesses of the cañons had a voice, if the blood that stains the sod could speak, if the night-wind could bear on its wings the cries that fell on unpitying ears, what a tale of horror would be unfolded ! But the dead are silent. The crumbling skeletons hidden under piles of rocks do not stir in their resting-places. The bottomless springs of the south, in which many a victim of priestly cruelty has found a grave, keep safely that which was committed to them, and the cries of the tortured captives in the Black Vault have never been able to pierce the thick walls and smite on the ear of the passer-by.

CHAPTER IX.

PLANS FOR ESCAPE.

IT is high noon upon the Wasatch peaks. The May sunlight, reflected from vast beds of untrodden snow, fills the whole atmosphere with a blinding glare. The mountain torrents, swollen by the streams that pour into them from every gorge, rush down their steep channels, and leap from ledge to ledge with a noise like that of an avalanche.

A few birds flitting in and out of the stunted timber along the gulch are the only living creatures in sight. A rough and narrow trail, rendered more uneven and difficult by detached masses of rock which have rolled down from the sides of the mountain, follows the course of the stream that takes its rise at the highest point of the divide which must be crossed in order to reach the valleys east of the range.

A wagon-road could not possibly be built over this divide, and the route would be considered impracticable by horsemen less accustomed to difficult feats than the pioneers of the Great Basin.

Under ordinary circumstances, travelers crossed the range by a road several miles to the north, which was passable for teams during the summer months ; but the two horsemen who could be descried a long way down the cañon had reasons of their own for choosing the southern trail.

The foremost of the two was Robert Kenyon, the husband of Catherine La Tour. He was a young man, not over three-and-twenty, but a giant in stature, and the cool and intrepid spirit which looked out from his gray eyes, joined to his skill in the use of arms, would have made him a formidable match for an adversary. Yet neither his strength, his skill, nor his courage availed him anything here, where, if he dared to assert his manhood, spies would dog his steps by day, and assassins lie in wait for him by night.

His companion was tall and slenderly built, with long hair and beard, once brown, but now thickly sprinkled with silver. His face was very pale, he stooped slightly, and his whole aspect was that of one lately recovered from severe sickness. This man was George Denys, the returned missionary whose wife had been given to Apostle Woodford.

About half way up the cañon the trail widened for a few rods, and in a little opening among the rocks the travelers dismounted for their noonday meal. The wind blowing from the snowy peaks made the day cold in spite of the sunshine, and Denys shivered perceptibly.

"Shall I light a fire?" asked his companion.

"Yes, if you will," was the reply. "This is as safe a spot as we shall be likely to find for talking over our affairs," glancing as he spoke at the sheer precipice that rose for a hundred feet above their heads, and the rushing, roaring torrent beside the trail.

When the meal was over, the two men seated themselves by the fire with their backs to the rocks, and in such a position as to command a view of the trail for a considerable distance above and below. Kenyon was the first to speak.

"If these precious scoundrels that run the Church don't change their minds between two days," he said, "I will be off by the end of the month—just think of it, on a mission: sent by the Prophet himself to build up and extend the kingdom in the western borders of the country that he claims by right of discovery. I could hardly help laughing in his face when he blessed me last week as a special preparation for this work. I wish I could get a report of the blessing pronounced on me when the old fox finds that I have outwitted him, and that Catherine and I are safe in California."

"I am glad to see you in such good spirits," was the reply; "but I must remind you that the need of caution will not cease when you reach Carson. A good many brethren who are weak in the faith meet with fatal accidents, or are 'killed by Indians,' even there."

"I suppose that is so; but you see, I shall not grow weak in the faith until I have shaken the dust of that place from my feet. I shall remain and attend diligently to all my duties until the next train bound for California or Oregon comes along, and then good-by. The only thing that troubles me is the idea of stealing away as I must—as anybody must who gets away at all—like a thief in the night."

"You are a happy man to have no greater trouble."

Denys dropped his head in his hands and was silent for some minutes. When he looked up again there was a spot of color on his pale cheeks, and his voice trembled slightly.

"I cannot do otherwise than wish you God speed," he said, "though your going will leave me without a friend to whom I dare speak. You deserve your liberty, and I pray that you may get it. You and your wife are here only because your parents brought you into the Church when you were too young to act for yourselves, while I deliberately abandoned a Christian home, and broke the heart of my gray-haired father, for the sake of joining myself to these wretches, and shut my eyes to the crimes they committed in the name of religion until I was made a victim myself.

That is the thought that always checks me when I am tempted to exclaim, ' My punishment is greater than I can bear.' "

" It is not a reason, though, why you should stay here until worse comes upon you."

Denys shook his head. " For me there is nothing worse to come," he said. " I had nothing in this life except Margaret, and after she was taken from me I was incapable of feeling any added wrongs. When she died, killed by the miseries that awaited her in that polygamous household, and by her own remorse, I knew they could not stab me again through her. If she had lived, they might have done so, for I loved her—loved her to the last."

Kenyon's face expressed both astonishment and incredulity. His companion observed his look and went on :

" You wonder that I did not hate her. Why should I ? The poor child only obeyed the doctrines that I myself had taught. Like you, she was brought up in this accursed community, and knew no other religion. How then could I blame her ? I did not blame her. I pitied her from my soul, and from my soul I was thankful when death released her from her sufferings."

" And yet, what she did or was led to do uprooted all your faith in Mormonism."

" True, because, as I have said, when other crimes were committed I was only a spectator ; this time I was a victim. If you could know how constantly the image of my wife was with me every day of those three years of absence, and how the hope of seeing her kept me up on our terrible return trip across the plains ! It was late in September when we reached Iowa, and common prudence warned us not to attempt the journey until spring ; but the other men had families in Salt Lake as well as I, and we thought we would brave anything rather than stay away from them six months longer ; at least that was the way I felt, and I persuaded the others to make the venture with me.

" You know a little of what we suffered, but you could not begin to realize our hardships without experiencing them yourself. Yet, as I said, the thought that every mile we traveled brought us nearer home kept us up, and then—and then—the message which told me I no longer had a home was brought to me just as I caught sight of the house that was mine once."

Again Denys buried his face in his hands, and shook as if in an ague-fit. Kenyon laid his arm gently around his shoulder.

" George, old friend, don't call that up," he said, as tenderly as a woman.

The giant carried an affectionate and impressible heart in his broad bosom, and the sight of this hopeless sorrow was more than he could bear.

' " Come, rouse yourself," he continued. " You are a man, and too good a man to stay among these cutthroats. In the world outside you may find, if not happiness, at least occupation that will keep you from brooding over your troubles, and friends who will stand by you. Promise me that you will make the attempt to get away."

" I can do nothing just now. There is no chance of my being sent west, but it is just possible that I may be chosen to accompany the emigration to San Bernardino in the fall."

" Now that you speak of it, I think I have heard your name mentioned in connection with that mission. You know, I suppose, that the *Prophet*"—Kenyon placed an indescribable emphasis on this word—" is well satisfied with your conduct, and has the greatest confidence in you."

" Yes, I know."

" And that puts you in a position to help others. Catherine feels much anxiety about her sister Louise, who is not allowed to go with us."

" Louise ! I thought her one of the Prophet's worshipers."

" Louise loathes and detests him and his teachings, and she has borne up so well under sufferings that would kill most women, it seems to me she deserves to escape ; but just now the way is barred. I think, however, that you may be able to do something toward helping her."

" I ?"

" Yes, if you go to San Bernardino. If she could get there it would be possible for her to communicate with her brothers, who are in California."

" No one could be more willing than I to help her or any-one else who wishes to get away from here ; but I cannot do anything to befriend her while she thinks me still a slave of the Prophet."

" I will find means to let her know where you stand, and will give you the key to the signals by means of which she and Catherine are able to say what they wish when in the presence of others. Poor girl ! She may need a friend badly enough when we are gone."

" I am surprised to learn that she feels as you say she does. The family seem very much attached to her, and I supposed she was with them from choice."

" You do not know her history then ?"

" No."

" Perhaps I ought to tell you. It can do no harm for you to know it now."

Then choosing his words as carefully as possible, but still keeping back no part of the truth, Robert Kenyon unfolded a tale which, so it seemed to his listener, should have caused the very stones at their feet to cry out against the stupendous system of villainy and outrage which had enthroned itself in these valleys under the name of religion.

"It is monstrous—incredible!" Denys exclaimed when the recital was ended; "and yet, why should it not be true? There is no form nor degree of crime that the leaders of this people are incapable of. Rest assured, Robert, that this poor girl will have at least one friend when you are away, and I will make for her the effort that it seemed not worth while to make for myself. If there is a possibility of getting her away from this valley I will find it out."

"That is spoken like yourself, George, and Catherine and I will go with lighter hearts, knowing that you will befriend her."

By this time the sun had declined perceptibly from the meridian, their fire had burned out, and Denys, rising, called his companion's attention to the fact that it was time for them to be on their way if they did not wish night to overtake them in the mountains.

The errand on which they were sent took them to a small settlement which had been recently made in one of the fertile eastern valleys.

"See how this curse is spreading," Kenyon observed to his companion as they came in sight of the valley.

"If the deluded Saints continue to gather to Zion at the present rate, in ten years Brigham Young will have his subjects scattered over the whole country between the Rocky Mountains and the Sierras."

"I hope before that time the Government will see the necessity of laying a strong hand on him," Denys said; "and if the nation does not hear something of his crimes, it will not be my fault."

Two weeks after the friends returned from their journey, Robert Kenyon and his wife left Salt Lake in company with about twenty families who had been ordered out to build up a Mormon colony within the limits of the present State of Nevada.   For many years after taking possession of Utah, Brigham Young devoted much attention to establishing outposts (called stakes of Zion) beyond the present territorial lines,* and the men selected as pioneers were, for obvious reasons, those on whom he supposed he could rely implicitly.   It occasionally happened, however, that his cunning overreached itself, and that men who wished to be sent to those outposts, in order that they might escape from his rule, were able to counterfeit loyalty to the Church so successfully that they were chosen by him to go on such missions without soliciting the privilege.

Apart from the hope of escape, there was nothing to tempt even the most adventurous to those distant settlements, and those who were not influenced by such hopes went only because they dared not disobey " counsel." The valleys of Utah are fertile, well watered and easily cultivated, and the climate is delightful ; but beyond the western limits of the Territory the face of the country is so mountainous and the narrow valleys are so sterile that even at this date few of them have an agricultural population.

The emigrant train set out late in May, 1855.   The women of the company took leave of their friends with tears, and the men looked depressed and anxious—all except Kenyon and his wife, whom the Prophet praised publicly for obeying counsel *cheerfully*.

Kenyon had found means to keep his word, both with Denys and with Louise, and they understood each other's true position ; but for more than two months they had no opportunity of communicating unobserved.

* See Appendix, Note I, page 344.

At length chance, or rather, shall we not say? the Providence which watches over the helpless and oppressed, opened the way for them to talk freely of the only plan of escape that seemed practicable. One of the Prophet's wives living at Provo, a settlement forty miles south of Salt Lake, sent for Louise to assist in the care of her sick child, and Denys, who owned a good team, was asked by Brigham to take her there.

It was not customary to make excuses when requested by the Head of the Church to perform any service, and Denys' ready consent awakened neither surprise nor suspicion. As for Louise, she made ready for the journey with the air of quiet resignation with which she obeyed all the commands of the Prophet; but she nevertheless contrived to leave the impression that she went unwillingly.

Their road lay through an unsettled portion of the country, bare of timber, as is the case with all the valleys of Utah, and affording no hiding-place for spies. For almost the first time since she left her mother's house Louise felt herself unwatched. The man beside her was her friend, and more than this, he rejected all the claims of the system that set spies and assassins on the track of those who dared to think for themselves.

They rode for a little way in silence; then as the signs of human habitation began to disappear, and they realized that they were alone, and, for a few hours at least, free from espionage, they began to talk over the chances of escape.

"It is now more than a year and a half since I returned to the valley," Denys said, "and if any one had told me at first that I could live so long while forced to breathe this accursed atmosphere of treachery, cruelty, and murder, I would not have believed him."

"I wonder you did not make an effort to get away last year," Louise remarked.

" You forget that I was sick for many months. I hoped I should die—that seemed the easiest and shortest way out —but I was disappointed, and with returning health came the feeling that perhaps there might be a life worth living somewhere beyond these mountains that shut us in. You know I did not come among the Mormons as a child. None of my people were led off with me, and my father's family would, I think, receive me even now."

" I am thankful for you that you have such friends. I have no one but my brothers, and my only hope is to reach them."

Louise did not look very hopeful as she spoke, for in her heart she was asking herself,

" How would my brothers receive me if they knew all ?"

Denys did not reply immediately, and when he spoke again it was to say,

" I suppose you know that the company bound for San Bernardino starts next month."

" I have heard so. Are you going with them ?"

" I can go if I wish. I have been offered the choice between San Bernardino and a mission to the States."

" But you will go to the States, of course," Louise said, and in spite of herself there was an undertone of disappointment in her voice.

Denys turned and faced her. " If I had only myself to think of," he said, " I should go to the States, but I promised your sister and her husband that I would help you, and therefore I am going to San Bernardino."

" And do you think it possible to gain permission for me to go too ?"

" Yes. There is one way by which I think I can succeed in getting you a place in the company."

" Name it."

" I fear I may both shock and pain you ; but I assure

you it is the only possible chance for you. You must go as my wife."

Louise's pale face flushed scarlet, and her eyes dropped.

"You have not heard my history, or you would not think of such a thing," she faltered, almost inaudibly.

"I *have* heard your history—all of it," was the answer, "and the knowledge of your cruel wrongs makes me doubly anxious to help you. Do you think that, in my eyes, the least shadow of blame attaches to you, because you have been made the victim of a system which I myself have helped to uphold?"

"You are good and generous," Louise said at length, after a long silence, "and you are the only friend I have now; but it seems like making a poor return for your goodness to consent to be your wife. I know nothing about such love as happier women have experienced—such love as Catherine feels for her husband—"

Denys stopped her. "My poor girl," he said, "I understand that. Neither of us can talk of marriage as men and women do who have not passed under this blighting curse; but I will take the best care of you that I possibly can, and do my utmost to bring a little brightness into your life, and I have no fears but that the friendship between us will grow into a more tender affection."

"There is one thing you have not taken into account," Louise said. "If Brigham Young knows that I desire such an arrangement, or that I consent to it even, he will never sanction it. The only way in which he can be brought to agree to it, will be by allowing him to think that I am unwilling."

"I see; but I believe I can manage that. I will go to him as soon as you return. He has already counseled me to take a wife, and he will expect me to fix upon some one before the company start. We all know that a woman's consent is thought to be a matter of small importance, and he will not be likely to ask me if I have secured yours. Are you willing that I should speak to him ?"

"I am. If it is for the best I think there will be no obstacles, and if it is not for the best—for both of us, I mean —I shall pray that some other way of escape may open."

"You still pray, then ?" Denys looked at her half pityingly, half inquiringly.

"Yes. I pray as my mother taught me to when I was an innocent child, with no foreboding of misery and shame."

There were tears in her dark eyes as she spoke, and Denys felt an answering moisture in his own.

"You are not altogether unhappy, then," he said at length. "I would to God I could pray, but I cannot. And yet, poor child, your wrongs have been greater than mine, and inflicted in the name of religion too. Maybe I should feel differently if I had not once *believed* in this accursed system, as firmly as I used to believe in my mother's God."

CHAPTER X.

THE BLISTERING DESERT.

EARLY in August, 1855, the families chosen to make the difficult and perilous journey to the coast by the way of Arizona, for the purpose of founding a Mormon colony, were instructed to hold themselves in readiness to start on a day's notice.

On the evening after receiving these instructions, George Denys repaired to the Prophet's office, in obedience to a message from him.

A few days before this he had signified his wish to marry Louise La Tour, and the man who held their destinies in his hands had answered that he would "think about it." From present indications it appeared he had thought favorably. He received Denys graciously, and said without preface,

"I am willing to give Louise to you, but I suppose you know it can be only a marriage for time. She is sealed to Brother Joseph for eternity."

"I am aware of that," was the reply. "Have you spoken to Sister Louise yet?"

"I have, and she is very sullen—more so than I have ever known her to be—but there is no question about her obeying me. She has never dared to rebel against counsel, and she knows better than to begin to do so now."

The sinister look that so many in Utah have abundant cause to remember, darkened the face of the Prophet as he spoke, and without another word he touched the bell on his table.   It was answered by one of the guards who always kept the door.

" Let Sister Louise know that I want her here," he said.

The man went out and returned in a few minutes with Louise, who appeared pale and downcast enough to justify the account of her sullenness.

" Louise," said her master, " Brother Denys, whom I wish you to look upon as your husband, is present."

Louise did not raise her eyes.

" Step this way," the Prophet commanded in his harshest tones.

The girl obeyed.

" Now, Brother Denys, stand up and take her hand."

As soon as this direction was complied with, the Prophet repeated the marriage service.   Louise's replies were inaudible, and her master's cruel satisfaction manifested itself in every look and tone.   He believed that he was sacrificing a reluctant and shrinking victim, and the satanic malignity which was so strong an element of his character made it a pleasure to him.   He would add this night's work to the list of his revenges, and yet the punishment which Madame La Tour had drawn down upon herself and her children would not be complete.

" Now, Brother Denys," he said, when the ceremony was concluded, " take your wife home with you. The train starts at nine o'clock to-morrow, and you have no time to lose. Never mind about your clothes, Louise, I will have them sent over in the morning."

" May I not say good-by to the children ?" Louise asked.

" No.   You should have thought of that before."

" Have you any farther instructions for me ?" Denys inquired.

" No.   Brother Calder has all the necessary orders for the company.   Good-night."

The Prophet turned to the papers on his table and the two who were thus dismissed passed out.

Once beyond the gate and in the sheltering darkness, Denys pressed encouragingly the trembling hand that rested on his arm ; but neither dared speak. Their prison doors were ajar, but a single word might close them again.

Denys was boarding at the house of the Ward Bishop, and it was necessary that he should introduce his wife to the rather numerous family of his host. Louise went through this ordeal with the same sad and subdued air that she had worn for days previous, and some of the women of the family made commiserating remarks as she left the room ; but others were of the opinion that she ought to be content with her lot.

•"She's a first wife now," observed Sister Ann, who was herself the bishop's fourth spouse, " and Brother Denys is so easy-tempered she'll have her own way in everything. I don't know, for my part, what she's got to complain of."

" Maybe she don't want to go on this mission," suggested Sister Emma.

" It is more likely that she wanted some one else," said the youngest wife, who, if report could be believed, had looked much more kindly on a handsome stripling in the neighborhood than on the gray-haired bishop.

Meanwhile the subject of their conversation was sitting with her husband in a room piled half full of luggage that should have been put into the wagons before night.

" I did not expect that we would start to-morrow," Denys said, " and I did not think that I should be allowed to bring you here to-night, or I would have made some better arrangements for your comfort. Indeed, I hardly dared hope that I should be permitted to take you with me at all."

" I do not believe that the Prophet made up his mind

until after he talked with me," Louise replied ; " but he got the impression that I was very unwilling, and that decided him."

" Just imagine what his feelings will be when he learns the truth," Denys said, and in spite of the dark past and the difficulties and dangers that lay before them, both smiled.

It was well indeed for them that their whispered conference was not overheard—well too that those who saw them start out the next day were confirmed in the belief that Louise went most reluctantly.

The emigrant train was composed of fifteen wagons, representing as many families.   The men were most of them young, and, like Denys, recently married.   Polygamous families could not be colonized in San Bernardino. The American flag yet waved over the whole of the vast Coast region which Brigham Young claimed as a portion of his dominions, and the day concerning which he uttered so many prophecies—the day when all human governments should fall before the power he represented—had not yet dawned.   The members of the company were all supposed to be sound in the faith they professed, and in every way fitted for their responsible mission.   They had been selected by the Prophet himself with especial care, and yet at least three of the men besides Denys intended that their departure from Utah should be a final one, and it happened eventually that not one of the fifteen families ever returned to the valley.

The emigrants were well provided with necessaries for their journey, not because the Church authorities had concerned themselves about making such provision, but because they had sufficient means of their own to supply them with ordinary comforts.   The first stage of their route lay through the settlements that had been made, at irregular distances, all the way from Salt Lake to the southern line of the Territory. This portion of the journey was not marked by any incidents worthy of notice, nor attended by any hardships, but after crossing the divide south-west of Mountain Meadows, the character of the country changed entirely. It was near the middle of September when the company encamped at Resting Springs—the last point at which pure water is found before entering the desert. They remained in camp several days to rest and recruit, for they knew that for the next hundred and fifty miles their powers of endurance would be taxed to the utmost.

At four o'clock on the morning of the 15th of September, the company broke camp, and were on their way before the first signs of day appeared in the east. It was necessary that they should make twenty-five miles or more before sunset, in order to reach the next watering-place—the Amagos, a stream so strongly impregnated with alkali that it has been named the Poison River by the unfortunate travelers who have tasted its waters.

The wheels of the loaded wagons dragged heavily. The mules sank to the fetlocks at every step, and the men who walked beside the teams waded ankle deep in the loose, shifting sand. As the day advanced, the sun beat down upon them with a pitiless glare, and not a breath of air stirred upon the face of the desert.

On every side, as far as the eye could reach, stretched an unbroken expanse of sand, gray as ashes. Not even a rock broke the monotonous view; not a hillock interposed between them and the farthest verge of the horizon where sand and sky met.

The sun sank at night in the gray waste; the stars came out overhead, and still the train toiled on. At length, just as the moon rose to light their way, the narrow channel of the Amagos came in view.

The shallow waters of the sluggish stream looked clear and bright in the moonlight, and the foremost drivers began to urge their teams toward it.

"Stop," cried Calder, the captain of the company. "Don't you know that these waters will kill every animal in the train? Halt where you are. There is a spring a little to the right that is safe."

The caution came too late. The loose cattle belonging to the train, tortured by thirst, had pressed forward to the brink and were already drinking.

The teams attached to the wagons were halted in obedience to orders, and a search was made for the spring, which, when found, proved to be brackish, but not unwholesome ; still, by Captain Calder's advice the company used for themselves only the water which they had brought in kegs from Resting Springs.

At starting, few of the emigrants had any adequate idea of the hardships and perils of the journey, but a single day's experience on the desert had given rise to grave anxieties even in the minds of those most inured to the difficulties of overland emigration.

Captain Calder had for his guidance a rude map, drawn by one who had been over the route before, and a few notes relating to the points at which water might be found ; but the sandy expanse over which they traveled afforded no landmarks whatever, and it was an easy matter to miss the sunken springs on which they depended. Their water-casks, which had been filled before entering the desert, held what was thought to be a sufficient supply for a four days' journey. This included a scant allowance for the teams, and a very small reserve to be used in case of delays, but a single day's trial convinced them that there had been a mistake in their estimates.

The heat, the fatigue, and above all the extreme dryness

of the atmosphere, aggravated thirst in man and beast, and it required all of Captain Calder's authority, in addition to the combined good sense of the company, to prevent drinking largely in excess of the day's allowance.

The second night on the desert was spent at Salt Springs. The teams already began to show signs of exhaustion, and it was necessary to drive carefully, for their losses from the effects of the poisonous waters of the Amagos had reduced their stock so that there were no relays.

The intensely salt waters of the springs would have been quite as fatal as those of the Poison River, if drank, and at this camping-ground the teams had to be supplied from the rapidly-diminishing contents of the casks. The third and fourth days' journey brought no changes, except that their progress was slower, and the allowance of water dealt out more scanty.

It was confidently expected that the train would reach Bitter Springs on the evening of the fourth day, but when the sun set on the wide waste of sand there was not the faintest sign of water in sight.

"We have traveled very slowly," Captain Calder said, "and it would not surprise me at all to find out that we have made at least ten miles less than we calculated upon in the last two days. The springs are only a little way ahead—that is certain—and it seems equally certain that we must reach them to-night if we expect to save our animals."

Acting upon this suggestion, the nearly worn-out teams were urged forward for three hours longer, but when the moon rose, nothing was visible except the same endless stretches of barren sand that daylight showed. Their animals could be driven no farther, and with the gloomiest forebodings they made their camp for the night.

All the lives in the company might now depend upon the

teams ; so the mules and oxen again received their share of the little water left in the casks, and at daybreak the wagons were lightened by throwing out the most cumbrous articles, and the train again put in motion.

On and on through the blistering sands they toiled till noon, and still no water ! The fear which had been gaining ground since morning now amounted to a certainty. They had lost their way. Whether the springs lay to the right or the left of the route they had passed over, it was impossible to tell. A council was called to determine whether it was wiser to turn back and make an effort to find them, or to push ahead to the sink of the Mohave ; and, in view of the slight chances of coming upon the springs if the search was made, the latter course was decided upon.

There was no accurate scale of distances on Calder's map, but as nearly as could be ascertained they had at least sixty miles to travel. The prospect was disheartening enough, and those who had joined the expedition only because they dared not disobey " counsel" were loud in their complaints, and quick to blame Captain Calder as being, in part, the cause of their misfortunes. On the other hand, those who looked upon the end of their journey as the door of escape from priestly tyranny, were courageous and calm, though by no means hopeful.

Captain Calder was not one of these. He had been put in charge of the company by a power whose decrees he did not venture to question, and his connection with Mormonism was of such a nature that he had no plans of escape, but he was the very man for the trying position he filled —brave, determined, enduring, fertile in expedients, and above all, patient with the murmuring, despairing company, who were ready to say with those of old,

" Why hast thou brought us into this wilderness to kill us with thirst ?"

Another day, and yet another, and still only the brassy heavens above and the burning sands below. On the evening of the sixth day the last drop of water was served out. Everything that could be left had been thrown out of the wagons, and even the weakest of the women walked by turns ; but in spite of all that was done to save them the teams began to drop by the way.

The tortures of thirst in an open boat at sea could not begin to compare with the sufferings of those whose last remnant of strength was taxed to the utmost to struggle through the deep, hot sand on foot, without a drop of water to moisten their parched tongues.

On the morning of the seventh day two men of the company and one woman were found to be unable to stand on their feet. In answer to their half-despairing, half-sullen request that the company would go on and leave them, Captain Calder had them put in the wagons that could best bear the added load, but when the train made the next halt their sufferings were ended.

A shallow grave in the sand received their bodies, and the survivors looked in each other's faces, mutely asking,

" Who will be the next ?"

" My poor child," Denys whispered to Louise, " I thought to save you ; but I have only brought you into the desert to die."

Louise's dark eyes were unnaturally large and bright, but she raised them to his face with a steadfast look.

" Better, far better, to die *here* than live *there*," she answered.

When the train again attempted to move, not more than half of the teams were able to drag the wagons, and the least courageous of the company broke out afresh into lamentations, but Calder silenced them with a gesture.

" Look !" he exclaimed, as soon as he could get their

attention. "Yonder are the mountains—I am certain of it, and the river is a long way this side of them."

"What of that?" was the despairing answer. "We can never reach it."

"Don't give up now," and the resolute tone in which he spoke was not without its effect ; "I will tell you what we will do. The river is not now more than ten miles from us. I have often heard that animals traveling over the desert can scent water that distance. We will set ours free, and the strongest men among us will follow them, and, believe me, before many hours we shall be back with water—plenty of it."

"We may as well try it," one of the men answered.

"When all's done, we can but die at the worst, and we are certain to die if we stop here another night."

"That is true," said Denys ; "and I believe with the Captain that the animals will be our best guides. How many are able to follow them ?"

Half a dozen men stepped forward at the summons. The rest had sunk upon the ground in the apathy of despair. Calder and Denys at once began the work of setting the oxen and mules free. The poor creatures staggered feebly forward, with their parched tongues hanging from their mouths. The men kept behind, but without making any attempt to drive them. When they had gone about half a mile in this manner, the foremost mule raised his head, snuffed the air eagerly, and started off in a straight line, followed by the others, who, like him, quickened their pace. The men kept a few yards behind, and were watched by anxious eyes, that were strained to keep them in sight until the moving figures merged into a black line, then a speck, a point, and they were gone.

How slowly the hours of watching dragged past ! The thirst that grew each minute more intolerable seemed to parch the whole frame. Some were sunk in a stupor, happily unconscious of their sufferings or of the lapse of time ; but to those who retained their faculties the sun appeared to stand still in the heavens.

Still they waited and watched, cheating themselves at times with the belief that they saw a moving speck in the dim distance, until at length the tardy sun dropped below the horizon, and the far-off mountains, the desert, everything, faded into the dull gray of twilight. Then the darkness swallowed up the landscape, and the awful stillness of a night in the desert settled down upon them.

" Wherever they are now," said one of the women, " they must stop until the moon rises."

" No," answered Louise, who still had strength enough left to encourage the others, " Captain Calder has his compass, and the stars are shining. They will not wait a minute for the moon."

The event proved that she was right, for the moon was just beginning to show its upper rim above the horizon when the night air bore to their ears a faint sound—the distant hail of those for whom they watched.

They replied with the loudest shout which their parched throats could utter, and then the women embraced each other and thanked God, while the men staggered to their feet and pressed forward toward their returning comrades. There were only five—Calder, Denys, and three others— among them a young man whose wife had begged piteously that he would not leave her.

It was almost like a resurrection from the dead when the precious drops that had been carried so far moistened the black lips and burning throats of the sufferers, and the good news that was brought with the water infused hope and courage into souls that an hour ago were sunk in the lethargy of despair.

They had found the Mohave.   The men they had left behind with the animals were camped where there was not only an abundance of pure, sweet water, but plenty of grass, and beyond the river the country was green and fresh.   They were out of the desert.

What a night of thanksgiving that was !   The sufferings of the past few days were almost forgotten in the joyous certainty that in the morning they would leave the desert behind them, and when, a few hours later, the three men who had been left on the river bank returned with their teams, there was an eager bustle throughout the camp, an activity that the night before would have seemed utterly impossible, as every one aided or attempted to aid in the preparation for starting.

Before noon all the company were resting in the shade of the timber that fringed the banks of the Mohave.   No, not all, for three of their number rested under the sands of the desert ; but even the sincere sympathy that was felt for those who were bereaved could not dampen the joy of the survivors in the first hour of their deliverance.

• After a week's rest in the valley of the Mohave, the march to the coast was resumed, and a little past the middle of October they entered San Bernardino.

As we have previously intimated, Brigham Young showed his sagacity in the choice of men. for this colony, by fixing upon those who had means of their own. So it had happened that these settlers had money enough to establish themselves comfortably on the lands near the town ; but Denys and the three others who had decided to cut loose from the community announced that they wished to look around a little before deciding upon a location, and they " looked around " to such purpose that within three weeks they had taken passage at San Pedro on a steamer bound for San Francisco.

CHAPTER XI.

A CALIFORNIA GULCH.

THE autumn of 1852 lingered long in the northern valleys of California, as if to give the busy miners ample time to prepare for winter. Late comers to Yreka Flat rejoiced in the mild October weather, and prospecting was pushed vigorously along every creek and gulch within the limits of what is now known as Siskiyou County.

The La Tour brothers, who had steadily declined buying the various "rich claims" offered them, joined this army of prospectors in company with Lucky Jim, whose overflowing cheerfulness and unflagging courage were not his only good qualities : Jim had never made anything for himself, but he had more than once helped others to make something. He had a keen eye for "indications," and if he had been so minded might have told as many stories of discoveries as the redoubtable Columbus ; but he had a constitutional antipathy to work, and if by any chance a few hundred dollars came into his hands, the money was sure to vanish like the dew.

Guided by him, the La Tours started out toward Shasta Butte, a solitary peak rising in the form of a sugar-loaf to the height of fourteen thousand feet, with a crown of eternal snow. From this proud elevation the mountain looks down upon the timbered spurs that guard the approaches to it, and the bristling tops of the firs and cedars that fill the cañons.

Here nature showed an untamed front. No human sound broke the silence. The hand of man had left no impress upon the face of the wilderness. To the little party of three, who were the first to invade these solitudes, the gloom of the forest in which they camped for the night was most oppressive, but when sunrise dispelled the shadows of the valley, and the lofty trees whose branches shut out the sky grew vocal with the songs of birds, their courage rose, and they felt themselves equal to an encounter with the Spirit of the Mountain.

Their camp was upon one of the numerous creeks which are fed in summer by the melting snows of the peak, and whose channels even in winter contain sufficient water for mining purposes.

Somewhere along this creek it might be that they should find the El Dorado they were seeking, and immediately after breakfast they started out on foot to explore the gulch through which it flowed, leaving their horses picketed within a few rods of the embers of their fire. Each man carried his gun ; and the remainder of the luggage, the chief items of which were the pick, shovel, and prospect-pan, was impartially distributed. Lucky Jim had given "the boys" various lessons while on their journey, regarding the signs they were to look for, and this morning he repeated and emphasized his instructions as they walked along.

" You see that black sand," he remarked ; " well, though that is not always an indication of gold, it's a pretty sure thing, and if you don't find it you may as well try another gulch. Then these boulders—they're quartz, and maybe there's no gold in them ; but in this country, where you don't find quartz you won't find gold. I call the quartz and the sand together good indications ; but for a *sure* thing you want something like this," stooping as he spoke to pick up a rough fragment of rock which his experienced eye at once perceived to be " rich."

The brothers pressed closer to look at the bit of quartz that lay in his open palm. It needed no magnifying-glass to show the yellow specks in its broken surface.

"You see, boys," he continued, "this hasn't traveled far, otherwise its edges would be rounded, and its sides worn smooth. The ledge must be very near, and we will move on a few rods until we find a favorable place for sink_ ing a shaft, and then get to work."

A little more than two hundred yards up the creek the gulch forked, and another stream came in from the left.

"This is the place to stop," Jim said, indicating a little flat below the junction of the streams. "The ledge may be in either gulch, but we are quite safe in sinking a shaft here."

It was still early in the morning, and Jim, announcing that he would "take the first shift," seized the pick and went to work with a will. Like many other people who dislike long tasks, he could put in some very vigorous strokes at the beginning, and the brothers, who had done more hard work during their four years in Oregon than he had in his lifetime, looked on and admired the rapidity and precision of his movements, as he broke the ground and tossed out the gravel. After about half an hour's work he stopped, posed himself gracefully, with the han- dle of his shovel as a support, and began to descant on the various theories of placer-mining. Francis allowed him to talk for a few minutes, and then claimed the pick and shovel, and applied himself so diligently to increasing the depth of the shaft that in less than an hour his pick struck the bed-rock.

Jim, who had been watching as well as talking, now filled the prospect-pan with some of the last dirt taken out of the shaft, and proceeded to wash it.

The operation of "panning," though simple enough in

theory, requires considerable skill in practice. The prospect-pan, which is much the shape of an ordinary milk-pan, except that it flares more toward the top, being fairly filled with the dirt, is held under the surface of the stream, shaken from side to side, and every few moments jerked up and down in such a manner as to cause an ebullition of the water, when the dirt and lighter gravel are washed out, while the pan is tipped a little to one side and shaken carefully to get rid of the black sand.

A miner who understands his business will go through the whole operation in five minutes, and have the precious dust left clean and shining in the bottom of the pan. At the expiration of that time Jim gave a triumphant shout.

"We've got her, boys ! Here she is ! Sing Hail Columbia ;" and with a few stronger expressions, that would not look well in print, he exhibited the result of his work.

"Half an ounce to the pan ! The boys will say that is one of Christopher's strikes, but all the same we've got it."

The glittering bait, which, once seen, never fails to lure the beholder onward through months and years of search in the hope of finding the hidden treasures of the earth, lay before their eyes—shining particles of coarse gold, like grains of sand, and in the mass a nugget the size of a pea.

The brothers felt a strange thrill, a quickening of the pulses, a sudden eagerness and elation. The gold fever had not impelled them to come, but it seized upon them now, with this evidence of the buried wealth of the mountains before their sight.

Lucky Jim, to whom the experience was not altogether new, was the first to come down to practical details, and in a few words he explained to the others what must be done in order to secure the benefits of the discovery to themselves. In conformity with his instructions, four claims, each two hundred feet long, were staked out, one for discovery and three pre-emption claims, and a notice was posted beside the shaft.

"We could organize a district by ourselves," he said, "for there's three of us, and that meets the requirements of the law; but the boys down on the Flat have always stood by me, and I'd like to give them a show. One of us will have to go back to the camp to-morrow anyway, to get a whip-saw and a few other tools, and the strike will leak out. What do you say, boys? Are you willing that the others should come in?"

"Why not?" said Francis. "The gulch is not ours. They made us welcome when we reached their camp, and I have no wish to keep out anybody who wants to come."

This sentiment called forth a hearty response from Jim, embellished with various emphatic expressions which we forbear to quote. He now felt that they had done nearly enough for one day, but the brothers were of a different opinion, and both of them worked so energetically that before night the bed-rock was stripped for a distance of five feet above and below the shaft, and the prospect-pan was filled and passed to Jim a score of times.

As may be supposed, none of the dirt "panned out" quite equal to the first sample, but at night, when Jim produced the scales he carried and weighed out the gold, the result of their first day's work amounted to a little over ninety-seven dollars.

"Now, that's what I call fair wages," he said, surveying the "pile" complacently. "What shall we do with it, boys?"

"Put it in the company's purse," said Charles.

"Yes," added Francis, "that purse you showed us yesterday. It will answer just as well as a banking-house for the present."

Jim accordingly produced from one of his numerous pockets a stout buckskin bag about sixteen inches long.

" This will hold five thousand dollars in dust," he said, " and after it is filled we can put the balance in yeast-powder cans and *cache* it under our fireplace."

In the morning their camp, which had been moved to the vicinity of the mine, was the scene of unusual activity, and soon after sunrise Jim started for the Flat, taking with him the two pack-mules to bring back supplies.

" We may as well lay in pretty much everything we want for the winter," he remarked, " for we are going to have work enough to keep us busy, and there won't be many days to spare for trips to the Flat or anywhere else."

Jim spoke in a matter-of-fact way, as though hard work was the staple of his life, and for the moment he really deluded himself with the idea that he was going to turn over a new leaf and " strike his best licks" on the Star of the West—for by this poetical appellation the claim was to be known henceforth.

He carried with him, in addition to the gold panned out the day before, fifty dollars advanced by the brothers to increase the funds of the company to an amount sufficient to purchase the necessary tools and supplies. He was likewise the bearer of a message to the Mormon boys, who were supposed by this time to have returned from Marysville. His last words on taking leave of his comrades were,

" I don't mean to blow about this strike of ours, but if the boys find out anything for themselves, I shall take it that you will make anybody welcome that happens to follow the trail."

During the day the brothers occupied themselves, as their more experienced partner had advised, in cutting down a beautiful sugar-pine that grew near their shaft, and dividing its straight, smooth trunk into logs twelve feet in length. These logs were to furnish lumber for the sluice-boxes that they proposed to construct.

As this lumber must be whip-sawed, it was necessary also to prepare a pit, and here their own knowledge of wood-craft proved quite as serviceable as Jim's instructions.

Two saplings about eight inches through, and growing within three yards of the side of the hill, were selected for the posts of the pit. These were cut off six feet from the ground, and one end of the logs, which were to be the sides of the frame, rested on the stumps, while the other end was bedded in the hill. A couple of transverse logs and the two short, movable sticks of timber called blocks, completed the pit, and then the miners had as good a substitute for a saw-mill as Northern California could furnish at that period ; or, at least, they would have when their whip-saw should arrive.

All this preparatory work took time, and the sun set on the first day of Jim's absence without a single shovelful of dirt having been disturbed in the vicinity of the shaft ; but on the morning of the second day they returned to the more fascinating employment of stripping the bed-rock and washing out the gold.

These men of eight-and-twenty were still young enough in heart to feel a boyish delight in being able to-day to manipulate the prospect-pan almost as skilfully as their instructor, and the gold which they deposited in the safe depths of a tin can glistened more brightly in their eyes because they had washed it out themselves.

Jim had told them that he should start out on his return trip long before daylight, and as the distance from Yreka Flat was only twenty miles, they began to look for him by the middle of the afternoon ; but the day wore away without bringing any signs of him until near sunset. Then a cheerful hail was borne up the gulch, and as they answered it they started down " to meet the supply train," as Charles observed. They had not gone many rods before they caught sight, through the trees, of the white horse that Jim rode, and in a few minutes the two pack-mules likewise emerged from the shadows.

Jim looked happy, but withal a little secretive, as though he knew something that was almost too good to tell.   In answer to their questions, he assured them he had had tip-top luck, but he did not get down to particulars until the mules were relieved of their packs, and he himself seated by the fire with a great mug of smoking coffee in his right hand.

" You see," he began, " I didn't talk much when I got to the camp, but just went around quietly buying up the supplies.   I paid out your money first, but when it came to weighing out the dust, the boys began to ask questions.   I told them we'd been at work for a while in the mountains, and had cleaned up a few ounces, but that didn't seem to satisfy them.   I started out before daylight, as I told you I should, but this horse of mine showed the way as plain as that pillar of fire they used to tell about in Sunday-school when I was a youngster, and by sunrise I could see a black line stretching away behind me toward the Flat— somewhere about a mile long, I should say.   I didn't wait for anybody to overtake me and ask more questions, but by the time I reached the timber they had got almost within hailing distance, and—hark !   What is that ?"

All three listened intently as the night wind bore a faint sound to their ears—a sound that grew more distinct and increased in volume, until they recognized the " O-o-oh J-o," the well-known hail of " the Coast," uttered by a score of throats.   They answered it in concert, and the sound was taken up and repeated, this time singly, until, as they conjectured, it had passed all the way down the gulch to the stragglers just entering the timber.

"Here are plenty of pine-knots," said Francis. "Let us make a blaze that they can see;" and

"On hospitable thoughts intent,"

the original pioneers of the gulch piled the fire with the resinous material at hand, until a ruddy column of flame shot upward to the branches of the tall trees, making fantastic lights among their dark shadows.

In twenty minutes more the head of the advancing column halted and dismounted at their camp.

"Right smart blaze, this yer is," observed a tall, lank, grizzled individual, with a free and easy air of good comradeship, "an' it was a cute idee of yourn to light it. We mought a' me-yandered round in this pesky timber all night an' not found yer, for the rocks mixes up sounds so's ter lead a feller offen the trail every time."

"Are the others near enough to see the light?" inquired Francis.

"Some on 'em is, an' the balance 'll camp in the edge of the timber till mornin', I reckon."

"How many are there?" asked Charles.

"Well, now, I couldn't rightly say. There was fifteen or twenty jest behind me an' Dick, but I looked back when we was on the last rise of ground outside the timber, an' it 'peared to me ez ef there was a percession that stretched pooty much all the way from Yreka to the foot-hills."

Here the conversation was interrupted by fresh arrivals. The new-comers scattered around among the trees, lighted other fires, and set about cooking supper. Lucky Jim did the honors of the camp in a style peculiarly his own, and the brothers treated their uninvited visitors with frank cordiality. Small parties of ten or twelve continued to arrive at intervals until after midnight, and when the camp finally settled down to repose, at least one hundred men were wrapped in their blankets and disposed in attitudes more or less graceful upon the ground.

With the first rays of light the whole camp was astir. Time was money, when the man who was only five minutes ahead of you might make the strike that you ought to make.

The Missourian who was first on the ground waked while the stars were yet shining, and rose so softly as not to disturb the slumbers of his "pardner" who shared his blankets ; but when he sought out the lower boundary of the "Star of the West," that he might locate a claim adjacent thereto, behold, a shadowy figure was stooping over a recently driven stake. Somebody was in the act of posting a notice on the claim that would have been his if he had waked half an hour earlier.

With a whispered ejaculation which did not include a benediction on the early riser, he silently paced off two hundred feet, and drove his own stake. He had barely affixed his notice (written over night on the back of an old envelope) when he heard a step behind him, and turning, faced "Vermont," a tow-headed, innocent-looking youth from the Green Mountains.

"Jest a minnit too late, wa'ant I ?" he drawled. "Curus, neaow, ain't it, heaow a feller kin make mistakes. I sot eaout to stake a claim jest above the Western Star, or whatsomever they call it, an' when I got to the fork I studied a minnit abeaout whether I'd better take the right or the left, an' I calkilate that's jest where I missed it. If I'd went straight ahead, I'd a' took the left, but arter studyin' on it I took the right, an' blamed ef I didn't stumble ag'inst a stake afore I'd went three steps. I struck a match, an' there was a notice that must a' bin posted last night by the feller they call the Parson. I was mad—some—but

I faced abeaout an' took t'other fork, an' there was Dick Turpin jest ahead of me. 'Twa'n't no use to pick a quarrel with Dick, an' so I come deaown this way ; but there's a notice stuck to the bottom of the Western Star, and here *you* be."

" Thet's so," said the Missourian with much decision ; " an' this yer camp don't go a cent on floatin' notices. 'Twouldn't be healthy, don't yer see ? I've bin in camps afore now whar sech things was done, an' the feller what did it dropped off mighty suddent ; but, see yer now, I hain't nothin' agin ye, an' I don't mind yer stakin' out a claim ter jine this yer one o' mine.   Dick's my párdner, ye know, an' I was kinder savin' it for him, but bein' he's located his'n already, ye'r welcome ter this," and with the air of a monarch bestowing a principality he waved his hand toward the lower boundary of his claim.

The recipient of this offer made all haste in the direction indicated, for it was now beginning to grow light, and moving figures appeared here and there in the timber, showing that the camp was fully awake.

Breakfast was postponed this morning in favor of the more important business of staking claims, but by ten o'clock most of the prospectors discovered that they were hungry, and for the next half hour they formed sociable groups around the fires that were kindled to boil their coffee.   After breakfast Lucky Jim announced that a miners' meeting would be held at eight o'clock P.M. for the purpose of organizing the district.

" Christopher Columbus orter be here now ter give the camp a name," suggested one of the new-comers, and the words were scarcely spoken when a gray felt hat, with a tuft of sandy hair rising through the crown, became visible above a boulder that obstructed the view of the trail up the gulch, and a minute afterward the great discoverer hailed his friends with the air of a man sure of his welcome. Columbus traveled usually on foot.

" A hoss is well enough ef yer hain't nothin' ter do but tend on him," he was wont to remark confidentially ; " but a man like me, thet hez other business, orter patronize Foot an' Walker's line."

It was by the above-named line that Christopher had arrived this morning. His luggage consisted of a gunny-sack and the half of a pair of blankets. The dust of travel still clung to him, but nothing could diminish the grandeur of his air or abate his cheerful readiness to advise and instruct the camp.

" Pooty well fur a starter," he observed, taking in the gulch, the stakes, and the prospect-holes at one comprehensive glance ; " but, boys, yer orter keep ter the right. That thar left-hand fork ain't no 'count. Color of the rock shows it. Country rock, every squar inch. Yer mought as well look fur a pay-streak in wood ashes."

Breakfast was over, but Columbus borrowed one of the still burning fires, and proceeded to toast a very small section of a rind of bacon.

" Yer hain't got a flapjack left over, hev yer ?" he remarked incidentally to his right-hand neighbor. " I wa'ant goin' ter miss th' strike ef I never had a bite of bread, an' I started off 'thout bakin' enny."

Half a loaf was tossed to him, and the bacon rind being now browned to the required crispness, he reached over and touched Vermont, who was gathering up his cooking utensils.

" Couldn't borrer a coffee-cup of yer, could I ?" he inquired. " Kem afoot myself, an' hadn't much show ter pack things."

The cup was handed out.

Next, Columbus interviewed Dick Turpin on the subject

of coffee, and got the quart cup filled with that beverage. Jim loaned the necessary amount of sugar, and the great discoverer proceeded with his breakfast. By the time he had finished his meal the prospectors were scattered up and down the gulch, no one remaining within speaking distance except Lucky Jim and his partners, who were consulting as to the ways and means of getting out the lumber for their sluice-boxes in the shortest possible time.

"The boys that travel on foot will be along to-day by dozens," Jim averred, "and plenty of them will be glad to work a little while for a grub stake. I can't handle a whip-saw myself—more's the pity. If my father had put me to that instead of studying law, I might have been good for something."

Christopher pricked up his ears at these words. The accomplishment which Jim had neglected to acquire he was a proficient in, or, in other words, he was a capital "top-sawyer," an artisan much in request and not always to be found in new camps. He sauntered slowly toward the group, and addressed the partners with the air of one willing to grant a favor at any cost to himself.

"I wuz sorter wild, ez a boy," he remarked ; "an' my old man put me ter' whip-sawin', kinder in hopes ter tone me down. I wuz sot alwuz ter make a clean job of what I undertook, an' I put my mind ter thet thar whip-sawin' tell thar wa'ant a man could hold a candle to me in th' hull kentry. Now, seein' ye'r sorter put to it fur hands, I don't mind takin' holt fur a week, jest ter 'commodate yer."

Jim managed to convey a hint to his companions that Christopher could really do what he boasted in this particular line, and Francis asked him to name his terms.

"Waal, now," he said reflectively, "I hadn't considered thet thar. I sh'd like ter 'blige yer 'thout mentionin' wages—I shd reely now—but I wuz recknin' ter prospect some this winter, an' I sh'll want suthin' fur a grub stake. What d'ye say ter ten dollars a day and board ?"

Francis glanced toward Jim, who made an affirmative sign.

"All right," he said. "You may consider yourself engaged. Are you ready to go to work now ?"

Columbus hesitated a moment.

"My breakfast wuz rayther light," he said, "owin' ter my not havin' enny show ter pack pervisions from t'other camp. P'raps it 'ud be as well ter cook dinner fust."

Jim's blue eyes twinkled, but he answered gravely, "That is so. Help yourself, old man," at the same time handing out a liberal supply of "pervisions," and pointing to the embers of their fire.

Jim and Francis now turned their attention to the work necessary to be done on their claim before putting in the sluices, while Charles held himself in readiness to accompany Columbus to the pit. Owing fo the confusion that had prevailed ever since Jim's arrival, this was the first opportunity Francis had found of speaking to him alone.

"Did you see the boys ? Had they got back from Marysville ?" he asked, as soon as they were out of Christopher's hearing.

Jim shook his head. "No, not the ones you mean," he answered. "The train got in four days ago, but the Mormon boys decided either to winter in Marysville or go farther south. They made a little raise on the Flat, and they want to spend their money."

La Tour's face showed his disappointment. Jim observed it, and added,

"You will see them in the spring, never fear. They will be dead broke by that time, and will come back to the Flat to look up their friends and go to work again. They are good fellows, every one of them ; but they have been so tied down all their lives that liberty makes them a little wild.''

''I can understand that,'' Francis said, and then abruptly changed the subject.

In the course of the day the stragglers to whom Jim alluded began to arrive on foot. They had, as a rule, limited wardrobes and scant luggage, but they were rich in expectations, and in every face shone the cheerful courage which sustained many a poor fellow through a long succession of reverses, until his comrades finally made a grave for him in the sands from which he hoped to dig his wealth.

These pilgrims increased the numerical strength of the camp to one hundred and fifty before night, and when, punctually at the appointed hour, the miners' meeting was called to order, the blaze of the pine-knot flambeaus lighted a sea of faces, rugged, bronzed, unshaven, but keen, resolute, and expressing in every lineament that tireless energy and unflagging perseverance which have done so much to build up the great State they helped to found.

The Parson, a tall, thin, solemn-looking native of the Middle States, who was said to have occupied a pulpit at some former period of his life, was duly elected chairman of the meeting, and Jim, whose penmanship was the wonder and envy of his associates, was chosen secretary.

The first business before the meeting was the adoption of a set of by-laws fixing the boundaries of the district, and the number of feet to be included in a claim ; also defining the conditions which must be complied with in order to hold such claim.

When the article relating to boundaries was read, Columbus rose to his feet, and waving his hand majestically, began :

" 'Pears ez ef them thar lines wuz pooty narrer fur a kentry like this. In the spring of '49 I helped ter organize Gouge Eye districk, an' we tuk in ten mile squar, an' 'lowed five hundred foot fur discovery an' five hundred foot pre-emption ; an' when I mined in South Ameriky—" Here the president's mace, otherwise the knobbed stick in the Parson's right hand, came down heavily upon the boulder that served as a desk.

" Time's up," he announced. " Only one minute allowed for remarks."

The article fixing the district boundaries was put to vote without further argument, and adopted. Then the second article, allowing two hundred feet for each claim, was taken up.

Poker Bill, who reached the camp just before sunset, and found notices posted all the way along the gulch, wished to offer a few remarks before this was put to vote. He thought that by allowing two hundred feet for pre-emption all the mining ground was virtually given over to a few monopolists, while poor men like himself, working-men, who were the bone and sinew of every camp, were deprived of their rights. In his opinion the claims should be cut down to one hundred feet, that all might have an equal show.

This proposition brought half a dozen holders of claims to their feet ; but the Missourian, whose grizzled head towered far above the others, was first seen by the chair, who ruled that he had the floor.

" A pooty arrangement ez ever I heerd on," he exclaimed. " A few on us must go ahead and prospect the kentry, make the trails an' take all the risks, an' then arter we git our claims staked out, in comes a lot o' lazy cusses that never struck a lick sence they wuz born, an' up an' sez, ' Half o' that, ef you please.' Now wat *I've* got ter say is jest this : the man ez wants half o' my claim kin come an' take it," laying his hand significantly as he spoke upon the shot-gun that rested against the tree beside him. These remarks were loudly applauded by a portion of the meeting, and when the question was put to vote, the article was adopted as first read, by a two-thirds majority.

After disposing of the by-laws, the only business before the meeting was the choice of a recorder for the district, and Francis La Tour was nominated and declared elected by a heavy majority. If there had been any other office of trust and profit to fill, the miners would have nominated his brother for it ; for the " Turtle Doves" had confirmed the good impression made by them on the night of their arrival at Yreka Flat, and they had the whole camp for their friends. Besides, the fortunate locators of claims that prospected well felt that they owed something to those who led the way to Shasta Butte, and the late comers who had no claims as yet were quite sure that the brothers had discovered diggings that it would pay to prospect to the very head of either gulch ; for, in the face of Christopher's decision several parties had staked claims in the left-hand fork and panned out coarse gold in considerable quantities.

Viewed in any light the new camp was a promising one, and the men who had just organized " Chespar District" felt comfortably certain that they had " struck it rich."

CHAPTER XII.

A THOUSAND MILES AFOOT.

" FATHER, are you *sure* that God has called us to gather to Zion in this way ?"

" My child, how can I doubt it ? He has not left himself without a witness in these last days. It is now as it was in the beginning. Signs that none can gainsay follow the preaching of those who have counseled us, in his name, to undertake this journey. Have faith and patience, my daughter, and these light afflictions, which are but for a moment, will work out for us a far more exceeding and eternal weight of glory."

The person to whom this exhortation was addressed rose slowly from the ground on which she was sitting, as though fearful that she might be doing wrong to rest by the way. She was a slender, delicate-looking girl of sixteen. Her golden brown hair fell in a mass of tangled curls almost to her waist. Her face, fair still in spite of exposure to sun and wind, was perfect in its outlines, though thin and pale as if from sickness or starvation. Her violet eyes, large, liquid, and just now full of tears, were cast down as she received her father's gentle rebuke, and her beautiful mouth quivered like that of a grieved child.

Had she done wrong to put such a question ? And yet, who could help it ? Here they were—she a delicate girl, and her old father who had never before known hardship— far from home, friends, and country, and plodding wearily on foot across the American wilderness, whose rugged mountains, and sandy wastes, and rushing torrents that must be forded, were in such sad contrast to her dreams of a land flowing with milk and honey.

The company to which they belonged numbered six hundred, and all of them, young or old, sick or well, strong or infirm, must make the terrible journey of a thousand miles on foot ; and more than this, they must drag their scanty outfit of bedding and clothing and a portion of their food in hand-carts.

They had left the Missouri River late in August. It was now November. But little more than half their journey was accomplished, and their road, marked already by the graves of those of the company just ahead who had fallen by the way, was strewed with the dead bodies of the weaker ones, who had started out with them full of hope and faith.

The weather grew each day more inclement, the streams they had to wade were icy cold, and, worse than all, their scanty rations began to fail so rapidly that death by starvation stared them in the face.

Jessie Wilton and her father were living happily in their English home when the emissaries of the Mormon Church sought them out, and so wrought upon the credulous, simple-hearted old man by their "miracles," "prophecies," and "gifts of healing" that he was induced to sell all he had, and after placing the proceeds in the hands of the elder who had charge of the emigration, set out with his motherless child on this journey, whose goal was the Zion hidden in the mountains—a city fair as Jerusalem the Golden—so the girl's dreams and the old man's simple faith pictured it.

The hundreds who had started with them on their toilsome pilgrimage were sustained by the same faith. Somewhere in the valleys of the mountains God had promised to hide his chosen ones until the evil days were overpast, and now he called them to witness the fulfillment of his promise, and share the security and peace of his Saints.

Alas for their simple trust, for the hopes that day by day grew weaker, as cold and starvation thinned their ranks, and the pitiless storm beat upon their unprotected heads! No wonder that the faith of the most devoted began to waver, when the bitter winter of the northern Territories overtook them midway on their journey; for those who told them of the glories of the Zion beyond the mountains had prophesied that "the seasons and the elements would be controlled for their benefit, and though they would hear of storms on the right and on the left, not one would be permitted to break upon their path."

Jessie had been dragging the hand-cart since morning, for her father had grown so weak from exposure and hunger that he was barely able to totter by her side. At Florence, where the final arrangements for the journey were made, one hand-cart was assigned to every five persons; but there were many little children and even babes in arms in the company, which reduced the number of those able to draw the carts to three in each squad, and often there were only two, who divided the labor between them.

Fathers put their little children, too young to walk, upon the already overloaded carts, and dragged them until nature gave out. Husbands attempted to carry their sick wives in the same manner, and feeble old men and women with frost-bitten hands and feet were helped as far as possible by those who were younger and stronger; but day by day the number of those able to help others, or even to help themselves, diminished, until at last Death, the Friend and Helper of a humanity that can bear no more, stretched out the only hand that was offered to the sinking victims.

The day was wearing away, and the biting wind chilled even the strongest to the very marrow. Jessie, who saw that her father was every moment growing weaker, begged him to get on the cart.

"I can pull you a little way, father," declared the girl, who had eaten nothing that day except a fragment of hard biscuit. "Look! there is a storm coming, and we are far behind the others. Do let me try to draw you along."

"No, my daughter," he answered. "Do you hurry on and send some of the men back to help me ; or, maybe I can go a little farther ;" but even as he spoke he tottered and fell.

"Father! father! I cannot leave you!" she cried in anguish. "You will be frozen to death long before any one can come for you," and with all her strength she tried to lift him, but could not.

"Oh, what shall I do ?" She wrung her hands as she looked in vain for some sign that they were missed by those ahead. "If I could only build a fire ; but I have nothing, not even a match."

She pulled the scanty supply of bedding from the cart, wrapped her father in it, and rubbed his stiffening limbs ; but his eyes were already dim with death.

"Listen, daughter," he said feebly, "for these are my. last words. The men who counseled us to take this journey were, mayhap, mistaken ; but never charge their mistake on our covenant-keeping God. Fifty years have I trusted him, and his goodness has never failed. I commit you to his tender mercies. Good-by, my Jessie, my little girl. I cannot see your dear face, but I shall see you where they hunger no more—where all tears are wiped away. I am going to your mother. Don't cry, Jessie—father's little girl."

The fluttering breath grew fainter, then ceased. The snow-flakes began to sift down upon the face that was as cold as they. The desolate orphan ceased to sob. Her head sank upon her father's breast, and in a little while she would have slept with him, but three of the strongest men in the company, detailed to look after the feeble ones who fell behind and to bury the dead, came up at this moment and lifted her, only half conscious, into the cart.

One of the men now hurried forward with the girl, and the other two, after satisfying themselves that life was extinct in the motionless figure before them, dug a shallow grave, and without coffin, without funeral rites, without a mourner (for those who laid him away in his last resting-place felt that he was to be envied), the body of the old man was committed to the frozen earth.

A couple of hours afterward, Jessie, restored to consciousness, began to ask,

" Where is my father ?"

" In heaven, child," said one who sat near.   " You surely do not wish him back ?"

" No.   Oh, no, I remember now ; but I was going with him.   Why did you hinder me ?"

There was little time for rest, and still less for tears, that bitter night.   The storm which began before sunset increased in violence, and the howling winds blew down the tents which were their only shelter, and drifted the snow into their feeble fires.   Morning found the living chilled and exhausted, with neither strength nor courage for the day's journey, and in the snow that surrounded the camp lay the bodies of five who, during the night, had taken the journey from which none return.

All the dead were hastily buried in one grave, and then the survivors, with little hope that another sun would rise on any of them, again pushed forward.

Numbers dropped by the way as they toiled slowly onward, but they dared not stop, for they knew that their utmost exertions would barely enable them to reach a camping-ground which would afford fuel for their fires. At length, just before night overtook the exhausted company, they were met by messengers who were as welcome as angels from heaven—two men who had ridden on in advance of half a dozen wagons sent out from the valley with provisions.

The good news they brought infused life into the perishing multitude, and superhuman exertions were made to reach a good camping-ground sixteen miles ahead, where also there were some abandoned log-cabins that would afford them shelter. By almost incredible efforts on the part of those who had charge of the train, this station was reached on the evening of the next day, but twelve more of their number were left dead in the snow.

Here it was decided to make the most comfortable camp possible under the circumstances, and wait for the relief which was on the way ; but on the first night in camp all that was left of their scanty rations was dealt out. The only food now remaining in the company was a few pounds of rice and hard bread, which had been reserved for the sick and for the youngest children, and for two days they endured the pangs of starvation.

There were fifteen deaths in these two days, and when on the morning of the third day the long-looked-for wagons drove into camp, many more were too far gone to be benefited by the food they brought. After a day's rest the train was again put in motion ; those who were unable to drag their carts being allowed to load their effects into the wagons, while those who could not walk were permitted to ride.

Thus heavily loaded, the wagons, drawn by oxen, moved slowly along with the hand-cart train, stopping every now and then to bury some one for whom help had come too late.

It was a noticeable fact that many women and young girls kept on their feet and continued to drag their carts, while the men beside them dropped to the ground dying or dead. In some instances the young girls were the only survivors out of a large family when the train finally reached Salt Lake.* Three bright young English girls saw father, mother, and five brothers die one after the other of cold and starvation, while they remained able to pull their carts, and entered Salt Lake in safety.

Jessie Wilton was among the number gifted with this power of endurance. She walked every step of the way from the Missouri to Salt Lake valley, and for more than two thirds of the distance dragged the hand-cart which had been assigned to her and her father at starting. When she reached Salt Lake she was thin and haggard from starvation, but no other consequences of the terrible journey were manifest.

She was ragged, shoeless, and penniless also, for her father's little hoard, which had been intrusted to the elder who persuaded them to come, had disappeared ; but, unlike many others, she had a home to go to. Her mother's uncle, a well-to-do Englishman who had settled in the valley three years before, received the orphan into his childless household, and in a few months she began to bear some likeness to the " singing bird," the old father's darling, who had made his home glad for so many years.

But, for a time, it seemed almost as though she had escaped the perils of the wilderness only to fall into greater perils in the Zion which she had long since ceased to compare to " Jerusalem the Golden." With returning health and strength all her winsome, girlish beauty came back, and from the glossy braids of golden-brown hair that crowned her shapely head to the tiny foot whose light pressure scarcely left a print on the earth, she was too fair to

* See Appendix, Note J, page 346.

know an hour's safety in that den of beasts, had she not been guarded as she was by her uncle, whose position, influence, and money made it a matter of policy with the authorities to conciliate him, and by her aunt, who at heart detested Mormonism and all things connected with it.

Though many of the leaders of the people looked upon her beauty with longing eyes, and more than one hoary-headed apostle with a score of wives asked her in marriage, Brigham Young refused to compel her uncle to sacrifice her. .

" The girl shall choose for herself," was his stereotyped answer to all petitions, until more than one came to believe that he designed her for himself. In this, however, they were mistaken. The reigning favorite in the Prophet's harem at this time was herself a beauty of no common order, and withal a jealous one, and her influence over him was sufficient to hinder him from taking a wife whom she would have regarded as a rival.

While matters were in this state, it happened that Philip La Tour met the violet-eyed maiden at her uncle's house. Philip was now twenty-four years old, and in spite of the advice of his elders he still remained single ; but possibly this was because the girls who arrived with each year's emigration were appropriated by gray-haired representatives of the priesthood as soon as they reached the valley.

Blanche, his only remaining sister, had lately been married to a neighbor's son, a young man whose good heart and sound principles had thus far survived the blighting influences of Mormonism, and thus Philip was left quite alone in the home that, by untiring industry, he had succeeded in making comfortable and even pleasant.

He was still as fanatical as ever in his religious belief, and the tenth of all his earnings, together with considerably more than a tenth of the money which he received

from time to time from his brothers in California, was
regularly paid into the Prophet's coffers.   Yet, in spite of
the continual drain consequent upon this payment of tithes,
he prospered, and in spite of Mormonism his daily life was
irreproachable, thanks to his inherited integrity and the
lessons his mother taught him in childhood.

He was a fine specimen of physical manhood—tall, lithe,
strong-limbed- and with a handsome face and a winning
smile that would have made him a dangerous rival of the
graybeards around him, had such rivalry been possible.

Jessie, who was not yet so thoroughly converted to Mormonism as to prefer exaltation in the next world as the
tenth wife of an elderly apostle, to happiness in this world
as the one wife of a man who loved her, found the handsome youth a pleasant acquaintance—dangerously pleasant
in a community where young men and maidens were so
closely watched, but where, after a couple of months, he
told the story that has been told so many thousand times
since the first pair of lovers met in Eden. Not even the concluding assurance that he had first sought and obtained
the Prophet's approval could dampen the joy that glowed
in the depths of her violet eyes and flushed her soft cheeks
as she gave him his answer.

But alas ! when the wedding-day came, there was that
to endure which not only dampened joy but well-nigh
crushed out life.   By the Prophet's express command, they
were to be married in the Endowment House, and the
hideous ordeal through which the poor girl was compelled
to pass inspired such terror and loathing that when she
knelt for the last time in the " sacred circle," and was
ordered to repeat with the others the fearful oaths of blood
and vengeance which completed the vows that made them
the slaves of the Prophet forever, she fainted quite away,
and was carried from the room insensible.   When she re-

covered consciousness, all the other candidates had passed
" beyond the veil" except her lover, and with him beside
her she submitted to the final ceremony and was ushered
into the sealing-room. Before her own marriage took place,
however, she was an unwilling witness of the nuptials of a
plural bride, while the first wife knelt beside the altar,
silent and tearless, but with such a look of anguish and
despair on her white face that the memory of it haunted
the beholder for years.

In spite of Jessie's loving faith in the man of her choice,
the torturing question,

" Shall I ever be compelled to act such a part ?" forced
itself upon her as she saw the wretched wife place the hand
of the youthful bride in that of her husband, and bow her
head in answer to the question,

" Do you give this woman unto this man, even as Sarah
gave Hagar to Abraham ?"

When it came her turn to kneel with Philip at the same
altar, the vision of that pallid face, stamped with the seal
of death—the death of hope and happiness and love—
seemed to rise between her and the man who held her hand
in a tender and loyal clasp, and at the very threshold of her
new life the sweetness of wedded love was mixed with the
bitterness of a nameless dread.

She could not say, even to herself,

" I fear that some day my husband will ask me to yield
my place to another."

She trusted him fully, she loved him wholly, and yet, as
they left the accursed mysteries of the Endowment House
behind them she felt that a shadow had fallen across their
path which the clear shining sun could not dispel.

Philip had done his utmost to make his home worthy of
his fair bride, and, on the summer evening when they took
possession of it, it looked pleasant enough to content them

both, had their hearts been quite at rest ; but Philip, no less than his bride, felt the effects of the ordeal through which they had passed, and the scenes they had been compelled to witness.

A honeymoon begun thus could not be filled with unalloyed happiness ; but the love that had drawn them together was strong and enduring, and Jessie's sunny temper and Philip's sterling goodness were proof against influences that might otherwise have turned the sweetness of married life into gall and wormwood.

Jessie's uncle, to whom the gentle orphan was as a daughter, gave her a marriage portion of three thousand dollars, and with this slender capital Philip became a merchant on a small scale. Here, as elsewhere, he was prospered, and by the end of the year was able to enlarge his business.

With the close of their first year of wedded happiness came also another gift, far more precious than the money that began to flow in—a dark-eyed baby boy, with his mother's smile lighting up his father's features. Now indeed the shadow that dimmed their sunshine seemed to melt away.

" Baby fingers, waxen touches" drove that nameless fear from the mother's breast, and Philip, now not only her husband but her baby's father, was her king, who could do no wrong.

For six months she lived in a dream of delight, only rousing herself to say sometimes to Philip, as both were gazing fondly upon the little head pillowed on her bosom,

" My love, I fear we are too happy. Something tells me that this cannot last."

It did not last. One night both were roused from sleep to find their idol struggling and gasping for breath, and when morning came nothing remained to them but a little waxen figure, still and cold, which neither wakened nor stirred when hot tears and passionate kisses were rained upon it.

After their baby was buried out of their sight, love, sanctified by sorrow, drew their bleeding hearts more closely together. In speaking, long afterward, of those days, the wife said,

" My husband was my all. I did not simply love him, I *worshiped* him. He was more to me than God or my own soul."

Are there not others whom sorrow has brought to cling, in the same way, to the one dear object left in a world from which all else that the heart delighted in has been taken ?

Another year passed, and then a sweet little blue-eyed girl came to brighten their home ; but though welcomed joyfully, and tenderly beloved by both parents, she could not fill in the mother's heart the place of the first-born.

Another year glided away, and little Lily was just beginning to totter across the room on uncertain feet, and lisp sweet baby words, when she too sickened, and in spite of all that love could do to save her, faded from their sight, and was laid beside her brother.

This time, when they returned from the burial of their little one and sat down beside the empty cradle, Philip put his arms around his wife and said tenderly,

" My love, in some way, though I know not how, we are displeasing God. He does not afflict willingly. I remember a text like that which my mother taught me long ago. When he punishes us it is in love—it is because he *must*. Let us try and find out what sin we are cherishing that calls for such bitter correction."

CHAPTER XIII.

THE LA TOUR BOYS AGAIN.

THE Shasta Butte diggings were rich—nobody disputed
that—but the ground that could be worked profitably was
limited in extent, and the " stampede" in the fall of '52,
which lasted until some weeks after the snow began to fall,
brought in rather more men than the camp had any use
for, and in the spring of '53 fully half of those who had
gathered there left, either to prospect on their own account or to follow up some of the new strikes that were
reported on every side.

The La Tours, who had worked their claim during the
winter as steadily as the weather permitted, sold out in
May and left the gulch richer by ten thousand dollars than
when they entered it the previous October. They had no
particular destination. Wonderful stories were afloat concerning the new discoveries made in Nevada County, and
they had some thoughts of turning their steps in that direction ; but first they must look up the young men from
Utah, whom thus far they had not been able to find.

Lucky Jim repeated his assurance that they would make
their way back to Yreka Flat in the spring " dead broke ;"
and partly on this account, and partly because Yreka was
the nearest outfitting point, they rode over there the morning after bidding adieu to Chespar District.

Yreka had met with a good many changes in eight
months. It was now an ambitious canvas town, with a
dozen lumber buildings besides, which constituted what

was proudly designated "the business block." Merchants in all sorts of wares reported "lively times," there was the usual number of saloons, and everything about the place indicated the process of transition from a camp to a town. The brothers put up at the Astoria, a hotel with log walls and canvas front, which was, as the rather highly-colored placard beside the door announced, "The only strictly first-class house in Yreka."

As if to prove Jim a prophet, almost the first words addressed to them by the landlord, after the conventional inquiry, "What will you take?" were,

"Them Salt Lake chaps that you fellers wor a-huntin' in the fall hez turned up. Got back last week with nary red. Cleaned out in 'Frisco. Sech is life."

The "Salt Lake chaps," three in number, were found, after a short search, sitting round the embers of the fire which had served to cook their scanty supper, discussing in a mood anything but hopeful the chances of obtaining work in the crowded camp. They did not recognize their visitors until they introduced themselves by name. The lapse of years had changed the boys who left winter quarters in 1848 into bronzed and bearded men, and the others whom Francis remembered as lads in their teens were now stalwart specimens of the California miner.

Only one of the boys, Dick West by name, really hailed from Salt Lake. The others were from the northern settlements. Dick, at first was very communicative, rattling off an amount of news about their mutual acquaintances which did credit to his imagination if not to his memory, but when Francis La Tour inquired after his own family the fluent young man grew silent and constrained. He hardly ever saw any of them except Philip, he said. The rest of the family kept themselves very close. Philip was growing up a likely sort of boy, but the old boss, by which irreverent term West designated the Prophet, kept a tight grip on him.

It was not until the next morning, when Francis found an opportunity of speaking with West alone, that the kind-hearted young fellow could be brought to tell what he knew. His story was the one commonly reported in Salt Lake with regard to Madame La Tour's disappearance; and as he with the others really believed that she wandered to the river in a fit of temporary insanity and was accidentally drowned, he gave the account with an air of sincerity that convinced his hearer of its truth.

Of the sisters he had little to tell. He knew that Louise taught the Prophet's children, and that the younger girls were with their brother, and he believed that all were safe and well.

"And I'll tell you what is the truth," he continued impressively; "you want to keep away from there. You could do no good to any of your family by being seen in Utah. You are apostates, and in all the sermons they preach nowadays they recommend sending apostates to the bottomless pit by the shortest route. Philip is a sort of favorite, and he and the girls will do well enough, but you would be blood-atoned without having time to say your prayers, if you were caught inside the Territory. I could tell you things that would make your hair stand on end— things that I've seen with my own eyes. It was something that happened almost at our door that made me think it was time to leave, and nothing on earth could persuade me to go back."

West was sincere: there could be no doubt of that; and his repeated assurance that the brothers would bring trouble upon their family instead of helping them, by making any attempt to get them away, finally caused them to give up the idea of returning to Utah. Here they were freemen, and an honorable career was open to them.   In the dominions of the Mormon Prophet they could only live as slaves, if permitted to live at all.

The most painful thing involved in their decision was what seemed to them the virtual abandonment of their sisters, whose rescue they were urged to undertake by every manly and fraternal impulse ; but West assured them that there was not the faintest possibility of succeeding in such an attempt—and he was right.   For twenty years no woman left the Territory without the Prophet's permission, unless under military escort, and more than one generous man who dared the consequences of attempting to release these victims of priestly tyranny paid for the desperate venture with his life.

*   *   *   *   *   *   *

1853 and '54 were prosperous years for the brothers ; so much so that buckskin purses and oyster-cans no longer sufficed as receptacles for their gold, and the books of the San Francisco banking-house in which their surplus capital was deposited showed the handsome balance of eighty thousand dollars in their favor.   They ought by this time to have been moderately happy, if success could bring happiness, but both of them were domestic in their tastes, and longed to end their wanderings and make a home somewhere.

The material for such a home as they dreamed of was not, however, to be found in California at this period.

There were a few families in San Francisco and the other towns which were beginning to take on the name of cities, but a large majority of the population were men like themselves, who had no certain dwelling-place.

In the late autumn of '55 they repaired to San Francisco, with their minds made up to take passage for the States. On the morning after their arrival, Charles, who was looking over the paper as they sat at breakfast, turned suddenly to his brother, saying,

"We are advertised for. I don't think anybody wants to arrest us, do you?"

Francis took the paper from his brother's hand and read aloud:

"Information wanted of Francis and Charles La Tour, who emigrated to Oregon in the spring of 1848, and who removed subsequently to Nevada County, Cal. Any person knowing the whereabouts of the aforesaid parties will be liberally rewarded upon communicating such information to Rand & Co., No. — M—— St."

"Rand & Co. are not detectives, that's one comfort," he observed. "I think I'll walk down there myself and claim the reward."

The place indicated in the advertisement was the office of a well-known law firm. Francis betook himself thither in the course of an hour, feeling no special curiosity with regard to the person inquiring for him.

"Some of the boys from Yreka want to hunt us up, I suppose," he said to Charles on starting.

It was no uncommon thing for "the boys," especially those who were "out of luck," to hunt up the Turtle Doves, who could never see an old comrade in trouble without offering to help him. This time the applicant might be Jim, whom they had lost sight of for a year or more. When last heard from he had got rid of the five thousand dollars that he made at Shasta, and was reduced to his normal condition of impecuniosity.

"I shall be glad to help Jim. Hope I can find out a way to do it without offending him," he soliloquized as he walked along, and with this idea in his mind he presented himself at the office of Rand & Co., and stated his name and business to the senior partner.

"La Tour ?　Ah, yes ;" said Mr. Rand.　"Very happy, I am sure, to find that our advertisement has reached you. The person inquiring for you is your brother-in-law."

"Brother-in-law !　I was—not aware that I had such a relative," La Tour said.

"The gentleman was accompanied by his wife when he called at our office," was the answer, "and the lady certainly bears a decided resemblance to you."

Francis was startled.　Could one of his sisters by any possibility be in San Francisco ?　If so, she must be the wife of a Mormon missionary ; and more than this, her own loyalty to the Prophet must be above suspicion, or she would never be allowed to travel with him.　It was not a pleasant thought ; and much as he had longed to see the face of one of his kindred, he set out to look up the address given him by the lawyer, in a frame of mind by no means enviable.

The name on the slip of paper he held in his hand furnished no clew to the identity of his unknown brother-in-law, for during the years that he spent among the Saints he had not happened to hear of George Denys.

When he reached the house he was somewhat reassured by the face and bearing of the man who offered him his hand, saying,

"This is a far better answer to my advertisement than I hoped for."

Francis asked at once for his sister.

"She is not very well," was the reply, "and I would like first to have her prepared for the interview.　Our escape from Utah was attended with perils and hardships from the effects of which she has not quite recovered."

"Your escape !"　Francis looked bewildered.　"Why, I thought—"

"You thought nobody escaped from that place, I suppose."

"No; that is not just what I was going to say. I thought you were a missionary sent out by the Church."

There was a look in Denys' eyes which the other could not fathom, as he answered,

"My last mission in behalf of the Church cost me too much, and I decided never to undertake another—but I am forgetting the explanation which I owe you. If you can wait an hour to see your sister, I will try and tell you why we are here, and what drove us from Utah."

It is needless to say that Denys had a deeply interested auditor while he related, in the fewest words possible, the story of the last two years. He did not allude in any way to his wife's previous history. He knew that her elder brothers had been kept in ignorance of the fact that she was sealed to the Prophet Joseph, and for her sake he hoped they might never learn anything of her relations to Kimball.

For himself he spoke honestly when he assured her before their marriage that in his mind no shadow of blame attached to her. In the eyes of the world she might be a disgraced and ruined woman; in his eyes she was, as he had said, only the victim of a system which he had helped to uphold; and though when he proposed to make her his wife he was actuated solely by pity, and a wish to rescue her from her surroundings, he had already learned to love her.

And Louise? It is true that, as she had told Denys, she knew nothing of such love as happier women feel, but gratitude to her preserver was changing into a tender affection. Those days of suffering on the desert had done more to draw them together than months of ordinary experience, and for the first time since she left the shelter of her own home she felt that she had some one to confide in and lean upon.

Yet there were hours when the memory of the horrors of her past life came upon her like a flood, and threatened to overwhelm her. At such times she could not bear to look upon a human face, not even upon that of the husband who was growing so dear to her, and he wisely left her to herself until her mind recovered its wonted tone. He knew that she at once desired and dreaded to meet her brothers, and it was this state of feeling quite as much as her health which made him anxious to prepare her for such a meeting.

Francis waited for what seemed to him a very long time in the room in which his brother-in-law left him. At length there were footsteps in the hall, the rustle of draperies, and the door opened, admitting a tall, pale, dark-eyed woman, whom Francis recognized as *La Belle Louise*, chiefly by her likeness to the mother, whose face was never absent from his memory.

The meeting between the long-separated brother and sister was most affectionate, and on one side altogether joyful, but Louise's happiness was alloyed by the bitter thought,

" If my brother knew all, he would cast me off."

In thinking thus she did him a measure of injustice, and yet it is certain that had the truth been told him she could not have been the same to him that she was in the days when the same roof sheltered them.

Before Francis left he learned that Catherine had also succeeded in reaching California with her husband, and that they were comfortably established on a ranch about twenty-five miles from the city. Both the brothers rode out to the ranch the next day, and found the place so much to their liking that the project of returning to the States was indefinitely postponed.

Catherine had no concealments and no bitter memories, and perhaps on this account there was something in her welcome which they missed in that of Louise. At any rate, the unpretentious house in which the married lovers had enshrined their Lares and Penates came so near to realizing their brothers' ideal of a home that they begged the privilege of sharing it, and formed a partnership with Kenyon, which was highly advantageous to the latter, who was richer in good sense and sound principles than in money.

During the winter that followed their settlement at the ranch, the brothers talked freely with Kenyon and his wife about their mother's disappearance. Catherine still adhered to her unsupported, and, to all except herself, unreasonable belief that her mother still lived; but Kenyon, when he talked with the brothers alone, put a different construction upon the single fact on which she based this belief.

"I have no doubt whatever that Catherine is right in saying that her mother never left the house alone," he told them; "but at the same time I feel sure that she was drowned, and from my knowledge of that accursed band of murderers I am equally certain that she did not drown *herself*."

This was only putting into words the suspicion that both the brothers had begun to entertain; but even if they had positive proof that their mother died by violence, it would be worse than useless to attempt to bring her murderers to justice. The Mormon Prophet, secure in his mountain retreat, was able to defy the law, and crimes committed by his orders would never be inquired into, much less punished. Kenyon could tell them of more than one deed of blood done in open day, and boasted of as a meritorious act, and the air of the valley was rife with secret whispers of other deeds that could not be so much as named among civilized beings.

CHAPTER XIV

PRAYER AND SACRIFICE.

IN all outward things Philip La Tour continued to prosper. His business increased, he built a new and handsome house, and filled it with the best furniture that the valley afforded ; his fair wife was daintily clad, and many a poor neighbor blessed both for the bounty that was freely bestowed ; but in spite of all this neither wore a look of perfect contentment.

It was now three years since the little daughter left them, and no other child had been given them to brighten their home. No one but a mother who has seen her baby carried out of the door for the last time could understand how Jessie longed to see a little sleeping head upon the cradle pillow, or how she woke in the night from a dream of her lost darlings and wept because her arms were empty, because there was no baby at her breast.

And alas ! Jessie now had sorrows which bereaved mothers elsewhere know nothing of. Because she was childless her husband was " counseled" to take another wife, and often this counsel was given in her presence, and she was sharply reproved for resisting the Spirit of the Lord by withholding her consent. It is but justice to Philip to say that he did what he could to shield her from these coarse rebukes, and that he assured her, with an air of sincerity which satisfied her, that nothing could induce him to do what his brethren all around him were doing. And yet Jessie knew that he accepted the doctrine of polygamy—that he believed it was enjoined by a revelation from heaven. Only the infatuation of a blind love could bring any feeling of security to the wife of a man who held such a belief.

Jessie knew that her husband was sincere in his acceptance of the Latter Day Gospel, and that in theory he did not reject even the doctrine of Blood Atonement,* which was preached openly and practiced year after year without let or hindrance. It is true that he was not selected as an actor in any of the bloody tragedies that occurred on every hand. The Prophet chose his instruments wisely, and he knew Philip well enough to be aware that he would be quite useless in the rôle of assassin, and moreover that the actual sight of the taking off of a Gentile or apostate would be apt to destroy his faith, not only in the doctrine of blood atonement, but in the divinity of the Mormon system as a whole.

The band of cut-throats who stood ready at all times to do the Prophet's bidding were men of quite a different stamp—men who were villains by nature, and who did not need the impulse of fanaticism to bring them to the point of shedding blood.

And yet these men were Philip La Tour's *brethren.* He joined with them in prayer. He invited them to his house, and they sat at the table with him and his refined and gentle wife. They filled offices of trust and authority. Some were members of the Territorial Legislature, others were judges of the probate courts or mayors of cities, but every one of them had blood on his hands ; every one of them had been engaged in deeds of darkness for which devils might blush.†

It happened one day that Philip brought home two of these men to dinner. Jessie, who always shrank from meeting them, pleaded a headache, and did not appear at the

* See Appendix, Note K, page 346.   † See Appendix, Note L, page 348.

table ; but her own room adjoined the dining-room, and as the door was slightly ajar, every word of their conversation was distinctly audible to her.

" I suppose you think, Brother La Tour," said one of the men, " that we ought to have accepted of this Governor they sent us from Washington, instead of driving him out of the Territory."

" No," was the answer, " we were not obliged to accept of him ; but still we had no right to mob him. There are more dignified and reasonable ways of dealing with an un-welcome official."

" Ha ! ha ! That is good. Just hear him, Brother Grove. Dignified and reasonable ! Don't you wish he could have seen the boys laying on their ox-whips ? I tell you the Governor took some dignified steps before they got through with him ; and I guess they *reasoned* with him in a way that he could understand."

Brother Grove did not appear to share his companion's mirth.

" I don't see anything to laugh about," he growled. " That job was managed just as I knew it would be when it was left to boys. The fellow got away, and now we must expect to take the consequences of the stir he will make in the States about his treatment here."

" And you are really afraid that President Young don't know how to turn that very thing to our advantage ? Brother Grove, I gave you credit for more sense. Who is going to prove that the boys were *counseled* to do the work ? It is the easiest thing in the world to fasten the responsi-bility on them, denounce them publicly for it, and have them arrested. That will quiet all feeling in the States, and put President Young before the people there in the light of a man determined to punish such an outrage on a Government official."

" That's all very well," Brother Grove responded, " if the boys don't tell their own story and put the responsibility where it belongs."

" Never you fear, Brother Grove. The boys won't tell anything," * and the Danite, who was also a member of the Territorial Legislature, drew his hand across his throat with an expression of countenance fairly diabolical.

He sat facing the bedroom door, and Jessie not only heard him but saw the look. She turned cold from head to foot. What if she should be suspected of listening to this murderous revelation ? Her husband rose and moved toward the door. She closed her eyes and feigned sleep, trembling in every limb. He came into the room, took a paper from his desk, glanced toward the bed, and went out, shutting the door after him. She listened again, with senses preternaturally sharpened, and heard him say,

" Here are the names that I promised to give you."

Did that refer to the subject which had been talked over, or was he only trying to turn the conversation into a less dangerous channel ?

What she had heard already she understood only too well. The instruments of the Prophet's vengeance were to be " taken care of," partly to punish them for failing in their mission, and partly to insure silence with regard to the high-handed outrage which the Church had authorized.

Was Philip a murderer too ? No, she could not believe that ; she would not wrong him by harboring the thought for a moment. And yet, were they not all in some way responsible for crimes which were the legitimate fruits of the doctrines they professed to believe ? The fearful oaths of the Endowment House yet rang in her ears—oaths by which she, with the others, was supposed to be bound.

* See Appendix, Note M, page 349.

" And I am one of them—one of this band of assassins,"
she said to herself. " Oh, God, my father's God, if thou
yet livest, make some way of escape for me."

Was there any God ? Every crime committed here,
every deed of blood that tainted the air and stained the
earth was said to be divinely ordered, and the Bible that
she learned to read at her dead mother's knee was quoted
daily to justify treachery, rapine, and murder. She knew that
the assassins, who were even now sitting at her own table,
would kneel in prayer before going out to arrange the details of the crime they were to commit. She knew that a
" prayer-circle" had preceded one wholesale slaughter of
men, women, and children, and that red-handed murderers
wiped their bloody knives, and said as they looked upon
their expiring victims,

" Oh, Lord, receive their spirits, for it is for thy sake we
do this."*

Strange indeed that such a faith should retain any hold
upon sane minds, and yet the Old Testament Scriptures,
often misquoted it is true, and always perverted, were
made the standard by which these acts were tried, and those
who sickened at the knowledge of the crimes committed in
the name of religion said,

" If we give up Mormonism we must also give up the
Bible."

Jessie knew that her husband shared this feeling, and
that he dared not appeal to his own conscience or to the
customs of the Christian world in deciding the question of
right or wrong. He had not yet begun to ask,

" Is there any God ?" and Jessie shuddered at her own
thoughts as she found them taking the form of this question.

* A fact established by the testimony of responsible witnesses in
open court.

" Yes," she said almost aloud, " there is a God, and he does not justify murder. I know the Scriptures do not mean what they would have us believe here. The Bible never bore any such fruits elsewhere."

There was so much comfort in this thought that she determined to speak of it to her husband, carefully concealing, however, her knowledge of the conversation at table.

In the course of an hour the unwelcome guests took their departure, and Philip came in to see if she was awake.

" Have you rested, love," he asked, in the tender tone he always used toward her.

" Rested enough to feel a little better," she answered, detecting his ill-concealed anxiety to know whether she had really slept while his guests were in the house.

" I was afraid we might disturb you," he continued, looking relieved, " and I am glad you are better, because I must go away this afternoon, and I may not. be back for a couple of days.

Her fears instantly put a construction upon this statement which almost broke down her self-control ; but calming herself by a great effort she asked him where he was going.

" Only to Ogden on a little business," he answered ; but though she had never doubted his word before, she did not believe him now.

The wretches who had just left the house had brought him some order which he dared not disobey—she was sure of that—and he was going to execute it. And yet, even if he was to be sent out to commit a crime like that named in her hearing a little while ago, she must be silent.

Can happier women in Christian lands understand the tortures which this wife endured while her husband was absent on his unknown errand ? Can they conceive the feelings of other wives (and there are scores of such in Utah) whose husbands were called from their beds at midnight to aid in some deed of darkness, returning home in time to change their blood-stained garments before the day broke ?''

Many a woman is to-day dragging out the remnant of a miserable life, carrying always the burden of a terrible secret, the disclosure of which would cost the life of one she loves. Many another woman has sunk into an untimely grave because not strong enough to bear the knowledge of her husband's crimes.

And this is not all. The men who have imbrued their hands in blood in obedience to counsel have found nothing in their religion to quench the fires of remorse or banish the torturing visions called up by memory ; and while some have been driven to madness, others have ended their lives by their own hands, and taken a fearful leap into the dark in the vain hope of finding forgetfulness beyond death.

Philip La Tour, as we have said, was a man altogether unlikely to be chosen by the Prophet as an executioner, and he was not now ordered to undertake anything that involved bloodshed. Two men who had become dissatisfied with Mormonism were preparing to leave the Territory secretly with their families, and as they occupied farms at some distance from the settlements, and upon the northern route to California, they thought they had a fair prospect of succeeding where others had failed.

They could not sell their farms or take their stock or household goods with them. All that they owned, with the exception of a light load for each wagon, must be left behind ; but this was a small price to pay for freedom. As they had no near neighbors, they hoped to be able to get two or three days' start before their absence was discovered, and with good teams they could then distance their pursuers. It was a vain hope, as the sequel will show.

Months before, some unguarded expressions had betrayed the weakness of their faith in the Prophet, and from that time they had been closely watched. Now the details of their intended flight were almost as well known to the Danites as to themselves, and the plan that was laid to intercept them was one that did credit to the peculiar genius of the individual who had the matter in charge.

As soon as the exact time of their departure and their intended route became known, it was arranged that a dozen armed men should lie in wait for them about ten miles out.

The fugitives started soon after dark, intending to make about twenty-five miles before daylight. It was now November, and the length of the nights favored them. They thought that the weather favored them also, for a storm was raging which no one would be likely to brave except on an errand as urgent as their own. They had bidden good-by cheerfully to the homes they had reared, and turned their faces westward with unabated courage, for was not freedom just ahead ? Full of this thought, the men urged their teams forward as rapidly as the darkness would permit. They knew every foot of the way, and their horses knew it also.

They were not in the least likely to meet other travelers ; one of the drivers was just giving expression to this thought when the sharp crack of a rifle was heard, and a bullet whizzed past the horses' heads, followed by the command '' Halt !'' spoken in stentorian tones.

It was not an order to be disregarded when backed up by a dozen guns, and the teams were stopped.

The only men in the wagons were the two who were driving. The remainder of the party were women and children. Their captors surrounded them and ordered them roughly to get down. The men obeyed in silence. Then the women and children, who were sheltered by the canvas covers of the wagons, were compelled to get out and stand by the roadside in the storm.

"Very sorry to discommode you," said the Danite captain, who was no other than the facetious member of the Legislature who had dined the day before at La Tour's; "but we are obliged to borrow your teams; hope it won't fatigue you much to make the rest of the journey on foot. Good night." And before the astounded fugitives could comprehend the situation two of the horsemen who had intercepted them jumped into the wagons and drove off at a rapid rate in the direction in which they had come, followed by the others. The little party, left standing in a pelting storm in the middle of a dark November night, had no alternative but to retrace their steps. The children were small—each of the women had a babe only a few months old---and they would perish before many hours unless they could reach shelter.

There was no house nearer than their own, and had there been, no door would open to apostates; so with heavy hearts they turned their faces homeward, and a little after daylight reached the place they had left with such different feelings the evening before.

They found no traces of their teams or wagons. These were the legitimate prey of their captors, some of whom found much amusement afterward in calling upon their victims, clad in the coats which formed part of the spoils taken with the wagons.

Was Philip La Tour a willing participator in this outrage?

This question might be answered in two ways. When he was told that his help was required to keep a couple of men, who had grown weak in the faith, from leaving the

Territory, he consented readily, for he was still fanatical enough to believe that there was no salvation for one who apostatized and forsook Zion.

At starting he knew nothing of the plans of the captain, and when he found that the women and children were to be left on the road, exposed to the storm, he remonstrated earnestly, but with no effect except to call out a sharp reproof for daring to oppose a measure that had been " counseled."

He made still stronger opposition to the robbery that was included in their arrangements, but was told that after approving the undertaking as a whole it did not become him to object to details.

When he reached home he found his wife ill from anxiety. She had never had any concealments from him before, and the effort she made to hide her suspicions and her fears was too much for her strength. It was useless, also ; for in spite of herself she betrayed so much of what she felt that her husband easily guessed the whole, and finding that her fears pictured something much darker than the affair in which he had been engaged, he thought it best to tell her the truth.

*   *   *   *   *   *   *

Mormonism blights and poisons whatever it touches, and no one who receives it in its entirety can retain either purity or integrity.

Philip La Tour had theoretically accepted Mormonism as a whole, but practically he still rejected its leading tenets. Polygamy, robbery, and murder were crimes so foreign to his nature that not even the blindness of fanaticism could hide their repellant features. It is true that he listened without comment while the leaders of the people explained that polygamy was God's plan for peopling the earth with a race uncontaminated by the vices of the Gentiles. He was also silent when, by way of justifying their own deeds of violence, they quoted Old Testament examples of the slaughter of the wicked by the armies of the Lord, and the spoiling of the Gentiles by his chosen people ; but in his heart he was deeply thankful that *he* was not called to engage in such a work, and he never visited a polygamous family without contrasting the discord and misery he witnessed with the happiness that he found in his own home.

.As for Jessie, the little faith she had in Mormonism received its death-blow on the day she went through the Endowment House, but for her husband's sake more than for her own she kept silent. As long as her home was not invaded by polygamy, and her husband's hands were unstained by blood, she would endure all things, and some day it might be his eyes would be opened too. If she had been older and wiser she might have looked forward less hopefully to the future ; but she had been married when little more than a child to the man whose image filled her girlish heart, and she was still so young, so blindly devoted to·him, and so sure of his love and loyalty, that the possibility of his becoming in all things like those around him never occurred to her.

CHAPTER XV.

THE TEST OF LOYALTY.

THE winter of '62–'63 was by no means a quiet one in the Mormon capital. The United States military post established the previous autumn on the heights above the city was regarded as a standing menace from a hated foreign power. The new Governor sent in the place of the one driven out of the Territory was a man not to be trifled with, and the Federal judges appointed at the same time actually had the temerity to talk of enforcing the laws of the United States in the dominions of the Prophet. It seemed that the open war between the Saints and the Government which had been inaugurated east of the Mississippi was about to be renewed, but now as in the past Brigham Young proved himself more than a match for his adversaries, and by a judicious combination of force and cunning made himself master of the situation. Still, it cannot be denied that the troops stationed in the Territory, and the expressed intention of the Government to hold the Saints amenable to the civil law, gave him much uneasiness and convinced him of the necessity of strengthening his position by every means in his power.

There was also another source of trouble that promised to increase year by year. The presence of the troops gave the disaffected courage ; and as seceders from the Church whose lives were manifestly in danger were allowed to take refuge at Camp Douglas, the number of apostates multiplied without any corresponding increase in the instances of blood atonement.

It had always been the Prophet's policy to outlaw his followers, and thus prevent the possibility of their return to civilized society. This policy he now pursued with more intentness than ever before, and those who were unfitted by nature for deeds of violence were compelled to take plural wives, in the face of a recent act of Congress which was designed especially to reach and punish such offenses in Utah.

Philip La Tour was among the number of those who fell under the Prophet's displeasure on account of his refusal to comply with what the Mormon leaders designated as '' the higher law.''

He had no leanings toward polygamy. He loved his wife devotedly, and his home was the dearest spot on earth to him—dearer now than ever ; for with the earliest flowers of spring a tiny guest had come under their roof—a dark-eyed baby-boy, so like the lost first-born that it seemed almost as though he had returned to them.

For months the Prophet counseled Philip, sometimes affectionately, sometimes sternly, to take another wife, but in vain. At last when, as he said himself, the utmost limit of forbearance had been reached, he summoned his disobedient follower to a private conference.

It was evident to Philip as soon as he faced the leader of the people that the Prophet was very angry—too angry indeed to waste any words—and in the most concise terms possible he was informed that he would be allowed just one week to choose whether he would take another wife or be cut off from the Church and delivered over to the buffetings of Satan.

Philip sat as if stunned. To be cut off from the Church ! For him who had never known any other faith, this was equivalent to a sentence of eternal death. And then he was to be delivered over to the buffetings of Satan. He knew very well what that means. His property and his life would thenceforth be at the mercy of the Danites—and their tender mercies were very cruel.

He was incapable of uttering a single word in reply to the question thrust upon him, and the Prophet continued :

" I know what is keeping you back. It is the fear of what your wife will say or do ; and I want you to tell her from me, that the judgments of God have rested on her these many years because of her rebellion against his will. Every child that has been given her has been taken away again, because she would not hearken to counsel ; and mark my words"—here the Prophet's face grew terrible— " the child that she holds in her arms to-day will lie in the grave a month hence if she does not submit to the law that has been given to this people."

" You will give me a week to decide ?"

Philip hardly knew his own voice as he pronounced the words.

" Yes, just one week, and not a day over. You may go now ; I have said all that I had to say," and with a look on his face as hard and cruel as when, fifteen years before, he gave Madame La Tour the choice of alternatives which brought her to the valley, the Prophet pointed to the door.

Philip groped his way out blindly. The sun was shining, but he saw nothing. When he reached the street he stopped and tried to think. He could not go home—could not face Jessie, who sat even now with her baby in her arms, singing a soft lullaby, while the blue-veined lids drooped over the bright eyes.

The baby ! What a stab went through his heart as he recalled the Prophet's words.

Do you, whose lot has been cast elsewhere, scoff at him because he *believed* what had been said to him ? Remember that since his childhood he had heard nothing except

Mormonism—that all his life, almost, the word of the Prophet had been, to him and all around him, the voice of the Almighty. Remember also how in every age creeds which have been handed down from father to son have dominated the intellect and the will, no matter how false and monstrous they may have been in themselves.

Philip La Tour, in accepting the dictum of the Mormon Prophet as absolute truth, did only what you and I have done in receiving without question the beliefs which our parents bequeathed us. He did not use his reason in the matter, simply because he regarded everything connected with religion as above the domain of reason.

He was called now to pass through an experience more bitter than death ; but if the call was indeed from above he might not disregard it.

Was it true that the judgments of God had rested upon him and his wife because of their disobedience ? Over and over he asked himself this question during the wretched day that followed his interview with the Prophet.

Hour after hour passed. It was almost night, and Jessie would be anxious and disturbed if he stayed away longer, so at last with the courage of desperation he turned his face homeward, resolved to speak out at once and come to a decision before another sun rose.

"Poor Jessie ! Was it for this I won your heart ?" he said to himself as he came in sight of his own house.

His wife was at the door, holding up the baby to welcome him. Both faces were bright with smiles, and one was as unconscious as the other of coming evil.

"How can I ever tell her ?" he thought, and for a moment a wild wish to seize wife and child and fly far from the cruel fate that threatened them all possessed him, but only for a moment.

"I cannot fly from God."

This was his next thought, and the Deity of the Mormon faith—remorseless, cruel, unrelenting—seemed to his excited imagination to stand in the way with a drawn sword, barring all escape and driving him forward to the destiny he dreaded.

"Philip, what is the matter ? You are surely ill."

It was the sweet voice of his wife that fell on his ear, but the words smote him like a blow. How could he bear her tenderness, her wifely solicitude, when he was about to strike her to the heart ?

With a mighty effort he controlled face and voice, and answered her calmly. She must not suspect anything yet. Let her have another happy hour—the last she would ever know on earth.

The minutes of reprieve which the wretched man had allowed himself flew rapidly. Supper was placed on the table, and he went through the form of eating and drinking. Then baby was rocked to sleep and tucked in his downy nest for the night.

His wife came and seated herself on his knee, asking again if he was ill. For a minute he strained her to his heart, covering her face with passionate kisses ; then putting her away from him and pointing to a chair, he said, in a strange, hoarse voice,

"Sit down, Jessie. I have something to tell you."

She obeyed, with an amazed look on her sweet face, and yet as plainly unconscious of the blow that awaited her as a lamb of the uplifted knife.

Twice her husband essayed to speak, but his voice failed him. At last, summoning all his strength, he began :

"Jessie, President Young sent for me to-day to tell me that he had already borne too long with my disobedience to counsel, and that I must now take another wife or be cut off from the Church, and—he has given me one week in which to decide."

Jessie's cheek blanched, and for a moment she could not reply ; but composing herself directly she spoke bravely,

"If we are cut off from the Church they cannot harm us. We can go to Camp Douglas, as others have done, and we will be safe there ; though, of course," glancing around the pleasant room, " we shall lose the house, and I suppose the store too, but we shall be *free*, and we shall have each other and our child."

As she finished speaking her eyes kindled, and the color came back to her face. How sweet liberty would be after all these years of bondage !

Her husband perceived her thought. He saw, too, that she had not even glanced at the alternative. How should he go on ? What could he say to make her share his own dread of bringing down the vengeance of Heaven upon them all by continued disobedience to a divine law ?

"Jessie, you do not understand me," he said desperately. " I am not afraid of them that can only kill the body, but I fear Him who is able to destroy both soul and body in hell."

" Philip, you do not mean—you cannot mean that—" Speech failed, and the unhappy wife, upon whom a possibility which she had never before contemplated dawned at last, could only clasp her hands in mute appeal.

" I mean that I fear we may be fighting against God. President Young says our children have been taken because we have been disobedient, and if we continue to rebel our baby will be laid beside the others before another month."

" And you believe that ?"

" God speaks to us by the voice of his Prophet. I *must* believe. If I doubt one word I must give up all."

"Give up all then. Oh, Philip, this religion is false—as false as it is cruel. It yields nothing but discord, and misery, and wickedness. Look at the families where they say they have obeyed the law of God ! The wife, if she is not changed into a fury, is dying of a broken heart ; the other women pass their lives in the midst of strife and jealousy that kills all the good in them. And then the children ! I had far rather bury my baby to-morrow than have him grow up like them."

"Jessie, wife, hear me. If God commands a thing, we must not question his wisdom. We must look beyond the present for results. He knows that it will cost me more than life to obey him in this thing, and he would not require such a sacrifice of me if no good could come of it."

"Philip !" She rose to her feet and stood before him. "Answer me plainly, and at once. Do you believe that God requires *you* to take another wife ?"

"Jessie, have a little pity on me. That is the question I am trying to decide. I have been trying all day. I dared not come home. I could not face you ; and I feel now as though I were going mad."

The stern look faded from her face, and the fire in her eyes softened. She was again the tender, loyal wife.

"Forgive me, love," she said, laying her hand on his bowed head. · "I did not mean to make the trial harder for you."

It is needless to dwell upon the struggle, which did not end with the night, but lasted throughout the week. The result was what might have been foreseen. Fanaticism triumphed over nature, reason, love—over everything that had hitherto saved their home from profanation, and when the time arrived for making his decision known to the Prophet, Philip said,

"I will obey."

Jessie did what hundreds of wives in Utah have done—submitted to the inevitable—and after the first day said nothing to influence her husband's decision. She had lived too long in the midst of such scenes not to know what the end would be, and she read her death-warrant in Philip's face before a single word was spoken to reveal the choice he had made.

And now comes the strangest phase of those tragedies which have been enacted year after year, ever since Mormonism raised its unclean altars in Utah.

Jessie La Tour did not believe in the divinity of the system which called for the cruel sacrifice she was about to make ; she felt as she had said, that Mormonism was false to the core—a foul superstructure of tyranny and crime, resting upon a foundation of lust and blood ; and yet, *for her husband's sake*, for the sake of the man she had worshiped with a blind devotion since the day he first won her girlish heart, she consented to the last, the most barbarous rite enjoined by *his* religion (not hers), and went with him to the Endowment House to place in his hand the hand of the bride chosen for him by the Prophet.

Through the days of martyrdom which she endured before the fatal time arrived, she shed no tear, made no moan.

Only her white face showed what she suffered, even when the new bride's relatives came to the house to talk the matter over with her husband, and the Prophet visited them to give the counsel he thought they needed.

The same power of endurance which had kept her alive during that fearful winter march, while strong men dropped dead beside her, enabled her to bury her anguish out of sight and sit calmly beside the grave of her dead hopes.

But when the day of sacrifice came, and she walked beside her husband to the Endowment House, she felt that she must speak once, or die, and turning her pallid face toward him, her wild eyes glowing like coals of fire, she said,

"Philip, I am going to lie to you and lie to God : I am going to perjure myself before Heaven ; for I must say that I *consent* to this marriage, when I had rather die a thousand deaths than have it take place."

"Jessie, God knows I would lay down my life to spare you this," was the only reply the wretched husband could make, and pity for him kept her silent.

She knew something of the terrible battle which he had fought out alone. She saw its marks in his face, which had grown old and haggard ; in the silver threads which had begun to mingle with his dark locks.

The bitterness which filled her soul was not against him, but against the man who had commanded this sacrifice, against the religion which had compelled it.

She had never crossed the threshold of the Endowment House since the day when her own marriage took place ; but when they entered the sealing-room, all that she witnessed there seven years before came back, fresh as the events of yesterday. She saw again the wife with the corpse-like face kneeling beside her husband, saw her place the young bride's hand in his ; and her senses reeled as the bride of to-day, a slender, dark-eyed girl of sixteen, took her place at the same altar.

It was surely a hideous dream, from which she would awake by and by.

Nothing was real, not even the face and voice of the tyrant who had brought this curse upon them, and who now stood before her asking,

"Are you willing to give this woman to your husband ?"

No sound came from her white lips in reply. She did

not even incline her head ; and when the command was given to place the bride's hand in that of her husband, she made no sign that she heard it. There was a moment's pause, and then the Prophet himself joined the hands of the pair before him, frowning darkly as he did so, and the ceremony proceeded.

There were a few witnesses present, and among them Philip's sister Blanche. When the party left the Endowment House Philip accompanied the bride to her father's house.

Jessie turned from the door alone. She was conscious of nothing but a dumb longing to fly to some covert where she might hide her misery forever from mortal eyes.

The unnatural strength which had sustained her through the day was fast failing, and before she had gone a dozen steps she staggered, and would have fallen but for Blanche, who put a supporting arm around her, and pressed her hand tenderly, in token of the pity that she dared not express in words.

The fate which was her sister's to-day might overtake her to-morrow. Blanche believed Mormonism to be true, because she had never heard of any other religion, but her woman's nature rebelled against polygamy, and her tender heart bled for Jessie, whose silent anguish was more terrible to witness than the most violent demonstrations of suffering. She longed to say something to comfort her, and yet she felt instinctively that for sorrow such as hers there was no balm and no healing.

When they reached the door of the house that now, alas ! was no longer *home*, Jessie seemed to wake slowly as from a nightmare.

"You are very good," she said, speaking for the first time ; "but now I want to be alone."

"I know it," and the sympathizing eyes filled with tears ;

"but I may come to-morrow, may I not? and to-night—to-night I will pray for you."

"Don't pray to the God they worship *there*," and Jessie pointed with a trembling hand toward the building they had left.

Blanche could not reply. She could only kiss the white face, while her own cheeks were wet with tears, and turn away.

Jessie, left alone, stood for a moment irresolute and bewildered. Why had she come here? This was Philip's house, and Philip was the husband of that dark-eyed girl. Would he bring his bride here to-morrow? And if he did, where should *she* go? She looked away toward the distant mountains.

"Oh that I had wings like a dove! Then would I fly away and be at rest."

Where had she heard such words? She put her hand to her forehead and tried to think. It was in her home, the dear old English home, whose vine-covered porch she could see even now. Her father used to read those words. Did he know now how his child longed to fly far, far away from this valley of death?

A sound broke her trance. It was her child's cry, and maternal love, stronger than death, drew her toward the cradle in which she had left her sleeping baby. He was awake now, and reaching out his tiny hands for her. She lifted him in her arms, and pressed his little head against her bosom. She had something left yet to live for, and somewhere in the world there might be a place of refuge for her and her baby; or if not in the world, then out of it. Maybe God—the God her mother used to pray to—would pity them and take them both to himself.

CHAPTER XVI.

PLURAL BLESSEDNESS.

"Before the glass, as usual. I do believe, Ruth, that you are vainer than ever."

The person addressed pirouetted across the room, shook her ringlets, smoothed out her draperies, and settled herself gracefully in a chair before replying.

"Don't be cross, Myra, there's a dear. I *have to* take a little pains with my looks when people are dropping in almost every hour in the day ' to see the bride.' "

"The bride! Oh, yes! I beg your pardon ; I had almost forgotten that your honeymoon is not over. And now, seeing that we are alone, tell me : *is it* a honeymoon altogether ?"

"It would be, only for one thing. Philip is just as sweet as he can be, but then he is so awfully religious. You know they pretend that it is a man's religious duty to treat all his wives just alike, and Philip actually believes that ! The first week after we were married he stayed here, of course ; but the second week he told me it was his duty to go home—just.think of it—*home*—and every blessed day of that week he stayed with his first wife. Last week he was here again, and now he is away. That's something that I didn't bargain for, and I don't mean to stand it."

"I confess I don't quite see how you are going to help yourself."

"Just wait a little, and you *will* see. How is it in other families ? Don't the last wife get all the petting and all the attention ? How is it in President Young's family ?

When Emmeline was the favorite, you know he stayed with her right along ; and now since he has taken Amelia, how many times do suppose he has spoken to any of his other wives ?"

" Not very often, perhaps ; but with you the question is, not what other men do, but what course your own husband is going to take."

" Oh, I'll manage him, never you fear. By the way, how ugly his first wife is growing. She has changed so within a month that I declare when I met her on the street yesterday I hardly knew her ; and I suppose now she will go and tell Philip that I wouldn't speak to her—the spiteful thing !"

" You ought not to talk in that way, Ruth. The poor woman sees trouble enough, I have no doubt."

" Well, I can't help it, and I'm sure it isn't my fault. If she didn't want Philip to marry me, why did she give her consent ? People ought to know their own minds, and not agree to a thing one day and make a fuss about it the next. And if she is growing old and ugly, I am not to blame for that, and Philip is not to blame either for wanting a wife that doesn't look like a grandmother."

" Ruth, how old are you ?"

" I shall be sixteen next birthday."

" My poor child ! I pity you."

" Now, Myra, that is just like you—always trying to spoil my good times. I don't know, I'm sure, why I should be pitied, unless it is because Philip insists on taking rooms right here at father's, instead of giving me a house of my own ; but I'll have different arrangements in six months, as you'll see. If I don't manage to be the mistress of his new house by that time, my name is not Ruth."

" Indeed ! And what will you do with Jessie ?"

" Oh, she can have the old house. It's comfortable

enough, and she don't care anything about style. She looks like a dowdy lately. Why, the dress she had on yesterday was a perfect fright."

"Perhaps she has too much on her mind just now to care about dress."

"If she knows anything at all, she ought to know that dress goes a great ways when you want to please a man. Last week when Philip came over here, he looked as if he'd just been to a funeral—I dare say Jessie had been giving him some awful lectures—but I had studied what to do, and I was ready to meet him. I had the new silk he gave me made up lovely, and I wore tea-rose ribbons —just my color, everybody says—and Jane Taylor came over and dressed my hair. She said I looked like a picture, and I believe Philip thought so too, for he brightened up wonderfully after I came down stairs."

"Well, Ruth, I am sure I want you to take all the comfort you can ; though, if I were you, I am afraid I should look forward sometimes to the day when I would be obliged to step aside and give place to some one else ; and you know you have just said it is the *last* wife who gets all the attention."

"Now, Myra, you are really too bad. I don't think there is another person in the world who would say such things to me—and in my honeymoon, too."

Here an embroidered handkerchief was produced, and the bride buried her pretty face in its folds.

"Don't cry, Ruth. I did not mean to make you feel bad."

The face came up again from its hiding-place.

"I *won't* cry and spoil my eyes, for I am going down to the store, and I want Philip to think I look lovely. I know he'll *think* it, though he won't say it—the provoking man. How is my dress ? And do you suppose my hair would look better if I should loop these curls back—so ? Did you ever hear of Philip's oldest sister ? They say she was so lovely that she couldn't walk the street without people stopping to look at her. Well, Aunt Margaret, who used to know her, says I have her style of beauty, and she says, too, it's my own fault if I don't make Philip worship me. She says he's worth a great deal of money now, and making more every year, and if I manage right I can have such a house and furniture and such dresses as I've never dreamed of."

"If those things will make you happy, I hope you may get them. For my part, if I ever marry, I want a husband who will not belong to any one but me, and then I think I could be contented with a crust of bread."

"It's no wonder, Myra, that you are an old maid, with such notions. How are you going to get a husband who will not belong to any one else ? If you are the first wife, you will never know what day your husband will bring home a second. Aunt Margaret said to me,

"'Whatever you do, don't think of being any man's first wife, for you will live a life of dread before he takes his second, and a life of misery afterward.' Aunt Margaret has got sense. She's a fourth wife. She is petted, and has her own way in everything, and she knows her husband won't take another ; but her sister, who is a first wife, is put off on a sage-brush ranch, and don't see her husband once a year."

Do any of our readers object to the foregoing style of conversation ? If so, we beg leave to remind them that it only exhibits the practical, every-day application of a religious principle which our Government has regarded as so sacred that for many years it has been an effectual shield from the penalties of a law which is openly and persistently violated by a whole people.

Ruth, Philip La Tour's new bride, was a fair specimen of the girls brought up in Utah—no better and no worse than the majority of those around her. She believed polygamy to be right because she had been so taught from her cradle, and she regarded her own marriage as legal and binding because no opinion to the contrary had ever been uttered in her hearing. If any one had intimated that she had wronged and outraged Philip's wife by assuming the relation to him which she now held, she would have lifted up her pretty hands in horror, and resented the imputation with hot words and angry tears.

It is true that she was shallow, vain, and selfish; but then girls of that description may be found outside of Utah, and Mormonism cannot be justly charged with developing traits that are quite as common among the adherents of other systems.

She really thought it too bad that she, who was so much younger than Jessie, and in her own estimation very much prettier also, should have no more of her husband's society than the first wife; and it was an unheard-of thing that a bride with so many attractions should live in a couple of plainly furnished rooms, while the woman whom she regarded only in the light of an obstacle to her complete triumph had a handsome house all to herself.

She was fully resolved not to submit to such an arrangement, and in the end she had her way, for though she did not succeed in turning Jessie out of doors, she tormented Philip until, glad to purchase peace at any price, he bought a pretty cottage for her, and fitted it up with the best that money could buy.

In other things, however, she found that her influence over the man she called husband was very slight. He still continued to spend every alternate week with his first wife, and when Ruth ventured to speak disrespectfully of

her he reproved her so sharply that even she was convinced it would not be safe to repeat the experiment.

After six months of married life, the opinions so confidently expressed in her honeymoon were greatly modified.

" Philip cares no more for me than he would for a kit-
ten," she declared petulantly. " If I talk to him half an
hour without stopping to take breath, he never hears one
word. Sometimes he doesn't answer me at all, and sometimes he asks, ' What did you say ?' in a way that would
provoke an angel. I've half a mind to ask President
Young for a divorce."

" Why don't you ?" inquired her friend Myra, to whom
these complaints were addressed.

" Well, you see, with all his faults, Philip isn't a bit
mean about money. I don't know any other man who
would be likely to buy me such a house as this ; and as for
dresses, you know yourself that half the girls in the city
are ready to die with envy when they see mine. Then besides—but I forgot : I haven't showed you his last present."

Ruth tripped into the next room, and came out with an
inlaid box in her hands.

" He gave me this on my birthday," she said, opening
it and displaying a gold watch and chain and a pair of
bracelets of elegant workmanship.

" Did you ever see anything so perfectly lovely in your
life ? I showed them to Milly Allen yesterday, and she
looked ready to cry. She was married the same week I
was, and she is wearing her old things yet, and has to live
in the house with two of the other wives, and they order
her around as if she was a little girl ; but then, Milly
never did have any spirit. She couldn't speak for herself,
no matter how she was treated."

" Brother Allen treats her well enough himself, does he
not ?"

"That depends on what you call good treatment. He isn't cross to her, but he tells her he can't afford another house, and it's no use talking about it. You see, the trouble is, he was sealed to Milly and Sarah Spencer on the same day, and Sarah happens to be the favorite. *She's* got a place of her own, and new things, and he spends half his time with her, which is about all that could be expected of a man with six wives."

"I am sorry for Milly," Myra said. "She used to be a good girl when I knew her, and she deserves a good husband."

"Well, I'm sorry for her too, of course; but she ought to have had more sense. When a man marries two girls on the same day, one of them is going to be neglected—anybody knows that. I told Milly how it would be, but she didn't believe me."

"After all, Ruth, I think you ought to be pretty well satisfied. You have a fine house, fine furniture, and fine clothes—things you have always wanted—and your husband spends half his time with you. What more can you ask?"

"I want him to spend more than half his time with me, and to act as if he cared for me;" and then, to her friend's surprise, Ruth buried her face in her hands and began to sob—not angrily, but in a wretched, heart-broken way, that brought Myra to her side at once, and caused her to put her arms around her and ask tenderly,

"What is it, dear?"

Ruth lifted her head and dashed away her tears.

"I'm a fool, I know, to feel so, but I can't help it," she said.

"Come into my bedroom, Myra. I haven't told a single soul—not even mother—but I'll tell you."

Myra followed her wonderingly into the next room, and

Ruth closed the door and locked it. Then opening a drawer she took out a pile of tiny garments and spread them on the bed.

"Look there!" she said. "You know what that means. I am only sixteen—sixteen last week—and I shall be a mother in three months. Philip don't care for me, and he won't care either for the poor little baby, that isn't to blame for anything, if I am," and again Ruth sobbed bitterly.

Myra tried to comfort her, but she had seen too much of polygamy in her own father's house, where four wives claimed a love that could only be given to one, to be able to console her with the hope that she might yet win her husband's heart.

"He loves that baby at home—Jessie's baby," Ruth said, as she dried her tears. "He had it down to the store the other day, and he looked as if he worshiped it. I heard him say, too, 'Papa's only comfort.' Just think of that! I tell you, it is all Jessie's fault. If she was out of the way I believe I could make him care for me, but as long as she lives he will love her best ; and I hate her—I hate her."

"Hush, Ruth ! You frighten me. It is wicked to feel so."

"I don't care if it is. I think it is a shame for a man to take a girl as young as I was and make her his wife, when he knows she will be miserable. What did he marry me for if he didn't care for me ?"

"I suppose he thought, as they all say they think, that it was a religious duty to take another wife."

"Bah ! I know better. I've seen too much at home to believe that, and I never cared anything about religion. I just wanted to have nice things and enjoy myself, and I've never hurt anybody, and never done anything to deserve such trouble as I have now."

It was vain to attempt to convince Ruth that she was not the most ill-used of wives.

A spoiled child, petted and indulged from infancy by a mother who had been forced to surrender her husband to others, and who had nothing left to live for except this one daughter, she had grown up with the idea that *her* interests, *her* comfort, and *her* happiness should be considered first, last, in the midst, and always.

To say that she *loved* Philip would be overstating the fact ; but she liked him, wanted him to admire her and pet her, wanted to be first in his regards ; and now, when filled with a vague dread of the trial that she must pass through, really longed for some token of sympathy and tenderness.

Philip, on his part, regarded her as a pretty, teasing child, and as the passing months made him better acquainted with her faults, he found the weeks that he was forced to spend in her society more and more irksome. It is due to him to say, however, that he did his best to conceal this feeling. He was always patient and gentle with her, gratified her whims, bought everything for her that her fancy coveted, and was considered by all her friends a model husband.

Yet to Ruth, who in spite of her shallow nature had a woman's insight, all this outward kindness was a very thin mask, which failed to hide his real feelings. She knew that he loved Jessie, and would never love her.

Jessie would always be first, and Jessie's child would be dear to the father, who would look upon *her* child with as little tenderness as he felt for the mother.

When these unwelcome truths were forced upon her, she suffered as much as she was capable of suffering—not enough, however, to altogether destroy her pleasure in the new dresses and trinkets with which Philip sought to buy immunity from the hard task of simulating love. . . .

Meanwhile, in the home that only a few months ago was so peaceful and happy, an evil spirit sat enthroned. The wife, after a season of apathetic despair, woke to a full sense not only of her misery, but of her wrongs ; and bitter jealousy for the girl who stood between her and her husband, and hatred of the tyrant who had placed her there, seemed to change her whole nature.

She would not feel so—she might get over it all in time, and bury the memory of the happy past—so she told herself—if every alternate week did not bring Philip back to the house ; if she did not see his face and hear his voice day after day, knowing all the time that the tenderness which he tried to show toward her would be lavished on another woman next week ; that the kisses which her outraged love refused would be given to that dark-eyed girl, whom she hated with a vindictiveness that frightened her when she stopped to reason about her feelings.

" I don't wonder they say that a wife who rebels against polygamy is possessed by devils. I feel as though I had a legion of them in my heart."

This was Jessie's confession to Helen Woodford, who was her friend as she had been the friend of Philip's mother years ago.

Mrs. Woodford was now fifty, but a stranger would have thought her much older. Her once queenly form was bent and wasted, her face deeply graven with lines of suffering, and her hair white as snow.

In reply to Jessie she said, with a strange far-away look in her eyes,

" I felt just as you do once, long ago—it seems ages now—but I got over it."

" And how ?"

" By outliving my love for my husband. As long as I loved him I suffered—suffered the torments of hell. You know the house in which he used to keep two of his women—I cannot so far forget what is due to myself as to call them wives. At night, when he was staying there, I used to walk the floor of the room until it seemed that I must go mad unless I could escape from the place—from everything. Then I would rush out into the street and go to that house. I would walk round and round it, feeling as though I could tear the walls down with my bare hands, growing every minute more like one possessed with devils, until my boy, missing me, would come in search of me and lead me home."*

"I know how you felt." Jessie's eyes gleamed, and she set her teeth, and breathed hard. "I am glad Philip did not bring that girl into my house, because—because I should have killed her."

"Ten years from now you will look back and wonder that you ever could have suffered as you do to-day from such a cause. I wonder at myself—wonder that I should have prized as I did the love that was not strong enough to shield me from wrong and outrage—the love that withered in a moment before the word of the man they call the Prophet of the Lord.

"To-day my husband is nothing to me. He comes home sometimes—I believe I have seen him twice during the past year—but his coming or going affects me no more than it does the walls of the house."

"*I* shall never feel so—never. I love Philip; I shall love him till I die. I can't help it; I try to shun him—I do speak harshly to him and turn away from him—and all the while I am longing to throw myself into his arms and sob out my anguish upon his breast, as I used to do in every other trouble."

* See Appendix, Note N, page 350.

"Poor child." The older woman laid her hand tenderly on the bowed head. "Is it so bad as that? I loved my husband too, for years after he inflicted an irreparable wrong upon me, but from the hour that I discovered the truth I was no longer his wife. I would not permit so much as the clasp of his hand—the hand he had given to others. But in one sense your wrongs were less than mine. Your husband did not add deceit to his broken marriage vows, while mine lied to me year after year—lived in adultery with the women his Prophet had given to him, while I believed myself a loved and honored wife. I could forgive anything sooner than that."

"I cannot blame Philip, even when I try to, for I know how he suffered. I know what agony he endured before his decision was made, and now I know that he is unspeakably wretched. That girl"—Jessie's face darkened as she pronounced the words—"torments and humiliates him with her silliness, her petty tyrannies, and her odious temper, until he would be glad to fly anywhere to escape from his life with her; and yet, according to his ideas, she is a *wife*, and he is bound to treat her as—as he used to treat me. Then when his week with her is ended he comes home and finds me cold, or sullen, or furious, just as the evil spirit within me moves me to be. If my father could come back from the dead he would not know his child. I do not know myself."

CHAPTER XVII.

THE DEAD TELL TALES.

WITH the fall emigration of 1863 one of Jessie La Tour's old schoolmates came to the valley with her husband, from England.

She was a fragile-looking woman, often ill, and always homesick for her own country and the friends she had left. Like many others, she was sadly disappointed when she reached the "Zion" whose glories had been so eloquently portrayed by the missionary who induced her and her husband to emigrate. The existence of polygamy in the valley was also a source of constant terror to her, and she importuned her husband to seek protection from the troops and leave the Territory ; but he had expended most of the money they brought with them in the purchase of a house and lot, and he was not willing to sacrifice his property for the sake of getting away.

Jessie went often to see this old friend, Mrs. Stanwix, and did her best to put aside her own troubles for the time and devote herself to the task of cheering and encouraging her.

In the spring her own affairs kept her at home more, and she had not seen her friend for several weeks when a message came one evening to say that Mrs. Stanwix was very ill and wished her to stay with her during the night.

She went at once, and on reaching the room in which the invalid lay, she could not repress an exclamation of astonishment and distress. The woman looked like one on the brink of death. Her face, always pale, was ghastly, her eyes were deeply sunken, and her thin hands were cold and clammy.

"Why did you not send for me before?" Jessie said. "If I had known how ill you were, I would have come any day or hour."

"My husband has been with me," was the answer, "but to-night he was obliged to go away."

Then raising her voice with difficulty, she said to the boy who had brought the message,

"You can go home now, Edward. This lady will stay with me until morning."

The boy availed himself of the permission at once, and as soon as the sound of his retreating footsteps died away, Mrs. Stanwix said, in a hurried whisper,

"Go down stairs, lock the outside doors, fasten all the windows, and don't leave a light anywhere."

Jessie obeyed, with a little doubt of her friend's sanity, and returned to the room as quickly as possible.

"Take that chair," the sick woman said, pointing to the one beside her pillow.

When her request was complied with, she clasped her friend's hand in both her own.

"Thank God that I see you once more—and alone. I thought that was never to be," she said.

"I would have come at any time," Jessie replied, as before.

"You do not understand me," she said. "They were afraid to have me talk with anybody. My husband has stayed with me night and day since I have been sick, and this morning, when he had to go away, he left me in Katrina's care. She hardly understands a dozen English words, he knew I could not talk to *her;* but to-night she was taken sick herself, so I sent the boy after you, and told her she might go home."

"I must not let you talk too much either," Jessie said. "You are excited now. You will make yourself worse."

"No, it relieves me to speak. Wait till you know what has brought me down to this bed, and you will not wonder that silence is killing me. Give me a little of that cordial yonder, and let me rest a few minutes. Then I will tell you."

She drank the cordial and lay back among her pillows, silent and exhausted. Jessie hoped she might sleep, but her large dark eyes remained wide open, and with the same wistful, terrified expression in them that at first made her friend fear her reason was going.

After half an hour's silence she turned her face toward Jessie and asked suddenly,

"Do you know that this place they call Zion is a den of murderers?"

The question was so unexpected and startling that for a moment she was unable to speak. She might have answered truthfully in the affirmative, but not wishing to do so, she only said,

"What makes you think that?"

"I don't *think* it," was the reply; "I *know* it, and this very house has been the scene of a crime so dreadful that I cannot put what I have learned of it into words."

She stopped again, panting and breathless, but recovering herself after a few minutes she went on:

"You know it was late in the fall when we bought this place. It was sold to us by the bishop of the ward, who held the property, but the house had been empty a good while, and everything in-doors and out was going to decay.

"We put off making repairs until spring. Then with the first fine weather we set about painting the house and putting the grounds in order. In one of the rooms down-stairs there were dark stains on the floor. I could not wash them out, so I had them painted over, little thinking what they were.

" The next week my husband went to work in the orchard. Two rows of trees down the middle were dead or dying, and he said he would take them all out and plant others.

" I liked to be out in the orchard with him while he worked.   One day I stood beside him, and—I cannot tell it, and yet I must—he was digging a deep pit for a large tree he meant to set out, when his spade struck some loose rocks.   He rolled them away, and oh, the horror of the sight !   It will haunt me till I die.   There were the remains of seven dead bodies which had been thrown in together, dressed in the clothes they wore in life : so we judged from the shreds that still clung to them.   They seemed to have been those of a man, a woman, and some children.

" I did not stop to see more, but fled to the house.   My husband followed me in a few minutes.   He said he did not try to examine the bodies—they were in such a state he could not—but they were lying on their faces, and he could see that even the little children had their hands tied behind them ; and of the children there were five.

" ' I must lose no time,' he added.   ' This must be reported at police headquarters before night.   I shall fill up the pit as well as I can and go at once.'

" I begged him not to leave me, but he said it would not do to wait.   Then, as if struck by a sudden thought, he told me to go to bed and stay there.

" ' It may not be wise to let any one know that you were with me,' he said.   ' I will report that you are sick and unable to leave your room.'

" I did as he bade me, and in truth I was sick : hardly able to stand.

" He did not come in again before going down town ;

but when he got back from the City Hall he was as white as a sheet.

"'I made my report,' he said, 'and what do you think the answer was? Why, just this: "Never speak of what you have seen, if you value your own life; and whatever you may hear about your premises to-night, do not look out: and ask no questions." I tell you, Mary,' he continued, 'this accursed discovery will end in your murder and mine unless we are dumb as death itself, and I warn you never to speak of it even to me. From this hour we will bury all memory of it.'

"It was easy to say that, but impossible to do it, as he knew well enough. That night, when I heard sounds in the orchard, I crept from the bed and looked out of the window.

"A wagon stood close beside *that pit*, and half a dozen men were putting *something* into a box that stood on the ground. In a few minutes my husband woke and called me in a terrified whisper. I went back to bed, and he said,

"'For Heaven's sake, Mary, what makes you do so? You are risking both our lives. I tell you we shall be murdered if the first breath of suspicion gets abroad.'

"I said nothing; indeed in a few minutes I was incapable of saying anything, for the excitement and terror brought on one of those attacks of hemorrhage which I had in the fall. I have not left my bed since, and he has watched me night and day, as I told you, in mortal fear that I will reveal something, while I have lain here feeling as though I had abetted that horrible murder by helping to cover it up." *

Jessie was silent. What could she say? It would not

* See Appendix, Note O, page 350.

lessen the horror of the deed, whose shadow seemed to fill the house where they were, to say that it was done by authority—that it was only an example of the swift and sure punishment which was visited upon covenant-breakers— for with no further knowledge of the facts than she could glean from the recital to which she had listened, she was certain that the victims of the tragedy enacted under this roof had fallen under the curse invoked in the Endowment House upon those who fail to keep their oaths.

The father and mother had revealed the iniquitous mysteries which they had sworn to keep secret, and their children had perished with them, because the bloody code of Mormon vengeance declares that the sin of the parents shall be visited upon the children unto the third and fourth generation. Or perhaps the children had been killed, like those at Mountain Meadows, lest they should some day bear testimony against the murderers of their parents.

" Why do you not speak ?" Mrs. Stanwix said at length. " Do you too think that I should keep silent ?"

" It was right to speak to me," was the reply, " if you felt that it would relieve you to do so ; but do not breathe a word to any one else. Your husband spoke truly when he said there was no safety except in silence, and to reveal what you know could be of no possible benefit. Crimes committed in obedience to ' counsel ' are never inquired into and never punished."

" I am glad that it is possible to die—glad that my own death is so near. This valley, that I foolishly believed was like heaven, would be hell instead if there were no way out, and I see none except through the grave."

" You speak truly," Jessie was about to exclaim, but she checked herself.

" For many years there *was* no other way out," she said after a little silence, " but now it is sometimes possible to escape with one's life. Why do you not go to the fort and claim protection?"

"For two reasons. All we have, almost, is in this place, which we dared not make any attempt to sell ; and now it would cost me my life to be moved. Not that I am troubled about that myself ; I have only a few weeks to live at the longest : but my husband believes I will recover, and he is trying his best, poor fellow, to save me."

"I am not taking the good care of you that he has a right to expect," her friend said ; "and for the remainder of the night I am your nurse only, and you must not talk to me."

The sick woman acquiesced in this arrangement ; indeed she was now too much exhausted to speak, and after another hour Jessie had the satisfaction of seeing her sink into a quiet slumber.

Morning brought the husband, who looked anxious and disturbed when he found his wife in other hands than those of the servant with whom he had left her ; but the explanation Jessie gave, together with her quiet manner, and the assurance that his wife had slept well during the night, appeared to disarm his suspicions. When she took her leave, she expressed her willingness to come again at any time and Mr. Stanwix answered that he would send for her should there be a change for the worse.

"I hope he is satisfied that I have heard nothing," she said to herself as she walked away.

Two days later she was again summoned in haste to her friend's bedside, but when she arrived life had fled. Another attack of hemorrhage had silenced the only witness who would have had the courage to reveal the crimes committed under that roof.

"*She* has made good her escape," was Jessie's first thought as she looked at the now peaceful face. "Is there no way open for me ?"

Truly life had become a heavy burden to her—heavier now than ever ; for Ruth lay on her sick-bed, with a tiny, wailing babe beside her, and Philip, from a sense of duty which his wife in her jealous misery mistook for love transferred from her to her rival, spent all his time with her.

It was now more than a month since he had been home, except for an hour on Sunday. At first Jessie tried bravely to school herself into a willingness to have him stay with Ruth until her health was restored ; but as the weeks passed and his whole interest seemed to center in her sick-room, to the neglect of his home, of her, and of the bonny boy who could say " Papa" so sweetly, when, alas ! there was no father there to listen to his call, a flood of bitter feeling swept away her resolves.

" You have no father," she would say to the wondering child, as he climbed into her lap and tried to wipe away her tears. " We have lost him—you and I."

Then the little fellow, understanding only the one word " father," would prattle over again the name he was so proud of being able to speak, sure in his baby heart that he was comforting mamma.

It was hard, very hard, to be thus neglected by the husband who had shared her every thought for so many years ; hard that this girl should win from her the love which was hers by right, if the unreserved surrender of her own heart, if wifely loyalty and devotion and the self-abnegation which had not refused even the last and most cruel sacrifice which could be demanded of a woman, gave her any rights.

Surely her husband must have transferred his love to Ruth, when he could not tear himself from her side for a single day ; and then the jealous pain at her heart grew so strong that she did not wonder at Helen Woodford, " walking round and round the house where her husband stayed, feeling as though she could tear the walls down with her bare hands."

She did not know all that Philip could have told her of Ruth's exacting nature, or of the tears and hysterics called forth by the slightest intimation of a wish to go home for a day—and this too at a time when doctors and nurses assured him that the least agitation might cost her her life.

Jessie had done at first all that she considered her husband had any right to ask—and more. She had gone to see Ruth, had taken the tiny baby in her arms—Philip's child, but not hers — and had forced herself to speak kindly to the pale young mother. In this she had taxed her powers of endurance to the utmost, and when, on the following Sunday, Philip said to her,

" If you and Ruth could be reconciled to each other, our family might yet be a happy one," the restraint she had put upon herself gave way wholly, and she answered him with words more bitter than she had ever spoken to him :

" Reconciled to the woman with whom you are living in adultery—never !"

Her face was white as death when she spoke, and her eyes flashed dangerous lightnings. She was in a mood in which her husband had never yet seen her, and in spite of himself he quailed before her look.

Living in adultery ! Never until now had Jessie put her thoughts of him into plain words ; and notwithstanding the sincerity of his belief in the system that enjoined polygamy, a feeling of guilt oppressed him.

Besides, though he would not acknowledge the fact even to himself, an actual experience of the effects of plural marriage had brought up the question,

" How can anything which God ordains bear such evil fruit ?"

This question he tried to put aside as a temptation of

Satan ; but it recurred again and again with every instance of domestic discord, every exhibition of jealousy and heart-burning which he was forced to witness.

Jessie was wrought up now to a pitch of excitement that defied control, and the feelings which, for his sake, she had so long repressed, found utterance in words that burned themselves into his brain.

" Look at our home," she cried ; " the home that was heaven once, and tell me what it is now. It is hell, and you know it ; and day after day, while you are spending your smiles and your substance on your mistress, I sit here alone enduring torments worse than those of a lost soul ; and this is what *your religion* has brought me to—*your* religion, but not *mine*. I thank God that I can remember a religion which made a man faithful to his marriage vows, which did not set up adultery and murder as sacred duties. It is this memory, and only this, which has kept me from taking my baby in my arms and finding rest at the bottom of the river."

" Jessie ! Jessie !" Philip exclaimed, as soon as he could stem the torrent of her indignant words, " if you felt in this way, why did you not say so at the first ?"

" Why ? Because your mind was made up, and nothing would turn you from your purpose. Did I not humble myself to plead with you—I will not say as I would have pleaded for life, because it would have been easy to give up my life if you had asked it ; but as a woman pleads for the last, the most precious thing left her in earth or heaven—and what then ? Why, you put my prayers aside, you trampled on my heart, and all because your Prophet bade you do so. If I had thrown myself into the river your wedding would have gone on all the same, for that would have been what your religion enjoins. Only yester-day this woman right at our door, who has been driven nearly mad by the *religion* that has made her husband bring a girl right in before her face to share his bed and claim his love, went to Eliza Snow for counsel, and what did she get ?   Why this :

" ' Pray for resignation.'

" ' I do pray,' said the poor creature, ' but I cannot be resigned ; and if that girl stays in the house I shall die.'

" ' Die then,' was the answer.   ' There are hundreds of women up in the burying-ground who have gone there because they could not be resigned to the order of God.'

" And that is the kind of God you believe in,—you, who used to tell me you would shield me from suffering with your own life !' '

" Spare me, Jessie," he said appealingly, " for I too have suffered.   How much do you suppose my life is worth to me—the life I am living now ?   And yet, neither life nor that which is dearer than life may be withheld when God calls for the sacrifice."

But even while he spoke, the question that he had striven for months to silence—the doubt whether the command which he had obeyed at so great a cost was indeed divine —haunted him and checked his utterance.

What if, after all, this religion in which he believed should prove to be false !   What if he had sacrificed home, love, wife, all that a man holds dear, for naught !

The conflict between reason and superstition—the conflict waged in all ages and under so many forms of belief —had begun.   How would it end ?

CHAPTER XVIII.

THE LION AND THE FOX.

THE inevitable changes which time brings are not confined to any particular locality or people, and as the rapid increase of population in the United States augmented the tide of emigration to the yet unsettled portions of its territory, the Great Basin shared in the influx of colonists who were attracted by reports of the agricultural and mineral wealth of the country beyond the Missouri.

Within the boundaries of the " Free and Independent State of Deseret," as organized by Brigham Young and his coadjutors in 1849, the Gentiles, who were to have no part nor lot in this inheritance of the Saints, had already settled to the number of hundreds of thousands.

Wyoming, Idaho, Nevada, Arizona, and California—all of them within the limits of the territory claimed by the Prophet " in the name of the Lord"—were occupied in spite of his dominions, and the country was rapidly filling up with a population inimical to him and to the system he represented.

These unwelcome intruders already hemmed Utah in on every side, and the day seemed not far distant when they would lay claim to the sacred soil of Zion itself ; but as yet the Prophet held his own, and not only ruled his subjects with a rod of iron as heretofore, but kept out the Gentile, who was not to have so much as a place to set his foot within the borders of Zion. It is true, it sometimes happened that an outsider was found foolhardy enough to undertake to pre-empt land beyond the boundaries which he was forbidden to cross, but in such cases the rash invader was baptized in Jordan—and left there; and his land fell to heirs not named in his will.

The only representatives of the world they hated, who could not readily be driven from their midst, were the troops at Camp Douglas. General Connor, notwithstanding many intimations that the Territory would be made too hot for him, still professed himself satisfied with the climate, and his batteries continued to frown upon the city, the Tabernacle, and even the sacred inclosure within which the Prophet held his court.

But this was not all. The chaplain at the post, Rev. Norman McLeod, a man of dauntless courage, as the sequel will show, actually procured and opened a place for Christian worship within half a dozen blocks of the Tabernacle. At first his congregation was drawn chiefly from the garrison and the families who had taken refuge at the fort, but gradually many who in their hearts had renounced Mormonism began to find their way to the building that, with a just conception of one of the first needs of a people so long enslaved, was named Independence Hall.* As might be supposed, many of those who went secretly to this place of Christian worship were women, whose bruised hearts longed for some message of hope and consolation: something which would remind them that the God of whom they had heard in their childhood—a God of infinite tenderness and compassion—still lived.

Who shall blame them if, borne down by the miseries of their daily life, and cut off from hope, they had felt as though he was not—had said, in the bitterness of their souls,

> " We sit unowned upon our burial sod,
> And know not whence we come, nor whose we be."

*See Appendix, Note P, page 351.

Among the first to go openly to the hall was Jessie La Tour. Others had gone veiled and disguised to the evening service. She went in broad day, and without making the least attempt at concealment. The first time that she defied the authority of the Church in this way the boldness of the act seemed to paralyze those whose duty it was to watch her, and nothing was said or done by them ; but on the second Sabbath a note was thrown into her open window after her return. She unfolded it, and read as follows :

"Remember your oath. Remember also what is the penalty of disobedience. You have offended twice. The third time, that which you imprecated upon yourself when you took your vows will surely befall you. Be warned in season."

Jessie's lip curled contemptuously as she read, and she made a motion as though to tear the paper in two, but checked herself and handed it to Philip, who happened to be at home in the afternoon. He read it, and turned very pale.

"Jessie ! what have you been doing ?" he said, with a degree of agitation which showed plainly that the missive meant something—to him, at least.

"What have I been doing ?" she answered. "Why, I thought you and everybody knew. I went last Sunday to Independence Hall to attend a Christian service. I have been there again to-day, and I mean to go next Sunday."

"You must not go again. You are risking too much."

"What do you mean by that ? Does this paper, which I should have thrown into the fire without reading, frighten you ? I hope not; for just as surely as I am alive, and well enough to walk there, I shall go to the hall next Sunday, and every Sunday."

"Jessie, listen to me for our child's sake, if not for my

sake or your own.   I tell you, it will not be safe for you to disregard the warning you have received."

"Why ?   Do you think I should be dealt with as Mrs. Jay and Mrs. Morse were ?"

He rose from his seat and put his hand on her shoulder.

"I love you," he said, in a voice scarcely audible, "love you better than my life, though you do not believe it ; but I could not save you by giving my life for yours if you should do as you say you will."

"You want me, then, by submission, to strengthen the hands of the man who has people killed for attending Christian worship ?   That is what makes him the tyrant he is. If even a few of the people had courage enough to defy him, his power would be broken ; but just as long as everybody fears him, persons who offend him will continue to *disappear*, like those two women who have never been seen since they passed through the Eagle Gate."

"I beg you, Jessie, not to speak of *them* again."

"Why not ?   Do you know what became of them ?"

Jessie would have continued her questions, but there was a look on her husband's face that checked her —an expression not only of agony, but of horror and dread.

"He *does* know," was the thought that forced itself upon her, and then her own face grew white ; for whispers of a deed so dreadful that none dared name it aloud had been afloat for weeks past.

Two women had been accused of revealing the secret rites of the Endowment House.   They had been summoned to trial, and since then had never been seen ; but the belief prevailed that the penalties prescribed by the bloody code against which they had transgressed had been inflicted on them in full.*   Death, in itself, was not considered a suffi-

*See Appendix, Note Q, page 352.

cient punishment for exposing the secrets of the Endowment House.

To mete out the full measure of vengeance which the culprit had called down upon himself, death must be preceded by tortures from which the imagination recoils, and which no pen could describe.

Philip La Tour now held an office which made it his duty to be present when offenders were tried and sentenced. If he had been present when these women were tried, he surely knew enough to make him dread a like fate for his own wife.

In spite of her fearless nature, Jessie trembled and grew faint as these thoughts passed through her mind. There were no crimes of which these wretches were incapable. She dared not even conjecture what would be the fate of one who was in their hands wholly and without remedy.

" I will not fall into their hands," she said aloud, replying to her own thoughts. " I will take my boy and go to the fort to-day. The guard that accompanies the chaplain is in town. I will ask protection. There are a few men, even here, who will protect a woman."

" Jessie !" and something in his voice compelled her attention.

" There is another way. Only be patient and wait a little while. There are changes coming of which you do not dream. Grant what I ask. Stay away from these meetings for the present, and act as though you submitted to the authority of the Church, and better days will dawn for both of us."

What did he mean ? Was it possible that his eyes were being opened to see the iniquities of the system that he had believed was divine ? Jessie's heart beat quickly at the thought, which something in his face as well as in his words seemed to confirm. If this were true, she would do what he asked —do anything for him.

"It shall be as you wish," she said at length, hardly daring to trust her voice lest it should betray all the joy she felt at the possibilities that opened up before her.

It was now two years since the day (never to be forgotten by him) when the expression of a wish that she and Ruth might be reconciled to each other had called forth the indignant words which stung into life a feeling of remorse, a sense of guilt, which could not co-exist with a firm belief in the divinity of the system which enjoined polygamy.

Nor was this all. During these two years many facts had come to his knowledge which had greatly shaken his faith in the Prophet. He was beginning to see what an impartial observer might have seen from the first—that Brigham Young and his coadjutors were using all the machinery of the Church for their own aggrandizement, and that the poor were oppressed and the whole people systematically robbed to fill the coffers of those men.

Only one thing more was needed to complete his disenthrallment, and that was to be brought face to face with the shocking barbarities involved in the rite of blood-atonement. This final blow to his faith in Mormonism came at the very time when a few Christians were making an effort to publish the long-forgotten gospel of peace and good-will among the subjects of the Prophet. It is true he was not an actual witness of the sickening horrors of the Black Vault, but he knew the victims who were taken there, and knew the fate to which they were doomed.

Yet while his whole nature recoiled from such scenes of blood and cruelty, and the inevitable effect of his knowledge of them was to overthrow his faith in a religion whose altars were red with human sacrifices, he had not attained to the courage necessary to throw off the yoke of the Prophet and take his place openly among those who were known as apostates.

That better days were coming he fully believed. From present indications it seemed impossible that the Gentiles could be kept out of the Territory for another decade.

The mineral wealth of Nevada and Colorado, which had attracted so many immigrants, might one day find a rival here. Already valuable deposits of lead and silver ores had been discovered by parties attached to General Connor's command, and the report of these discoveries was certain to bring miners from the neighboring Territories in such numbers that they would be able to defy the Prophet.

In such an event, the disaffected element within the Church would certainly join the foe from without in an attack upon the despotism which made life, liberty, and property dependent upon the will of one man.

There were many besides Philip La Tour who waited for the coming of such a day of deliverance as his hopes shadowed forth—many who had been as sincere as he in their acceptance of Mormonism, and who had made even greater sacrifices for the sake of their faith.

Ever since the bloody days of the " Reformation,"* when an unsupported accusation was sufficient to doom a man or woman to death, or a fate worse than death, without even the form of a trial, the number of those who only waited for an opportunity to throw off the Prophet's yoke had been steadily increasing.

Husbands whose wives had " disappeared," wives whose husbands had been called out of the house in the dead of night to meet the knife and bullet of the Destroying Angels, and parents whose sons had been given over to the tender

---

* A reign of terror inaugurated in 1857 by the preaching of such fanatics as Grant, Brigham's Counselor. The Reformation was at full tide when the Mountain Meadow massacre took place, and that most atrocious butchery was in accordance with the doctrines taught by the Mormon press and pulpit at the period named.

mercies of the Danites, could hardly be expected to remain firm in their loyalty to the Church whose teachings sanctioned these atrocities. Yet so absolute was the despotism under which the people lived, and so great was the terror inspired by the summary punishment visited on those who were even suspected of apostasy, that but for the presence of the troops no whisper of dissent would have been heard among the masses.

Not even to his wife did Philip La Tour venture to confess all his distrust of the Prophet, and his horror of the crimes perpetrated by his order ; and though by this time he had little doubt that plural marriage was likewise a crime against both human and divine law, he continued to acknowledge Ruth as his wife, and to spend half his time with her—not because he cared for her, but because he dared not renounce polygamy openly.

After the scene described in a former part of this chapter, Jessie found her life more tolerable ; for though Philip still spent every alternate week at " the other house," she could not help seeing that he went there reluctantly and returned to her gladly ; and, strange as it may appear to those who have seen nothing of the domestic life of the Saints, she began to take unusual pains with her dress, her table, and her household arrangements, and to make the time which her husband spent with her wear a holiday garb.

Do women who have never been within sight or hearing of such lives as hers wonder that she could forgive the past, and solace herself with the hope of a future in which her husband should be all her own ?

There are scores of women in Utah to-day who have extended such forgiveness to husbands who cast them aside in obedience to the requirements of a false faith, and whose late repentance has involved not only the breaking of other ties, but the loss of property, position, and friends.

When Philip at length found courage to talk freely with his wife, and explain his difficulties, he found her more patient and considerate than he had dared to hope she would be ; and when he begged her to bear with him until the way opened for him to renounce polygamy and Mormonism together, she answered that she could bear all things with the prospect before her of a day in which he would be a free man.

In many respects he was better situated than others who wished to sever their connection with Mormonism, for he had but one plural wife, while some of his brethren had half a dozen whom they must give up, together with their children. According to the teachings of the Mormon pulpit, when a man was cut off from the Church, all of his wives and children were to be taken from him and given to others. Even the first wife, with her children, could be disposed of in this manner. There are many instances on record where a man suspected of apostasy and compelled to flee for his life has returned to the Territory in after years only to find the wife of his youth in the harem of some member of the priesthood, who claimed his children also.

Philip knew that by the exercise of a little caution he could provide for the safety of his wife and son, and he was quite willing to give up Ruth, who had no children ; for the frail baby, the innocent cause of so much bitter feeling, lived only a couple of months.

Then, too, his hands were unstained by crime, while others who longed for freedom were held back by their enforced participation in some of the dark deeds " counseled" by the authorities of the Church.

When Jessie thought over the matter by herself, it

seemed to her as if there was really no hindrance except their property, which must be sacrificed if they left the Territory, and which, on her part, she was quite willing to sacrifice ; but then, if Philip did not see his way clearly yet, she would wait, and wait patiently.

In the mean time, true to her promise, she kept away from Independence Hall, and attended the services at the Tabernacle instead—in short, conducted herself as Philip had advised, so as to give the impression that she was completely subdued.

Some of her neighbors, however, continued to go regularly to the meetings in spite of threats, and the Sabbath-school proved so great an attraction to the Mormon children that no degree of punishment availed to keep them from it.

It is not to be supposed that such a state of things could be suffered to continue. Mobs, armed and organized in such a manner as to leave no doubt that they were acting under instructions, surrounded and filled the hall at the hour of service. The meetings were broken up, the life of McLeod threatened, and finally Dr. Robinson, one of his strongest supporters, was murdered in cold blood.

McLeod was not a man likely to succumb to threats or violence, and he determined to assert his rights as an American citizen and continue to hold religious services in the building that he and his friends had paid for ; but official changes soon after called him from the Territory, and the movement he had inaugurated, deprived of his courageous leadership, seemed for the time at an end.

Other influences, however, were at work to change the condition of affairs. Rumors of the mineral wealth of Utah reached the surrounding Territories, and hundreds of hardy miners, most unpromising material for subjects of a despotism, began to crowd in.

At first the authorities of the Church ordered the Danites to drive all prospectors out of the cañons with shot-guns ; but in a very little while the Prophet discovered that the game was one which two could play at, and this order, though not rescinded, became practically inoperative. .

Then another foe, more dreaded even than the miners, was reported on the way. The iron horse was speeding across the plains over which Mormon pilgrims dragged their hand-carts only a few years since. In a little while Deseret, the kingdom that was never to be moved, must be brought face to face with the world from which its founders had fled, and the old strife between civilization and barbarism would be renewed.

But the Prophet proved himself equal to the emergency. The Lion of the Lord, as he was wont to style himself, became a very fox in cunning and duplicity ; and though he did not succeed in keeping out the invader, he saved his kingdom from overthrow, and made all who came from without realize that they dwelt in Zion only by sufferance.

The only perceptible change consequent upon the new order of things was that blood-atonement, instead of being preached and practiced openly as heretofore, took the form of midnight murders committed under secret instructions. Gentiles and apostates were no longer shot down in broad daylight ; but men who knew themselves to be obnoxious to the priesthood kept in-doors after dark, or, if compelled to go out, armed themselves doubly, and took the middle of the street.

In other respects, however, the despotic rule of the Prophet was in nowise affected by the presence of the Gentile element in his dominions. If he chose to appropriate the property of his subjects the courts afforded them no redress, and polygamy, instead of experiencing any check, spread and increased.

CHAPTER XIX.

A MYSTERY SOLVED.

THE southern portion of Utah has been the scene of many a bloody tragedy besides that of Mountain Meadows, but as yet there had been no attempt on the part of the Government to seek out and punish the perpetrators of any of the crimes committed there ; and if in Salt Lake and under the guns of the fort some feeble effort was made by the Federal authorities to investigate the murders committed at their very doors, the accused had only to betake themselves south to assure their perfect safety.

The idea of arresting a Mormon in one of the southern settlements without the aid of an armed force was so preposterous that the most courageous of the Federal judges would not send a United States marshal on such an errand ; and even if the officers of the law should be sent after notorious offenders with troops at their back, it would be quite useless.

Brigham assured his people that he had prepared a retreat in the mountains of the south in which the whole people might hide—a spot of which no white man knew anything except those in his confidence.

This assurance was an exaggeration, like most of his public boasts ; but it is certain that in the heart of the mountains he described there has always been a safe refuge for those of his followers who, after years of delay on the part of the Government, have at length been indicted for some of their many crimes.

In 1867 and '68 many persons whose names were unpleasantly associated with open outrages committed in Salt Lake and vicinity found it convenient to move south, and among these were two men who were heavily indebted to Philip La Tour, and who had forgotten to settle their accounts before leaving.

Not wishing to lose so large a sum, he determined upon going down to the settlement in which they had located, hoping to make some arrangements by which a part at least of the debt might be secured.

It was a long distance—more than two hundred miles—and as railroads were yet unknown in Utah, and stage lines few, the whole journey had to be made by private conveyance. Such institutions as hotels were also yet in the future ; but in most of the settlements there was some house—often that of the bishop—at which the chance traveler could obtain lodgings.

On his return trip, and when still more than a hundred miles south of Salt Lake, La Tour stopped for the night at a small town, the center of a farming community, established there in the early days of the Territory. Mother Simons, his hostess, was a garrulous old lady, one of the original Nauvoo Mormons, and also one of the earliest converts to the doctrine of polygamy.

She had come to Nauvoo a widow, and bestowed herself and the property she brought with her upon an elder whose wife, like many other women in Nauvoo at the time, was kept in profound ignorance of the transaction until the Saints emigrated to Utah.

The first consequence of the avowal of these secret polygamous relations was generally a division of the domestic establishment ; and Mother Simons, who, besides being several years older than the lawful wife, was almost pathetically ugly, was given a home in this southern settlement, while the other members of the family remained in Salt Lake.

No sense of ill-usage or neglect, however, seemed to disturb the good woman's placid content, or affect in the least her loyalty to her master or to the Church. She was the most devout of Saints, paid her tithing with scrupulous regularity, and every spring and fall made the long journey of a hundred miles to Salt Lake, for the purpose of seeing the face of her Prophet and hearing his voice at the conference.

La Tour found tolerable accommodations at Mother Simon's place ; but as a chilly autumn rain set in on the evening of his arrival, he was glad to exchange the uncomfortable temperature of his own room for the warmth of the old lady's kitchen fire.

Mother Simons delighted greatly in new subjects, into whose ears she might pour the flood of gossip which her neighbors grew tired of listening to, and she made the most of the present opportunity. After La Tour had submitted good-naturedly to a long catechism with regard to his own affairs and " the news in Salt Lake," she proceeded to enlighten him upon the history of all the families in the settlement.

It must be owned, however, that her tattle was in the main good-natured, and she had no evil report to bring up until she came to the neighbor whose orchard adjoined her own. •

" They're that set up," she remarked, " that folks as works for a livin' ain't good enough for 'em to speak to, hardly. They've got a two-story house—the only one in the settlement—though what they want with such a place, with nary chick nor child around, nobody kin tell. Sister Mirandy won't have the second wife in the house neither, and she and Brother Wells and their Danish girl was

reckoned for years and years to be the only souls on the
place ; but a spell ago—'tain't more'n six months, I should
say—it leaked out that they've bin a-keepin' a poor crazy
creetur for nobody knows how long, in one o' the upper
rooms.   'Pears as if it's a relation of some kind ; and folks
that knows how graspin' Brother Wells has always bin
says they've got her property, and that's what's set 'em up
so, and give Sister Mirandy her fine shawls and things.''

Here the good woman stopped a moment to take breath ;
but as her listener showed no disposition to interrupt her
by a question, she went on directly :

'' Some of them that takes up for Sister Mirandy says the
woman ain't no kind of relation, but only a poor creetur
without friends, and that they're paid for her keepin' out of
the tithin', but that ain't noways likely ; for,'' dropping her
voice a little, '' things has come out lately that goes to
show that Brother Wells ain't much better than a 'postate,
and as for Sister Mirandy, she's always been set agin
plurality, and 'twouldn't surprise me the least mite to hear
her say she'd never had no faith in the gospel ; for them
that sets up to pick and choose for themselves what part
they'll believe and what part they won't, generally ends
with believin' nothin'.

'' I don't want to think no harm of my neighbors, and
there ain't nobody that kin say I go around talkin' about
folks behind their backs ; but I can't help mistrustin'
there's somethin' wrong in that family.   No soul in the
settlement has ever seen that poor creetur up-stairs ; an'
them that used to know Brother Wells kin tell you the
same as I, that he didn't have a dollar to his name when he
was in Nauvoo.   Now, what I want to know is, where's
his money come from, and what made him keep that poor
creetur out of sight for years and years ?''

Again Mother Simons paused, as though expecting to

elicit from some source the information she had asked for, but as it was not forthcoming she continued :

" But I ain't told the hull. The way it happened to come out that they was keepin' this poor creetur up-stairs, she was took sick, and it 'pears like all they could do for her didn't help her a mite, so they sent to Nephi settlement for Sister Perkins.

" Now Sister Perkins is a master hand at doctorin' with yerbs—I shouldn't be above ground myself to-day if it hadn't bin for her—and besides she's one of the kindest-hearted creeturs that ever breathed. She felt that bad about Sister Mirandy's aunt (for that's what they give out she was to 'em) that she couldn't keep still about her noways. Sister Perkins thought, and we all thought, that if the rights of the thing was told, Brother Wellses house, and all their fixin's that they set such store by, come out of the aunt's money ; and Sister Perkins said she didn't 'pear to her that crazy that she needed to be shut up all the time. Kinder strange like, she was, and wouldn't speak ; but that was all. But there was more to come. Seems as if the poor creetur kep' growin' weaker and weaker after that sick spell, and yesterday she dropped off. The neighbors that went to lay her out asked for her Temple robes, and Sister Mirandy up and says, as sharp as could be,

" ' She won't wear nothin' of the kind, for she wasn't in the Church ; and I won't put on her dead what she wouldn't have if she was alive.'

" That was a curus speech, and if it had a' bin any one else they'd bin called to account for it ; but the bishop, he's always bin easy with Brother Wellses folks, and he's that easy now that he's goin' to preach the funeral to-morrow mornin', though Sister Mirandy says as plain as can be her aunt never was in the Church."

Philip listened to his landlady's monologue at first with

profound indifference, but finally with a degree of interest for which he could not account, and when she finished asked the hour of the funeral.

"Ten o'clock in the mornin'," was the answer. "Maybe you'd like to go. The neighbors is all a-goin' to get a sight of the poor creetur that nobody's bin let to see while she was alive."

When morning came, the rain which had set in the night before was still falling, and the prospect of riding through such a storm was not a pleasant one ; but this alone would not have been sufficient to cause Philip to defer starting until the next day.

A curiosity as unusual as it was unaccountable possessed him to look on the face of the woman whose sad story had ended in death. Who was she ? And why had her existence been kept secret for so many years ?

When the hour appointed for the funeral arrived, Philip took the way to the house alone. The place looked like the home of a well-to-do farmer—a New England farmer, an observer from the States would have added—for there was an air of thrift and neatness about the grounds and buildings which, as a rule, was conspicuously absent from the homes of the Utah settlers at that day.

The appearance of the front room in which the funeral services were held kept up the impression of a home transplanted directly from the hills of New Hampshire or the valleys of Connecticut to the Great Basin, and the man who sat at the foot of the coffin, facing the curious crowd with grave composure, was unmistakably a son of the Pilgrims.

How came he in such a place and among such a people ?

But if his looks and bearing compelled this question, that of the woman beside him contrasted still more strongly with the surroundings.

A noble, spiritual face ; a head to which the silver locks were as a crown of glory, and a presence at once gentle and commanding, increased every moment the wonder of the beholder at finding her in such a company.

La Tour, seated near the door, could scarcely take his eyes from that face, which recalled dimly a life that now was little more than a dream to him—a life untainted by the deadly poison of the upas-tree that had taken fast root in these valleys.

Like a man but half awake he listened to the rambling discourse of the bishop, which included a reminder that it was the duty of the nearest of kin to be baptized for the dead, who had left the world without receiving the gospel ; listened to the doleful funeral hymn, and rose to his feet as the whole company, marshaled by the bishop, filed past the coffin.

He was the last in the line, and a feeling of reluctance that amounted to dread held him back, until he was left standing alone. Then the bishop, recognizing him as the stranger who had stopped in the settlement over night, beckoned him forward, and he moved slowly toward the spot where the dead lay at rest.

The body was robed in a plain shroud, the thin hands were folded on the breast, and on one of them was a ring —a ring he had seen before—and almost in the same instant that it met his eyes they rested likewise on the dead face.

Great Heaven !

His heart gave one suffocating throb, and then stood still.

It was the face of his mother ! No chance likeness, no resemblance that might cheat the eye for a moment, but in very deed the face that had bent over him in infancy, that had made the sunlight of his boyhood.

For death had brought back all the early loveliness of Marguerite La Tour, and but for the snow-white hair she looked as she might have looked if this dreamless sleep had overtaken her upon her bridal day.

While he stood as if transfixed, incapable of speech or motion, officious hands closed the coffin-lid, and before he could rouse himself from his trance they had carried it from the room. The assembled company followed, and he was left alone. The strong man felt ás helpless as a little child. Stunned, blinded by the shock of that awful discovery, he groped his way to the door. The wind that blew in sharp gusts, driving the rain into his face, roused his benumbed faculties and partly restored him to himself.

Mechanically he followed the path taken by those who carried the dead ; but he was a long way behind, and when he reached the place of burial the first shovelful of earth had been thrown upon the coffin. As his fascinated eyes watched the rapid filling up of the grave, all the terror and anguish of that long night-watch twenty years ago came back to him, and with it came also the memory of every word spoken by the man who had made him as well as his mother the victim of his unrelenting hate.

He saw it all now—saw the deliberately-planned scheme of vengeance which had cost him and his sisters a mother. How much it had cost that mother herself he dared not think.

The burial was over. The people whom curiosity had drawn together separated, and hurried homeward through the rain, which was still falling. No one remained beside the grave except the man and woman from whose house the dead had been carried out. Philip stood opposite them. They too were about turning away, when he stopped them.

"My name is La Tour," he said, speaking across the grave. "I saw and recognized the face of her whom you have buried here."

"Husband," said the woman, clasping her companion's arm, "have I not told you again and again that this hidden wrong would surely be brought out into the light of day?" The man turned toward Philip, "My friend," he said, "come with us to our home. What you should hear can be best spoken there."

Without another word he led the way down the path, and Philip followed silently. When they reached the house they entered, not by the way the dead had been carried out, but by a side door, which opened into a room that was warm and cheerful in spite of the storm.

"Take off your wet wrappings," said the host, "and sit down beside the fire, for the story we have to tell is a long one."

Philip made a negative gesture.

"Do not refuse to sit down in our house." It was the woman who spoke this time, and her face and her voice were full of pathetic entreaty. "We are not your enemies. We were not *her* enemies. Only hear what we have to tell you."

Thus urged, he seated himself by the fireside, but the questions he wished to ask died upon his lips. The man turned to his wife.

"The story is for you to tell," he said ; "for from first to last you have been blameless in this thing, and remorse will not tie your tongue."

"Fifteen years ago," the woman began, fixing her soft, dark eyes on the face of her guest, "we were asked to take charge of a friendless woman who had lost her reason. I need not tell you from whom the request came ; but when I consented to receive the woman I believed her case to be as I have stated. My husband knew the truth, but he dared not refuse to do as he was commanded."

"Say also," the man interrupted, raising his head, "that I was poor then, and the money that was offered me tempted me."

" That is doubtless true," she went on in the same quiet voice ; " but if nothing had been offered you, you must still have obeyed."

Then addressing herself again to Philip, she continued her narrative.

" We were not living here at that time. We were in Salt Lake—within a few blocks of your home—and the house in which the woman we were asked to take charge of had been confined for five years, was on the opposite side of the street."

Philip started from his chair. If this woman spoke the truth, how blind he had been—willfully blind, it seemed now.

" You cannot credit this," she said, " and yet it is true, and stranger things still have happened. Your mother"—her voice faltered a little as she pronounced the word—" was in the custody of James Sprague until he died, and after his death she was removed to our house."

" How came she in his hands ? How could she have been taken there in open day, against her will, and yet without the knowledge of the people around her ?"

The woman looked at him steadily. " Surely you are aware," she said, " that had all the people known of such a thing, not one of them would have dared to speak if counseled otherwise ; but in this case no force was employed. Your mother was decoyed to the house by a message that you had been injured by a fall from a horse and carried in there."

" And what then ?"

"She was confined in a dark inner room : kept under lock and key as a prisoner, and treated as a maniac."

Philip sprang to his feet, with a white face and flashing eyes. The spirit of his race was roused at last.

"My curse rest forever and ever on the man who placed her there," he cried ; "and God do so to me and more also if he escape my vengeance."

"Be calm," the woman said, her own face and voice unchanged. "You do not know what you are saying. He cares nothing for your curse, and only those who are stronger than he can mete to him the measure he has meted to others. Hear all that I have to tell."

"Your mother, perhaps, suffered less than you imagine. She was not beaten or starved, as has been the case with many a one imprisoned by the same authority, but she was fastened by day to the bed on which she slept at night, and during the five years in which she remained in that house she was not permitted to exchange a word with a human being—not even with her keepers, who had strict orders never to speak to her or answer her.

"You must understand that I knew nothing of all this when she was placed in my care, and it was years before the whole truth came to my knowledge ; but she had not been with us a week before I was convinced that she was not insane ; and as we had no special orders regarding her treatment except that we were not to allow any one to suspect her existence, I did my best to make her as comfortable as circumstances permitted, and talked with her when I could do so with safety.

"A year after she came to us we moved to this place. The land was bought and the house built with the money that was paid my husband for taking charge of her, and we were again strictly ordered to let no one know we had such an inmate. If the fact of her existence should be discovered by chance, we were to say that she was an insane relative.

" By this time I knew who she was, and soon after we came here I learned the whole of her sad story ; but what could I do ? What could any one do ? Were we not all slaves, bound hand and foot ? Had I told what I knew, no good would have come of it, but much harm to her as well as to us. Had I even let you know the truth, you would have been powerless to help her."

" That may have been so in the past," Philip interrupted, " but now there is a change. There are men in the country who dare not only to differ with Brigham Young, but to defy him."

" Have you dared to do so ?"

The question was asked kindly, but Philip's pale face flushed.

" I have been a coward in the past," he said, " but I will be one no longer. I am going home, to sever my connection with this iniquitous system, and to denounce the man who stands at the head of it."

" That is well. I pray that the way may open for others to do so," and she glanced at her husband. " I have felt that a day of deliverance was coming, though I knew not when nor how."

" That day may be farther from us than from you," the husband said, addressing Philip. " You have the troops to protect you, and the Gentiles are coming in, I hear, in great numbers ; but in this settlement there is not a man, woman, or child who dares to disobey counsel in the smallest thing, much less to say a word against Mormonism. And yet there are those here whose wrongs are greater than yours."

" Greater than mine ?"

" Yes. Deeds have been done within sight of this house

for which devils might blush, and done, too, in the name of the Lord ; and the still living victims, who envy the dead, dare not utter a word of complaint."

" As for you, the revenge that was planned against you and yours fell short of its mark ; for though your mother has been kept a prisoner, in all things else I have treated her as I would if I had been her own son."

Here the woman rose and opened a door at the farther side of the room.

" Come," she said to Philip, " and I will show you the place in which your mother spent the last years of her life."

He followed her through a long hall, and up a flight of stairs, but on the landing above she paused.

" I need not tell you," she said, " that I have already put my life and the life of my husband in your hands, and now that I am about to give you all that your mother has left behind her, I am putting trust in your wisdom as well as in your honor."

With these words she opened the door and admitted Philip into a room which he entered with feelings that were indescribable.

It was in no respect like the prison-cell he had at first pictured to himself. The floor was carpeted, a comfortable bed stood in one corner with an easy chair beside it, a table in the center of the room was covered with books, and a writing-desk filled the niche between the windows. The woman went directly to this desk, unlocked it, and took out a sealed packet.

" In this," she said, " you will find the history of your mother's life since the day she left you. She begged, almost with her last breath, that I would convey it to her children, and I promised, without knowing of any way in which the promise could be fulfilled ; but see, a way has opened already. The hand of God is in this thing."

Philip received the packet with irrepressible emotion.

" Did my mother know ? Did she hear anything of us during these long years ?" he asked.

" Until she came to us she heard nothing," was the answer. " If all of you had died she would not have known ; but since she has been here I have told her all that I could learn of you which was likely to give her any happiness, and that which I knew would pain her I have kept from her."

Philip dropped his eyes. He knew well enough that there was little in his own history which it would have made his mother happier to hear.

" It is strange," he said at length, " that you should not have known me, and that I do not recall either your face or your name as that of one who must have been our neighbor."

" Fifteen years have changed all of us," she answered ; " but I knew you again when you spoke to us at the grave. That you did not recognize us is no wonder, for we had been in Salt Lake but a little while when your mother came to us, and afterward we avoided you, as we were instructed to do."

" And yet you have done me the only kindness possible. You have cared for my mother as if she had been your own. I will never forget that."

The woman looked out of the window. " The rain is over," she said, " and the people will soon be abroad. For your own sake as well as for ours, you must not linger in the settlement. When you are a free man, remember us. If we have shown any kindness to you or yours, that will be the best return you can make."

CHAPTER XX.

THE SEALED PACKET.

" *Oct.* 10.—Once more, after so many years of darkness, I behold the light of day. Once more I look out upon the sky and the earth, whose face I never hoped to see again.

" Dear God, how fair is thy world ! And how sweet is a human voice—a kindly human voice—after the long silence.

" This day it is five years since I had the last sight of the faces of my children. I should not know—I could not reckon time in that dark cell into which day never penetrated : but this woman—no, she is not a woman, but an angel, to risk so much for me—has given me the day and the date ; and the date of that other day—the day on which I was torn from my children—is burned into my brain.

" Five years ! My little Blanche, my baby, is almost a woman now. Oh for one moment's sight of her sweet face ! Day after day I sit at this high window, and watch the street, and pray God to send my children this way, but they never come.

" Once indeed it seemed to me that Philip passed by on the other side—taller, more manly, than when I saw him last—that must be—but the form was like my Philip, and he carried his head as my brave boy did. His face was turned away, and yet it was he. A mother's eyes see clearly."

" *Oct.* 21.—My eyes are blinded with grateful tears, for this day I have seen my little girls from my window. My little girls ! They are women now, and Catherine's face is like the one I used to see in my mirror years—oh so many years ago.

"I owe it all to the good angel who watches over me in my imprisonment, for though she dare not speak to my children, or make herself known to them in any way, she has worked through others so that my daughters should pass by the house.

"How many hours I watched, and how I feared her plan would fail! I dread lest she should risk too much for me; and though I long—God only knows *how* I long for a sight of my lost darlings—I must not tell her all that is in my heart, for that would move her to try again to bring them near me; and there is danger, always danger, that she, my only friend, may be involved in my fate."

"*Nov.* 12.—I have news of Louise—my beautiful, my darling, my wounded dove. She is here, so near me, and ,yet she cannot know that her mother lives! Her mother, who has given more than life for her!

"My good angel tells me too that Louise is not unhappy. There is peace in her face and in her voice.

"She has learned, then, the secret that was taught me in those years of darkness. She is not alone and helpless in the hands of wicked men. Dear God, I thank thee!"

"*March* 1.—For months I have written nothing. A slow fever, brought on, I fear, by those longings and anxieties which I should not have indulged, has made me helpless—made me doubly a burden to my only friend. And yet she will not allow me to say that. She has tended me like a child, she has watched over me like a sister, and she says only this:

"'All that I can do is a poor atonement for your wrongs.'

"I can guess what she means, and yet it is not for her to make atonement."

"*March* 4.—I have learned to-day something that I never knew before—learned what took place that day after I was lured to my prison.

"My children believe me dead. They have been taught that my reason was gone, and that I drowned myself in the river! My helpless darlings! They could not think that anything but death would be able to keep their mother from them.

"I can see the terror in their faces when they came back to the empty house. I can realize what they felt when that cruel tale was told them. But they were very young, and God is good. He would not let that sorrow shadow their lives. My friend thinks the little home which Philip keeps for his sisters would be a happy one, if the man who took their mother from them did not take their bread also.

"This is hard—and hard to forgive—but One who suffered the utmost malice of cruel foes forgave them with His dying breath."

"*March* 10.—More news! My Catherine has been a wife for two months and more, and my good angel, unable to leave the house because I must be cared for, had not heard of it.

"A wife's lot here is full of bitterness—of more than mortal pain. God shield my darling!"

"*April* 4.—I am to go far away from my darlings. And yet, what does it matter, since, near or far, I am separated from them while I live?

"Still, here, at this window, I could watch, and hope that they might pass by, and that was something. The day could not be quite a blank when I could say in the morning,

"'It may be that one of my children will come this way.'

" And then I have really seen my little girls, and Philip twice. Once I saw his face plainly.

" But Louise—my Louise, my beautiful one—I have not had the faintest glimpse of her ; and how can I give over my watch for her, and go away without the sight of her face ?"

" *May* 21.—The journey is over, and had it not been that each hour took me farther from my children, they would have been happy days. I breathed the fresh free air, the sun shone on me, and whenever we were in lonely places, far from the sight of those who would have been spies on us, I might feel the dear earth, the soil of God's beautiful world, under my feet.

" How sweet is liberty ! It seemed sometimes as though I must break away from those who cared for me so kindly, and run toward the mountains, for beyond them must be freedom.

" Run ! I smile at myself now, for I could not walk for an hour, and a year ago I could not walk at all. My limbs were cramped. They had almost grown to the shape of the seat to which I was chained.

" No, liberty is not for me. Yet my soul is not in prison, and during those years of darkness, when chains were on my body, my spirit was free."

" *Aug.* 20.—My friend, my guardian angel, who has comforted me through all my sorrows, now needs that I should comfort her. Her home is invaded, her husband is taken from her, and another woman usurps the name and place of wife in the house. What are my sufferings now compared with hers ?

" She comes to my room, to my prison, which I may never leave alive, as to a sanctuary. It is her only place of refuge, the only spot where she is safe from curious, unsympathizing eyes, or from the sight of her husband and that other woman, who claims the rights of a wife. She does not complain—she is one of those who would die and make no· moan—but her dumb despair is more eloquent than the most impassioned lamentations.

"And yet she thinks that her husband loved her truly—loves her even now—and that he has taken that other woman only because he was counseled to do so, and because he dared not disobey. Would a husband believe still in the love of his wife, after she had brought another man into the house to usurp his rights and to claim her as his own?

"The patient endurance of these wives, and the love that outlives the husband's baseness and treachery, touches me, and yet it angers me. It was never meant that any good woman, much less an angel like this wronged wife, should waste her love on a man who tramples it under foot."

"*Nov.* 4.—A better day has dawned for my friend, if indeed there can be a better or a worse to a wrong like hers. The other woman has been sent away to a settlement twenty miles distant, and the husband goes there but seldom. He is forced to stay at home on my account—so I am told. The man who placed me here thinks a woman cannot be trusted to guard me, and so my friend is not left alone.

"I cannot understand her. She seems almost happy when week after week passes without the expression of a wish on the part of her husband to go to the other settlement, and yet she knows that he will go by and by—knows he calls that woman wife, and that she may be the mother of his children. What a life! What a fate! And yet, it may be the fate of my own daughters."

"*Dec.* 30, '55.—I have heard that my Louise is married, and married to a good man who loves her; and better still, that both she and Catherine have left the Terri-tory with their husbands, who have been sent on missions, the one west, the other south.

" Is not God watching over my children, and doing far more for them than I could if I were free ?   Neither of my daughters will ever return voluntarily—of that I am sure."

" *Feb.* 1, '56.—The winter passes slowly.   I find it hard to repress my longings for liberty.   Often I look to the distant mountains, and a wild wish to fly to them takes possession of me.   I know that escape is impossible ; and yet, now that I can look out on those who pass to and fro beneath my window, on the earth, that my foot must never press, on the stars—the same stars that looked down on my childhood—the thought of freedom is with me con-tinually.   I dream of it at night, and a feverish restlessness possesses me by day.

" This is not as it should be.   I was calmer in that dark cell, where I saw nothing, heard nothing.

" Death will open my prison doors by and by.   Until then let me wait in peace."

" *April* 10, '56.—Ought I not to be thankful and con-tent ?   Word comes to me through this dear friend, who puts aside her own sorrows that she may serve me, and does her utmost to get news of my children, that both my daughters are safe in California, and with their brothers. I have now only Philip and little Blanche to be anxious about ; and surely, since Heaven has so watched over the others, I may dismiss anxiety even for them."

" *Aug.* 12.—I have been very ill again.   I thought the hour of my deliverance was surely at hand.   Those who have gone before seemed waiting for me, and in the still-ness of the night a face like my mother's bent down and smiled upon me.

" Liberty, and rest, and peace seemed already mine, and

when the gates that were opening closed again, and I found myself left outside—left here—I could not help a feeling of bitter disappointment.

"Patience, my soul! The years that seem so long will be but a speck, an atom, when thou lookest back on them from the Paradise of God."

"*Oct.* 5.—Again I have been the witness of pangs which make my own afflictions seem light. The woman who has been taken into this family is a mother. The wife whose place she has usurped is childless, and the husband, when he learned that he was a father, sent for the mother and the babe. They have been brought here, and are in the house to-day.

"The father, proud of the little one, and forgetting everything else in his joy, has shown plainly that the mother of his child is dearer to him than the wife of his youth, who has sacrificed all things for his sake; and she, unhappy, helpless victim, after making superhuman efforts to mask her sufferings and treat the woman and child as though they had a right to be here, has at last succumbed to her anguish. Yesterday she sank upon the floor of my room in a swoon that was like death. Fortunately, I was able to restore her without help, and in an hour she recovered so far as to be able to creep down the steps, holding on to the railings; but at the foot of the stairway I heard her fall again.

"To-day I have been waited on by a servant, who had not previously been permitted to know of my existence, and who, it seems, has orders not to speak to me; so I can learn nothing of my friend's state from her, but I fear she is very ill. If able to leave her bed she would surely come to me, for now, as before, my room is her only sanctuary."

"*Nov.* 20.—To-day I have seen my friend again for the

first time in many weeks. She is only the shadow of her former self, and her hair has grown as white as mine, which was blanched in those years of darkness.

"The woman and child have been taken away, and she feels this to be a relief, but she no longer cheats herself with the belief that her husband's heart is still hers. She has talked with me more freely than ever before, and I realize something of the daily martyrdom endured by her and women like her—of whom, alas! there are hundreds on every side."

"*July* 9, '57.—I have heard to-day that both Philip and Blanche are married. There is nothing in Philip's marriage to sadden me, for he is like his father, and the woman who has given her happiness into his keeping will never have cause to regret it. Her love will be his guiding star, and his home will be the most sacred spot on earth to him. His wife will never know a fate like that of my poor friend, who is striving to bury her love for her husband in the same grave in which she has buried happiness and hope.

"But my little Blanche—my baby, who has grown to womanhood without a mother's care—what will *her* fate be ? Has she fallen into the hands of one who will sacrifice her to the demands of this monstrous system, as coolly as pagans elsewhere sacrifice a lamb ? Alas ! there are none near her to protect her, and whatever her sorrows may be, her tears cannot be shed on her mother's bosom.

"*Aug.* 12, '57.—I have not written anything of late, because the uneventful days pass with nothing to mark their coming and going except the rising and setting of the sun.

"In spite of myself, in spite of all the lessons of patience which I have learned, an unutterable weariness possesses me when there is nothing—absolutely nothing—to break the monotony of my imprisonment; and then when some-thing comes to my knowledge which rouses me from the stupor that is creeping over me, the old restlessness and longing, the feeling that makes a caged bird beat its wings against the bars of its prison, comes back to me.

" Yesterday I sat at my window, seeing for hours only the long stretch of dusty highway upon which not a living thing appeared, when at length, late in the afternoon, an irregular mass came in sight in the dim distance, and as I continued to watch it resolved itself into a long train of wagons, with horsemen, footmen, and cattle—some in ad-vance, some in the rear. The train passed directly under my window. The animals moved slowly, as though worn out with a long journey ; the teams seemed to drag the wagons with difficulty, and the people looked travel-stained and weary ; but there was something in the ap-pearance of the company which told that they were not seeking a home *here ;* and as they passed on I noticed that persons in the settlement who were by the roadside hasten-ed in-doors as the train drew near.

" In the evening, when I asked my friend the meaning of what I had seen, she answered,

" ' They are emigrants on the way to California.'

" But she seemed disinclined to talk about them, and no questions that I asked brought me any more definite information.

" On the way to California ! If I had known of their coming I might—what might I not have done ? It seemed to me at first that I should have let myself down from my window in the night, and found some hiding-place on their route, where I could lie concealed till they passed, and then throw myself on their protection.

" But if this had been as impracticable as all my other plans of flight, I could at least have dropped a letter as they passed, that would have told of my fate, and begged them to carry the word to my sons—my sons, who would move Heaven and earth to release their mother from prison.

" The chance that I have lost is perhaps one that will never be within my reach again, and a feeling of disappointment that amounts to wretchedness shows me plainly how much my soul needs to be disciplined to patience— how little I know of true resignation."

" *Dec.* 10, '57.—An awful crime—a deed whose blackness might quench the light of day—has come to my knowledge. I am suffocating with horror. Would that I had remained ignorant of it. A bloody vision follows me, haunts me, night and day, since the fearful tale came to my ears.

" After those strangers passed this way, and while I was still grieving over my lost opportunity, I began to perceive from my window the appearance of unusual idleness on the part of the men of the settlement, who are farmers, and should at this season have been attending to their crops. They were congregated in groups by the roadside, and those who were so near that I could observe their faces, I saw looked gloomy and sullen. Finally, one night, I heard the heavy tramp of many feet, going in and out of this house until midnight.

" I slept none that night. A vague uneasiness, a terror for which I could not account, kept me wakeful, and before day I rose from my bed, and sitting down beside my window watched the stars until they began to fade.

" When the day broke, my eyes were fixed on the highway, and presently a band of mounted men issued from a little lane near the house. Many of the faces I had seen before, as they passed day after day, and among them I recognized my jailer, whose wife, contrary to her usual custom, had kept away from my room the day before, sending the servant with my meals.

"All of the men were armed with guns, and as I watched them they rode away southward, two abreast.

"That day, and for many days afterward, I could not help seeing that my friend was in some great trouble, which she refused to confide to me. Thus nearly two weeks passed, and one morning, as I was looking southward, I saw the same body of men whose departure I had watched, riding into the settlement.

"As they came near I perceived that Wells was in advance, and that he carried something on his horse in front of him. As he reached the house I saw, to my surprise, that it was a child—a little girl, perhaps four years old. He dismounted at a side door, at the foot of the stairs leading to my room.

"I heard his wife open the door—heard her exclamation, not only of surprise, but of dismay and terror—heard the man say,

"'Hush, for God's sake!'

"And then both seemed to pass into an inner room.

"After that I saw no more of my friend for many days, and when she entered my room again she was changed more, it seemed to me, than even during those weeks of sickness the year before.

"I knew something was wrong. An air of mystery brooded over the house. I heard the child sometimes—once it climbed up the stairs leading to my door, and more than once I distinguished a plaintive cry of,

"'Mamma! mamma! Take me to my mamma!'

"It was a wail that pierced my heart. How often must my own children have uttered that cry!

"When I spoke to my friend about the child, she turned a white, terrified face toward me, saying,

"'How did you know? Have you seen—have you heard anything?'

"Why protract the recital? In the end I learned the whole dreadful truth. The company of emigrants had been followed by bodies of armed men from the settlements, surrounded, and butchered in cold blood. Neither age nor sex had been spared. Only a few of the youngest children were rescued at the last by men who could not quite forget their own children. The little girl in the house was one of these.

"I cannot bear to dwell here. There is only one thing which I feel compelled to leave on record, and it is this :

"The man whom this people look up to as their Prophet ordered the butchery, and the men who did the deed were only his instruments. Many of them went most unwillingly. Some of them took no part in the massacre, and returned home with their faith in this man and his teachings destroyed forever. My friend's husband is one of those last named. He declares to his wife that he cannot remain here, and that he will watch night and day for an opportunity to escape.

"Should this be so, I too may yet be able to flee from this blood-stained spot.

"*Oct.* 10, '58.—This day completes the tenth year of my captivity. At times I think that the hope and even the wish to escape has died out altogether, and that I shall wait in peace for the Angel of Death ; and then some word, some rumor breaks in upon my quiet, and for weeks I am in a state of unrest.

"Of late I have had news of my elder sons. They have been greatly prospered, and they dwell among a brave and generous people, who would aid them in any effort to deliver their mother from prison, if they knew—but they do not even dream that I am still among the living. Like my children here, they have mourned me as dead these many years.

"Perhaps, after all, it is better that they should not know the truth. They might try to help me and fail, for it seems that in these valleys the power of the man who decreed my imprisonment is absolute. No one even dares call him to account for the butchery of those helpless women and innocent children who were so cruelly put to death last year.

"And for me, does it matter how or where I spend the little remnant of my life? No. Time is so short, eternity so long, that even if I were doomed to live out my three-score years and ten within these walls, it would be but like tarrying for a night at an inn that did not please me.

"*April* 12, '62.—My sight, which began to fail four years ago, and which I thought I should have lost entirely, is in a measure restored, and yet the light is painful, and I can no longer solace myself with books or beguile the tedious days by watching the world outside from my window.

"At first I felt this to be a great affliction, but now I acknowledge in it the same Hand that has led me hitherto.

"Cut off once more from the sight of this world, I turn to the world of spirits—the world where my beloved, who have escaped from the straits and burdens, the turmoil and unrest of this present life, abide in blissful peace.

"My eyes, closed to thy creatures, are opened to behold thee, oh, Uncreated Good!

"I behold the love that rules and permeates the universe. I have repose and liberty, because that which has no metes nor bounds is at once my home and my resting-place."

"*March*, '65.—For the last time, perhaps, I attempt to trace here my thoughts and my wishes. Strength and sight alike are almost gone; but while a little of life remains, I desire to make a final request of my children, should this which I have written ever fall into their hands.

"I pray them all, and especially my sons, to harbor no thought of vengeance against the author of my wrongs. With all my heart, with all my soul, I forgive him, and I ask my children to forgive.

"No real harm has come to me. That which was evil intended has worked for good. I have peace, I have joy within these walls, and my prison has become a sanctuary wherein I dwell safely until the doors of my Father's house are opened to receive me.

"*Nov.*, '68.—For many months I have dwelt in utter darkness; but I know in my soul that the dawn of a perfect day is very near. The Angel of Death waits close at hand. I shall welcome him with joy—and yet, something within me pleads for my children—begs that they might be permitted to look once more on their mother's face.

"How clearly I can see them all, here in the dark—my little Blanche in her cradle, Catherine and Philip sitting on the nursery floor beside her, and Louise and her brothers at the round table between the windows. How the light that streams in above the table shines on their faces, on my boys' curls, on the baby's little hands!

"Dear God, wilt thou not suffer me to take this picture with me into thy heaven?

"It grows colder. My hands can scarce hold the pen with which I trace these words in the darkness.

"Farewell Life. Welcome Death.

"My children, my little ones, good-by. Dear God, keep them—may—"

The manuscript closed abruptly. The good woman of the house had sealed it up religiously, as she found it on the little table.

CHAPTER XXI.

THE REVOLT.

IT was. midnight. The rain beat against the closed shutters, and the wind that swept round the house and shook the leafless branches of the trees outside wailed like a lost spirit.

Within, the fire had burned low and the lamplight fell on two pale faces, bent together over a yellow and blotted manuscript, traced in a hand almost illegible.

Philip La Tour and his wife were reading the last words of the dead—reading with difficulty, for tears had stained the paper, and the trembling hand had more than once refused to obey the guiding will, leaving words and sentences unfinished.

Amazement and horror, fierce indignation against the author of such wrongs, and boundless tenderness for the patient victim, struggled together in their hearts as they followed the record of those years of captivity ; until at last the mother's farewell words to the children of her love quite overcame her son, and bowing his head over the paper which her dying hands had touched, the strong man wept like a little child.

His wife mingled her tears with his, and with those tears all bitterness and heart-burning melted away, and the two whom man had put asunder felt once more that God had joined them together.

" My mother asks me to forgive her oppressor," Philip said after a long silence. " I may forego the desire for vengeance —I must, since she asks it but if the law is ever able to reach him, I ought to aid in bringing him to justice."

" You will, if that time ever comes," the wife replied ; " but there is little probability that his crimes will be punished in this world. During the last month, while you have been away, he has compelled many of those who have been attending the services at the hall to make a public confession of their "sin" and take their children from the school ;* but that is not the worst. Many of the Gentiles are going away, and the people think there will not be twenty of them left here in the spring. It seems as though Brigham Young will rule while he lives, and continue to be the tyrant that he has been, unless, as I said a good while ago, some of us right here gain courage to defy him."

" Jessie !" Her husband spoke quickly, and with the glow of a newly-formed resolution on his face. " To-morrow is Sunday. Will you go with me in the morning to the hall ?"

" You need not ask that. I will be only too glad to go —and what then ?"

" We will be called to account in less than two days, and that will give me an opportunity of defining my position."

" They will cut you off from the Church."

" Yes, without doubt ; but I shall not wait for that to— Jessie, I cannot put in words what I mean, but I will not delay the only reparation I can make you. From this hour no one shall ever come between us. Before another week ends everybody shall know that I *call* no other woman 'wife.' "

The hour so long waited for had come at last !—the hour

*See Appendix, Note R, page 353.

for the rending of his bonds, the beginning of a new life, and the hour in which to make tardy atonement for the wrongs of years.

Does the reader wonder at the wife who could accept this atonement without betraying by look or word any memory of the bitter past? Does it seem a thing incredible that in the first moments of reunion all the jealousy and heart-burning, the anguish and despair of those miserable years, should be buried out of sight?

It may be equally hard to understand how a man could speak without emotion of sending away a woman whom he had called wife for five years, and who had borne him a child ; but in the present case Philip knew that Ruth cared for nothing except his money, and that the gift of the house she lived in and of the means to support her and to buy all the pretty trifles she coveted, would easily reconcile her to the separation. Had she loved him, his task would have been a much harder one, and in his heart he was thankful that the woman chosen for him had proved incapable of love.

*   *   *   *   *   *   *

Morning dawned, serene and cloudless—the morning of the day on which Philip La Tour was to assert his newly-acquired freedom. When ten o'clock came, and the streets were filled with people on their way to the Mormon services in the various wards, he set out for the hall with his wife on his arm, and leading his little boy by the hand. Neighbors and acquaintances passed him as he turned in at the gate, and the policemen appointed to watch those who entered the forbidden portals were so close to him that he could have touched them with his hand, but for the first time in twenty years he was acting without reference to the will of another, and he scarcely noticed their presence.

Inside the small, plain building about fifty persons were

seated, awaiting the hour of service.   Nearly one third of
this number were recusant Mormons, chiefly women.

All eyes were upon Philip La Tour as he walked slowly
up the aisle to a seat in full view of the congregation. Had
he come alone it is probable that his former friends would
have misunderstood his motives, but a man who brought
his family with him to such a place could not be a spy—
this was what the faces of those who knew him expressed
as he took his seat among them.

As he passed out at the close of the services, the policemen placed themselves directly in his way, so that he was
compelled to speak to them and ask them to make room
for his wife.

They moved a couple of steps, and one of them made
a sign which he understood perfectly well, but which, in
his present frame of mind, did not disturb him in the
least.

Before noon the next day he was waited on by a committee of his brethren and informed that it had been thought
best to give him an opportunity to explain his extraordinary conduct. This was an unusual act of grace, as he
knew, but the way in which he improved it was not calculated to lead to its repetition.

In the strongest language at his command, he denounced
the system which enslaved all who embraced it, and which
taught treachery, rapine, murder, and every species of
crime as sacred duties.

His wife, who was present, defined her own position
with equal clearness, and the members of the committee
withdrew in silence, but with a look on their faces that
boded no good to the rebels.

In a few days they were both summoned to trial.   They
paid no attention to the summons, and the day after the
one set for their trial they received formal notice that they

were cut off from the Church of Latter Day Saints and delivered over to the buffetings of Satan.

"Free at last!" These were Jessie's first words when her husband finished reading the notice aloud. "Such liberty is worth any price. We ought not to think it too dearly bought, even if it costs life."

"It will not cost life," was the reply. "The day that I told you, more than three years ago, would surely come, is here. You know we are not the first who have been cut off, and our friends are still alive. Our enemies have the will to destroy us, and, for that matter, the power also; but Brigham Young knows that any more violence, in the present condition of affairs, would be certain to react upon himself; so we are quite safe—at least by daylight."

"That is what I was just going to speak about," interrupted the wife, who, full of courage where she alone was concerned, yet trembled for her husband. "I don't think you will be attacked by day, but you *must not* go out after dark. Only the night before you came home, Henry R—— was fired at by some person in the shadow of the trees beside his own gate."

Philip could not smile at his wife's fears. He knew, better than she, the vindictiveness of the despot against whom they had rebelled—knew also that if he could be "taken care of" in such a way that the act could not be traced directly to the Church authorities, his life would not be worth a moment's purchase; but he was no coward (though when he looked back on the past he called himself one), and he faced the dangers of his position with the utmost calmness.

In the mean time his separation from Ruth had become an accomplished fact, and he once more had a *home*.

In the domestic life of Utah that sacred word is a mockery, and none felt this more keenly than the man who had conscientiously sacrificed his own happiness and that of the dearly-loved wife of his youth on the altar of a false faith. It is true that his case was exceptional, and that the majority of his brethren who had embraced polygamy had done so from choice; yet even among this class there were many who repented of the step they had taken, and who would gladly have given all the promises of future exaltation which their religion held out to them for a little present peace.

Women are the greatest sufferers from polygamy, but men who transgress the laws of God and nature do not escape the penalties of those laws.

Philip La Tour, pure-minded and honorable in spite of Mormonism, and loving his wife with the first and strongest love of early manhood, had suffered intensely when he was made to believe that God required him to give another woman the same place he had given her; but he suffered still more, if possible, in the years that followed, and the first hour of real happiness he had known since his second marriage was when he sat down beside Jessie to tell her that he was free from all ties save that which bound him to her.

Danger and death might lie in his path, the friends of a lifetime might become his bitter foes, his riches might take wings, but none of these things moved him while he had the approval of his own conscience and the restored trust of the woman he loved.

Nor was he altogether without friends and sympathizers outside of his own family. A number of prominent citizens had already been cut off from the Church—some because they refused to pay the exorbitant sums demanded of them as tithing, others because they had engaged in mining, a pursuit which all good Saints were imperatively ordered to have nothing to do with, and still others because they had questioned the right of the Prophet " to dictate to them in all things both temporal and spiritual"—a right which he proclaimed publicly in the very words quoted, as vested in him by a decree of the Almighty.

These men who had been lately excommunicated formed a community by themselves. They were not so thoroughly freed from the prejudices of years as to be able to affiliate at once with the Gentiles, whom they had regarded for a lifetime as their natural enemies. Many of them also still clung to polygamy—probably, as has been said, because it clung to them, and they could not easily let it go.

With La Tour, however, the case was different. As a Mormon, he had conscientiously obeyed all the requirements of the Church because he believed them to be also the commands of God, but the uprooting of his faith in that system included a renunciation of all that grew out of it.

Polygamy and hatred of the Gentiles belonged to Mormonism, and were renounced with it ; there was nothing, therefore, to prevent either him or his wife from joining themselves to the little band of Christians who taught the doctrines of peace and good-will to men. In their communion, realizing at last that

> " He is a freeman whom the truth makes free,"

Philip found it possible at last to reconcile the claims of conscience with the dictates of reason.

CHAPTER XXII.

EPILOGUE.

THE summer of 1871. In a pleasant home in the Golden State, the abode of wealth and refined taste, a family group awaits the return of the master of the house. The lady, young and fair, is a stranger to us, but the two bright-eyed little ones who rush out upon the veranda with a clamorous welcome for "Papa" remind us of some one that we have seen before, and the gentleman they have captured and are dragging in-doors has a face that is familiar to us 'in spite of the changes which time has wrought.

It is Francis La Tour, at present the happy owner of a home which, we venture to say, fully realizes the dreams that cheered him in the days when he wielded pick and shovel in Chespar Gulch. He has been absent for a day only, though one would judge from the excitement caused by his arrival that he had just returned from a voyage around the world.

The boy and girl, one on either side, present their captive to mamma with delighted cries. La Tour salutes his wife in a very lover-like fashion for a man who has been ten years married, and as soon as he can succeed in bribing his small captors to leave him at liberty for a few moments, draws his wife's arm within his and leads her into the next room, out of hearing of the sharp ears of the two youngsters.

"What does Kenyon say?" the wife asked as soon as the door was closed.

" Just what you thought : that there is no more real liberty in Utah than there was ten years ago, and that there is not the shadow of a chance that any Mormon will be punished for such a small matter as killing a few people in obedience to counsel. He says that while he was in Salt Lake he never ventured on the street after dark—and you know Kenyon is not a coward."

" And Philip—is he still determined to stay ?"

" Yes. He says that his work is in Utah, and he will live and die there."

" He does not expect that the Government will enforce the laws, and make Utah as safe a residence as California ?"

" No, none of them seem to expect that ; but the Gentiles are coming in in great numbers this year, and if the mines of the Territory turn out as well as they promise to, the immigration is likely to be larger each succeeding year. He hopes, and so do others, that in ten years the Gentiles may be in the majority, and in that case they will soon have a new set of laws, and new men to administer them."

The wife shook her head sadly. " I am afraid it will not turn out as they hope," she said. " We used to hope for the same thing fifteen years ago, but there is no change for the better yet. My father's bones lie unburied in the cañon where they shot him, and I dare not think of my sister's fate ; but to whom can I go to demand the punishment of the men who murdered my father and carried off my sister ? I tell you, Brigham Young will rule while he lives, and die at last in his bed, and be eulogized even outside of the Mormon Church as one of the greatest men of the age. This is my prophecy, and time will prove it true."

" Nevertheless, I honor Philip for his determination to stay and fight out the battle with fraud and oppression, and I shall always be a coward in my own eyes if I do not go to his help."

"Francis! You don't mean that you would take us to Utah? You know it was not the fault of those who followed us that mother and I escaped with our lives."

"I know. But, my dear little wife, you have some one to protect you now, and you would be in no more danger than Jessie, who rebelled openly against the authority of the Prophet years ago. There is a change for the better by the incoming of the Gentiles, and even if the past is not punished the present is less dangerous."

One October day, three months after the above conversation, the cars landed Francis La Tour and his family at Salt Lake. It was during the Fall Conference, and the city was filled with Saints from the outlying settlements. The streets were crowded also with miners, who had come in from the surrounding camps to purchase their winter supplies, and the sleepy Mormon capital which Elsie La Tour remembered seemed transformed into a busy, bustling Western town. Their brother Philip's home was on a quiet street at some distance from the main thoroughfares, and to reach it they had to pass in sight of the Tabernacle. The afternoon services were over, and at least ten thousand people who had congregated in and around the building were slowly dispersing.

"Look at those faces!" Francis whispered to his wife. "There were brigands and cut-throats enough among the Mormons when I left them, over twenty years ago, but they must have received large accessions from those classes since."

In truth, it would have been a difficult matter to find anywhere among the same number of people a greater proportion of men whose faces expressed an ignorant and brutal ferocity; but there was a special cause just now for the scowls and black looks which had caught La Tour's attention. The United States Court, then in session, had undertaken the task of investigating a few of the most notorious crimes committed by the orders of the Church authorities, and a grand jury, composed of men not bound by an oath to obey the Prophet in all things, had been impaneled by the United States marshal to hear such evidence as could be procured. As a result of these proceedings, indictments for murder had already been found against many men in high places, and among these was the mayor of Salt Lake, who occupied the position of Second Counselor to the Prophet.

" The Gentiles think they can succeed in their undertaking," Philip said to his brother the day after his arrival, " but we who have once been in the Church know better. The power of the Prophet was never more absolute than it is to-day, though he is wise enough to change his methods. He knows that to resist the law openly would be the very worst thing for him just now, but his cunning makes him more than a match for the Federal authorities, and all that the courts are doing will only strengthen the Mormons in the end."

" I cannot understand that," Francis said.

" Wait a few months and you *will* understand," was the answer. " This people have money and influence enough to get everything which has been done here reversed, and in that way establish their plea that they are persecuted for conscience sake."

The next week brought still more exciting news. The Prophet himself had been indicted for complicity in a number of murders, and there were rumors on the street that he had been arrested and taken to Camp Douglas.

" At last !" exclaimed Francis, " that wretch is to be brought face to face with Justice."

" Don't be too sure of that," Philip said.   " He has not been taken to Camp Douglas.   He is under nominal arrest in his own house, and you will see soon enough what that means."

Francis did see ; for the Prophet continued to take daily airings in his private carriage to visit his friends, and to attend the weekly balls with which the Saints enliven the dullness of the winter season.   He was always accompanied, it is true, by the deputy marshal who was supposed to have him in charge, but that officer treated him with such marked deference that strangers doubtless supposed him to be the Prophet's valet.

The winter passed slowly away.   One hundred and twenty-nine Mormons, most of them men who held important Territorial offices, were under indictment for capital crimes ; but none of them languished in prison, for the sufficient reason that all the prisons in the Territory were under Mormon control.   A few were under nominal arrest ; that is to say, they occupied quarters in some of these Mormon prisons, in which they received hosts of sympathizing friends, and had parties given in their honor ; but by far the greater number were out on bail, pending an appeal which had been taken to the Supreme Court of the United States.

During the winter Francis La Tour occupied himself in collecting evidence against the Prophet, and though his brother assured him that his efforts were useless, he would not be discouraged.   The memory of his mother's wrongs was always present with him, and since he had met her enemy face to face he felt more determined than ever not to rest until the penalty of his crimes was meted out to him.

Spring came, and with it the anxiously expected decision of the Supreme Court.   Philip's prophecy proved correct in every particular. The grand jury which had found the indictments against the Prophet and his subordinates was declared illegal because impaneled by the United States marshal, and in less than a month the columns of the Eastern press teemed with strictures upon the conduct of the Federal officers in Utah who had been engaged in " persecuting" the Saints.

Meantime the Gentiles and those recusant Mormons who had aided them in their efforts to bring notorious criminals to justice felt the full force of the Prophet's wrath. It is true that men were no longer shot down on the streets in broad day ; but if the Danites were instructed to put any one out of the way by poison, or in any other quiet manner, they could do so without hindrance, as, no matter how suddenly or strangely a man might die, no inquiry was made as to the cause of his death. Moreover, now that the United States courts were powerless, all questions relating to the security of life or property were referred to the local courts, presided over by Mormon high priests, and the arbitrary decrees of the Prophet were clothed with legal forms and fulfilled to the letter by his sworn adherents, who held all the public offices in the Territory.

While matters were in this state, and at a time when Francis La Tour was beginning to question seriously the wisdom of the step he had taken in bringing his family to Utah, Elsie discovered, by pure accident, the whereabouts of her sister, who was dragging out a miserable life as the neglected and abused plural wife of a man high in the priesthood. This sister, of whom mention has been made in the beginning of the present chapter, had been forcibly detained when Elsie and her mother made their escape from the Territory, and her fate was that of many another unprotected girl who fell into the hands of the Mormon leaders.

" Poor Julia !" Elsie said sorrowfully to her husband, " I could wish that I had found her grave instead. She dares not talk with me about what she endures, but her face tells enough, even if I had not seen the miserable hut in which she lives."

Elsie saw little of her unhappy sister, who was not allowed to visit her Gentile relatives. She lived in the outskirts of the city, more than two miles from the handsome house which Francis La Tour had bought.

Elsie went there a few times, but as her visits seemed to distress the poor creature, they were gradually discontinued.

" Julia seems more unwilling than ever that I should see her," she said to her husband one evening, after she had driven out to the wretched cabin that her sister called home.

" I suppose that is because the contrast between your lot and hers makes her more unhappy," was the anwer.

" No, I do not think that is the reason. She looked frightened when I came in this afternoon. I dare say that brute had forbidden her to receive me, and I am almost certain now that he beats her when she disobeys him. There was a livid mark across her face to-day. She said she had fallen and hurt herself, but to me it looked exactly as though she had been struck in the face with a whip."

" If I were sure of that," Francis said, " I should not deny myself the pleasure of breaking my cane over the fellow's head when I meet him on the street."

" Oh, Francis !" His wife looked alarmed. " In this place it will not do to interfere, no matter how badly a man may treat his family. There is a better way, if Julia would only consent to it. She has no children, as you know— nothing to keep her here—and I am almost certain I could get her safely out of the Territory ; but she will not go."

A few days after this conversation Elsie heard, through a neighbor, that her sister was sick. No word had been sent to her, and she knew that in all probability her presence was not desired, but she started at once to go to her. When she reached the cabin a couple of women were standing in the doorway, and to her hurried inquiries one of them answered briefly,

" She is dead."

Dead ! Elsie clutched the broken palings to keep herself from falling. In that moment the years vanished away, and she saw, instead of the miserable wreck of womanhood that met her eyes when she last visited the cabin, the baby sister with sunny curls, and eyes like April violets, whose tiny hands she held while she took her first tottering steps. And now the tired feet had ended their pilgrimage of sorrow at the brink of the grave, when no one who loved her was near to stay the faltering steps. How she must have longed for human love in the hour of mortal weakness ! How she must have looked, through the mists of death for the sister who did not come !

" Why was I not sent for ?" she asked of the two women, whose stolid faces never changed. " I am her sister."

" Her husband was with her," was the only answer.

" He is not here now ?"

" No."

" Then let me come in ;" for both women still stood in the doorway, barring entrance.

" I'm sorry ma'am," one of them answered ; " but Brother Benson left strict orders not to let you in if you should come."

Elsie was alone. Her husband had not known of her coming, and with no help near she was forced to submit to this harsh edict and turn away without looking upon the face of the dead.

Weeks afterward, Philip La Tour told his brother the story of the poor creature's tragic fate as he had learned it from others. " I would not have Elsie know the truth for the world," he said ; " but there is not the least doubt that her sister died by poison. She was accused of breaking her covenants, and now, as in the past, an unsupported accusation is all that is needed in the case of one whose death is desired. The poor girl was weary of life, and consented, I am told, to take the poison.

" It is strange that the story should have been allowed to get out," Francis observed.

" Such reports circulate in whispers, and at last reach ears for which they were not intended," Philip answered ; " but a few years ago it would not have been thought necessary to keep a case of blood-atonement secret."

" I might have asked last year if something could not be done about it," Francis said ; " but I have learned a great deal since then."

" You will learn more before another year," replied Philip. " You can see already that while our local laws are made and administered by the priesthood, Brigham Young is the actual ruler of the Territory, and that the presence of the Gentiles and of the Federal officers has no effect except to cause the Danites to do secretly what they used to do openly."

*   *   *   *   *   *   *

Two more years passed, bringing no material changes to the La Tours. Francis, who had invested a large sum in the mines, found it necessary to stay in the Territory and give personal attention to the development of his property. Philip was as determined as ever to see the end of the conflict between theocratic despotism and republican ideas, and as Congress had lately passed a law which made it possible for the Federal judges to resume their duties, he began to hope, not that past crimes would be punished, but that present abuses might be checked in a measure. The Prophet had determined to break up Philip's business, but for once he failed in his undertaking. The money brought into the Territory by the Gentiles, as well as much that was taken out of the mines, helped to enrich the Saints (who sold freely to the outsiders, though they bought nothing of them), but at the same time it saved from ruin those ex-Mormon merchants who had been "delivered over to the buffetings of Satan." The miners were Philip's best customers, and he was a far richer man in 1875 than he was ten years earlier, when the Prophet declared that he should be blessed in basket and store.

His wife, too, had grown young again in the five years that had elapsed since the shadow was lifted from their hearthstone, and the bonny boy who was his mother's only comfort in the days to which she could not look back without a shudder, now led about a little blue-eyed sister, while a rosy baby claimed the cradle in the nursery.

Thus far the Prophet's curse had borne no fruit in their lives; and though at first Jessie always watched anxiously for her husband's return when business detained him after dark, her fears gradually died away, as year after year passed without any token that the Danites were shadowing him. Still it was not usual for Philip to be absent until nine o'clock without telling his wife where he might be found, and when, one evening in the summer of '76, ten o'clock came without bringing the sound of the well-known footstep for which the wife was listening, the old dread began to oppress her, and though she told herself over and over again that she was foolish and nervous, when the clock struck eleven she could bear her anxieties no longer. An errand-boy employed in the store slept at the house, and waking him she sent him for Francis. It was nearly twelve when his brother came, and still Philip had not returned.

"I will go out at once and search for him," Francis said.

"Where could you search?" the wife asked, as the hopelessness of such an attempt presented itself to her mind. "If harm has come to him, the police have acted the same part that they did in the Robinson murder. You could get no help from *them;* but I will not believe yet that anything has happened. I spent a terrible night once years ago, when he did not come home until daylight. He was called away to the house of a sick friend, and the boy that he sent to tell me never delivered the message. Most probably something of the same sort has occurred now."

Yet while she tried to speak hopefully her face was so white that Francis rose once more to go out into the street, saying, "I will find him, wherever he is." But before he finished speaking they heard the gate open, and in a moment more Philip entered.

"I have caused a great deal of anxiety, I fear," he said, as soon as the door closed behind him ; "but I could not help it, and it is just as well that Francis is here, for he is as much interested as I in what I have to tell.

"It was late when I left the office, but I thought I would stop in a few minutes to see Blanche. I have fancied for weeks that she looked badly, but as, thus far, she has always obeyed counsel, and refused to confide in any of us, I could not find out whether she was ill or in trouble. To-night I knocked two or three times, and not getting any answer I took the liberty to open the door and go directly to the sitting-room, where I thought I should be sure to find her. The hall lamp was burning, but there was no light in any other part of the house. I struck a light myself, and there on the floor of her sitting-room the poor child lay insensible. At first I thought her dead. Poor little Blanche! It might have been better for her if she had been."

"Why, Philip! What can you mean?" his wife asked with a shocked face.

"Wait and you will hear. There was no one in the house with her, as I found after calling repeatedly for her husband and the servant. I tried first to restore her by dashing water in her face, but failing in this I hunted up some more powerful remedies, and in a little while succeeded in bringing her back to consciousness. Her first attempt to talk to me, however, ended in a fit of hysterical sobbing, and it was an hour more before she was composed enough to answer my questions. Jessie knows how positive Blanche has always been in her belief that her husband would never take another wife, and I own I shared this belief for a long time; but two years ago, when the Prophet determined to force the whole people into polygamy, in order to outlaw those who had not committed other crimes, I began to tremble for my little sister's happiness, and of late I could not help seeing that a great change had come over her and her husband. It seems Blanche has known that a strong pressure was brought to bear upon her husband months ago, to wring a promise from him to take another wife. The Prophet had managed to tie up all Richard's money in his co-operative schemes, and of course he would never see a dollar of that again if he disobeyed counsel; but there was another cause—one that Blanche never learned anything about until to-night—which operated more powerfully than the fear of losing his money to bring him to the Prophet's terms.

"Richard knew all the facts about Van Wirt, Clive, and some others who died after being so roughly handled by the police at the City Hall, and though he would have prevented those murders if he had been a free agent, he feels now that he is involved in the crimes of the city authorities, and no doubt the law would take the same view of his case. Blanche did not mean to tell me all this, but her wretchedness had broken down her caution as well as her pride, and before she knew it she was telling me her troubles as freely as she used to when she was a little girl, and 'Brother Philip' took the place of father and mother both."

" I can guess the remainder of the story," Francis said.

Jessie was silent. Her head rested on her hand, and her face showed that the old wounds which the years had seemed to heal were reopened.

" You may not be able to guess all," Philip said in answer to his brother's remark. " It was easy enough to foresee, months ago, that Richard would eventually be forced into polygamy ; but it appears the Prophet made up his mind that Blanche deserved a special punishment for her obstinate refusal to consent to the marriage, and so it has been decreed that Richard shall take as his wife a servant girl that Blanche discharged last winter—a bold, forward piece, who spent half her time curling her hair and dressing up to attract Richard's notice—that is what poor Blanche told me to-night, forgetting that she gave a very different reason at the time for dismissing the girl."

" And has Blanche so little spirit that she will submit to such an arrangement ?" Francis asked.

" How can she help herself ?" Jessie said, speaking for the first time. " You forget the law under which we are living—the law which says, ' If a woman refuse to give other wives to her husband, he shall take them without her consent, and she shall be destroyed for her disobedience.' Blanche has refused her consent, but the marriage will take place all the same, and her punishment will come afterward."

"I will go to the Federal authorities in the morning," Francis said, rising hastily. "I will lodge information against Richard, and have this thing stopped."

"How will you stop it?" It was Philip who asked the question this time. "When the courts are powerless to punish a plural marriage after it has taken place, how can you expect them to prevent such marriages? We know of more than one wife who has gone to the United States Court in this city to beg that her husband's second marriage might be prevented, but the answer has always been, 'We can do nothing for you.' Neither you nor I nor the Federal authorities can prevent Richard from marrying that girl to-morrow; but I have thought it possible that we may save Blanche from the punishment that, as Jessie says, is to come afterward. The Prophet has decreed that, to make this punishment complete, the new wife is to be brought directly home and made the mistress of the house. If Blanche will only institute a suit for divorce as soon as the girl is brought there, I think the judge will be just enough to decide that she shall keep the house in which she lives."

"Maybe he will not grant the divorce. You say no one is punished for polygamy."

"True, because in the first place it is impossible to get proof, in court, of a polygamous marriage, which takes place in the Endowment House, and is witnessed only by those who are bound by an oath to divulge nothing; and in the second place it is probable that when the criminal is tried there will be men on the jury who are bound by a similar oath to convict nobody; but if Blanche asks for a divorce it will be easy enough to prove that she is entitled

to that, and the Federal judge, and not a Mormon jury, will
decide the case."

"All I have to say, then, is, that if Blanche does not
avail herself of the only remedy the law offers her, she
does not deserve our pity."

These were the elder brother's last words as he took his
leave of the others for the night. Two days afterward
Philip learned that the second marriage had taken place,
but the bride had not been brought home. Blanche,
who in this emergency developed a spirit which had been
latent during the happier years of her life, had barricaded
every door and window, and announced her determination
to hold possession of the place at all hazards.

"If a few more of the women in this Territory would
take such a course, polygamy would be broken up in less
than three years," Francis said.

"Wait a little and see how the thing ends," his brother
advised. "You may not be so sure, six months from
now, that her course is the best one."

For two weeks Blanche was the sole occupant of the
house she had fortified. At the end of that time she fell
sick, and the doors were opened to admit Jessie, who
nursed her tenderly, and would gladly have offered such
sympathy as Blanche manifested in her own hour of mortal pain, in that dark past which she could never forget.
But the nature once so sweet and tender was embittered
and hardened by misery and despair, and Blanche turned
a deaf ear to her sister's pitying words. She did not pray for
death, as Jessie had done, but she seemed to wish to live only
that she might see such punishment as they deserved visited
upon her husband and the girl who had supplanted her.

"The law cannot reach them yet," she said to Jessie,
"but I shall live to see the day when it will. I shall live
to see them both in prison, branded as felons."

" You do not wish to see your husband there ?" Jessie ventured to say.

" I have no husband." The face of the wronged wife grew livid, and her hands worked convulsively. " I cannot go on loving as—as some women do. My love had received its death-blow the night that Philip found me."

Blanche was soon to learn that the law which was powerless to punish a man for breaking his marriage vows was strong enough when used as an instrument of vengeance against a woman who refused to give other wives to her husband. In three weeks from the day of Richard Barney's second marriage, the house which his wife had called her home for nearly twenty years was sold, and Blanche received formal notice from the purchaser to vacate the premises.*

" I will never leave the house alive," she declared to Philip.

" You cannot hold possession after the place is sold," Philip answered. " The man who has bought it and paid for it has a right to his property."

" I did not expect *you* to turn against me," Blanche said bitterly.

" My poor girl ! You know your brothers would still be your friends if all the world should turn against you. I am only telling you the facts. The court on which you rely for help will send officers to eject you from the premises if you do not give up possession."

---

* Under the laws of Utah a wife has no right of dower; consequently, when she displeases her husband he can sell the house in which she lives, or deed it to a plural spouse, and turn her into the street. The occurrence related above came under the writer's personal observation in 1876.

But Blanche would not be convinced, and in spite of her brother's efforts to persuade her to leave, remained in the house until the purchaser procured a writ of ejectment, and she was removed by force.

In other days the Prophet would have called upon the Danites to enforce the law which declares that a woman who refuses to give other wives to her husband shall be destroyed, but now he found it wiser to make the officers of the United States Government the instruments of his will. The writ which turned the disobedient wife into the street was issued by a Federal judge, and served by a United States marshal. When, a few weeks later, Blanche applied for a divorce, the same judge granted it, and decreed her the munificent sum of *six dollars per month* as alimony, and in less than a year the husband was released altogether from the payment of alimony to the wife who had dared to rebel against polygamy. No blame, however, could be made to attach to the judge in this matter, for the husband, anticipating the suit for divorce, had put all his property out of his hands, and when the case came to trial any number of Mormon witnesses were found ready to testify that he received no salary for his services in the Co-operative Mercantile Institution, but was working out a debt.

In his heart the Prophet doubtless felt that he had little more need of the Danites, and it was a noticeable fact that about this time the older and more trusted ones— those who knew most of the dark deeds of former years— began to drop off. They were men advanced in years, whose death might naturally have been expected, and as they adhered to the teachings of the Church and called no physician in time of sickness, but depended instead on the ministrations of the elders who possessed the gift of healing, no one competent to decide whether or not death was due to natural causes was present in their last hours. It seemed as though the ruler of the people had made a compact with Death to keep his secrets for him.

But that ghostly ally, whom he had sought to propitiate by the sacrifice of his trusted adherents, at last laid his hand on the Prophet himself.

"The tyrant is dead! Thank God!" In these words Francis La Tour announced the event to his wife.

"He died peacefully in his bed, as I prophesied years ago; is it not so?" she asked.

"He died in his bed, that is true, but it could not have been a peaceful death."

"And he will be eulogized, as I said. Men whose words have weight with the nation will praise him as the founder of a commonwealth, as one who has turned the wilderness into a garden, and peopled this Territory with hardy and industrious immigrants. I can see in my mind the very sentences that will be inscribed in his praise, while the system that he built up is proving a heavier curse than ever to the people."

Elsie La Tour did not lay claim to the gift of prophecy, but her words proved true. And to-day, though the Prophet is dead, Mormonism lives, and is strengthening itself and enlarging its boundaries year by year. Its rule is absolute in Utah, and it holds the balance of power in the adjoining Territories. The potency of the system is felt in the halls of Congress, and while its high priests are boasting loudly that the nation *dares not* interfere with a religion that teaches treason and murder, thousands of European immigrants are being brought to Utah to take the oath of unquestioning obedience to the authority of the Church, and of perpetual enmity to the Government and people of the United States.

For nearly half a century the Mormon leaders have been industriously engaged in sowing the seeds of disloyalty to the Government and hatred to the nation. What will the harvest be ? Let our statesmen answer the question.

APPENDIX.

UTAH : 1870–1881.

THE year 1870 may properly be characterized as the beginning of regeneration in Utah, for it witnessed the completion of the Pacific Railroad and the commencement of mining.

It is true that prospecting had been carried on to a limited extent for seven years previous to that date, and in Little Cottonwood and Bingham cañons Gentile capitalists had expended thousands of dollars in the partial development of mining claims that promised well ; but the ignorance of many who had the business in hand with regard to the proper treatment of silver-lead ores, the scarcity of charcoal and coke for smelting purposes, and, above all, the want of means of transportation (for previous to 1868 there was no railroad within a thousand miles of Utah), combined to render the mines unprofitable.

The year 1870, however, witnessed many changes. The completion of the transcontinental railway brought the isolated " valleys of the mountains" into direct communication with the civilized world. With freight across the plains reduced from twenty-five cents to three cents per pound, the miners were no longer dependent upon the Saints for supplies, and the bullion which the smelters turned out could be shipped to the States at a handsome profit.

Immediately following these changes came the discovery of the Emma Mine and the publication to the world of the enormous mineral wealth of the Territory.

During the summer and autumn of 1870 the " stampede" to the new mining country was continuous, and in the spring of 1871 the Gentile residents of Utah numbered at least five thousand souls. The majority of these were, of course, miners ; but in Salt Lake City there were a goodly number of Gentile merchants and professional men who had brought their families with them, and Corinne, a railroad town laid out in 1869, had a population of twelve hundred, all of whom were Gentiles.

With so large a representation from the outside world in the Territory, and with railroad communication open between Utah and the States, the Prophet saw the wisdom of abandoning the shot-gun policy, adopted in former years, to keep miners out of the kingdom ; but he was by no means at the end of his resources.

Every possible obstacle was thrown in the way of the miners, and as the political and legislative, and to a great extent the judicial machinery of the Territory was altogether in Mormon hands, the " possible obstacles" were many.

In the winter of 1871-72 a *coup d'état* was planned to rid the Territory of its unwelcome guests. The Utah Legislature (composed wholly of Mormon high priests) passed an act imposing a tax of twenty per cent on the gross proceeds of the mines. This act, had it become a law, would have compelled every mine in the Territory to shut down, except possibly the Emma, which was producing ore to the amount of five thousand dollars per day.

The Gentile Governor, being invested with the power of an absolute veto, nipped this precious scheme in the bud ; but at every subsequent session of this inspired Legislature bills have been framed and presented having the same object in view—namely, the complete destruction of the mining interests of the Territory.

In the May number of *The North American Review*, Mr. George Q. Cannon, late Delegate from Utah to the House of Representatives, alludes to the current rumor of the above fact, and denies it.

Mr. Cannon is hereby referred to Governor Emery's veto of the bill to suppress the smelters in the Territory (*Journals of the Legislature for* 1876, page 261) and likewise to his veto of the bill levying a tax on the mines and a double tax on their products. (*Journal* for 1878, page 321.)

In that portion of Mr. Cannon's article which relates to the mineral development of the Territory, I find the following assertion :

" Every person was at liberty to do as he pleased about prospecting for or opening mines."

On the 16th day of October, 1869, an article appeared in the *Utah Magazine*, published in Salt Lake, advocating the opening of the mines that were known to exist in the Territory. This article was written by E. L. T. Harrison, editor of the magazine, and indorsed by Wm. S. Godbe, the publisher. Both Godbe and Harrison were immediately summoned to appear before the School of the Prophets, and there in the presence of two thousand of the elders of the Church, Harrison was asked to rise and explain how it was that he *dared* to write the article in question. His answer not being satisfactory to the ruling powers, he was formally summoned to trial before the High Council.

Wm. S. Godbe was next called upon to define his position, the test question asked him being : " Do you believe that President Young has the right to dictate to you in all things, both temporal and spiritual ?"

A negative answer to this question let loose a storm of wrath on Godbe's head, and he too received notice to appear before the Council.

On the following Wednesday the trial took place. The

two men, both of them possessed of more than ordinary intelligence and culture, and both well known then and now in business circles, were held to answer for the heinous crime of advocating the development of the mineral resources of the Territory, and were cut off from the Church and delivered over to the buffetings of Satan. George Q. Cannon acted as prosecutor for the Church on the occasion of the trial. And yet George Q. Cannon says that every person was at liberty to do as he pleased about prospecting for or opening mines !

And if Mormons could not venture to express the opinion that the Territory would be benefited by the development of the mines, much less could Gentiles venture to explore the mineral districts of Utah with safety to themselves. General P. E. Connor, the commanding officer at Fort Douglass in 1862–3–4, made the first mining locations in the Territory, and he was obliged to detail soldiers to protect the men engaged in working the mines.

As late as February, 1876, when the mining population of the Territory numbered more than five thousand, and the annual production of the mines amounted in value to six million dollars, the Legislature passed an act declaring that the smelters (who had built on unoccupied lands at some distance from any settlement), should be suppressed as public nuisances.

Governor Emery promptly vetoed this bill ; but the fact that it failed to become a law did not discourage its framers, who are still bent upon driving out the miners, and confident that they will some day succeed.

Meanwhile, in spite of all the obstacles thrown in its way, mining has become a paying industry. There are more than fifty organized mining districts in the Territory, with not far from one thousand producing mines, and an unlimited and constantly increasing number of " prospects," many of which promise well and are likely to become paying mines in the near future.

In 1876 Utah stood third on the list of bullion-producing States and Territories. To-day her rank should be still higher, for there has been a great increase in the number of paying mines since that date, and it is confidently expected that the bullion produced the present year will amount in value to ten million dollars.

Speaking from personal knowledge, obtained during nine years' residence in the midst of her mines, I have no hesitation whatever in saying that the mineral wealth of Utah is incalculable, and practically inexhaustible.

Take a single example.

Within the limits of a square mile, on the divide between two cañons known respectively as Big and Little Cottonwood, a few mines, only partially developed, have produced silver-lead ores to the amount of *twenty million dollars* in the last eight years, and from present indications the same mines are likely to be largely productive for many years to come.

In the vicinity of these mines, but on the opposite side of the range, is the Ontario, producing gold and silver-bearing ores. This mine has for four years past paid regular monthly dividends, aggregating three million dollars over and above all expenses.

On the west side of Salt Lake valley is the Oquirrh range, in which the first mineral discoveries were made in 1863, by parties attached to General Connor's command. The mines in this range contained immense bodies of low-grade smelting ores—that is, lead ores carrying a very small percentage of silver. These mines were industriously worked, and yielded large profits to their owners until the fall in lead.

When that metal was quoted in New York at prices that

would not pay for shipment, the plucky owners of the lead mines, instead of sitting down in despair, began to look around for something else, and the result was that the Oquirrh range was found to be ribbed with gold. Both quartz and placer mining have already become important industries in the Oquirrh cañons, and the gold bricks that are shipped monthly to Salt Lake are pleasant reminders of old times to the " Forty-niners" in that city.

The southern portion of our Territory was the last to admit the miner—the last, indeed, to yield in any way to the pressure of civilization. Remote from railroads, hemmed in by mountains, its valleys inhabited by a population ignorant and fanatical to the last degree, with a large sprinkling of notorious criminals who had fled from the north at the first intimation that the Government proposed to investigate the dark deeds of the past twenty years, southern Utah possessed few attractions for the Gentile immigrant.

Five years ago, however, the irrepressible prospector, to whom difficulty and danger are attractions in and of themselves, began to penetrate the cañons and climb the mountains of the South, and at the present date the largest bodies of silver-lead ore yet discovered in the Territory, or perhaps in the world, are being opened up in that section.

Late explorations have also convinced experienced miners that these immense ore bodies are in a mineral belt which extends from Colorado through Utah and southern Nevada to the coast, and at the present writing numerous prospecting parties are outfitting here for an exploring expedition, which they believe will result in opening up new and rich mining districts along the line which separates Utah from Colorado.

But gold, silver, and lead are by no means the only mineral products of Utah. Copper ores are abundant;

iron exists in immense quantities ; bismuth and cinnabar are found in certain districts ; coal abounds in different parts of the Territory ; there is salt enough to supply this world, and sulphur sufficient to meet all demands in a certain quarter in the next.

Fire-clay is plentiful ; also potter's clay ; there is excellent building-stone, including granite and marble of a superior quality. Black lead, alum, borax, and gypsum are disseminated throughout the Territory, and in the southern districts are immense beds of paraffine.

Should the reader be disposed to ask why the mineral wealth of Utah fails to attract attention, or why capitalists are slow to make investments in the Territory, the answer is easily found :—

The mines are under the ban of the priesthood, and as Church and State are here one and inseparable, those who are aware of the existing condition of affairs decline to place themselves under the rule of the Mormon hierarchy. In a word, the un-American aspect of the Territory, viewed both from a social and a political standpoint, deters American citizens from either making it their home or investing their money in its mines.

It is from this cause, and this alone, that Territories which were settled ten years later than Utah have vastly outstripped her, and become prosperous States, while her resources remain undeveloped. Is it, then, a thing to be wondered at, that the non-Mormon residents of Utah have determined upon organized and unswerving opposition to priestly rule, or that they petition Congress year after year for such legislation as will secure to them the common rights of American citizens ?

I have alluded elsewhere to the doings of the Utah Legislature.

As before stated, this Legislature is composed of thirty-nine Mormon high priests, thirty-six of whom are living in polygamy. These law-makers hold their offices year after year, seldom dying and never resigning. I say their *offices*, for nearly every one of them fills two or three official positions besides that of member of the Legislature.

They are supposed to be elected by the people, but the election is a farce which might easily be dispensed with. Good Mormons, who thought they were stating a fact which spoke well for their people, have said to me,

" The election is only a form ; we are all of one mind."

The marked ballots which are placed in the hands of the voters by the priesthood are understood by them as a notice that Brother So-and-so has been appointed to a certain office by the President of the Church, and that ends the matter.

The Head of the Church selects a man to fill a certain position, and the people have nothing to say ; indeed, the majority of them have grown so accustomed to the yoke that they do not *wish* to have anything to say.

When Hooper, a monogamist, was superseded as Delegate to Congress by Cannon, the husband of four wives, Brigham Young said,

" I have chosen Brother Cannon to represent us in Congress, because I mean to cram polygamy down the throats of the American people."

Mr. Cannon stamps this statement, which has been often made, as a fabrication. A gentleman who was present when the Prophet made use of this expression said to me only a few hours ago, that it was one of the things which Cannon should not have attempted to deny, inasmuch as it was a part of a boastful and intemperate address which Brigham Young delivered in the Tabernacle in the hearing of many hundreds. As I was a resident of Salt Lake at the time, and heard of it, probably the same day that it was used, from several parties, I am forced to conclude that Mr. Cannon's memory has again proved treacherous.

Delegate Cannon was *selected* by the Prophet; the burlesque called an " election" was not in the least necessary, except for outside effect.

In like manner the members of the Legislature have been chosen to fill their present positions, and they are the servants, not of the people they are supposed to represent, but of the Head of the Church, who can remove them at pleasure should they prove disobedient. They meet once in two years, the Government pays them their *per diem* and mileage, and they spend forty days legislating industriously in the interests of the Church.

If it were not for the absolute veto power possessed by the Governor, they would have legislated the Gentiles out of the Territory long ago. As it is, they are hindered somewhat in their laudable efforts to purify Zion, but occasionally they accomplish something that pays them for years of toil and disappointment.

For example, in 1872 they passed an act depriving the first wife of her dower, and of any and all claims upon the property or earnings of her husband. This act, in some way not yet understood by the Gentile residents, obtained the Governor's approval and became a law; consequently any man may sell his home, put his wife and children on the street, and leave them to shift for themselves. In Mormon families this power which the husband is known to possess is held as a sword over the head of a wife who is disposed to protest against the introduction of a plural into the household.

During the same session of the Legislature a number of bills equally outrageous were vetoed by the Governor; but the legislators, nothing daunted, returned to the charge the next session, and when the Governor vetoed their pet measures they passed them over his head by what they called a joint resolution.

It is true the organic act of the Territory impaired the efficacy of these joint resolutions, but when circumstances made it possible for them to carry out their own behests they pursued the even tenor of their way, unhindered by organic acts or anything else.

For instance, one of the acts passed by joint resolution was an appropriation bill which turned the entire contents of the treasury over to the Mormon leaders ; and as the auditor and treasurer were both good Saints, who dared not disobey counsel, the provisions of this bill, which the Governor had disapproved in a most emphatic message, were carried out to the letter, and the brethren emptied the treasury in an astonishingly short space of time.

In 1876 a bill was passed designed to shield all the perpetrators of crimes committed in obedience to counsel during Utah's darkest days. By the provisions of this act all murders committed more than ten years ago were declared outlawed, and prosecution was forever barred.

The Governor vetoed the bill, in a message couched in very decisive language, but the brethren betrayed no consciousness of defeat. With witnesses and jurors entirely under their control, they felt safe for the present, and they had faith in the future.

Previous to 1869 the probate courts, presided over by some of the most ignorant and fanatical members of the priesthood, claimed both common law and chancery jurisdiction, and the district courts, presided over by judges appointed by the Federal Government, might as well have been located in the moon.

Many of the United States judges were driven from the Territory, others were shamefully insulted and maltreated, and under the most favorable circumstances the court had no power to enforce its decrees.

In 1869, however, two judges were appointed who soon convinced the people that they had come to stay, and that all the power conferred on the district courts by the organic act of the Territory would be claimed and exercised. These judges—C. M. Hawley, of Illinois, and O. F. Strickland, of Michigan—were lawyers of solid attainments, and possessed likewise of judicial firmness, and of a proper sense of their obligations to the Government they represented. From the day on which they ascended the bench the district courts began to afford redress to the victims of Mormon tyranny, and a panic seized upon the blood-stained wretches who were known as the Destroying Angels of the Church.

In August, 1870, Chief Justice J. B. McKean arrived in Utah. To-day, after death has embalmed his virtues and silenced his calumniators; to-day, when his memory is enshrined in the hearts of thousands as that of a spotless Christian, an incorruptible judge, the friend of the oppressed, the unswerving foe of wrong, it is possible to review impartially the years of his administration—years from which the smoke of battle has barely cleared away.

The year previous to Judge McKean's appointment, Associate Justices Hawley and Strickland, with a full knowledge of the manner in which the execution of the law had been defeated by grand and petit juries composed of Mormons who recognized no law except the will of the Prophet, had issued orders to the United States marshal to impanel juries in their respective districts. In conformity with the order of court, United States marshal M. S. Patrick proceeded to summon grand and petit juries composed of Gentiles and recusant Mormons of known integrity. The Saints, through their legal advisers, objected to these juries as not having been impaneled according to the laws of Utah. · Chief Justice McKean rendered an able decision, sustaining the course taken by his associates, and at the terms of court held in the different judicial districts during 1870 and 1871 the juries impaneled by the United States marshal were composed altogether of Gentiles and seceders from the Mormon Church.

During these years one hundred and twenty-nine persons were indicted for the commission of murders, unspeakable mutilations, and other atrocious crimes.

Brigham Young was indicted for complicity in a number of murders. He was not, however, imprisoned, but was allowed to remain in his own house under surveillance.

Four indictments for murder were found against D. H. Wells, mayor of Salt Lake, but he was allowed to remain at large upon giving bonds to the amount of fifty thousand dollars.

In the mean time an appeal from the decision of the Supreme Court of the Territory had been taken to the Supreme Court of the United States, and in the spring of 1872 a decision was rendered *reversing the decision* which had been rendered by Judges McKean and Hawley, and concurred in by Judge Strickland.

The Mormons were triumphant. Their Prophet assured them that Heaven had interposed in their behalf, and defeated their enemies. The district courts were again powerless, and the probate courts claimed and exercised the jurisdiction which they had assumed for twenty years past.

Judicial affairs in the Territory remained in this state until June, 1874, when the passage of the Poland Bill by Congress defined the status of the probate courts, reaffirmed the chancery and common law jurisdiction of the district courts, and gave a jury law, clumsy and inefficient, it is true, but still a little better than none.

This jury law, which is still in force at the present writing, provides that the probate judge (always a Mormon priest), shall select one hundred names, and the clerk of the district court one hundred names, and that these two hundred names shall be written upon separate slips of paper and thrown into a box. From this box the United States marshal draws, in open court, a sufficient number of names to constitute a panel. The names drawn are Mormon or Gentile, as it may happen, but when the jurors are challenged for cause, chance no longer rules. The Gentile jurors are men who read, and also men who have some regard for the sanctity of a judicial oath; hence it happens that most of them, upon examination, will admit that they have read or heard of the case in hand. The Mormon jurors, on the contrary, regard no oath as binding which conflicts with their Endowment oath. Of course, if a brother Saint is to be tried, it is their duty to get on the jury and save him, and it is edifying to observe the uniformity with which they swear that they have never heard or read of a case which has filled the newspapers and been publicly commented upon by all classes for months and years. It is due to the causes indicated that the juries impaneled to try notorious Mormon criminals are almost always Mormons, who are bound to acquit the accused, even in the face of the most positive evidence. This, too, has a bearing upon Representative Cannon's article.

In spite of the difficulties which they foresaw as consequences of the partial and imperfect provisions of the Poland Bill, the United States judges once more entered upon their appropriate duties, and although (owing to the features of the jury law mentioned above) it was seldom possible to convict a Mormon of any crime, the fact that those who had so long defied the law were now held amenable to it acted as a wholesome restraint, and the property and lives of Gentiles and apostates became comparatively safe.

In March, 1875, Brigham Young, for refusing to comply with an order of the Third District Court, was adjudged guilty of contempt, and Chief Justice McKean sentenced him to twenty-four hours' imprisonment therefor. In obedience to the mandate of the court, the United States marshal conveyed the Prophet to the penitentiary, four miles south of Salt Lake City, the only prison in the Territory not in Mormon hands.

This penitentiary, which is United States property, is every way worthy the pencil of Nast. While Brigham Young filled the office of Governor of Utah, Congress appropriated thirty thousand dollars to build a United States penitentiary in the Territory. The money went where a great deal of money went in those days—namely, into the Prophet's coffers—and a few score of poor Saints were allowed, as a special favor, to work out their arrears of tithing by making adobes from the mud of the penitentiary quarter-section, and building with them a prison, which the Government was expected to regard as an equivalent for the thirty thousand dollars.

The result of their labors was an adobe wall which an enterprising woodchuck could dig through in two hours. This wall incloses an acre of ground, in the center of which was a species of dug-out divided into half a dozen compartments.

When the United States marshal took possession of the premises in 1871 he found nothing inside the walls except a hole in the ground, Rockwood, the Mormon warden, having carried off the roof of the dug-out and the bricks which sustained it.

The marshal had no funds for building penitentiaries, but Congress, when the facts were laid before that body, appropriated a small sum to erect a block-house, a building better fitted for a sheep-corral than for the purpose it was intended to serve.

Outside the walls and immediately adjoining them stands the warden's house, a rickety three-story building which Rockwood, the Mormon incumbent, used for years as a harem for his numerous wives.

To this place the Mormon Prophet was brought on a certain afternoon in March, 1875, in the custody of the United States marshal.

The Gentiles had at last laid an impious hand upon the Lord's anointed! The whole city was in an uproar. A procession of about twenty carriages followed the one in which the Prophet rode, but on reaching the penitentiary gates the occupants of these carriages were informed that they could not be admitted.

A little later in the afternoon two wagon-loads of arms and ammunition were brought out to Brigham's factory, about half a mile from the penitentiary, and when darkness began to settle down upon the valley, seven hundred armed men, some on horseback, some on foot, surrounded the prison walls and the warden's house, bent upon rescuing the Prophet at any cost.

The warden had fourteen prisoners inside the walls, and only two guards to aid him. He had besides, in an upper room, his wife and his little children, one of them a baby only a few weeks old.

The threatening demonstrations outside increased, but fortunately neither the prisoner nor his would-be rescuers had any idea of the weakness of the garrison.

The Prophet, in consideration of his age and infirmities, had been allowed by the marshal to spend the night in the warden's office. Early in the evening one of his own servants, who had a pass from the marshal, was admitted with the prisoner's mail. By this time the armed mob were within a few feet of the doors and windows. The warden, as he returned from viewing the situation, was asked by the Prophet what he thought of the demonstration outside.

" I think," was the reply, " that a good many of those fellows stand a fair chance of getting killed. Every man I have is at his post, well armed, and with orders to fire upon the first one who advances a step nearer."

The Prophet's notorious cowardice manifested itself in an instant. He was in the hands of his enemies, and held too as a hostage for the good behavior of his followers—so his fears caused him to think—and with a white face and a shaking voice he exclaimed,

" Don't let us have any bloodshed ! I will order them to disperse."

And turning to his retainer, he added,

" Go out and tell the men I wish them to fall back and remain quiet."

The order was given and obeyed. The mob withdrew, and though a mounted patrol, composed of the Prophet's most trusted adherents, continued to pass and repass until sunrise, there were no further hostile demonstrations.

At the expiration of his twenty-four hours' sentence, the Prophet was escorted home by a portion of the armed crowd who had remained in the vicinity of the prison.

Days passed. The sun rose and set as usual. No convulsion of nature indicated that the Gentile court had called down the vengeance of Heaven by its daring act ; but just as the loyal portion of the community began to hope that the example of official firmness which the people had witnessed would cause them to respect the majesty of the law, word came from Washington that the President, influenced by considerations which Utah Gentiles do not understand to this day, had deposed the incorruptible judge, whose only fault was the faithful and fearless performance of duty.

The Saints were again triumphant, and the moral effect of the President's unwise action is still felt among us, though years have passed away, and Judge McKean has gone to a world where all wrongs are righted.

The history of the United States courts in Utah from that day to this is a history of futile efforts, of seeming success and real defeat, whenever they have attempted to investigate and punish the crimes of the Mormon priesthood.

In three instances only has conviction been secured when the crimes sought to be punished have been committed in obedience to counsel! In 1876 John D. Lee was sentenced to death for his share in the Mountain Meadows massacre, and in March of the following year his sentence was executed; but Lee's conviction and execution *would have been impossible if Brigham Young had not determined to sacrifice this man to save himself.* And Representative Cannon's article in the *North American* accordingly allows the responsibility of " this dreadful massacre" to rest upon Lee's shoulders.

I am at a loss to determine the reasons which have led Mr. Cannon to allude to a matter that, for his own sake and the sake of his people, should have been kept in the background.

In 1874 several persons implicated in the Mountain Meadows butchery were indicted for murder, and among them Bishop (also Colonel) Dame of Parowan, a town in Southern Utah. I saw Dame while in the hands of the officers of the law. I had then recently furnished an article to one of the Washington papers, giving an account of the massacre, and Dame, aware of this fact, asked :

" Did you say anything about me ?"

" No," was the answer.

Dame. " Do you think me guilty ?"

The Writer. " I shall wait to hear the evidence before forming an opinion as to your guilt."

Dame. " Before God, madam, I am innocent. I did not give the order for the massacre, and I am not responsible for the orders that were passed over my head."

Dame, it will be remembered, was the *superior officer* of John D. Lee, who was made a scapegoat by the Mormon leaders, and sacrificed to save the real instigators of the massacre. The orders which were, as Dame said, " passed over his head," must have emanated from *his* superior officers. Lee is in his grave, but his dying confession, which has been abundantly corroborated by the testimony of old residents of the Territory, is extant, and contains accusations that will not down, even at the bidding of ex-Delegate Cannon.

The following are some of Lee's dying statements :

" The Mountain Meadow Massacre was the result of the direct teachings of Brigham Young, and it was done by the order of those high in authority in the Mormon community. After the massacre I was sent to Brigham Young to make a report of it. I went and *told him all.* I said, ' Sustain me, or release me from my endowment oath to avenge the blood of the prophets.'

" Brigham sent me away, telling me he would commune with God and let me know the result. The next morning I went back to him and he said : ' Brother Lee, the people did just right—only they were a little too hasty. I have evidence from God that the act was right. I sustain you and the brethren in all that you did. All I fear is treachery on the part of the brethren. Go home, tell the brethren I sustain them ; and keep all as secret as the grave. Write me a letter throwing the blame on the Indians, and I will report it to the government as an Indian massacre.'*

" Young was fully satisfied with me then and for years afterwards. He gave me three wives after that, and appointed me Probate Judge of Washington County. Nothing but cowardice has made him desert me now."

" It was the first plan to have none but Indians take part in the massacre, but as William C. Stewart, Joel White, and Benjamin Arthur were coming to the Meadows on Wednesday night they met young Aden and another man from the emigrants' camp going to Cedar City for help. They told of the Indian attack and asked aid from the settlers. The only reply was a shot from Stewart which killed Aden. The other man, who was wounded by White and Arthur, escaped and carried word to the emigrants that the whites had come to help the Indians. After that the authorities said there was no safety except in killing all who could talk."

Lee gives the names of many men holding official positions in the Nauvoo Legion and in the Church, who were leaders in the bloody work. Five of these men, Bishops and Presidents of Stakes of Zion, fled to the mountains as soon as it was known that the massacre would be investigated, and remained in hiding until after Lee's execution. Should any person be disposed to ask why Lee was the only one of the fifty-eight white men engaged in the massacre who was ever brought to trial, I refer him for an answer to the prosecuting attorney at the time of the Lee trial.

Three of the men whose names are conspicuous among the Mountain Meadow murderers—Haight, Higbee, and

---

* Brigham Young was at that time Governor of Utah and Indian Agent.

Stewart—are still hiding from justice, remaining much of the time in the mountains, but occasionally visiting those Mormon settlements in which there are no Gentile residents to give information against them.   I am informed by the judge who tried and sentenced Lee that these men might have been taken at any time during the past five years if means had been provided for their capture, but as the general government *does* not, and the Territorial authorities *will* not furnish money to defray the expenses of arresting them, it is not probable that they will ever be held to answer for the atrocious crime committed by them in obedience to the " council" of their spiritual teachers.

In the same year George Reynolds was convicted of polygamy and sentenced to imprisonment in the penitentiary, but the execution of his sentence was delayed more than two years by an appeal to the Supreme Court of the United States ; and meanwhile he continued to live openly with his plural wife, and was elected to one or more municipal offices by his admiring fellow-saints.

In the spring of 1879 one John Miles was convicted of the same offense, but the convict is still at large, and happy in the belief that his appeal to the Supreme Court will result favorably.   This completes the list of convictions.

Mr. Cannon's statements with regard to the testimony of parties traveling through Utah, to the " remarkable security of life and property there," should be qualified somewhat.   A good many travelers who attempted to cross the Territory previous to 1870 are not now in a condition to give testimony, as, for example, the Aiken party, robbed and murdered by the Danites ; the party murdered in Kimball's barn ; and many others.

On page 460 of *The North American Review*, Mr. Cannon says : " The whole foundation of the charge about ' blood-atonement' is that the people believe in the Biblical doctrine that men who commit murder, adultery, and other gross crimes, should be executed."

The following affidavit may serve to show just how the doctrine of "blood-atonement" is understood by Mr. Cannon himself.

" UNITED STATES OF AMERICA, ⎫
       TERRITORY OF UTAH,   ⎬ *ss. :*
    COUNTY OF SALT LAKE,   ⎭

" Adolph Razins, a citizen of the United States, resident in said Territory and County, deposes and says that on or about the first day of March A.D. 1855, at the City of Salt Lake, one George Q. Cannon told affiant that according to the doctrine of blood-atonement as believed, understood, and practised in and by the Church of Latter Day Saints, or Mormons, it was, and always is the duty of each and every member of said Church to shed the blood of his neighbor for salvation's sake. That is to say, the said George Q. Cannon did at the time aforesaid attempt to impress upon the mind of this affiant that when any co-religionist was thought to be in a state of sinfulness, or disobedience to said Church, its doctrines and priesthood, it was then and in that case the justifiable privilege and duty of any other co-religionist to kill such offender. And having argued and explained to affiant the said doctrine of blood-atonement, the said George Q. Cannon did then and there inform affiant that Almon W. Babbitt, Secretary of Utah Territory, had transgressed the laws of said Church, and had disobeyed the commands of its President in divers ways ; and that for such transgression and disobedience, the blood of the said Almon W. Babbitt should and must be shed, to redeem and save his soul from sin. That thereupon the said George Q. Cannon told affiant that said Almon W. Babbitt was then, in March, 1855, intending to go from

Salt Lake City to Washington, D. C., advising and urging affiant to accompany said Babbitt on the journey as aforesaid, and on the journey to shed the blood of the said Almon W. Babbitt, according and in obedience to the teachings of said Church. The affiant then and there earnestly and conscientiously refused to commit or have any part in the commission of the murder so advised and counseled by the said George Q. Cannon. Affiant further says that he did accompany the said Almon W. Babbitt to Washington, D. C., but did not return to Utah with him. That afterwards, in the summer of 1856, the said Almon W. Babbitt was assassinated on his return from Washington, and this affiant believes said assassination was an act done in accordance with the laws or doctrines of said Church and by agents of said Church, instigated thereto by the advice and counsel of George Q. Cannon as aforesaid, and other persons in the authority of said Church. Affiant says that in March, 1855, as aforesaid, he was a member of the Church of Jesus Christ of Latter Day Saints, or Mormons, as hereinbefore stated, and that said George Q. Cannon was a member of said Church holding office in its priesthood at the same time. That the said George Q. Cannon is the same person who is now Delegate in the House of Representatives from the Territory of Utah, in the Congress of the United States. And further deponent saith not.

" A. RAZINS.

" Subscribed and sworn to,)
   before me, this 9th day }
    of March, A.D. 1874,)

" ALFRED S. GOULD,
"*Clerk, Supreme Court of Utah Territory.*"

> U. S. of America.
> Supreme Court.
> Terr. of Utah.

It is not my purpose to answer in detail the article containing Mr. Cannon's statements. In Utah, it needs no answer, for no person who has resided here for any length of time can be deceived by it. Outside of the Territory, however, the history of the "peculiar people" of these valleys is not so well known as to preclude the possibility of anybody's receiving a wrong impression. It may be well, on this account, to notice one more of Mr. Cannon's positive assertions and see what foundation it has.

Mr. Cannon says (page 458), "For many years after the settlement of Utah, not a liquor saloon existed in the Territory." The ex-Delegate's memory is certainly at fault, or possibly the places in which liquor was sold were not called "saloons" in the days to which he refers.

What are the facts? In 1850, just three years after the Prophet took possession of Salt Lake Valley "in the name of the Lord," the business of distilling whiskey from the grain raised in the valley was commenced. The next year, 1851, a person named Moon, a good saint, and ranking high in the priesthood, established a distillery in the First Ward in this city, and another saint, Badley by name, started the same business in the Eleventh Ward. Currency was scarce at the time, and the usual method of laying in a supply of whiskey was to take a certain number of bushels of grain to the distillery and barter the same for spirits. Moon and Badley continued in business until about 1855, and were growing rich. The Prophet, who had a keen eye to business, even in those days, was not slow to perceive that the money these men were making might as well be made by the Church. Accordingly, both Moon and Badley were sent on missions, and their distilleries were seized and appropriated by the city authorities. Then as now, Church and State in Utah were one and inseparable, and the Mayor and City Council were creatures of the Prophet. The Church, as represented by the city authorities, enjoyed a monopoly of the liquor business for more than ten years, and coined money out of it. When Gentile liquor dealers first came to Salt Lake, the city fathers, not relishing the idea of competition in a business which they had found so profitable, sought to drive them away, first by demanding exorbitant licenses, and afterward by sending the police to raid the saloons. Englebrecht, a dealer whose conflict with the city authorities became somewhat notorious through a suit which was carried to the Supreme Court of the United States, had upwards of twenty thousand dollars' worth of liquor emptied into the streets at one time by Mormon policemen.

After the days of monopoly were over the Church still continued in the liquor business. The present writer well remembers some windows on Main Street in this city, which used to be ornamented with the inscription " Holiness To The Lord" surmounted by something intended as a symbol of the All-seeing eye. In these windows, and directly below the inscription named, stood an array of bottles labeled severally : " Old Tom Gin," " Honey Dew Whiskey," " Put Up Expressly For Zion's Co-operative Mercantile Institution."

We turn now from the consideration of Mormon peculiarities to a retrospect of the social and moral progress of the people of Utah within the last decade, under the zealous labors of the " Gentiles." Christian teachers and laborers of every name and of no name, filled with pity for the masses, whose condition even to-day is unspeakably wretched, have worked faithfully and earnestly to raise the fallen, to rescue the victims of priestly tyranny, to succor the distressed, and above all to save the children, the innocent sufferers for the sins of others. It would be asserting too much to say that they have accomplished all they hoped to, but they have done a great work.

The Mormon leaders proclaim to the world that the Gentiles in the Territory are "carpet-baggers," "adventurers," and "broken-down political hacks," whose only object is to drive out the Saints and seize their homes.

This senseless cry is sometimes taken up by the Eastern press, and I have seen similar charges in the columns of the leading papers of the United States within the past four years.

Let the facts speak for themselves. These Gentiles, who constitute a little more than one tenth of the population, own mines which produce six millions annually, and mills and smelters aggregating in value many hundred thousands of dollars. Only one of the nine banking-houses in the Territory is in Mormon hands ; all the others are owned by Gentiles. Many of the most elegant private residences in Salt Lake belong to Gentiles, from whom more than one fourth of the revenue of the city is derived. The Gentiles have built and endowed three hospitals, the only ones in the Territory. They own many substantial church and school buildings, and conduct the only schools in which free tuition can be obtained.

There are hundreds of Gentile merchants in Utah who have invested large sums in their business, and the Gentile lawyers and physicians of Salt Lake are gentlemen who would rank high in their respective professions in any city in the world.

I subjoin here a brief sketch of the different non-Mormon religious bodies in Utah, and of the work accomplished by them within the past ten years. I have taken the utmost pains to procure a careful and trustworthy account of the rise and progress of this work, and I commend the following pages to all who have been accustomed to regard the Gentile population of Utah as composed chiefly of adventurers.

CONGREGATIONAL CHURCH, SALT LAKE CITY.

This is the youngest, and yet, in one sense, the oldest church in the city. In its present form it was organized in May, 1874, and yet it claims connection with a work that was started nine years before this, and an organization that antedates all the churches of Utah.

In January, 1865, the Rev. Norman McLeod came to this city by the invitation of several prominent Gentiles and the Young Men's Literary Association. He labored under the auspices of the American Home Missionary Society, and at first met with great success. A society was organized, with such men for trustees as Major C. H. Hempstead, Chief Justice John Titus, General P. E. Connor, and others.

He organized his society and Sunday-school in the building known as Daft's Hall, on Main Street, provided for him by the Young Men's Literary Association.

A lot was secured and a chapel built known as Independence Hall. This was the first rallying-point of the Gentiles in Utah.

In the spring of 1866 Mr. McLeod went East to secure funds for the erection of a larger chapel. During his absence his Sunday-school superintendent, Dr. J. K. Robinson, was assassinated as described in this book, and Mr. McLeod was warned not to return. So the work was suspended for several years. Independence Hall was used in the mean time, first by the Episcopalians and then by. the Methodists.

In May, 1872, Mr. McLeod returned, and began the work anew, but the old hostility manifesting itself, he remained but a year, and the work was again suspended for six months.

On Christmas, 1873, the Rev. Walter M. Barrows arrived from the East, having been sent here by the American Home Missionary Society. He preached the first sermon in Independence Hall January 18th, 1874. Beginning with only four or five families, he was yet able, on the 23d of May of the same year, to organize a church of twenty-four members.

This is now one of the strongest societies in the city. The church owns a large and valuable lot on Third South Street, and on the rear of this lot is a comfortable chapel in which they worship at present. If the society continues to grow as rapidly as it has during the past few months, a new church building will be a necessity.

SALT LAKE ACADEMY.

Mr. Barrows early became impressed with the fact that mission work in Utah resembled that in foreign lands, and that the same reasons which influence the missionaries in Japan and India to start day-schools in connection with their church work would apply with equal force to Utah. So in the winter of 1878 he went East for the purpose of securing assistance to inaugurate educational work.

As the result of that visit, the Salt Lake Academy was established, being incorporated under the laws of Utah with a self-perpetuating board of trustees.

This unsectarian academy, the only institution of the kind in the Territory that is free from all ecclesiastical control, opened its doors September 9th, 1878. Professor E. Benner, of Lowell, Mass., was secured for principal, and he has already exhibited rare qualifications for the

position. He is assisted by an able corps of teachers, and
the institution is in a very flourishing condition.

THE NEW WEST EDUCATION COMMISSION.

One purpose in founding the Salt Lake Academy was to
raise up teachers for the rest of the Territory, but this requires time. How can the present need be met ? An organization has been formed in Chicago for this purpose.
It is called the New West Educational Committee.

Rev. Dr. Noble is president ; E. W. Blatchford, Esq.,
is secretary ; Col. C. G. Hammond, treasurer.

The object of the commission, as defined in the constitution, is,

" The promotion of Christian civilization in Utah and
adjacent States and Territories, by the education of children and youth under Christian teachers, and also by the
use of such kindred agencies as may at any time be deemed
desirable."

Under the auspices of the commission flourishing
schools have already been established at Park City and
West Jordan, and others are about to be opened at Hooper-
ville, Kaysville, and adjacent towns.

THE CATHOLIC CHURCH.

The history of the Catholic Church in Utah commences
with the year 1866, when Rev. E. Kelly was appointed
pastor by Right Rev. Bishop O'Connel, of Marysville,
Cal.

In the beginning of 1871 the Most Rev. J. S. Alemany,
Archbishop of San Francisco, Cal., appointed Rev. Father
P. Walsh pastor of the Territory. Rev. Father Walsh,
immediately after his appointment, opened a subscription

list to raise funds to build a church on the lot purchased by Rev. E. Kelly in 1866. The present handsome and commodious brick structure that stands on Second East Street affords ample testimony of his labors, and of the generosity of the people of Salt Lake and of the whole Territory.

Rev. Father Walsh remained in charge till 1873, when he was succeeded by Very Rev. Father L. Scanlan, who is the present incumbent.

Father Scanlan has, through persistent zeal and hard labor, succeeded in the past seven years in erecting two churches and three school buildings, and establishing two hospitals, of each of which we append a brief history.

These are St. Joseph's Church, in Ogden ; St. John's Church, School, and Hospital, in Silver Reef ; St. Mary's Academy, in Salt Lake City ; the Academy of the Sacred Heart, in Ogden ; St. Mary's School, in Silver Reef, and the Hospital of the Holy Cross, in Salt Lake. The schools and hospitals are chiefly under the direction of Sisters of various orders ; and the efforts of the early Catholic priests in the country were so highly appreciated that Gentiles of all religious denominations and of no denomination united in giving them pecuniary aid toward erecting the buildings for their churches, schools, and hospitals. Of the latter an additional word will be of interest.

The Hospital of the Holy Cross, Salt Lake, was opened September 26th, 1876, and is conducted by the Sisters of the Holy Cross. Three physicians visit there regularly. During the four years of its existence *nineteen hundred* patients have been cared for. Considering the many successful surgical operations performed in this hospital, it is an incalculable benefit to the community at large.

After the erection of the Catholic Church in Silver Reef, the citizens and miners held a mass meeting, and decided upon furnishing Father Scanlan with pecuniary means, by voluntary contributions, for the erection of a hospital, if he would take charge of the same. To this proposition he assented, and commenced to build in April, 1879. The building was nearly completed in June, but was used as an asylum for those who were left houseless by the great fire.

The Sisters of the Holy Cross, five in number, took charge of it August 1st, 1879.

There are thirty-nine Sisters in the Territory, five priests, and over a thousand communicants. Archbishop Alemany, of California, has episcopal charge of the Territory, and he has appointed Father Scanlan as his representative, and endowed him with the power and title of a vicar-general.

THE HEBREW CONGREGATION IN UTAH.

Samuel Kahn, Esq., of Salt Lake City, president of the congregation, which numbers one hundred and fifty souls. The Hebrew citizens of Utah are generally respected for their integrity. They are friends of law and order, and are always ready to assist, both with money and personal effort, in every good work. They have two benevolent societies, which during the past year have disbursed over twenty-three hundred dollars to the poor. They are among the most liberal supporters of our schools, and are about erecting a school building of their own, in which both English and Hebrew will be taught.

Utah is the only spot known on earth where the Hebrew is termed a "Gentile." Our Hebrew fellow-citizens were among the earliest non-Mormon settlers, and in the dark days previous to 1870 were among the foremost of the trusty few on whom the representatives of the Government could rely for aid.

THE PRESBYTERIAN WORK.

The first point occupied by the Presbyterian Church in Utah was Corinne, a Gentile town on the Central Pacific Railroad.

A church was organized here in 1870. It is supplied at present by Rev. S. L. Gillespie, of Brigham City.

The first missionary effort in Salt Lake on the part of the Presbyterian Church was made by Rev. J. Welch, who commenced his labors in October, 1871. A church of twelve members was organized the following November.

In 1873 a lot was purchased, containing a house suitable for a parsonage, and in 1874 the church building was completed. The entire cost of house and lot was about $30,000, which, with the school building erected in 1877 on the same lot, makes a valuable property.

In the spring of 1875 the Salt Lake Collegiate Institute was organized, with Professor J. M. Coyner, of Indiana, as principal. This school now occupies a neat and well-arranged building, with accommodations for 160 pupils. It has three departments—primary, intermediate, and academic—presided over by competent teachers. In excellence and efficiency this school is not surpassed by any school of a similar character in the States.

More than half of the pupils receive their tuition *free*, either in whole or in part. The importance of this statement will be understood when it is remembered that the Mormon population of Utah have *no free schools*.

Outside of Salt Lake, Presbyterian missionaries are occupying every point where they can gain a foothold. They have ten congregations in the Territory, nine church buildings and chapels, and thirteen schools in successful operation, with an attendance of eight hundred and seventy-five pupils.

They have eight ministers and eighteen teachers employed, and they expect to increase this number during the present year, and to open eight more schools within the present year.

Their stations at present stretch along a line extending from the Idaho boundary to the southern border of Sevier County—a distance of three hundred miles—and their arrangements are completed for establishing mission schools all the way to St. George, the southern capital of the Territory.

It is only necessary to add, in conclusion, the words of one of the chief promoters of this work :

" We have come to Utah to *stay*."

METHODISM IN UTAH.

The missionary work of the Methodist Episcopal Church in Utah was begun by Rev. G. M. Pierce, who, under appointment of Bishop Ames, commenced religious services in Salt Lake in 1870, and opened a school in the same year, known as the Rocky Mountain Seminary.

At the present time the Salt Lake Methodists have a church building worth about $55,000. This building also contains the school-rooms and class-rooms of the Rocky Mountain Seminary, which for several years had an attendance of nearly two hundred pupils under the care of an efficient corps of teachers. In 1879 this school was temporarily closed, but it has since been reopened.

The total number of Methodist day-schools in Utah is five. These schools have an attendance of five hundred and eighteen pupils, and employ ten teachers. There are six church buildings owned by the Utah Methodists outside of Salt Lake. The aggregate value of these buildings is $25,000. They own also three parsonages valued at

$3500. There are seven Methodist preachers in the Territory, and two hundred and ten church members. There are twelve Methodist Sunday-schools in Utah, with an aggregate attendance of nine hundred and thirty-four scholars, and eighty-two officers and teachers. The Methodists also sustain a monthly paper, the *Rocky Mountain Christian Advocate.*

The Methodists, being among the pioneers of religious and educational work in Utah, met with much opposition, and had many difficulties to overcome. They have expended much money and more labor in their efforts to benefit the people of the Territory, but they begin already to reap the fruit of their toil, and they believe that much of the good seed sown, like "bread that grows in the winter night," will spring up in after years, making spots that now seem as barren as the rocky peaks that wall in our valleys,

" Fair as the garden of the Lord."

THE PROTESTANT EPISCOPAL CHURCH IN UTAH.

In April, 1867, Rev. Bishop Tuttle, being in charge of a diocese which included Utah, sent two clergymen, Rev. T. W. Haskins and Rev. G. W. Foote, to Salt Lake to establish a mission there. They arrived the following May, and opened services at once. Independence Hall was secured for their use, and within two years and a half they baptized one hundred persons and admitted ninety communicants, many of whom were of Mormon antecedents.

St. Mark's Grammar School, the first Gentile school in Utah, was opened in July, 1867, with only sixteen pupils, but the number soon increased to one hundred and forty. In 1871 they erected a substantial church edifice, at a cost of about $45,000. Churches were also built at Logan and

Ogden, and schools established at these places, and also at Plain City.

In Salt Lake a school building was erected capable of accommodating over four hundred scholars.

Right Rev. D. Tuttle, bishop of the diocese, resides in Salt Lake.   There are, besides, five clergymen employed in the Territory.

The statistics of the Church in Utah for the present year are as follows :

Communicants in the Territory......... 300

Salt Lake Sunday-school.
Scholars............................... 415
Teachers............................... 29

Ogden Sunday-school.
Scholars............................... 140
Teachers............................... 7

Logan Sunday-school.
Scholars............................... 65
Teachers............................... 5

Plain City Sunday-school.
Scholars............................... 35
Teachers............................... 4

St. Mark's Grammar School.
Scholars............................... 460
Teachers............................... 23

Ogden Day-school.
Scholars............................... 125
Teachers............................... 2

Logan Day-school.
Scholars............................... 65
Teacher............................... 1

Plain City Day-school.
    Scholars.............................. 52
    Teacher 1

In all the above schools pupils unable to pay the required rates receive *free tuition*. St. Mark's Grammar School was the first school in Utah to offer the benefits of education without money and without price.

ST. MARK'S HOSPITAL, SALT LAKE.

This hospital, established in 1872 under the auspices of the Protestant Episcopal Church, was the first hospital ever opened in Utah. During the eight years of its existence it has been the means of an incalculable amount of good. An efficient corps of nurses is employed, and physicians and surgeons of superior qualifications attend the patients.

By mutual agreement, all miners in the Territory who wish to avail themselves of the benefits of St. Mark's Hospital in case of sickness or accident subscribe and pay into the hands of the treasurer one dollar per month. This monthly payment entitles them to board, care, medical attendance, and surgical treatment when needed.

When we take into consideration the fact that Utah Mormonism has always been hostile to education, and that *the Territory makes no provision whatever for free schools*, the work now being done by the twenty-eight schools established and conducted by Gentiles becomes specially important. And when we remember that Utah knows nothing of public charities, and that those who govern the Territory are interested in nothing that relates to the public good, we are prepared to appreciate the hospitals which owe their existence to Gentiles.

Previous to the entrance of these "adventurers" into the Territory, the poor were left to suffer unrelieved or pine in unvisited and untended sickness, unless helped by neighbors, who often had little enough to give ; but now, in addition to every other form of good works, the various non-Mormon religious bodies in Utah sustain benevolent societies whose work is to feed the hungry, clothe the naked, and visit and help the sick.

It is to these agencies mainly that Utah must owe her regeneration. The Gentile residents have " besieged with unavailing prayers" the law-makers of the nation, lo ! these many years. They have exhausted every form of appeal to the Government and people of the great country whose citizens they are, but help does not come from without.

The Mormon problem is still unsolved ; the Mormon priesthood still rules.

A former historian of the Territory, writing in 1871, said :

" The opportune death of Brigham Young would simplify matters somewhat."

In 1877 Brigham Young died in his bed, thereby cheating the gallows, as many of his associates in crime have done ; but his successors yet rule the people with a rod of iron. Every year witnesses a large Mormon immigration, chiefly from Europe, and each immigration is an accession to the mass of ignorance and fanaticism which is so dangerous a power in the hands of unscrupulous men, such as the present Mormon leaders.

THE gravest problem presented to the American statesman of to-day is that which is found in the attitude of Mormon Theocracy towards our government. There are perhaps two hundred thousand Mormons in Utah and the adjoining States and Territories—that is to say, two hundred thousand of the inhabitants of our common country who are bound by oaths which make them at once the slaves of their spiritual leaders, and the sworn enemies of the nation within whose borders they dwell.

Salt Lake City, the capital of Utah, is the centre from which emanates the power that controls the one hundred and thirty thousand Mormons in this Territory, and the seventy thousand Mormons in Idaho, Wyoming, Arizona, Colorado, and Nevada. When the President of the Church speaks, he is obeyed as implicity by his subjects outside of Utah as by those who dwell in sight of the Temple. The present head of the Mormon Church is John Taylor, an Englishman, who on the death of Brigham Young was elevated to that position by the foreign-born Saints, who greatly outnumber the Americans.* Taylor has a profound contempt for republican institutions, but, like his predecessor, he knows how to make them subservient to the interests of the Church. Thus the ballot, which was little valued before the advent of the Gentiles in the Prophet's

---

* This remark applies to adult Mormons. The children of foreigners born in Utah give the native-born population a preponderance in the census tables.

dominions, is now prized as the bulwark of priestly power in Utah, and as a means by which the adjoining Territories are to be brought under Mormon rule.

In Utah the law confers the right of suffrage on men above twenty-one years of age who are either native born or naturalized, and who are also tax-payers. Women enjoy the right of suffrage without these qualifications. Alien women who have been less than a month in the Territory may and do vote, if married (polygamously or otherwise) to a citizen ; and while the law requires that a single woman shall be over twenty-one years of age in order to be a legal voter, practically this qualification is not insisted upon when she votes for the Church candidate. As the population of Utah is constituted at present, the Mormons, who vote as one man under the direction of the authorities of the Church, can return a majority of ten to one over the Gentiles. In nearly three-fourths of the precincts in the Territory, not a single Gentile vote was returned at the last election, and as the Saints do the counting, and count as well as vote in obedience to '' counsel,'' the heaviest Gentile immigration that can reasonably be expected will not affect the election returns much for ten years to come.

As a matter of course, with the ballot controlled and directed by the President of the Church, the same individuals exercise both spiritual and temporal power. All Territorial offices are filled by men who hold official positions in the Church. But this fact does not begin to express the measure of temporal power wielded by the spiritual masters of the people. In order that the domination of the Church may be complete the whole Territory is divided into municipalities. Nearly every Mormon settlement is a '' city,'' and the authorities of these cities (some of which, with a population of a few hundred, have a charter covering thirty-six square miles), are invested with powers only a little less absolute than those of the Autocrat of Russia. It is needless to add that every city official, from the Mayor down, is likewise a member of the Mormon priesthood.

Outside of Utah the President of the Mormon Church holds the balance of power in those Territories in which neither political party has a heavy majority. In Idaho the Mormons are already strong enough to control the Legislature. In proof of this assertion it is only necessary to call attention to the recent action of that body in tabling the portion of the Governor's message which relates to polygamy. Mormon emigration to Arizona is continued year by year, and in a little while President Taylor will be able to dictate the course of that Territory in relation to Mormon institutions. In Colorado and Nevada the success of the system is not marked· as yet, but the trusted adherents of the Church are quietly colonizing in both these States, that they may be on hand when either political party shall make a bid for the Mormon vote.

It is a well known fact that the laws of the United States are not, and never have been, enforced in Utah. This fact is not a reflection upon the officers of the government, who are doing their best in the difficult position in which they are placed. The remedy for the anomalous state of affairs in Utah is not in their hands.

Let it be remembered that when a criminal is arraigned before the court for an offence which is the direct outcome of the Mormon creed, nine-tenths of the people of the Territory are pledged to defeat the ends of justice. When the Governor performs his sworn duty, he can only count on the support of one-tenth of the population. For eight years past Utah has been represented in Congress by a polygamist who is shown by the records of the court to be an unnaturalized foreigner.　The present Governor of the Territory refused this man a certificate of election to the Forty-seventh Congress, holding that the votes cast for him were thrown away because he was not a citizen of the United States, and that, as he was a polygamist, his disabilities could not be removed before the time should arrive for taking his seat.

This act, performed by the Governor as a duty which his oath of office made incumbent upon him, has arrayed the entire Mormon Church against him.

Since 1858, when Brigham Young was superseded as Governor of the Territory by a Gentile, no Federal officer has ever been warmly welcomed by the saints, and the various governors, in particular, have been the objects of a bitter animosity on the part of the Mormon leaders.　In former times these unwelcome officials were driven out of the Territory by the Danites,* but for ten years past they have suffered no annoyance beyond newspaper abuse and covert threats of personal violence.　It is hoped therefore by the friends of Governor Murray that his straightforward performance of official duty will not be followed by serious consequences.

The monstrous doctrine of Blood Atonement (the offering of human sacrifices) is as much an integral part of the Mormon system to-day as it ever was, though masked and modified in its practical application through fear of the United States laws ; and Polygamy, the curse and blight of the homes of Utah, instead of being on the decline, as some of our astute statesmen suppose, is entrenching itself more firmly in Utah itself and spreading into adjoining States and Territories.　*More polygamous marriages were contracted during 1880 than during any year since the*

---

* The sworn band of "Destroying Angels," who perform the extreme commands of the Church authorities.

settlement of the Territory. If the vigorous treatment of the Mormon problem, which President Garfield has outlined in his message, could become an accomplished fact, there might soon be a change for the better in Utah, but, judging the future by the past, we have little hope that Congress will do anything until compelled by the pressure of public sentiment.

Visitors from abroad often ask, " What would be the effect of enforcing the laws of the United States in Utah ?"

If polygamists were disfranchised, and the Territorial Legislature superseded by a Legislative Council composed of law-abiding citizens, there would be loud threats of armed resistance, but in the opinion of the Gentile residents these threats would not be carried out. Mayor Little, of Salt Lake, said to a reporter in the East only a few weeks ago : " We number two hundred thousand, and if the authorities at Washington are wise, they will not interfere with us." The present writer has heard John Taylor say, when addressing an audience of six thousand people : " Let the government *dare* to lay so much as a finger upon us, and we will soon show the people of the United States what we can do."

But persons who indulge in this sort of bravado are not usually made of such stuff as would fit them for leaders in an armed conflict, and their threats alarm none but the most timid. It is true that Taylor has neither the caution nor the foresight of his predecessor, and if left to himself he might rouse his ignorant followers to a pitch of fanatical fury which he could neither direct nor control ; but he has advisers who are far too wise to risk the steadily increasing political power of the Mormon Church by permitting an outbreak of any sort. These men will not counsel war until the Mormons believe themselves strong enough to dictate terms of peace.

Let us hope that enlightened statesmanship will solve the Mormon problem before that day arrives.

It is the belief of those best qualified to judge of the situation in Utah that *if polygamists were disfranchised and made ineligible to office*, the Mormons would shortly receive a " revelation" directing them either to give up polygamy or to seek " fresh fields and pastures new," outside the boundaries of the United States.   In any event, the disfranchisement of polygamists would break down the political power of the Mormon priesthood, and pave the way for the Congress of the United States to " secure a republican form of government " in a United States Territory in which the will of one man has been the supreme law for more than a quarter of a century.

It needs only the assurance that the laws of the United States will be enforced in Utah and the common rights of American citizens guaranteed to all residents, to bring to the Territory that class of immigrants who must be depended upon for the development of the mineral wealth of Utah.   This wealth is beyond computation, but while the temporal power of the Mormon priesthood is supreme, capital will not seek investments in it.   Once let it be known that the Territory is a ward of Congress in fact as well as in name, and that the President of the Mormon Church no longer holds the reins of temporal power, and Utah, with her unequaled natural advantages, will invite immigration and capital from all parts of the Union, and in another decade will be ready to take her place among the most enlightened and prosperous of the Pacific States.

NOTES OF REFERENCE.

NOTE A (PAGE 18).

THE following extract is made, by permission, from
the *Salt Lake Tribune* of October 21st, 1879. The writer,
J. R. McBride, Esq., a member of the Salt Lake bar, is
well known to our citizens as one of the oldest pioneers of
the coast, and his statements can be relied upon as correct
in every particular :

"In the face of undeniable facts to the contrary, the
priesthood of the Saints prate of having made a garden in
the wilderness, built a commonwealth in the Great American Desert, and made it blossom as the rose ; of having
subdued the wilds of the savage to the use of man, built
towns and cities, tabernacles and school-houses, railroads
and telegraphs, and so on *ad nauseam.*

"Whenever these untruthful boasts are exposed, the
priesthood fall back on the statement of some Eastern
editor who has been duped by them into crediting the
Mormons with Utah's progress, and again quote the old
lie started by themselves to confute the well-known facts.

"There are many Mormons who actually believe that
this country was first discovered by the Mormon people.
Brigham once, on the witness-stand, in a noted cause
pending in the courts, denied that the owners of lots in
Salt Lake derived title from the United States, and boldly
asserted that he claimed the Emporium Corner 'by right
of discovery.'

"To the facts. The valley of Great Salt Lake was as

well known to travelers in the Far West—years before the Mormon chief squatted here to pass the winter of 1847, before resuming the journey to California—as the valley of the Sacramento, or that of the Willamette. It was no 'desert,' but a beautiful, grass-covered meadow, waiting to be appropriated. Its *isolation* was its protection, not its 'sage-brush soil' or its 'untamed savages.' The labor of subduing it then was nothing comparatively.

"The writer was here before the Mormon settlement was made, and knows that the pretense of reclaiming 'alkali soil' and subduing the Indians is utterly groundless. From Soda Springs to the head-waters of Salt Lake Valley to the south, there were not a hundred resident Indians. The Utes lived to the south and the Bannocks to the north, and the settlers had nothing to do but to enter into and possess the land, and work it to secure a fruitful result. One might as well talk of subduing or reclaiming the prairie soil of Illinois or Iowa as of 'subduing' or 'reclaiming' the lands of Utah.

"There were stretches of miles upon miles of meadow lands, with grass mid-sides to a horse, where even irrigation was not required, when the Saints came into the valley. All that was needed was ordinary industry.

"I assert that the lands were, in the early settlement of Utah, more easily brought to bear fruitful returns than the ordinary wild lands of any of the Western States. All this talk and sentiment about the hardships of pioneering in Utah are pure fustian.

"Those who crossed the plains when the writer did, anterior to the occupation of Utah, know that the real difficulties and dangers of that long journey were after we had passed Utah; the deserts of Nevada, the Snake Plains, the alkali water, the alert and dangerous Indians were all to the west. . . . They 'made the roads' forsooth!

Not less than 15,000 people and 3000 wagons had passed through Utah to the West before a Mormon ever set foot in Salt Lake Valley.

" The road from Fort Bridger to this valley in 1847 was as plain as the road from Salt Lake City to Sandy is to-day. This I know, for I had traveled it prior to that time. General John Bidwell, now of Chico, California, and Captain Bartlett, of Jackson County, Missouri, went to California with an ox-train in 1841. Lansford W. Hastings and A. L. Lovejoy, both yet living, led a large party of wagon emigrants through to the Pacific Coast in 1842. In 1843 the regular annual overland emigration to Oregon and California began, and between that date and the time of the Mormon arrival in the valley in 1847, thousands had passed through Utah to the West ; while the Saints are now boasting that ' these valleys of the mountains ' were discovered by the Lord to the Prophet Brigham, who then by inspiration opened a ' road to Utah,' though that road had been regularly traveled for years . . .

" The Saints neither discovered the country, nor built the roads, nor subdued the Indians : there was no such work to be done. The fact was, they entered into a beautiful, un-inhabited, inviting, and fertile valley. They were poor and isolated, and endured the ordinary hardships of their poverty and isolation. In that respect their condition and surroundings were far better than those of the early pio-neers of the Mississippi Valley. And when we consider the advantages they have enjoyed, and their want of enter-prise and energy, until the stream of progress from Gentile sources has forced them into a sort of unenviable notoriety —unenviable because of their opposition to the develop-ment of the Territory—the reactionary tendency and un-American character of their institutions becomes mani-fest." . . .

NOTE B (PAGE 38).

I have heard men of intelligence, who in the early days of this Territory were leading Mormons, but who have since renounced that faith, attempt to explain Brigham Young's power over the people in the same way that the old Nauvoo Mormons accounted for Joseph Smith's influence—viz., by attributing extraordinary magnetic or mesmeric gifts to him.

My own observation inclines me to a different belief. Brigham Young was a man utterly without heart or conscience, and being possessed of an iron will and gifted with an extraordinary degree of perseverance, it is not strange that he was able to make such use as he did of the engine of superstition which he found ready to his hand, or that he succeeded in bringing the ignorant and unthinking among his followers to regard him as God's vicegerent.

It is a significant fact that the masses who have remained faithful to the Mormon Prophet are, for the most part, ignorant almost beyond belief, while the ranks of the apostates from Mormonism are being continually recruited from the more intelligent and better educated classes. Indeed, it is safe to say that at the present time the only intelligent and educated men who are to be found within the pale of the Mormon Church are those who are kept there by pecuniary considerations, or who are bound to their leaders by fellowship in crime.

NOTE C (PAGE 39).

I have in my possession the names of a number of married women, some of whom were "sealed" to the Prophet Joseph in Nauvoo, and were, at his death, "sealed for time" to Brigham Young, while others were taken from their husbands by Brigham after Joseph's death. A regard for the feelings of innocent relatives, who are still living, alone induces me to withhold these names.

I will give but one instance out of many that have come to my knowledge, which may serve in some degree to explain the bitter feelings with which the Mormons in Illinois were regarded by their Gentile neighbors.

A married woman, whom I will call Mrs. L——, young, beautiful, and of hitherto unblemished reputation, fell a victim to the arts of the Prophet Joseph, and was induced to be sealed to him as his plural wife. Her husband being a Gentile, it was important to keep the matter from his knowledge, and within a few months after Mrs. L——'s intimacy with the Prophet began, the husband died, as it happened many men died in Nauvoo whose presence was not desired by the Saints. When the Mormons fled from Nauvoo, Mrs. L—— found a home in Iowa. She had one child—a daughter, the offspring of her " spiritual" marriage. She had a large amount of property, which her deceased husband had left her, and being besides, still young and fair, her hand was sought by one who was not of her faith, and who knew nothing of the dark page in her history.

After a few months she married Mr. C——, and was induced by him to promise to give over following the fortunes of the Saints. They lived happily together for a few years, and two children were born to them. Then Mrs. C——'s brother (who was a Mormon elder with seven wives) paid them a visit, and tried to induce them to emigrate to Utah. Failing in this, he talked with his sister alone, and endeavored to exact a promise from her to leave her husband and gather with the Saints at Zion.

In this attempt he was also unsuccessful, and exasperated by what he called her obstinacy, he told her she would soon be glad to claim his protection and a home among his people.   After uttering this prophecy, he went directly to her husband, and told him the whole shameful story of her past life, asserting that the little daughter of whom she was so fond was the child of the Prophet.

The result was exactly what he had intended.   Mr. C—— confronted his wife with the charge made by her brother.   She did not deny it, and a speedy divorce followed.   The discarded wife fled to Utah, glad to hide her misery and shame among a people who called crime "virtue."   She is living here to-day, a heart-broken, desolate woman, devoid even of the comfort of being able to believe in the teachings that caused her downfall.

NOTE D (PAGE 62).

The family which figures here under the name of La Tour I have known intimately for nine years, and from the members of it who never believed in Mormonism I have obtained the facts of their history.   I have, of course, made changes in their story, and have blended with it some incidents (of fact) from other lives.

To-day the grave covers Louise and her sorrows from mortal eyes ; but I knew her years ago, after she had made her escape from Mormon despotism, and I promised myself then that it should be my work to denounce those at whose hands she had suffered such cruel wrongs.

In this book I have told only a small part of her story ; and in deference to those who complain that the tragic character of my former history of life in Utah is unrelieved by a single gleam of light, I have tried to dwell most upon the brighter days that followed her deliverance from the hands of her enemies.

NOTE E (PAGE 64).

A brief description of the ceremonies of the Endowment House may not be out of place here. Though these ceremonies have been changed from time to time in many particulars, the oaths which the candidate is required to take remain substantially the same.

The Endowment House in Salt Lake is a two-story adobe building, presenting the appearance of an ordinary dwelling-house. It is situated in one corner of what is known as the Temple Block, a large square surrounded by a wall twelve feet high. This inclosure contains the Tabernacle, a large wooden structure nearly the shape of a tortoise-shell, which rests upon a very substantial rock foundation. East of the Tabernacle, and also within the walls, stands the Temple, a magnificent granite building which, after halting just above the ground for twenty years, is now rapidly approaching completion.

Certain days of each week in the year are set apart by the priesthood for what they term "giving Endowments." On the morning of the appointed day, the candidates, perhaps twenty in number, repair to the building already described. After giving their names, ages, etc., to the officiating clerk, the men and women are ushered into separate dressing-rooms.

Here they are required to disrobe, and wash from head to foot. Then the officiating priest or priestess anoints every part of the candidate's body with oil, after which each one puts on the garment of salvation—an article of apparel made exactly like a child's night-drawers, cut in one piece from the shoulder to the ankle.

This garment, once put on, can never be left off. When the wearer changes it, one arm or leg must be changed at a time.

Over this garment the women put on a white skirt, and the men an ordinary shirt.   Thus attired, all the candidates are marched into Room No. 2, where they are seated, the men on one side, the women on the other.   They are now told by the officiating priest that if they are not strong enough to go forward, they may stop where they are, and return home without their Endowments, *but that if they repeat anything relating to the ceremonies through which they have already passed, their throats will be cut from ear to ear !*

They are next ushered into Room No. 3, supposed to represent the Garden of Eden.   In former days the scenes enacted in this " garden" are said to have been disgraceful beyond description, but at the present time the candidates are merely treated to a crude theatrical representation of the temptation and fall, after which each one is clothed with a robe consisting of a straight piece of linen four yards long, gathered upon one shoulder and belted at the waist.   Over this robe they tie a fig-leaf apron.   They also put on the Temple head-gear, that worn by the men being similar to a baker's cap.   The women put on a cap composed of a square of Swiss muslin, one corner of which is so arranged as to form a veil.

All good Mormons are buried in their Endowment robes, and the veil worn by the women covers their faces when they are consigned to the grave.   In the morning of the resurrection this veil is to be lifted by the husband ; otherwise no woman can see the face of the Almighty in the next world.

After being thus clothed, the candidates are driven out of Eden into Room No. 4, called the World, where they encounter many temptations, the chief of which is the false gospel preached by Methodists, Baptists, etc.   Finally St. James and St. John appear and proclaim the true gospel of

Mormonism, which they all embrace gladly ; after this they receive the first grip belonging to the secret signs of the Church, and are ushered into Room No. 5.

Here the candidate raises his right hand in such a manner as to form a square with his arm, and swears on the square to avenge the death of Joseph Smith on this nation, and to teach this vengeance to his children and children's children unto the fifth generation. He then imprecates upon himself the following curse :

"*If ever I reveal the secrets of this House, may my tongue be torn out by the roots, and my heart and bowels cut out while I am yet alive ; and if I escape in this world, may all these penalties overtake me in the morning of the Resurrection.*"

The candidates now pass into Room No. 6, where all kneel in a circle and join hands. Kneeling thus, they take another fearful oath of eternal enmity to the Government and people of the United States. They also swear to obey the rulers of the Church in all things without question. After receiving a little more counsel concerning the duty of taking vengeance into their own hands, they are thought perfect enough to pass beyond the veil. This " veil " consists of a white curtain stretched across the room. The candidate is directed to stand with the breast, limbs, and abdomen touching this veil, while a person behind it who represents Deity passes his right hand through an opening in the curtain and cuts the mystic signs in the sacred garment.

As soon as the candidates receive these signs they pass behind the veil into Room No. 7, which is the last room to be entered, except by those contemplating marriage.

Candidates for marriage are ushered into Room No. 8, which is the sealing-room. Here husbands and wives who have been married outside of Utah are instructed that their

Gentile marriage is null and void, and they are offered the privilege of being sealed to each other for time and eternity. This offer they may accept or decline.

If they decline, they are free from each other, and the wife may be sealed to some other man.

If they accept, they kneel at an altar, and an ordinary marriage ceremony is gone through with, concluding with a formula of blessing which seals them to each other for eternity.

Candidates for plural marriage kneel at a similar altar, and the first wife, if obedient, kneels beside them and places the hand of the new bride in that of her husband. Should the first wife prove rebellious, her presence at the ceremony is dispensed with. The same service that unites a man to his first wife is used to "solemnize" a plural marriage, but at its conclusion this blessing is pronounced on the pair :

"Forasmuch as you have entered into the holy covenant of celestial marriage, all manner of sins shall be forgiven you, and you shall inherit eternal life."

* * * * * * *

The above information with regard to the rites of the Endowment House I have obtained from a number of persons at different times and places, and in all important particulars the witnesses agree perfectly. I have purposely omitted the grips, signs, pass-words, etc., together with the "counsel" of the officiating priest.

The ceremonies are very tedious, lasting fully eight hours, and a complete description of them would fill a volume.

NOTE F (PAGE 101).

In proof of the assertions made in this chapter, I subjoin a copy of a petition which I drew up, by request, in the winter of 1872, when great fear was felt by the Gentiles and by those who had left the Mormon Church that Brigham Young would succeed in his schemes for getting Utah admitted into the Union (in which event the petitioners would have been deprived of the protection of Congress and left wholly in the power of the Mormon priesthood).

This petition was signed by nearly five hundred women, most of whom had been residents of the Territory for many years. It is proper to add, also, that in 1872 there were very few Gentile women in the Territory, and women who had once been Mormons signed the petition at great personal risk. Many women to whom the memorial was presented said,

"Every word in it is true, and we want to sign it, but we *dare not.*"

"*To the Senate and Representatives of the United States in Congress assembled:*

"We your petitioners, residents of the Territory of Utah, the mothers, sisters, and wives of her loyal citizens, appeal to you, in the name of justice and humanity, not to withdraw your protection from us. Our sole dependence is upon you. Only the strong arm of the Federal Government can secure to us, and to our husbands, brothers, and sons, the enjoyment of the rights guaranteed us by the Constitution of our country.

"For more than twenty years, Utah, though a Territory of the United States, and as such nominally under the jurisdiction of Congress, has been in reality governed altogether by the Mormon priesthood. Let history tell the nature of their rule !

"No more bloody despotism has disgraced the earth in modern times. Brigham Young, in the self-appointed character of God's vicegerent, has held the lives, liberty, and property of the people in his hands. Disobedience to him has been accounted a crime not to be atoned for except by blood.

" Nothing that the people possessed could be called their own except by his will. Not only were they required to pay into the Church treasury one tenth of all their property, but they were liable at any time to be ordered to give up their homes to the Prophet; and this order none dared disobey. Many of your petitioners have been robbed thus in years past. Women who, by the labor of their own hands, have earned the shelter of a roof for themselves and their little ones, have been deprived of that shelter by Brigham Young's commands. The bread has been taken from the little children's mouths to swell the revenues of the Church and enable its rulers to add house to house and field to field.

" But these robberies are a little thing compared with other enormities perpetrated by the despotic rulers of this people in the name of religion. During all the years that their will has been law in Utah, no man's life, no woman's honor has been safe, if either stood in their way. Never, in this world, will the history of their dark and bloody deeds be fully written, for the victim and witness of many a tragedy are hidden together in the grave.

" For twenty years none dared lift their voices in complaint or condemnation ; and now, when liberty of speech, so long denied, is vouchsafed, it is fitting that woman's voice should be heard, for woman has been most cruelly wronged.

" Will not the representatives of this great nation listen to our appeal ?

" We adjure you, in the name of the mothers who bore you, of the wives you love, of the sisters whose honor is dear to you, not to turn a deaf ear to the cry of those who ask protection from the tyranny of a system that, throughout its whole existence, has sought only to crush and degrade womanhood. Thousands of women in the Territory of Utah are to-day in a condition of abject slavery. Many of them would proclaim their wrongs to the world if they dared. We appeal to you not to take any step that will cut off all hope of their deliverance.

" We know it has been urged that polygamy, the curse and blight of the homes of Utah, is hastening to its death, and that even if the people do not agree to relinquish it, it will shortly fall before an attack of natural forces consequent upon being brought in contact with the Christian civilization of the nineteenth century ; but do the facts which are constantly transpiring support this assertion ?

" During the past three months polygamous marriages have rather increased than diminished. Since the first of November scores of young girls have been led up to the Endowment House, and sealed to men who had already from two to five families.

" Is it reasonable to suppose that a people who defy the law thus openly, while under the direct supervision of Congress, will order their internal affairs more in harmony with the Constitution when invested with the prerogatives of a State Government ?

" But the continuance of polygamy is not the only ground upon which your petitioners deprecate the admission of Utah into the Union. There are other crimes and other tyrannies that will most assuredly be perpetuated in such an event.

" The Constitution of our country guarantees to every one of its law-abiding citizens the rights of life, liberty, and the pursuit of happiness. The principles which govern the majority in Utah make these rights dependent upon the will of a single man, who has already been guilty of incredible abuse of power. The history of his *reign* (for it is nothing else) is written in characters of blood. Some of your petitioners have known what it is to incur his displeasure and tremble for their lives ; others have had their property torn from them, and their dearest interests ruthlessly trampled upon by him. Will Congress consign them again to the tender mercies of this man and his coadjutors ?

" A number of your petitioners have become residents of Utah within two years past. Relying upon the protection of the Federal Government, we, with our families, have sought homes here ; but though we, our husbands, and our sons, have been peaceably engaged about our private duties, and have in no way interfered with the rights of the earlier settlers, we have been regarded as unwelcome intruders, and have been forced to live as though in an enemy's country.

" We have been told repeatedly, through the columns of the *Deseret News* (the official organ of the Mormon Church), that in the event of Utah's becoming a State, if we do not choose to be ruled by the majority, we can leave—the railroad is open.

" We are duly sensible of the graciousness of this permission, but there are some obstacles in the way of our availing ourselves of it. Many of us have our all invested here, and would be forced to leave empty-handed. Still, that would be preferable to remaining here under the rule of those who have shown themselves incapable of either justice or mercy, and determined to ignore every principle which lies at the foundation of our republican institutions. Our prayer to you, the representatives of a free people, is that you will not take such action as will force upon us either alternative."

(Signed) Mrs. WM. S. GODBE,
and four hundred and seventy-three other signers.

Read and referred to the Committee on Territories, and ordered to be printed, with the names of the petitioners and the accompanying letter:

"SALT LAKE, U. T., March 12, 1872.

"*To Hon. S. Colfax, Vice-President of the United States, and ex-officio President of the Senate:*

"SIR : We have this day forwarded to your care, per Wells, Fargo and Co.'s Express, a petition to Congress, strongly deprecating the admission of Utah into the Union at the present time. This petition is signed by more than four hundred of the loyal women of the Territory. A large majority of the signers have been residents of Utah and members of the Mormon Church for many years, and numbers of them have a personal and very bitter experience of the practical workings of polygamy. They have every reason to believe that their wrongs would be intensified by the admission of Utah into the Union, and the consequent accession of power to the Mormon priesthood. In the name of these women, who have been so cruelly wronged, we earnestly request you to lay this petition at once before the honorable bodies to whom it is addressed.

"MRS. A. G. PADDOCK,
"MRS. B. A. M. FROISETH,
"MRS. O. P. MILES,
"MRS. H. W. LAWRENCE, *Committee.*"
"MRS. J. B. KIMBALL,
"MRS. WM. S. GODBE,

NOTE G (PAGE 103).

The facility with which divorces have always been obtained in Utah is a suggestive commentary upon the peculiar marriage system of the Saints. Again and again

parties have been sealed to each other " for time and eternity," and in less than six months divorced by the same
power that sealed them.

It has been well said by one of the elders of the *Reor-
ganized Church* (a sect which, although it accepts the Book
of Mormon repudiates polygamy) that multitudes of
women in Utah have been divorced and remarried so
many times that they scarcely know themselves by name.
It is a common thing to find women living in polygamy
who have been divorced three or four times from as many
different husbands.

An Englishwoman who, a few years ago, abandoned her
husband and children for the purpose of gathering with the
Saints to Zion, has been divorced and remarried five times
since she came to Utah. The present writer has lived
within half a block of a woman who, after being divorced
from five husbands, is now living in polygamy with the
sixth ; and one of our district judges reports the case of an
elderly Saintess, living·near the place in which he holds
court, who has been divorced *fourteen times*.

NOTE H (PAGE 107).

The incident related happened in the family of a personal friend of the writer, and it is an example, by no
means unusual, of the manner in which the tithing has
always been collected, and the priesthood enriched at the
expense of the people. Whatever " the Lord" calls for
must be given up at once, and while Brigham Young lived,
he was, as Heber Kimball was accustomed to say in his
sermons, " the only Lord that this people had anything to
do with."

But the collecting of tithes to the extent of taking the
poor man's last cow was by no means the only plan re-

lied upon by the leaders of the people for filling their coffers. A friend of the writer, belonging to a respectable and wealthy family in the Eastern States, relates the following :

"In 184- my father was induced by a Mormon missionary to emigrate to Nauvoo. He went in advance of the family, taking a large sum of money with him. Soon after his arrival he wrote for us, stating that he had bought a house and lot, and that we would find a good home awaiting us. We started at once, but when we were within a few miles of Nauvoo we were met by the Missionary referred to, who told us that father had died suddenly.

"On reaching the city we were unable to learn anything of the time or manner of his death. We never found out where he was buried, or, indeed, whether he was buried at all ; and from that day to this we have never been able to get any information about the house and lot that he bought, or about any of the property that he left."

NOTE I (PAGE 120).

The present boundaries of the Territory of Utah differ much from those of the "kingdom" which Brigham Young set up in the Great Basin, after taking possession of the same "in the name of the Lord."

When the Mormon pioneers entered Salt Lake Valley, in the summer of 1847, the country belonged to Mexico, but in March, 1848, five months before the arrival of the emigrant company for which they had prepared the way, it was ceded to the United States by the treaty of Guadaloupe Hidalgo.

Such a small matter as this treaty was, however, of no consequence to the Saints, to whom the lands of the Gentiles had been given for an inheritance, and a year afterward (March 18th, 1849) they met in convention and or-ganized

" A free and independent government by the name of the State of Deseret."

I quote from their own words, as found in a copy of the original document now before me.   The boundaries of the State of Deseret, as set forth in this document, embrace the whole of the present State of California, together with half a dozen other States and Territories.

Soon after the organization of this " free and indepen-dent State," Brigham Young sent a delegate to Washing-ton avowedly to open negotiations looking to the admis-sion of Deseret into the Union ; but the tone he assumed was very like that of a foreign power demanding recogni-tion.

The following year (September 9th, 1850) Congress, cruelly ignoring the great State of Deseret, organized the present Territory of Utah within much narrower limits, reserving to itself the right to cut up said Territory when it should be deemed expedient, and annex portions of it to other States and Territories.   This high-handed proceed-ing on the part of Congress was, however, toned down a little by the appointment of Brigham Young as Governor—an office which he announced that he should hold until the Almighty ordered him to resign it ; as, in fact, he did.

Up to the day of the death of its " founder," the State of Deseret existed *de facto*, with Brigham Young as Gov-ernor, and the aforesaid State still exists in spite of the Territorial organization.

Once in two years the Utah Legislature (composed of thirty-nine Mormon high priests, thirty-six of whom are at present living in polygamy) convenes, and the Federal Government pays the members their *per diem* and mileage. During the life-time of Brigham Young, he, in the character of Governor of Deseret, convened them as a State Legislature on the day succeeding the adjournment of the Territorial Legislature, and the business of the State was then and there transacted.

Since Brigham Young's death, John Taylor, who succeeds him as President of Church, inherits likewise the office of Governor of Deseret—for Church and State are here one and inseparable. Comment is unnecessary.

NOTE J (PAGE 160).

Those who have any curiosity to become acquainted with the details of the hand-cart emigration to Utah in 1856 are referred to the tragic account given by Mr. John Chislett, in Stenhouse's " Rocky Mountain Saints."

Mr. Chislett was one of the captains of hundreds selected to take charge of the emigration across the plains, and it was due in a great measure to his heroic exertions that so many of the people lived to reach Utah.

Mr. Chislett, in common with hundreds who left England with him, was at that time a sincere believer in the New Gospel ; but his experiences on the way to Zion and after his arrival in the Valleys of the Mountains, convinced him that Mormonism had, to say the least, no claim to a divine origin, and he severed his connection with the Church at a time when such a course involved much personal risk.

NOTE K (PAGE 176).

The sermons of Brigham Young and his two counselors, Grant and Kimball, as reported and published in the *Deseret News*, the official organ of the Mormon Church, furnish abundant information as to the doctrine of blood-atonement, and it is from these sources that I have collated the following :

Blood-atonement, as preached by the Mormon leaders and practiced by the people, means the offering of human sacrifices for the remission of sins. Brigham Young says :

" There are certain sins which the blood of Christ cannot wash away ; but when a man's own blood is shed, and the smoke thereof ascends as sweet incense to Heaven, then are his sins remitted."

He likewise taught the people, in his published sermons, that to love their neighbor as themselves meant that they should be willing to shed their neighbor's blood, in order that in the next world he might be exalted among the gods.

J. Grant, Brigham Young's counselor, taught that in order to make the sacrifice of blood in a manner pleasing to Heaven, altars of unhewn stone should be erected, and the victim laid thereon, and his throat cut with a knife, and added,

" I wish we were in a situation to obey the laws of God in this thing without hindrance."

Closely allied to the doctrine of blood-atonement is the " principle," so called, that the Church has a right superior to the right of the civil government, to inflict the penalty of death upon offenders ; and this idea obtained so firm a hold in Utah that persons either in or out of the Church who were accused of anything which the Mormon code pronounced a crime, had no chance whatever to vindicate themselves in a court of law, but were either shot down by Danites who lay in wait for them, or arrested, and killed while in the hands of officers.

I will give a single well-known instance, the sequel of which I witnessed myself.

A young man named Skeen was suspected of a disposition to apostatize. Thereupon he was accused of cattle-stealing, and upon this accusation was arrested and held in custody by the sheriff, who was also a Mormon high priest.

The place of his confinement was a school-house, in which he was guarded by Ricks, the sheriff, and a man named Chambers. After Skeen lay down to sleep, Ricks said to Chambers,

"Whatever you may see to-night, your business is to keep still."

Not long afterward, when the sleeper's breathing showed his slumber to be sound, Ricks placed his gun to the young man's breast and fired. The victim sprang up, ran to the door, fell, and in a few minutes expired. It was afterward given out that he was killed in attempting to escape, but the testimony of Chambers, who was an eye-witness of the whole affair, was corroborated by that of several other men who ran to the school-house when the shot was fired, and who testified that the gun which inflicted the fatal wound had been held so close to Skeen's breast as to set his clothing on fire.

Yet in the face of this positive testimony a Mormon jury pronounced Ricks "not guilty," and his fellow-saints escorted him home with a band of music, flags flying, etc.— a procession which I saw and of which everybody understood the meaning.

It is proper to add that the witnesses at Ricks' trial were men who, after the murder, left the Mormon Church. No Mormon could by any means be induced to testify against a brother Saint.

NOTE L (PAGE 176).

Out of a multitude of cases that might be adduced in support of this statement, I will quote two of the most notorious :

Bill Hickman, the Danite, who according to his own confession committed nineteen murders, was a Mormon in good standing throughout his career of crime, and was a member of the Utah Legislature at a time when he was killing men in obedience to " counsel" every few months.

John D. Lee, one of the principal actors in the butchery of Mountain Meadows, was rewarded for his share in the massacre by a seat in the Legislature, though at the time he held several other offices of trust and profit ; for a plurality of offices is allowed in Utah as well as a plurality of wives.

NOTE M (PAGE 178).

The occurrence here alluded to is a matter of history. In 1862 J. W. Dawson, of Indiana, was appointed Governor of Utah. He was unwelcome, as Federal officers were apt to be.

Brigham Young caused some charge to be made against him, and he was ordered to leave the Territory.

A number of young men who were charged with the business of seeing that this order was carried out, gave the Governor a severe beating, but either because they misunderstood their instructions, or because of an unwillingness to shed blood, they allowed him to escape with his life. Brigham believed with Napoleon that a blunder is worse than a crime. He caused the arrest of the young men, and the officers having them in charge, who could not afford to misunderstand *their* instructions, coolly shot them down.

The bodies of two of the young men—brothers—were left at their father's door with the laconic order :

" Bury them."

Brigham Young took pains to be present at their funeral. He commanded the mother not to shed a tear for her unworthy sons, and told the women present·not to offer her any sympathy; and so absolute was the power he exercised that those whose hearts were full of pity for the bereaved mother turned away from her without a word.

NOTE N (PAGE 207).

I have given here the exact words of a woman whom I number among my personal friends : a woman of fine mind and noble presence, worthy, every way, of a better fate. It was her misfortune, when very young, to become the wife of a man who was afterward a Mormon apostle. When she had a family of little children, this man was sealed to two girls on the same day. He afterward took *eight* more women as his plural wives.

He is living to-day, and is one of the strongest advocates of polygamy.

NOTE O (PAGE 213).

A number of years ago, when the Government was making some effort to ferret out evidence concerning a few of the more atrocious crimes committed in Utah by the Mormon priesthood, a detective placed in my hands the following statement :

" In the year 186–, a person who had recently come to Utah bought a house and lot in the 19th Ward, Salt Lake City. Soon after making the purchase, and while engaged in uprooting some of the trees in the orchard and setting out others, he broke into a pit containing the remains of seven human beings—a man, a woman, and five children. The bodies were in an advanced state of decomposition, but the rawhide thongs with which the arms of each one were bound were still in place.

" The man who made this discovery was a Mormon, but

he was new to the Territory and ignorant of the doctrine of blood-atonement, and he supposed it to be his duty to put the officers of justice on the track of the crime whose evidences he had unearthed. He therefore repaired at once to police headquarters, and told his story.

" He was there informed that his only duty with regard to the discovery he had made was to say nothing about it, and ask no questions.

" That night a detachment of the police force took up the bodies and reburied them outside of the old city wall.

" When I was made acquainted with the foregoing facts, I sought out the spot indicated as the second place of burial, and dug up the remains, which by this time were skeletons. The skulls of the children as well as of the grown persons were crushed in, as if from a blow with a bludgeon or crowbar. I also found in the pit the rawhide thongs which had been used to bind the victims.

" I made a detailed report of the matter to the Federal authorities in the Territory, but they were not clothed with power sufficient to trace or punish the perpetrator of the crime, and so far as my knowledge extends no effort has ever been made in that direction."

(Signed,)   S. G."

NOTE P (PAGE 221).

Independence Hall was a small adobe building capable of seating about two hundred persons. It has since been remodeled, enlarged, and neatly furnished, and is now known as the Congregational Chapel. It is situated on Third South Street, half a block west of Main Street.

While General Connor commanded at Camp Douglas, Rev. N. McLeod, post chaplain, conceived what seemed then the chimerical idea of establishing a Christian mission in the very heart of the Mormon capital, and being a man of great courage and firmness of purpose, he finally succeeded. The building afterward known as Independence Hall was erected by the aid of the officers at Camp Douglas and a few others who felt an interest in the undertaking, and, in spite of the threats of the Mormon hierarchy, regular services were opened, followed by a Sunday-school. In the first place, almost the only attendants were the soldiers, the few Gentiles in the city, the officers and their wives, and the families who had taken refuge at the post; but soon disaffected Mormons began to drop in, and the Sabbath-school proved so great an attraction that Mormon children went again and again, though punished for going as often as the fact was discovered.

This state of affairs could not continue long. Recalcitrant Mormons who had been to the hall were notified that if they went again their lives would be forfeited, mobs broke up the meetings, and finally the superintendent of the Sabbath-school, Dr. J. K. Robinson, was brutally murdered within a few yards of his own door and of the hall, into which his bleeding body was carried.

NOTE Q (PAGE 223).

The penalties attached to the Endowment oaths are revolting beyond belief, and it would be impossible to publish the details of the punishments which the Mormon code prescribes for offences of every degree. The simplest and mildest penalty invoked upon covenant-breakers is that their throats shall be cut from ear to ear, and in many instances this penalty has been (mercifully ?) commuted and the offender shot instead.

In at least one well-known instance (that of Julia H —,

an unfortunate plural wife, whose husband at present fills an important office in this city), the victim was allowed the alternative of death by poison ; but in the case of the two women to whom I have alluded in this chapter, trustworthy testimony makes it only too clear that they were sacrificed with attendant barbarities which could not be paralleled outside of the darkest abodes of paganism.

NOTE R (PAGE 260).

In 1867, less than a year after the murder of Dr. Robinson and the breaking up of McLeod's school and congregation, Christian missionaries were found courageous enough to make a second attempt in the same direction. In that year religious services were commenced and a school opened under the auspices of the Protestant Episcopal Church, and in spite of opposition and threats the missionaries maintained their ground and continued to exercise a powerful influence for good among the many whose faith in Mormonism had been uprooted by a discovery of the crimes of the leaders and the inherent evils of the system.

THE END.